J. S. Campion

On Foot in Spain

a walk from the Bay of Biscay to the Mediterranean

J. S. Campion

On Foot in Spain
a walk from the Bay of Biscay to the Mediterranean

ISBN/EAN: 9783337237950

Printed in Europe, USA, Canada, Australia, Japan

Cover: Foto ©Andreas Hilbeck / pixelio.de

More available books at **www.hansebooks.com**

ON FOOT IN SPAIN.

A Walk from the Bay of Biscay to the Mediterranean.

BY J. S. CAMPION.

Author of "On the Frontier."

SECOND EDITION.

𝕴𝖑𝖑𝖚𝖘𝖙𝖗𝖆𝖙𝖊𝖉 𝖇𝖞 𝕺𝖗𝖎𝖌𝖎𝖓𝖆𝖑 𝕾𝖐𝖊𝖙𝖈𝖍𝖊𝖘.

LONDON:

CHAPMAN & HALL, 193, PICCADILLY.

1879.

TO

THE TRAVELLING PUBLIC,

WHOSE STEAMER IS THEIR SOFA, AND WHOSE RAILWAY CARRIAGE IS A
LIBRARY CHAIR,

AND TO

ALL PEDESTRIANS FOR PLEASURE,

This Work is most respectfully Dedicated.

PREFACE.

As a majority of Anglo-Saxons delight in foreign travel, while those whose circumstances or avocations forbid indulgence in personal experience gladly substitute genuine narratives thereof, the Author has felt emboldened to publish the notes made by him during a recent pedestrian trip across Spain. Nor does the fact that many and valuable works on that country are accessible seem a sufficient reason for not doing so, because the experiences of a traveller over an un-hackneyed route, journeying in a different manner from any preceding him, must be more or less unique and novel—therefore, if conscientiously told, interesting.

The following pages are full of trivialities and minor incident. But truly the small things of life, taken in the aggregate, are the most important;

and, as a general rule, comprise all that in it is entertaining.

He who reads will find more gossip than guide-book ; more frank confession than egotism. The Author has tried to convey ideas of persons, things, customs, and occurrences, precisely as he found, saw, and experienced them. He has also preferred being reliable to being startling ; has chosen the rather to risk a charge of commonplaceness than to aim at " dignity of narration," perchance only to achieve pomposity and dulness. To paraphrase the oft-quoted " Veni, vidi, vici," he has seen, returned, told ; has done his little best to fulfil the wish of Catullus to Veranius :

Visam te incolumem, audiamque Iberum
Narrantem loca, facta, nationes,
Sicut tuus est mos.

CONTENTS.

CHAPTER XVII.

CHAPTER XVIII.

CHAPTER XIX.

CHAPTER XX.

CHAPTER XXI.

CHAPTER XXII.

CHAPTER XXIX.

CHAPTER XXX.

CHAPTER XXXI.

LIST OF ILLUSTRATIONS.

ON FOOT IN SPAIN.

CHAPTER I.

Where would I go ?—The Affair decided—Preparations—My Little All—The "Pleasant Land of France"—Run from Bayonne to San Sebastian—The Land of Historic Romance—Disarmed—Irun—The Gibraltar of Northern Spain.

THE winter of 1876 was fast approaching, and I found myself an idler who had no programme, absolutely without engagements, having no special inducements to go anywhere in particular, nor reason to remain where I was. And so the wandering spirit born of past adventures—that feeling, near akin to the impelling instinct of migratory birds when their time of flight draws near, which becomes part and parcel of the man who has travelled far and wide —irresistibly tempted me, like them, to spread my wings and take a flight. Like them also I would seek a better clime, for an English winter has few charms for me.

Where would I go ? Not, if possible, on a tourist beat ; certainly not anywhere I had been before. Spain at once presented itself to my mind, a country I had long wished to see something of, and the nearest one not tracked over

B

by holiday travellers, as a rabbit-warren is by runs. I
would go to that museum and last coign of refuge of all
the odd ways, customs, and trains of thought that have
existed in Europe since the beginning until now. And
the better to observe the same, and amuse myself, would
make my sojourn in that country a pedestrian trip.

Considering Murray the best practical guide to any
country he treats of, I at once procured his " Spain ; " and
though an admirable handbook, which, had I not feared to
overweight myself, I certainly should have taken along, I
must confess to disappointment at finding it to be, to so great
an extent, but the reprint of what was written for the last
generation, which though good in its time, is now, like the
country treated of therein, rather behind to-day in matters
of practical utility. A glance through its leaves greatly
strengthened my resolve ; and when I read on page 22 :
" As a pedestrian tour for pleasure is a thing utterly unknown in Spain, walking is not to be thought of for a
moment," the affair was decided. I would prove a pedestrian trip in Spain, and a longish one, too—for my walk
should be from the Bay of Biscay to the Mediterranean—
could be achieved. Surely, if the man who makes a blade
of grass to grow on a before barren spot deserves to be
well spoken of, he who shows a new path available to the
pedestrian would in these times of pleasure pilgrimages be
doing to the fraternity of wanderers a service he might
contemplate with satisfaction.

To find a congenial companion, a friend, who with the
physical qualification requisite to sustain, without serious
inconvenience, the probable hardships of the undertaking,

uniting a natural or acquired disposition towards patience, contentment, and compromise, would, I well knew, more than double its enjoyment, halve its trials. Such a one I unfortunately did not find, so a pleasure excursion in solitary selfishness alone was decreed. One substitute for the companionship of a friend presented itself to my mind : I would make a comrade of my note-book, repeat to, or rather in it, whatever should happen that was not confidential, whatever I should see and hear that was interesting, everything that might be useful to be known to others following in my steps, my impressions and my reflections as they came to me. While to give a link with humanity to my labour, I would do so with a hope the result would prove sufficiently interesting to warrant publication. That so, I should, in fact, have many companions travelling with me—companions who, while spared the fatigues and worries, would enjoy the pleasures and charms of the excursion, and who, however much I might ultimately try their patience, I should certainly not quarrel with by the way. I would write up my journal from time to time, as occasion served, and revise it only so far as to extract vain repetitions and cut down verbosity ; for to review and modify first impressions by the light of after experience, though it might prevent self-contradictions, would certainly not be making a reader a travelling companion, while to indulge in " dressing up " or " pointing " of the scenes and incidents, though so doing would make the narrative more amusing, would be to totally deprive it of its only value— the being an unexaggerated account of personal experience. Indeed, I determined rather to err, and have probably done so, on the other side, preferring to be somewhat flat in description than unreliable in fact.

Preparations were soon made, and an outfit, light, portable, and compact, provided. Having found the inconvenience of a knapsack, out of which, without stopping and unharnessing, nothing can be taken, into which nothing put, I had made for me a substitute, which prior experience had taught is a far better arrangement as a carryall.

Out of waterproof canvas, from a full-sized pattern in calico cut out and stitched together by myself, to prevent mistakes, was constructed an affair of many pockets in one, like the skirts of a gamekeeper's shooting-jacket. It is supported by webbing straps, disposed after the fashion of trouser-suspenders, extends round the hips and fastens, when wished, in front by strap and buckle. Slits, an inch in length, with opposite metal slides, placed along the edge of the opening to the outside, and enclosing pocket, and a running strap, to be passed through them, fastening at each end by snap padlocks, furnish the means whereby its contents are, when advisable, made secure from the over curious, or from the plundering of petty pilferers, who care not to betray a robbery by use of knife or scissors.

A change of under-clothes, a couple of pairs of socks, half-a-dozen handkerchiefs, some paper collars and cuffs—to "put on airs" with—a barber's comb and toothbrush, a towel and piece of soap, is my ample outfit of personal effects. To buy and throw away as I go along will be better than to burthen myself. Indelible-ink-pencils, a small and well-filled writing-case, a compact little housewife, the necessaries for smoking, my Foreign Office passport in a case, and a map of Northern Spain take but little room. A large powder-flask, full of Curtis and Harvey's best, a shot-pouch, caps, wrench, screwdriver, and other etceteras, necessary to have if one carries a muzzle-loader, are, however, both bulky and heavy. I take a gun on the advice of a friend, a Spaniard. He said I must have a gun with me, and for fear of difficulty about fixed ammunition, a muzzle-loader. A money-belt, worn under my shirt, carries my circular notes and all coin, excepting such as is wanted for immediate use. An old greatcoat that has seen many a day's and night's service, a soft felt hat, a fishing suit, and a pair of ankle-jacks, comprised my costume. I burdened myself with a gun and apparatus not merely as a protection, as insisted on by my Spanish friend, but because of vague but glowing accounts concerning the shooting to be had in Spain, and the hope that by experience of a sport that is one of my chief delights, I may obtain reliable and definite information for the benefit of brother-sportsmen.

A railway trip through the pleasant land of France was not devoid either of interest or incident, for the journey was broken at many places, at which short stays were made, to renew old friendships and revisit once-familiar scenes ; and on the 14th of November I found myself making its last stage, the run from charming Bayonne to the Spanish frontier, and the proposed end of my railroading—San Sebastian.

From Bayonne to San Sebastian is not far, only fifty-five kilo. The road, however, is one whose construction must have presented some engineering difficulties, and cost much ; for the country is mountainous all the way, four rivers have to be crossed, and many miles of gradient has been blasted out of the solid rock.

It is an interesting and picturesque journey, that turning of the west flank of the Pyrenees. Pretty dells, little mountain valleys, rocky gorges, timber-covered slopes, open grassy glades, willow-fringed streams, present themselves in ever-changing combination. The rugged and serrated combs of the distant mountains in the east, now seen, then lost, always reappearing with changed aspect, afford an ever-varying background, and give additional interest and finish to a succession of most charming natural pictures. The weather was perfect, and except during the *arrête* at Hendaye station I spent the time pleasantly, luxuriating in the prospect, enjoying the balmy, invigorating mountain air, and trying to recall some of the stirring incidents connected with the country I was passing through ; for I was in the land of historic romance.

Soon after leaving Bayonne, the ruins of Chateau Marrac suggested the story of Charles IV., for therein he had been a prisoner ; then of the shameless act of villany perpetrated in that very chateau by the first Napoleon, for there, outraging the sacred laws of hospitality, violating his pledged faith, the conqueror of Europe and greatest scoundrel of the age sent his invited guest, Ferdinand III., " from his table to a dungeon." Then came a peep at the cathedral of St. Jean de Luz, scene of the nuptials of Louis XIV. and the Princess of Philip IV. of Spain, the ill-fated Maria Theresa. A little farther on appeared the ancient Chateau d'Urtubie, where Louis XI. and the kings of Aragon and Castile met in state ; and then the frontier stream, the historical Bidassoa.

On the right bank of the Bidassoa stands the Hendaye station, and there I had to pass the custom-house, and also change trains ; for, with a precautionary eye to a possible future invasion from France, the Spanish Government insisted on a break of gauge where the railway crossed the frontier line, so that trains carrying troops could not be run into Spain ; but foolishly, it appears to me, they fixed on a wider gauge instead of a narrower one. It is no great trick to raise the rails on one side of a road and put them down again closer to the others. To widen a narrow track, having "ties" with nothing to spare, is a heavy contract.

My first experience with Spanish officials was unpleasant. As I stepped over the air line between the two national jurisdictions, as I put my foot in Spain, I was disarmed, my double-barrel was taken from me. It was of no avail that I showed my "Derby," and explained my gun was for sporting purposes solely. I must give it up ; there was no remedy ; their orders were imperative. A superior officer came and explained to me. The province of Guipuzcoa was in a state of siege ; a proclamation had been issued ordering the disarming of all its inhabitants unprovided with a Government licence to carry weapons. All custom-house officers and frontier guards were instructed under no pretence to allow arms to enter from France, and to arrest anyone attempting to smuggle them. But, he added, your gun is only temporarily withheld from you ; it will be returned on your producing an order for it from the

Governor of Guipuzcoa, which you will have no difficulty
in obtaining, and it shall be taken good care of. This
relieved my mind, and resigning myself to the inevitable,
and my gun to him, I resumed my journey, reflecting that,
considering the recentness of the late civil contest, the fact
that the Carlists had obtained their arms chiefly across the
French frontier, and the apprehension entertained of
another rising, I could not reasonably consider myself
ill-used, though it was a nuisance and a bore. But the
striking view before me, the associations connected with
the points of interest in sight, drove for the time being all
thought of petty annoyance from my mind.

Stirring episodes of history had been enacted all around
me. "The dolorous rout" of Roncesvalles is as identified
with the town, whose ruined fortifications and quaint old
buildings appeared to my sight, as that of the Saxons is
with Hastings, while, coming into view below, Fuenterabia
recalled a flood of half-forgotten history. There more than
half-a-million French soldiers entered to conquer Spain,
over 300,000 of them never to see France again. There our
"great captain" forced the river and defeated Soult,
driving him from an almost impregnable position. To the
left rises San Marcial, scene of an earlier French defeat.
There, in 1522, Beltran de la Cueva overthrew the troops of
Bonnivel; while again, in 1813, it witnessed 18,000 French
repulsed and routed by 12,000 Spaniards. Below, in the
centre of the river's bed, lays an island, small in size but
great in renown—l'Ile de la Conférence, where Louis XI.
and Henry V. negotiated the marriage of the Duke of
Guienne; where Francis I. was exchanged by his captor

the great Charles V., for his two hostage sons ; where the treaty of the Pyrenees was concocted by Cardinal Mazarin and Don Luis de Haro. Then came Irun, captured by De Lacy Evans from the Carlists in 1837, after a desperate assault, that cost the enemy 700 men ; soon after Pasages, a picturesque old town, apparently situated on the shore of a lovely little mountain lake, surrounded by redoubt and tower-crowned heights—really a land-locked harbour ; and at last San Sebastian, " the Gibraltar of Northern Spain," the end and terminus to my railway travelling. Thenceforth I would foot it.

CHAPTER II.

NOVEMBER 20, 1876.—The San Sebastian railway station
is on the north side and close to the banks of the river
Urumia. The city lies on the south. I walked across the
bridge, the Puente de Sta. Catalina, and took up my quarters
at the first hotel arrived at : a large house of good appearance called Hôtel du Commerce. From its windows is a
fine sea view. It was sufficiently well furnished, clean, and
comfortable ; the attendance and commissariat very good ;
the proprietor and his family attentive and polite.

After breakfast my first care was to obtain an audience
with his Excellency Don Laureano Casado Mata, the
governor of the province, to arrange the matter of the
recovery of my gun. This I did without difficulty. I was
courteously received, and assured that to-morrow an order
from him on the custom-house for it would be issued
to me, but that it would be first necessary for me to
take out a licence to carry arms, and that when my gun

was delivered there would be a duty to pay. "Return to-morrow," he said, and "Go with God"—a polite dismissal.

Leaving the Oficinas de Gobernacion, I strolled off to the sea-wall at the mouth of the river, attracted by the roar of a magnificent surf: immense rollers from the Bay of Biscay breaking on the shore in glittering spray. Seated on the stone parapet were some fishermen whom I watched with interest. They were catching gray mullet. I entered into conversation with them, and learned the season for good sport was over, but that in summer and autumn the wall was lined with fishers whenever the tide served, and not an instant passed without a capture along the line, while frequently as many as twenty fish might be seen in the air at once, as they were being slung out of the water. Then also many other varieties of fish were to be caught; the takes being, too, not only more numerous, but including larger fish, many seven and eight pounders. However, the four fishermen I was watching seemed to me to be doing well enough. I remained a long time, and they averaged, to the man, a mullet to the quarter of an hour, the fish running from half a pound to two pounds in weight. The water was so clear I could see the rocks at its bottom, and swarms of little fishes swimming about. Occasionally, also, I saw a passing mullet take the bait with a rush like that of a lively trout. The tackle used is a rod of about twenty-four feet in length, the butt pine, the rest a bamboo cane. A long twisted hair line, salmon-gut points, three small white-metal sea-hooks, baited with pieces of salted and dried fish, a cork float, and a lead sinker. The "swim" is constantly ground-baited by lumps of mashed refuse-fish being thrown in, and a sharp eye and quick wrist are necessary to strike at the right moment.

At dinner acquaintance was made with two fellow-guests, a captain of cavalry and another of artillery, pleasant gentlemanly men and great dandies, and the evening spent smoking *cigarios*, sipping cognac, and chatting with the three daughters of the house who joined us, the mother occasionally looking in by way of playing propriety, I suppose.

Next morning I applied for the licence to carry arms, and was informed my request must be made in writing on stamped paper, and accompanied with a payment of eighty reals—sixteen and eightpence—made in government revenue stamped notes to that amount, which I could obtain at a tobacconist's. I got them, wrote out my application, signed it, returned to the governor's office, and handed it to the proper official. He bowed, told me to " Return to-morrrow " and " Go with God "—pretty phrases, but becoming too frequent. I remonstrated ; said I was in a hurry ; should like the licence directly. He said, " Impossible ; besides, to-morrow will be soon enough."

" Ah ! " said one of the officers, when in the evening I was relating to him my experience at the Government House, " this is truly the land of to-morrow, though not as much for foreigners as for us ; you, perhaps, will get the papers you want to-morrow ; were you a Spaniard, you would be in luck to obtain them in a week or ten days. Two hundred years ago a witty Spanish author wrote a work called ' Volver Mañana ' (return to-morrow) ; we are just as bad now."

And next morning I did get both order and licence. The latter, I found, was good for a year from date, and practically, leave to shoot all over Spain, for I learnt that only near a few towns in the south was any attempt made to preserve or to drive off trespassers. When, in reply to the official's question, as he handed order and licence to me, "When are you going for your gun?" I answered "By the next train," he was perfectly aghast. To make but one day's work of getting the documents and the gun was a display of energy evidently unprecedented. "Impossible!" said he, "they will never give it you the day of the date of the order; wait till to-morrow and go with God."

My travelling experience on the continent of Europe is, that to expect to "take mine ease in mine inn" is to foster a delusion. I have found hotel living there not only much more expensive, but not nearly as comfortable as furnished apartments and eating at restaurants; so, though I had no fault to find with the house I was stopping at, I started out to seek lodgings, or some good boarding-house, for I had been told Spanish ones were often comfortable and pleasant.

San Sebastian being, in the season (summer time), one of Spain's most fashionable watering-places, I found this town was full of *Casas de Huespedes*, and, so, soon discovered my affair. I am domiciled, *piso segundo*, in one of the best-located houses in the town. A small bedroom, fair-sized sitting-room *en suite*, and both well furnished— the former containing a most comfortable bed, and plenty of washing and toilet apparatus — are my apartments.

Three meals daily ; namely, at nine o'clock, or earlier if wished, chocolate, rolls, &c. ; at noon, breakfast *à la four-chette;* at seven, dinner, comprises the board. For all these mercies I thankfully pay the sum asked of one dollar per day and no etceteras, wine, attendance, and everything included. On taking my room the landlady told me she was a widow, her *clientèle* chiefly military men, and that the company then staying in her house consisted of the secretary of the leading bank in town, a staff captain, a major of artillery, and another of the military administration ; and that a general of brigade and wife, and one of his aides, who were expected to arrive in a few days, had engaged all the remaining rooms, excepting the two she had given me. The class of inmates was recommendation of the house enough for me ; otherwise, not being used to Spanish cheapness, I should have, in spite of the good appearance of the rooms, doubted the firstrateness of one dollar a day board, and so gone farther to have, perchance, not fared so well. My bill at the Hôtel du Commerce was at the rate of eight *pesetas* a day inclusive, and no little French swindles about attendance, candles, soap, &c., &c., nor did anyone on my leaving ask mutely or otherwise for a *pour boire;* but I noticed a little money-box near the front door inscribed, " For the servants," and dropped what I thought right into it. It struck me as a modest, considerate way of soliciting vails, and far preferable to being mobbed on the doorstep by the whole *posse comitatus* of an inn's staff after the French and English manner.

On the morning of the 16th I took the ten A.M. train, and retraced my way to the frontier to get my gun. Arrived there I caught a commissionaire, tipped him the usual fee (two-and-a-half *pesetas*—two shillings and a penny), and after seeing, with him, some half-dozen officials, at as many bureaux, and paying ten *pesetas* duty, for which a custom's receipt was given, at last I recovered it. Part of four days, no end of trouble and bother, and some expense, to transact an affair that in England or France would have been one of only as many minutes. I have laid the lesson to heart. My first experience of how things are done, or rather, if avoidable, not done, in this country, has determined me, under no circumstances, to allow myself to become impatient while in Spain, that only so can I comfortably sojourn or travel in this country.

As I passed the pretty *embarcadero* of Pasages a familiar-looking craft caught my eye. A glance under her sternboard told me it was the *Miss Evans*, Aberystwith ; she brought a flood of home recollections to my mind. By-the-bye, that reminds me that the first time I went into the Plaza de Guipuzcoa (the chief square), I was astonished at seeing, staring me in the face, carved in gilt letters each a foot square over one of the handsomest shops there, my own surname. I went in, asked a gray-eyed, light-haired, prominent-nosed man, who was reading a newspaper, if he was the señor whose name was over the shop. He was, could he do anything for me? I bought some trifle, entered into conversation, and incidentally asked what countryman he was, remarking his name seemed to me foreign. He replied, " Not so ; we are a Spanish family and of this place." I was rather pleased by his reply ; it is in many ways convenient, when travelling in a strange country, for one's name not to stamp a man as a foreigner, or, as is sometimes the case, be unpronounceable by the natives. But it was a strange coincidence, and I mentioned it at dinner. The artillery captain asked me, "Was your grandfather ever in this country?" "Yes, and remained here. He was an officer in the unfortunate Sir John Moore's expedition, and died at Corunna." "All is explained," said he, with a quiet smile and wave of the hand. "That man is your cousin. When one's grandfather has been an officer on foreign service, one never knows where one may meet with cousins." Then everybody laughed. The girls seemed to think it an excellent joke. But the strangest thing is to come. A day or two after I was again in the shop, and an old man entered from the street, having in features, complexion, and expression a great likeness to one of my ancestors. I said to the proprietor of the shop, "That's your father."

"It is," he replied. "How do you know?"

"I see a family likeness."

"I do not, but perhaps I shall look like my father when I am eighty."

I was quite intrigued, and have taken considerable trouble to find out all about the family; not a difficult thing in this country of genealogies. They are a branch of an old Pampeluna family, who came to Spain early in the sixteenth century, from Naples. There certainly is not a particle of an Italian look about the father and son. And I am told their Pampeluna relations are notorious for their light hair, fair skin, gray eyes, and family look. That it is one of the rare cases of preservance of type in a family occasionally occurring, strikes me as the only possible solution. Perhaps the captain was right when he said, "That man is your cousin," but by how many generations of removes?

Each day I have a look at the fishermen. The river-wall is such a nice place to take the after-breakfast smoke on, and the view thence is glorious. On several occasions some of these anglers were fishing for bass, using a different tackle from the mullet catchers. They were provided with a strong hemp line, sixty feet long; no rod; a gimp or wire trace, a foot in length; a heavy lead sinker (3 oz.), and large white-metal sea-hook, on which, in precisely the same manner the hook of a trimmer set for pike would be baited, is placed a sardine. I saw many splendid fish taken. The *modus operandi* is as follows: You coil your line carefully on the parapet of the sea-wall, take hold of it a dozen feet from the hook, swing it round a few times, and launch it into the breakers. Then you feel the line lightly till you get a run. You will know it when you do. It will be snatched with a rush, and your capture will give plenty of sport to land.

I am told, but not on authority I know to be reliable, that trout are to be caught three or four miles up the river. But there is no doubt the Orio, within a day's easy drive, contains plenty. And I was informed sewin and salmon abound also.

I have made the acquaintance of several ardent sportsmen, and eagerly sought information from them. I find the immediate prospect for sport is very bad. The weather has been too warm. Since my arrival the thermometer has

only ranged between 24° and 27° Réaumur, in the shade,
night and day. Not a speck of snow has fallen on the
mountains. And, as the "passage" takes place between
the first and twenty-fifth of this month, only a few days
remain. Such a season is unusual. November generally
sees the peaks of the Spanish Pyrenees white with snow;
and a northerly storm or two is regularly expected to
accompany the advent of this month. In such cases the
flights of cock alight as they arrive—there are thousands of
birds I am told—till the country is alive with them; and
the marsh grounds and rivulet banks swarm with snipe.
Once settled they remain till spring, and the shooting, of
its kind, is not to be surpassed. Resident game, however,
such as partridges, hares, rabbits, and so forth, have become
almost extinct in this neighbourhood. They were killed
off by the Carlists during the war, who were mostly
armed with shot-guns, had opportunities in plenty to get
sporting ammunition; and the mode of warfare being a
" Return to-morrow—go with God " affair, pot-hunting was
a regular pastime and the order of the day. Ducks, usually
plentiful and in great variety at this season, are also very
scarce, owing to the mildness of the weather. In the
mountains there are a few boucketins and bears, and wild
boar are plentiful. None of them, however, can be got at
until after the fall of the leaves, the cover being now too
thick for stalking to be possible. I am too late for the
quails, whose season here is the latter part of summer,
when the country is literally alive with them. Foxes are
innumerable, and hunted with avidity. They are in fact
the sportsmen's (?) chief game. Here foxes are "done to

death " with shot-gun and dog, in a like manner as hares are in France, and are sought after for their skins.

I have had a specimen of Spanish postal arrangements. My daily call at the *Correo* was invariably a disappointment, and I had commenced to wonder why I never got any letters, when one day a stranger, a Frenchman, stepped up to me in the street and saying, " I think this is yours," produced one from his pocket and handed it to me. It was properly directed after the Spanish manner :

Al Señor Don Juan S. Campion,
San Sebastian,
Guipúzcoa,

Lista de Correo.   España.

There was no excuse for mistake. And it ought to have been delivered to me at the office.

This is the history of that letter's adventures. The summer visitors here have introduced the bad custom of tipping the letter-carriers who bring them their correspondence ; hence, instead of, as by law bound, leaving foreign *Lista de Correo* letters to be called for, they hawk them about town to find the owners and get the tips. I had been tracked to the Hôtel du Commerce and my letter taken there. But I had left. So also had a recent French guest. The landlord did not know my name, nor where I had gone ; neither did he know the name of the French traveller who had just left his house. But he did the place where he had gone to, so, on spec, forwarded my letter to the Frenchman, then sojourning at a little village in the mountains called Atocha. The Frenchman was out when it arrived, and the letter was left. On his return, seeing it was not for him, he pocketed it; and the first time he came to town asked amongst his friends if they knew of such a person as myself. One of them was fortunately a lately-made sporting acquaintance, and describing my appearance accurately, enabled the holder of my letter to recognise me. I went to the *Oficina del Correo* and presented the officials with a piece of my mind. I hope they liked it.

Wishing to have a look at the country and to see if I could find any game, though the weather had remained fine and as warm as the hottest English summer-time, I started out yesterday for a day's shooting. Leaving home at a quarter to seven, without breakfast, of course—no man expects to get anything to eat at that early hour in Spain —but I laid in a supply of bread at an early-opened bakery that I passed, and at a *ventorrillo* disposed of a "go-down" of *aguardiente*. Awful stuff—liquid lightning.

The temperature of the morning was so warm that I dressed very much in my old Arizona style: a loose flannel shirt, no collar, no necktie; trousers without braces, no underclothes; cotton socks, and the peasant shoes of the country, *alpargatas*, or, in plain English, linen shoes with soles of thick hemp-webbing and without heel-taps, looking much like, and feeling exactly the same to walk in, as Mexican Indian moccasins.

Crossing the river Urumia by the *Puente de Sta. Catalina*, I took a road leading diagonally up its course, recrossed it by another bridge, and found myself on an alluvial flat of about fifteen hundred acres. A tract of land partly cultivated, partly in rush-grown ponds and waste ground. Evidently the sea backed the river water up, at high tide, to beyond the head of the flat, and to protect it from overflow was an enclosing embankment, and several transverse ones ; while to drain it were intersecting ditches, crossing in all directions ; most of them about the width of an easy jump, all nearly choked with reeds, rushes, and flags. Around this flat the river curved for more than a half-mile. For the remainder, its edge was met by hill sides, covered with low trees, with tangled brakes, and beds of fern ; hill sides full of little springs, miniature bogs, and rills of water. If there were any cock, snipe, or duck in the country, before me was the ground to find them on.

I first tried the flat ; beat it closely and carefully. No go, nothing on it. While doing so, the sky became overcast, and ere long it commenced to drizzle, a soft, warm rain, but very wet. At last I flushed two plover. They were of a kind unknown to me, and got away, far out of shot. As I was leaving the flat to try the hills, I put up a fine snipe. He rose at thirty yards, and I covered him before he had gone ten feet ; but it had been raining then for two hours, a fine soaking rain, my gun hung fire, and a miss was the result.

While wandering amongst the hills, or more properly speaking, mountain spurs, I came across a ruinous old water-mill, a most dirty, tumble-down, miserable hovel ; but having an announcement over its entrance that wine was procurable within. It was an opportunity not to be missed. I could there make my breakfast, and pleasantly reverse the state I was in, for I felt dry inside and very wet without. In the mill were two men cobbling up the wheel's machinery, which to English eyes, albeit those of one who had been a backwoodsman, seemed totally wrecked, and quite unmendable. The living-room contained some half-dozen children, most of them girls, and two young women busy doing nothing. A bloated goatskin lying on the window-sill, stained a dark blood colour, and having a piece of bamboo reed, stopped with a spigot, sticking out of one corner of it, was ocular evidence there was wine in the house. It was *Vino de Navario*, and in quality a fine, full-bodied, fruity burgundy, very grateful to a wet and tired *chasseur*. I drank two big tumblers full of it while eating my bread, smoked a pipe, and felt refreshed. The flavour of the skin, in the wine, I did not quite like (I am told strangers do not, but soon get accustomed to, and then rather prefer it), otherwise it was better wine than I have ever got in France, and it cost me less than three halfpence per tumbler—a *real* (twopence-halfpenny) per pint. *Vino de Navario* proved much stronger than I supposed, for notwithstanding wet and exercise, it got into my head, and very nearly into my legs too.

I beat the cover on hill and mountain side until three o'clock, and only saw one cock. It was flying, and too high up to be shot at, with any possibility of success ; then I faced for home. Soon after four o'clock I arrived as wet as the false-keel of the Ark when it grounded on Ararat, and quite satisfied I had been correctly informed, that as yet there were no cock or snipe to speak of in the country, and as sure I had never, in as many hours, walked over better cock and snipe ground before.

It has been raining steadily ever since yesterday morning, and looks as if it might continue to do so till doomsday, but it is a warm rain. What little wind there is comes from the south, and the prospect for birds is very bad. It is just the weather for them to travel; but while the wind holds in its present quarter they will continue going north, and not alight this side the Pyrenees.

CHAPTER III.

NOVEMBER 24, 1876.—I have been staying in San
Sebastian much longer than I intended. At this rate I
shall never get to the Mediterranean. But really the place
is a hard one to leave. I am very comfortable. Politeness
and kind attentions have been showered on me from all
sides. The country and town is so thoroughly Spanish,
notwithstanding its proximity to France, as to be quite
new and strange ; and since the rain ceased—it only lasted
two days—the weather, with a slight exception, has been
delicious, and my time most interestingly occupied observing the inhabitants, their ways and customs, and in
viewing the neighbourhood, taking long walks to the
numerous points of special interest, and vainly looking for
game.

These Guipuzcoans—the peasantry—seem a hardy,
good-sized, stout, industrious, and when not fighting,

energetic people. In every little field—and they are little, for ground level enough for cultivation is scarce, and in small patches—I was sure to see some of them at work, working, too, with a will, not "putting the time in," like English farm labourers. Still, these people live in wretched hovels. Not that the buildings in which they sleep always were such; on the contrary, they are the remains of good, substantial, occasionally large, solidly-built, stone houses—ancient *casas solares*—whose fronts are frequently adorned with armorial shields, sculptured in stone. But they all look, not only some centuries old, and as if no repairs had ever been done to them, but also as though they had been regularly battered and sacked, which, indeed, every one of them has doubtless been many times. One or two rooms in these ruinous buildings, more or less roughly roofed over in recent times, is the present dwelling-place of the farmer and family, his help, and his cattle. The largest and most remarkable of these old places that I came across is situated some distance up, in fact, on a spur of the mountain immediately south of the San Sebastian bathing-bay. Its roof has gone—literally gone—to grass, ever so long ago. Its windows are ragged holes in the walls. The only thing in tolerable preservation about it is an admirably well carved in stone coat-of-arms, most elaborately quartered, and surmounted with a many-pointed crown—one like the David's crown of Bible pictures.

On the height immediately above are the remains of an old fort of the redoubt order, apparently the key of the position ; for the whole summit of the mountain has once

been intrenched, and the traces of the zigzag, which cork-
screws up its face, lead immediately thereto. A Spanish
gentleman of this place informs me the fortifications are of
the time of the Emperor Charles V., but can tell me
nothing about the old house, or why there is a crown over
the coat-of-arms above its entrance. Most certainly the
crown is not an imperial one.

The personal appearance of the females of the peasantry
is a daily source of astonishment to me. They are continually exposed to the weather, wear nothing to protect
their faces, their head-dress is but a party-coloured kerchief,
bound round their back hair ; yet the majority of them
have really beautiful complexions, not swarthy, not rough,
but fair and quite delicate, with a rosy tinge and very
smooth skin. The thoroughly fair type is, however, scarce ;
most of these women having very dark brown eyes and
raven hair, enhancing greatly by contrast the fairness of
their skin. I suppose the Northmen conquest of the
country in eight hundred and something is the remote
cause of their fairness of complexion. These women on
working days wear neither shoes nor stockings, and have a
reckless *naïveté* about the displaying of their limbs, generally very good ones, that is not surpassed by even the
Boulogne shrimp-girls when following their vocation. They
seem a good-natured, cheerful lot ; there are always groups
of them to be seen round the pumps, springs, and wells,
some washing, some drawing water ; others balancing,
without help of hand, huge oriental-looking water-jars on
their heads ; and all laughing, chatting, singing, and
making sport. The shop-girls of the town seem quite of a

different type. They, or I mistake greatly, show more or less Jewish blood.

The hauling of the country is chiefly done by oxen, smallish, but well-built, active animals ; in shape a little like Devons ; all of one colour—light dunnish bay. These draught animals are yoked by the horns ; a troublesome way of hitching, but unquestionably the method enabling them best to use their strength. Over the yoke is drawn a sheep-skin with the fleece on, and round the forehead of the steers is bound an ornamental fringed fillet. The waggon is generally a two-wheeled affair, made after a most ancient pattern, the wheels being solid discs of wood. The "iron work" of many of these primitive vehicles is raw hide, and the axles of all of them are "greased with curses " only. You can hear them squeak and groan long before you can see them.

The town is at present full of military—*migueletes* mountain militia ; and a permanent provincial force, *guardias civiles*, the Spanish equivalent for the gendarmerie of France, and the regulars of all arms, swarm everywhere. Guipuzcoa has the garrison of a country conquered but not trusted. These troops, officers and men, are very well uniformed. Ease, elegance, and utility are combined in a way that is an example to England, France, and even most practical America.

I perceive the officers here have the same custom as obtains in England, with regard to the wearing of their uniforms ; only doing so when on duty. Directly they come off, so does their harness, and they clothe themselves in mufti. When *en paisano*, these Spanish officers are dressed more like Englishmen than Frenchmen, as far as style goes, and have all a thoroughly well-groomed look about them, and a quiet repose of manner. In fact their " form " is excellent. And they must certainly take great care of their hands, which, as a rule, are small, well-shaped, soft, and white.

The Spanish newspapers I have come across are but poor affairs, and their foreign intelligence is, I suspect, like a good deal of the cognac drunk in England, chiefly a domestic manufacture, flavoured to suit customers' palates. At dinner, I regularly hear the political news of the day discussed. Sunday last there was great excitement. Two coalitions had been formed, and war was about to be declared—Russia, Germany, and Italy against Turkey, England, Austria, France, and Spain. "Why Spain?" I innocently inquired. "What earthly interests has she in the matter, calling for the extravagance of going to war?" One of the officers gave triumphantly the—to all except myself—conclusive answer: " Spain cannot permit a European war to take place and remain inactive, not take the front position her rank amongst nations demands ; and Spain, England, and France, being the leaders of civilisation, *must* pull together." It all sounded very queer to me, premises and conclusion ; I give it as a specimen of Spanish sentiment.

In pursuance of a promise, I have made a commencement at beetle-collecting. My first step was to get laurel leaves ; for, I had been told, mashed laurel leaves, in a closely-stoppered bottle, would quickly kill these insects. It took me half a day's searching to find any laurel trees.

At length, spying some in a walled garden, I made a rapid raid, committed trespass and petit larceny, and fell back on my base of operations, with a pocketful of tender upper leaves. Then I went and bought the bottle—an old sulphide of quinine bottle—at an apothecary's shop. I told the chemist what I wanted it for. He disgusted me by saying no beetles were to be found in winter, no matter how warm the weather was; that in summer, any quantity of numerous varieties could be procured, but not so now. However, I cut and mashed my laurel leaves, filled my bottle with them, ate my twelve o'clock breakfast, and sallied forth. I turned over rocks and stones, exploited a quarry, tried the cliff's face, the roots and bark of trees, hedge bottoms; I nettled myself well, disturbed a colony of ants, was charged by their entire army, well bitten, and ignominiously put to flight. At last I made two captures—two wretched, half-dead-looking, black beetles. They were all I could find, and I bottled and took them home. Those are the two most contrary, disobliging, aggravating little monsters I ever heard of. They won't die. They walk about in the bottle, and fatten on those leaves. I found them looking miserable and half-dead; they have grown proud, and mightily exalt their horns. If those beetles continue in their present outrageous course, I shall, at the expense of the loss to science of their interesting carcasses, take them to a blacksmith's shop, lay them on an anvil, and try if they can be killed with a sledge hammer. Apropos of insects, I have been pleasingly disappointed by the absence of "the midnight marauder." Already I have been some little time in Spain, and, contrary to expectation, have not encountered " the wicked flea." But " the oldest inhabitant " assures me that, in summer, they, like the beetles, are not scarce.

More rain, but not for long, only an afternoon ; a steady, soaking, warm rain, with a light westerly wind. Then a clear up. After the rain, I took my usual evening's constitutional round the *Plaza de Guipuzcoa.* The air resounded with the cries of migratory birds, hovering and wheeling over the town, attracted by the lights. The companion of my promenade told me that when, during the passage of the woodcock, it was good " settling " weather, flights of them often alighted in the *plaza,* and were flushed by the early risers who first crossed it in the morning.

Eating being an interesting incident of life everywhere, I will give a fair specimen of a San Sebastian boarding-house breakfast, at the latter end of November. Table covered with a clean white cloth ; a ditto napkin ; and a roll of fresh bread before each person. In the centre of the table a handsome bouquet of natural cut flowers— heliotropes, roses, carnations, &c. &c.—all grown out of doors. Set around, are little plates containing cheese—a sort of gruyère ; fresh butter—very good ; excellent grapes, apples, walnuts, and other fruit. A neat, clean servant-girl goes round and pours out a large goblet of wine and a tumbler of water for each person, and the following courses are handed round : a beetroot salad, omelettes, sausages on toast, mutton chops and fried potatoes, pastry, black coffee, and *cigarios.* During the meal, wineglasses are refilled by the servant as often as emptied. Everything that ought to be hot is so—piping hot. The dishes are passed through a sliding panel in the wall, from the kitchen to the waitress in the room, and plates, knives, forks, and spoons changed with each course. The meal lasts about an hour, and there is to spare of everything.

Dinner of the same day. Table set out as at breakfast, excepting that there are no flowers. Wine helped and courses as follows : vermicelli soup ; boiled gray mullet and parsley sauce ; lentils, potatoes, and chopped cabbage; pieces of boiled beef and sausages; rissoles made of no man knows what, might have been veal, perhaps fowl, or possibly—but hold ; if, as is said, confidence is necessary to the enjoyment of love, how much more so is it to that of Spanish rissoles? Sufficient to say they were egged, bread-crumbed, nicely browned, and very good. Then, beef *à la jardinière ;* salad ; custard of some kind unknown, for I do not usually eat such things. In search of information much may and ought to be done, but a line must be drawn somewhere : I draw it at experimenting on my stomach with sweets and pastry. Finally, a dessert of all fruits in season, black coffee, the weed, and topics of the day.

The night succeeding the afternoon rain there was a light white frost, and thinking some of the birds, whose cries I had head, might have settled, I turned out early the following morning for a *chasse.* It was a magnificent, bright, clear, warm day, but I was again disappointed, and did not see any game, excepting two snipe, who got away out of range. During the day's tramp I saw a native sportsman with a cross-bred dog, one between setter and pointer ; also two others with a couple of highly-bred red setters that were ranging and quartering their ground beautifully. Neither party had seen any cock ; evidently there are none in the country now.

Last Thursday night the principal theatre opened for a short season, though it is the deadest time of the year ; not only are there now no visitors here, but the resident gentry are all away wintering at Madrid, or farther south, the good country houses being almost all empty and shut up. It was my first opportunity to attend a Spanish theatrical performance, and was not neglected. I found the theatre a very pretty, well-arranged one, much after the style of the Princess's, and admirably ventilated and lighted. All the evening, its temperature left nothing to be desired. Wishing to see and hear to the best advantage, I took a *butaca*, the equivalent for a stall, the most expensive place in the house, but only costing seven *reals* (one shilling and fivepence-halfpenny). I estimated the building would conveniently contain eight hundred persons, but this is probably an under estimate. In round numbers, there were four hundred present. A very well-conducted audience ; no shouting, stamping, or catcalling, in the gallery—if it was only twopence-halfpenny admittance ; no oranges, pop, and trash hawked about ; no talking while the acting was going on. Everyone seemed there to attend to the play, and not to annoy other people. There was no full dress, as we understand the term. The gentlemen were in calling costume, the ladies *en toilette de ville*, and very well dressed too were both the sexes. There were present many good-looking women, hardly any really plain ones, and some downright beauties. I counted them—there were seven. I am tolerably sure I never saw seven as handsome girls at one time in a London theatre.

Between each act most of the men went into the corridors and walked up and down them, smoking *cigaros* and chatting, or they paid calls on the ladies of their acquaintance in the *palcos* and *butacas*. There was no refreshment-buffet, and I do not think anyone left the building to " take a drink." Applause was only occasional and judicious. I had been told the company was indifferent, that it was one of no reputation. That being true, I am anxious to see a Spanish one that has a reputation, for the acting was capital. The troupe consisted of six performers, three men and as many actresses, and of a few "sups." It was a very even company, and nothing "sticky" about any of them ; no awkward pauses, no hitches, no exaggerations. They were dressed to their parts, not beyond them. And they did not "act "—that is to say, there was no posturing, mouthing, or obvious making of points. Altogether it was a very pleasing performance, and, from its excessive naturalness, a refreshing novelty. Three light comedy pieces composed the bill. The first, principal, and best, was entitled " *Un Inglese*," and was a " take off" on the travelling "*Milor*." The Englishman was got up to perfection. I declare when he came on the stage he looked so typically the London middle-aged swell, that had I met him in the street, I should have thought it

somebody I knew but could not exactly place. I was told
the actor was a Spaniard, who did not know any English
excepting the words in his part, so the way he talked
broken Spanish with an English accent, and mixed in
correct English phrases, was very clever. The orchestra,
twenty-eight performers and a conductor, was a fair one.
The performance commenced at eight sharp and finished
at eleven. There were no carriages in attendance, and
the ladies of the audience all walked home without don-
ning wraps, and either bareheaded or with only light lace
veils on. It said much for the climate.

While on the subject of amusements, "*Pelota*," the
national game of Northern Spain, that country's equivalent
for cricket, the game *par excellence* of the people, must not
be passed over. There is a very fine pelota court here,
and I have lately been a spectator at a grand match. The
game resembles in many respects both fives and rackets,
and can only be properly played in a court constructed
purposely. But it can be indulged in, after a fashion,
wherever there is a high wall and open space. And, in
spite of notices forbidding, and announcing fines for so
doing, the street *gamins* are eternally at it, making every
public building and ecclesiastical edifice in town a make-
shift pelota court, the forbidding notice serving admirably
as "the line." So early does the young idea here learn to
practise the Spanish maxim as to how an unpopular law is
to be observed —*obedecido pero no cumplido.*

The pelota ball weighs three ounces, and is as like as
may be to a racket-ball. It is "served" with the naked
hand. But the rest of the players are each furnished with

a species of racket ; a strong leather glove firmly bound on their right hand, and having a wicker-work spoon, two feet long and six inches wide, stiffly fastened to it, being used.

The match in progress was between crack players, and tolerably heavy betting was going on. The playing was very violent exercise for such hot weather, and considerable address, activity, and expertness displayed ; and judging by the frequent and hearty applause, the play was very good. However, not understanding the game, I could not properly appreciate the points.

The markets here are scenes of considerable interest to me. They are held daily, Sundays included. The principal are, the fruit, flower, vegetable, and game market ; the meat and fish one ; and in an open square a general mart of all kinds of frippery, earthenware, pots, pans, and charcoal—the last brought to town on donkeys, and sold by charcoal-women, looking like so many duchesses disguised as sweeps. The daily supply of vegetables and fruit is astonishing, both for its variety and quantity. All English summer vegetables and French autumn fruits are in profusion, as are also many, to me, new and strange ones ; and as the gardeners are now busy planting out young cabbages, cauliflowers, and lettuces, it looks as though they always had summer vegetables here. Indeed, the large oleanders and heliotropes, which flourish unprotected in the gardens all the winter, vouch for the mildness of the climate.

Nor is the fish market less well supplied. Indeed, the variety of fish seems almost infinite. Unfortunately, not being a learned piscatorial swell, I cannot give a list of them. I really do not know the English names for any, excepting the red and gray mullets, the bass, and the sardines. The last-mentioned fish are caught here in tolerably large quantities; though smaller they are much better flavoured than their Mediterranean cousins. I can vouch that when just caught, fried crisp and brown in new olive oil, and eaten with cucumber, salt, and cayenne, they are delicious. As yet, no sardines are "put up" here. The bulk of the takes are purchased by some Frenchmen of this place, who expedite them to Bordeaux; but intend, when sufficiently "ahead of the game" to have the necessary capital, to start canning works, and export them, cured and boxed, in the usual way.

The market-houses here are large, commodious, sweet, and airy; would be a credit to any place. The chief one is a handsome stone, iron, and glass edifice; in shape a hollow square, whose sides of one hundred and ninety feet each in length enclose an open flagged yard, having a fine fountain in its centre. It is quite lofty—about sixty feet in height from floor to ceiling. The fish and meat market is a large semicircular building, equally well arranged, lighted, and ventilated. Both these market-houses are kept scrupulously clean.

At present game is not plentiful, the few partridges and hares exposed for sale coming from Navarre. But poultry of all sorts and eggs are in profusion. I find the markets a pleasant lounge before breakfast, and a capital place to study the peasantry, especially the pretty girls from the mountains, and the hardly less comely fish-maids;

these latter being here, as everywhere else, seemingly belonging to a race apart and to themselves.

I have been disappointed by a lack of picturesqueness and variety in the peasant-costume of the province. This is the usual male one: On the feet, *alpargates*—no stockings—trousers and blouse of blue cotton, just like a French peasant's; under the blouse a coarse white linen shirt; round the neck a loosely-tied kerchief; in many folds and winds a wide red stuff sash, encircling the waist; surmounting all, and completing the costume, the Biscayan *gorra*, a head-covering wove all in one piece, looking like a compromise between a cricketing-cap and a Lowland Scottish bonnet, and having a tuft on its top. These caps are all either red or dark blue. Red is Royalist; blue is Carlist. For one red cap, fifty blue are to be seen.

After doing the markets—not being a purchaser, the fair vendors do not *do* me—the market-houses being close to the sea-wall, I usually go and spend a short time watching the fishermen. On the last occasion, though the sun shone in a clear sky, and the air was balmy, it was evident that either a gale was blowing to seaward, or there had recently been a storm in the Bay of Biscay; for the rollers that coursed one another up the Lazurriola, and with flashing light and thunder roars broke into snowy clouds of spray at the mouth of the Rio Urumea, swept in, in height and volume like unto the surf of the Pacific on a coral reef. Just within the breakers' edge, right in the churning foam, a long-line fisherman was trying his luck. I had not watched him two minutes before he got a run, and struck and landed a splendid fish, a rock bass, in excellent condition, and very deep and thick, at least two feet in length, and whose silver sides glistened like a salmon's. He gave it to a companion, who took it immediately to the fish market to sell "all alive ho!" rebaited with a fresh sardine, and resumed his fishing. Before long he had another run. The line was snatched right out of his hands, and twenty yards carried out before he could catch hold of its coil. After a short and lively tussle the fisherman landed his capture—a different and much larger fish than the other. Being close to him as he unhooked his captive, I had a good chance to inspect it carefully, but did not recognise the species. The fish was as silvery as the bass, had very small scales, and spots like a salmon trout. The fishermen called him a luena, but that may be only a local name. These Guipuzcoans have one for everything. But whatever he is called, that the fish is good eating, firm, flaky, and delicate of flavour, I do know, having done my part at table in the demolishing of several.

Sunday morning I attended a requiem mass in the Iglesia de Santa Maria, the chief church in town. The congregation was numerous, well dressed and devout, and the music good. In the afternoon the military band of one of the regiments stationed here played in the Boulevard. This promenade is a wide opening right through the centre of the town; it runs from the sea-wall of the river Urumea at its east end, to that of the Aconcha, the bathing bay, at its west extremity. It is about five hundred yards long, well planted with shade trees, has a pretty fountain at each end, and there is a pleasant draught of air almost always drawing through it. For the occasion the Boulevard was crowded with listeners walking up and down, principally servant-girls, soldiers, and peasantry. The band was a wretched affair; the twenty musicians played about as well as, and their instruments were, in tone and accord, like unto, a London street German brass band; but, if possible, in worse condition. They—the instruments—were as dirty as could be; had certainly never been cleaned since issued. I have never seen dirtier brass in any marine store. What a contrast to the, in every sense, splendid French band I had so lately heard at Bayonne!

The relative value of the copper coins in use here seems at first a conundrum which "no fellow can find out." But this question, like "Bradshaw," is to be understood by giving one's whole mind to it, and though it seems a very small matter to trouble about, is yet really worth while mastering, because in all countries a display of ignorance of small change stamps a man as a stranger unused to the business ways of the locality; in fact, as a person to be overcharged and otherwise imposed on in greater matters. Legally or theoretically—the two expressions are often convertible terms in Spain, I fear—the question is easy. The peseta, a silver coin worth twenty-one French sous, and practically replacing our shilling, consists of one hundred centimos, and is the standard of value; and the centimos are coined in copper pieces of one, five, and ten centimos, value respectively; but, practically, values are almost always reckoned in reals, a silver coin worth twenty-five centimos, or else in cuartos and ochavos, dos-cuarto pieces replacing our penny as a circulating medium. Now there are in general use here two dos-cuartos, each of different value, *i.e.* the old coinage and that of Isabella II., so I have tabulated their relative values for my guidance and convenience :

> 2 diez-centimos and 1 cinco-centimo ⟩
> 3 dos-cuartos, 2 cuartos, and 1 ochavo (old coinage) ⟩ = 1 real.
> 2 cuartos and 1 dos-cuartos (Isabella coinage) ⟩
> 17 ochavos ⟩

An old coinage dos-cuartos is much heavier than an Isabelleta cuarto, and yet it takes four of them and one ochavo to make a real, while four Isabelleta cuartos are taken for one real; verily, it is at first puzzling, and the reason thereof not obvious, nor can I see what the cuarto piece is a quarter of. The new one-centimo piece passes for an ochavo, so does any ancient or foreign copper coin, an English farthing or penny, an old French liard, or a two-sous piece. I am sequestering all strange ochavos that come to me as change, forming a collection of them. I have already put by a modern centimo, an old Egyptian inscribed coin, several Moorish ones of the period when the Moors governed Spain, a coin covered with Arabic characters, one of the Kingdom of Castile, a Roman one, a Gibraltar "two-cuarts" of 1842, a Don Carlos VII., and a Waterloo halfpenny ; this last coin bearing on one side the head and bust of the old duke. He is represented as wearing a laced uniform coat and epaulettes and a huge frill shirt ! Round his head is a wreath of bay-leaves and the words, "The Illustrious Wellington ;" on the obverse an Irish harp and the date 1816. I am told by a collector it is a very scarce piece in Spain. A gentleman showed me the other day some very rare old Roman coins in a splendid state of preservation, which he had received as ochavos when making purchases in the market. He would not part with them. One of my Moorish coins is as heavy as an old English penny, another weighs about the sixth of a farthing ; to-day they are of equal value, both ochavos. It seems queer to have such coins handed to one in change. Until habituated to the fact that he is in the old curiosity shop and museum-corner of Europe, a man wonders how they ever all got here.

CHAPTER IV.

NOVEMBER 28, 1876.—I am getting more in love with this place every day. The air is so soft and balmy, the sea so blue, the encircling mountains so charming. My only regret is that now is not the bathing season, for La Concha is an unsurpassable bathing beach. It lies to the south-west of the town, and is the inner edge of a circular bay, something over a mile wide. This bay is the harbour of San Sebastian, and has but a narrow opening to the sea, its mouth being more than half closed by the Isla de Santa Clara, a handsomely-wooded, rocky island, rising to the height of one hundred and sixty feet, and surmounted with a lighthouse. This island breaks the swell of the ocean into gentle waves. The water of the bay is clear, clean, bright, and warm, and there is absolutely no current. The sands are sloping, without a stone, shell, or rock, firm and smooth. The Perla del Oceano, or range of bathing-rooms, is admir-ably convenient for toilette arrangements. Ropes floated by buoys extend out nearly two hundred yards. In short, every care has been taken by the municipality for the safety, comfort, and convenience of bathers, of whom, I am told, hundreds at a time are to be seen, dressed in all varieties of costume, sporting in the water; for San Sebastian has of late years become a fashionable resort from Madrid and other large Spanish towns, and in the summer and early autumn is full of gay company. Then, too, is the time for bull-fights, and the large bull-ring is crowded with beauty and fashion. Now it is shut up, for which I am sorry, for Guipuzcoa is famous for fine and strong bulls ; and though much may be said against bull-fighting, it is certainly a sight to be seen occasionally, and if seen at all, may as well be seen thoroughly well done.

San Sebastian is evidently determined to be up to the times. On the old walls of the Plaza de Toros are flaming advertisements of a new skating-rink. Thus is a sport dating anterior to the Dark Ages and the last modern invention for amusement brought into close connection.

Yesterday I met a town-crier. In the most important particular of his office he exactly resembled the crier of Old England, for no man could make out what he was proclaiming. But he differed from his English equivalent in that he had no bell. He had, however, a striking substitute. A young man accompanied him, bearing a treble drum, on which he from time to time beat a roll to attract attention. Both crier and drummer were dressed in a neat—it might almost be called handsome—municipal uniform : dark blue frock-coat and trousers, brass buttons, and narrow silver-lace facings, and a glazed cap with a silver-lace band.

I have got a companion for my journey; I have bought
a dog, a setter, aged fifteen months. He is not exactly
the style of dog I should have chosen, were there choice to
be had, but there is not; for though I have seen plenty of
high-class, well-broken pointers and setters here, there is
no buying them, there are none of them for sale. I object
to the one I have obtained on two accounts. His size, for
he is the biggest, heaviest setter I think I have ever seen,
and it may bother me to keep him in condition on the trip
before me; and to his tail, which is inclined to the "club"
order, and carried too straight upright. However, he has
his good points—splendid feet, a fine intelligent head,
magnificent eyes, and great power. His late owner parts
with him because he cannot find a good man to break the
dog, does not go out sufficiently often to do so himself,
and has the promise of a thoroughly broken one from his
brother. He tells me the dog has had a few quail and
cock killed over him; that he possesses an excellent nose,
and ranges well; is tractable and affectionate, and of clean
habits. This gentleman has invited me to join a wild-
boar hunt, now being organised, and to come off as soon
as a snow-storm in the Pyrenees drives the game into the
foothills; but there is no immediate prospect of a change
in the weather, and the delay is too indefinite; besides,
snow is the very thing I fear and wish to avoid; a heavy
fall would play the mischief with a pedestrian trip in this
nest of mountains. I am promised, if I stop, a certainty
of sport, for the breeding-season has been very propitious.
Two litters have been the rule, not the exception, and wild
boar are in plenty; a herd of forty-seven has already been

marked in one of the high valleys, and the snow will drive down numerous more such herds.

The hunt is a regular *battue ;* those having guns are posted in likely places, in a circle extending miles, and a crowd of persons armed with clubs, forks, spears, pikes, &c., and hounds and curs, dogs of high and low degree, make a regular drive. The sport is not devoid of danger. My friend possesses the stuffed head of a boar, at whose killing he assisted, who sold his life at the price of that of three men. The hunter stationed where he attempted to break the line struck him in a vital spot with an ounce ball, but without stopping him. Making a last desperate charge, the boar floored his man and ripped him up, and two out of the number of beaters and hunters who rushed to the assistance of their fallen comrade were so badly injured as not to recover ; really we English have no right, as we often do, to assert the Anglo-Saxon is the only true sportsman. The boar's head was an immense one, and I am credibly assured that the wild boar of the Spanish Pyrenees dwarfs in size and ferocity the ordinary European wild boar to a " pig."

To-day is Alfonso's fête-day, and all the flags are flying. The troops are *en grande tenue.* Bells are ringing, powder is burning. "Viva Don Alfonso! El Rey de las Españas!" For how long ?

This afternoon, in honour of the day, there was a review of the garrison, three thousand men, infantry detachments from several regiments, a general's escort of cavalry-chasseurs, and the artillerymen from the forts. Several regimental bands attended, all about much of a muchness with the one I have described. The general, a fine soldier-like man, and his staff and escort, were in gorgeous array. I was struck by the marching of the men. It was most admirable. Though in heavy order, carrying knapsack, haversack, overcoat, &c., they went past at a killing pace—the *pas gymnastique*—and though they continued at the same speed, marching and countermarching for over half an hour, they looked as fresh as though they had been standing still ; indeed, it seemed as if they could keep at that gait all day. I inspected their arms and accoutrements. Nothing was rusty, dirty, or muddy ; but nothing was clean as a British sergeant would understand that word. All metal-work, gun, bayonet, buckles, &c., though they had been wiped often enough, had certainly never been scoured ; a system that has two practical advantages : the men lose less time cleaning, and there is nothing bright about their accoutrements—nothing that by catching a ray of sunlight might give a flash, betraying from a distance their movements to a foe.

After watching for two hours march and manœuvre, I came to the conclusion that the infantry before me were admirable to form the skirmish line of an advance through a difficult country. There was an "on my own hook" look about them and their movements, and they had the physical appearance of men who could stand hard work, fast marching, and short rations. Comparisons may be objectionable, but they are permissible to convey a clear idea. It seemed to me such soldiers could easily, in a rough hard campaign, out-march, out-starve, and perhaps, *after so doing*, out-fight British soldiers ; but under ordinary circumstances they would be no more able to meet their charge in the open than would so many children. They would go down like ninepins, or scatter like sheep ; the individual weight was not there, nor the solidity in mass, to give them the remotest chance in such an encounter. May it never occur.

The cavalry, so far as the rough material of horseflesh went, were very well mounted, their steeds being strong and serviceable, with a fair turn of speed and considerable dash of blood about them ; though as for being chargers, they would have been considered but unbroken horses in England, and they looked as wild as rabbits. The saddles were as much as could be after the fashion of English hunting ones, which surprised me, for I expected to see in use a modification of the old Spanish saddle, one like that now used in Mexico and California—a saddle which in my humble opinion is in every respect superior for campaigning purposes to the hunting-saddle. The men rode very well as individuals. Once they passed at a gallop. They were supposed to be in the formation column, four abreast. They went by in a ruck, like a close Derby finish, or a charge of wild Arabs.

To-morrow (D.V., and weather permitting), I shall take up my line of march—horse, foot, and artillery ; in other words, dog, self, and gun ; for, after much trouble and more advice, I have got my itinerary, and, subject to unforeseen alterations, my route as far as Zaragoza is decided upon. My best and most reliable informant has been a banker here, Don Pepé Fuliano, who in his younger days has often travelled the country in question on horseback, and quite lately gone through it several times by rail. My halting-places are to be Tolosa, Lecumberri, Pamplona, Venta de las Campanas, Tafalla, Caparroso, Valteirra, Tudela, Mallen, Alagon, Zaragoza—all long marches apart for a man carrying gun and ammunition, heavy overcoat, and all his baggage. I am assured that at many of these places I shall find the accommodation wretched ; that some of them are not fit for Christians to enter, much less to eat and sleep in.

"But you are not going alone ? " said Don Pepé.

"Indeed I am."

"Impossible ! Look you, two companions may travel the whole of this country—excepting parts of Andalucia, where there are organised banditti, with the utmost safety ; but a solitary man must not. In this country occasion makes the robber. Some men working in the fields, some peasants travelling the road, will see you ; will say, ' See, there is a man travelling alone ; let us run ahead of him, hide, jump on him from behind, and kill him ; nobody will know.' You may get as far as Pamplona without danger, for the peasantry of Guipuzcoa and Navarrette are quite honest ; they are smugglers. Below, thieves and bad people are not scarce, and if you travel alone beyond Tudela, something evil will certainly befall you. I would not undertake to do so for any money. You must absolutely have a companion, or——" And he executed a most impressive pantomime.

Don Pepé's opinion was corroborated by a Frenchman with whom I talked the matter over ; one who had lived ten years in Spain, and who not only talked Castellano

(Spanish) perfectly, but the Vizcayan and Catalan dialects. He said :

"I have travelled all over the country you are going through, most of it alone. You certainly risk being assassinated, if only for your gun and clothes."

"But if you have gone in safety alone, why not I ?"

"Look at this," pointing to the cicatrice of a gash across his cheek ; "and at this," opening his shirt-front and showing the mark of an ugly stab in the ribs. "Those are what came of travelling alone in the byways of Northern Spain. But," he added, "you are an Englishman, and may get through all right. You English are not *vive* as we are. You do not meddle with what does not concern you ; do not, when there is danger or excitement, lose your heads. But be very careful. Never give a light from your pipe or cigar to a stranger, for, doing so, you give him the drop on you ; and sleep with a weapon handy."

The officers with whom I mess say this is all bosh. If I make a point of travelling exclusively by daylight, do not tell anyone where I am going, make my payments out of an old rubbishy Spanish purse, with many coppers, little silver, and no tempting gold in it, wear old clothes, and mind my own business, I shall run no danger. They prophesy the chief fear is my being snow-blockaded at some miserable roadside tavern, with a vile bed, abominable and scanty fare, fleas, and low company. However, it seems to me that an Arizona pioneer, one who has gone through some Indian warfare, and several first rushes, ought to pull through without difficulty. We shall see.

In conclusion, I will give a short description of the

E

scenery surrounding San Sebastian.   Take all the mountains in Wales, north and south, tear them up by the roots,
pitch them endways in heaps all over the country ; cover
the portions lying uppermost with heather ; clothe the
lower slopes, when not so steep as to be bare rock, with
thickets and woods of oak and chestnut ; fill every ravine
and hollow with brawling streams, having swampy sides
and fringed with cock covert ; scatter through it, wherever
the ground approaches to a workable level, small and far-
apart fields of from a quarter to half-a-dozen acres in size ;
crown every eminence with ancient and modern entrench-
ments ; place ruinous old stone mansions, straggling
villages, apparently built in the Middle Ages, and big old
churches in every valley ; enclose with a rock-bound sea
and towering mountain ranges—and you have it.   No
wonder the Carlists held it so long.   Cavalry is useless,
cannon cannot be moved in it.   There is no question of
finding an impregnable position ; the difficulty would be to
find one that was not.   The country is one vast natural
ambush.   Apache Indians would hold it against the whole
Spanish army *ad infinitum.*   But Carlist troops had to be
paid ; that beat Don C.

NOVEMBER 30, 1876.—Wednesday's sun rose in a cloudless sky, a light balmy breeze blew from the south, and after despatching my little cup of chocolate I sallied forth on my long walk. A blessing on Spanish chocolate, Mexico's best gift to Spain, better than all its gold and silver. Speaking generally, we English have not the remotest idea what a good cup of chocolate means, and the Pope and College of Cardinals who have decided drinking it does not break fast; to the contrary, notwithstanding, it is the Spanish national, and for a person who takes an eleven o'clock meal, a really sufficient *break-fast.* Made thick enough nearly to stand a spoon up in, it is full of nutriment; and a glass of cold water drunk immediately after a complete preventive to its causing biliousness.

My gun was slung, coat rolled up and strapped to my

E 2

back, haversack swung from my shoulders, my new dog
Juan secured by a strong collar and chain, and taking
the road going south-east, I started for the Mediterranean.
So soon as the town was left the way commenced to
ascend, and an hour's climbing brought me to the top of
the first summit ; there I turned to take a last look and
bid farewell to San Sebastian and the Bay of Biscay.
The white clean houses of the town, the crescent bay, the
winding river, the fort-crowned mountains, the blue ocean,
on whose surface occasional flaws of wind and catspaws
glistened in the morning sun, seemingly so many splashes
of liquid gold, formed indeed a lovely view.

Juan behaved in a most extraordinary way. Evidently
he did not object to leave his native town ; on the contrary,
instead of my having to drag him he dragged me. The
way that dog threw his weight into his collar and determinedly hauled me along was most fatiguing. But it was
no use remonstrating by word of mouth. Ere gaining his
affections I dare not do so by word of whip. I had
therefore to submit, and suffer him to fill the contract
to do the hauling he seemed to consider that he had
undertaken.

Early in the day I arrived opposite a conical hill
whose side seemed inaccessibly steep, and which was
crowned with the fort of Hernani ; an ancient fort refitted
and rebuilt, and, as I could see, containing a garrison, for
its ramparts were paced by sentinels. Leaving it on my
left, and rounding the hill, the first valley seen since
starting came in sight, lying a few hundred feet below
me. A long narrow valley, with steep rugged mountains

beyond ; and in its centre, on the banks of a mountain trout stream, the town of Hernani, a poor dilapidated place, looking almost deserted, although " returned " as having a population of four thousand souls.

It was clearly perceivable that the town of Hernani is a place of antiquity, and also that it was for its protection that the fort on the hill had been originally built. Its recent way of fulfilling such mission had been, judging by the appearance of the houses, the lack of roofs to many of them, the round ragged holes in their walls, to knock it into a cocked hat.

The only chance for refreshment I saw at Hernani was a tumble-down little bakery, whereat I purchased, for *dos-cuartos*, some stale rolls for self and dog; and, after walking along a few hundred yards of comparatively level road, I again commenced to climb. Soon a bend to the right brought me to another little valley and village, also with its commanding fortified eminence ; for on a low but very steep and rugged flat-topped mountain of bare rock, overlooking valley and village, was another fort. On looking back, it became evident the road had curved more than a semicircle, and that this little village also was under the guns of Fort Hernani. Whether the two forts had had a long range duel and caught that poor little place between, or they purposely had been paying their respects to it during the late civil war (if a succession of skirmishes, surprises, assassinations, and running-aways—especially running-aways—can be called war), I do not know, but that village had certainly come to most unmitigated grief.

At Andoain, two miles farther on, a dilapidated, tumble-down, poverty-stricken mountain town, I had intended to breakfast; but failing to find any place where such a meal could be had, I hunted up a *ventorillo*, walked in, called for a tumbler of wine, and sat down to breakfast on it and a roll of bread, which had remained in my pocket.

The host of this wayside tavern and a well-to-do-looking customer were the only individuals present besides myself, and their manner of returning my salutations was uncordial almost to rudeness. By-and-by the customer asked what Department of France I belonged to, and then, learning I was English, his and the *ventero's* countenances and manners changed to great friendliness, and they assured me, with much *empressement*, it gave them the utmost pleasure to welcome an Englishman, for, said they, the English are a good people, helped us against the c———*jo* French, saved San Sebastian in the old war, and furnished money to Don Carlos.

After conversing awhile on politics, these men showed me some rich specimens of argentiferous galena, alleging it came out of a mountain quite close by, and we had a long talk on mining matters. I think they suspected me of being a "prospector." The wine at that rubbishing "Deadfall," drawn as it was out of an old goat-skin bag, was the best I have yet drunk in Spain—Navarra wine of the first quality. It was too strong for me to venture on a second tumbler, for the tumblers were very big; what I took cost the equivalent of three-halfpence. It was better wine than I ever got in a French restaurant at any price.

A continuously ascending walk, through rugged mountains, and passing by villages of most ancient aspect,
brought me towards the close of evening to Tolosa—the
end of my day's tramp. It was a charming walk. The
latter half of it had led along the edge of the Orio, a clear
stream of about the size of the Usk in South Wales, from
below Brecon. On its banks were some paper and several
flour mills. It was joined by numerous mountain rills,
and being a succession of deep pools, falls, and rapids,
was the very beau-ideal of a trout stream. A peasant, of
whom I made inquiry, informed me it was full of fish,
especially trout, the latter running up to four pounds in
weight, but that it was much fished by casting-net and
worm-angling. I could not make him understand my
inquiries as to its being fly-fished, and when I showed
him some flies I had in my pocket-book he was much
astonished. He had never heard of such a mode of
fishing. The peasants along my route (for the present)
only talk Basque, and before leaving San Sebastian I was
assured I should neither comprehend a word they said, nor
be able to make them understand what I wished to convey
to them ; but I am glad to find such is not quite the case.
I have adopted the plan of putting my questions into the
simplest form possible, and into plain, slow Castellano,
accompanied with expressive signs, and then to immediately repeat them in French, using the same signs. So
far, I have always succeeded in rendering myself intelligible ; indeed, to my great satisfaction, I not only find that
I comprehend tolerably well their answers, but that I have
already commenced to pick up a few words of Basque, the

which I do not fail to fire away at every peasant I meet,
and during the day they have been continually passing me,
accompanied with their pack-asses. These *burricos* are
the very smallest donkeys I have seen since I left Mexico
—very dwarfs of asses. Occasionally, too, I met small
trains of covered waggons, two-wheeled concerns, each
drawn by from six to eight mules. These fine animals
ranged from fifteen to sixteen hands in height, and were
harnessed in single lines by rope traces. The waggons were
all heavily loaded with wine, in casks and skins. The
peasants seen during the day had quite the characteristic
mountaineer air and gait, walking with a springing step
and independent swagger; men, women, and children,
true mountaineers, every inch of them.

I arrived at Tolosa about four o'clock, having walked
at a fair pace six-and-a-half hours, exclusive of stoppages.
The continual climbing, the weight of my traps, and the
way that powerful brute of a dog pulled at his chain, had
quite tired me out ; in fact, my arms felt as though I had
been driving a runaway four-in-hand all day. I was
hungry too. At that time of day a meal was not to be
expected in Spain ; but I hunted up an hotel, to engage a
room, and relieve myself of my burden and my hauling
dog.

Tolosa can boast of two hotels. I chose the one
looking least objectionable ; but it had a most forbidding
aspect. It was a dismal old stone building, with a gloomy,
dark, dirty passage entrance, leading to a rickety flight of
wooden steps. There was nobody to make inquiry of ; no
bell or knocker visible. Preceded by Juan, who did not

seem to care a rap where he went so long as he went
ahead, I clambered up the stairs, opened the first door I
came to, and walked in. I found myself, to my surprise,
in a large, clean, nicely-furnished reception-room, and, on
clapping my hands, a really stylish-looking woman, showily
dressed, whether maid or mistress I could not tell, appeared. By her I was shown into a nice clean room,
having a well waxed and polished oak floor, containing a
large and comfortable bed, with snowy linen, but where the
toilette appliances were on a very reduced scale from what
I had been furnished with at San Sebastian. Perhaps
Spaniards do not wash much when travelling, for fear of
catching cold.

After making myself comfortable, and leaving Juan
chained to a leg of the bedstead, with a promise of a
thrashing if he got on it, I strolled out to see the town,
and kill time until six o'clock should bring dinner.

Hearing martial music, I walked in the direction the
sounds came from, and arriving in a wide boulevard
planted with young trees, found myself fronting extensive
barracks and a *pelota* court. At the gateway of the
barrack-yard a number of buglers were playing, and
immediately on my arrival, out poured the soldiers, at the
same terrific pace those seen reviewed at San Sebastian
marched at. Five hundred men were coming out to
drill. I watched them go through many manœuvres. The
men appeared to be principally new joined, for though
they seemed anxious to do right, and the officers, who
evidently knew their business, took great pains with them,
they had a most hazy notion of what they were about,

and got continually fogged. The patience and temper of the officers, from commander to corporal, were quite pleasing to see.

Tolosa is a long straggling town, with nothing striking about it, that I saw, except its church—the Santa Maria—which, though a plain square building of rough stone, ugly on its outside, is singularly beautiful within. It is Gothic, with a very lofty groined and carved roof of stone, supported by six pairs of admirably-proportioned monolith pillars of fine-grained sandstone ; is profusely decorated with marble of the country; has a gorgeous shrine and altar ; while high up on each side, close to the roof, are three pictures in a row of Bible subjects, those on the right being from the New, and those on the left from the Old Testament. The six pictures are in fresco, their composition excellent, their drawing and colouring good. They are undeniably works of great merit, but by what artist I could not ascertain. The church was lighted by small stained-glass windows, just under the eaves, and by numerous candles on the shrine, and there was a simplicity and beauty of proportion about that interior which was most impressive.

At dinner—an excellent dinner by-the-way—I met five paper-mill men, well-dressed, well-mannered dons. They were surprised at hearing I had walked from San Sebastian, and still more so when informed I intended walking to Pamplona ; but they agreed it was the proper way to see a country, one of them adding : " Many foreigners have rushed through this country by rail, from city to city, and gone home and told a pack of lies about it and us because they knew nothing of what they were talking about, except what they had heard or suffered in hotels kept by rascally thieving Swiss and French. From their carriage-windows they saw men looking exactly like the brigands of the opera, but who were really honest hardworking peasants in the garb of the country, and so they have reported that out of the big towns we are a nation of robbers. You will find we are no such thing. The only thieves you will meet with are the innkeepers. From them there is no escaping. And recollect our proverb :

Ventera hermosa
*Mal para la bolsa.**

These gentlemen said that before arriving at Irurzun I should pass the *hacienda* of Don Ramon, a gentleman who owned iron and copper works at a place called Las Dos Hermanas, and that I ought not to pass without seeing them. They gave me a card of recommendation, signed by all, assuring me I should be well received, and we parted for the night ; for being tired, and not wishing to sit up late, I declined their invitation to accompany them to a café.

I persuaded the *ventera hermosa* to bring me a couple of eggs with my chocolate next morning. My bill was four-and-a-half *pesetas.* I gave her a *propina* that fulfilled the proverb, and again started, Juan in the lead as before.

The morning was a cloudy, windy one. The mountain peaks, hemming in the view, were from time to time

---

* A handsome hostess is bad for the purse.

enveloped in thick mantles of vapour, and heavy gusts of wind rushed frequently down their gorges and ravines with a violence that sometimes brought me to a standstill.

The winding road led up the narrow valley of an east fork of the Orio, in many places scarped out of the face of the bare rock on one side, and built up with solid masonry on its other; a wide, well-engineered and constructed highway, with a continuous stone-wall parapet, two feet high, on its precipitous side. The numerous bridges by which the stream was crossed and recrossed were massive in construction and of good design, but after a most ancient pattern, and evidently quite old. Soon the valley became a close cañon, the mountains closing in on each side and becoming almost perpendicular; but every little patch of available ground was under cultivation, and there was considerable timber in sight growing in side cañons, and on flattened summits—chiefly chestnut and walnut trees; these, though probably wild, planted there by Nature's hands, were nevertheless attended to and taken care of. Little diagonal trenches, in soil and rock, intercepted and brought to their roots the surface drainage from rainfalls; and as before the door of every house I passed lay large heaps of husks, doubtlessly these chestnut and walnut groves and woods furnish the inhabitants plentifully with a cheap article of food.

In most of the little fields the soil was being turned up for the reception of seed by a method quite novel to me, a laborious but most thorough one. The implement employed was a two-pronged steel fork. The prongs were over two feet long and six inches apart, and joined together

with a square shoulder from which a straight wooden
handle three feet in length extended. These tools weighed
altogether ten to fifteen pounds, and were very strongly
made. The operation is as follows : The diggers, generally
five in number, stand in a row close together, working
backwards. Simultaneously they raise their forks perpendicularly up, as high as possible, and then bring them
down with all their force, driving the sharp prongs eighteen
inches more or less into the hard ground ; then, taking
hold of the extremities of the handles with their two
hands, to get the utmost leverage, they throw themselves
backwards, each prizing up a huge chunk of heavy soil.
Two other labourers follow in front, and, armed with
heavy hoes, break all extra large chunks to pieces with
smart blows. Seven men so working get over the ground
astonishingly quickly, and turn it up in a most effective
manner. A heavy wooden harrow, of primitive construction, drawn by a yoke of oxen, finishes the preparation of
the soil.

Wherever a break in the mountains afforded a site for
building was perched a dilapidated and decayed-looking
old village with its huge church or two. Not unfrequently,
also, a big church, convent, or some other ecclesiastical
edifice appeared without any village. It seemed as though
the country had been monopolised for clerical use and
benefit, and that the villages were but the shelters for
the necessary working population to supply the creature
comforts to the inhabitants of religious strongholds.

The numerous little rills, trickling down the mountain
sides, fell into a paved ditch, constructed on the upper side

of the road ; which, in many places, was almost choked
with delicious watercresses.

Ere long the rain descended in a steady pour, and
when at noon I arrived at a little village through which—
unlike those I had passed—the road ran, I was thoroughly
drenched.

The first building I came to was a *posada*, a rough-hewn
stone house, its windows small square holes in its walls,
without glass or sash. It was shut up, and looked uninhabited. A few heavy knocks on the double door brought
a face to one of the holes, and the demand, "What is
wanted ? " It was the face of the *posadero*, who seeing a
stranger demanded admittance, descended immediately and
let me in. The entire lower story of the inn was one huge
stable and coach, or rather, waggon-house, but at the time
there were no animals there, excepting fowls ; but hay,
litter, old harness, wrecks of waggons, and rubbish of all
kinds, was strewn plentifully around. A flight of wooden
steps led to the upper story, and following my host, I
found myself in the dwelling portion of the building ; for
we emerged through a hole in the floor immediately into
a long, narrow, low chamber running directly across the
house, and having in one of its corners a large bench-like
oak table, black with age and old dirt, and two correspond-
ing-looking wooden benches, one on each side of it. A
cupboard resembling an old watchman's box, and a bloated
wine-skin completed the furniture. I told the landlord I
wanted breakfast.

"All right ; are you very hungry ? "

" Yes, I am."

"It is well. Behold! Eat and drink."

Then he produced out of the watch-box a large loaf of white wheaten bread, a big-bellied bottle of wine, and a goblet, and left the room. I thought that was the breakfast, so sat down and commenced, for I was hungry. Presently mine host returned and asked would my worship like some soup. Certainly I would ; and I stopped eating the dry bread. Soon he reappeared, placed before me a clean napkin, laid a white tablecloth across one end of the table, and placed in position plates, knife, fork, and spoon. Then he brought in the soup. It was contained in an old iron utensil, in appearance exactly like the bottom of an immense, badly-battered old candlestick, and consisted of slices of bread boiled in olive oil, with a handful of lentils mixed in, and a poached egg in its centre, the mess being nearly solid. But though the bread I had eaten had taken off the edge of my appetite, I yet found the soup very good, for it was savoury, hot, and well-seasoned ; and not knowing when I should get my next meal, or how bad it might be, I tried to eat it all as a matter of precaution, and had nearly succeeded, when in came another course, a hot plateful of black pudding, containing morsels of fat, chopped herbs, and cabbage sprouts. It was absolutely delicious ; and so, giving the remainder of the soup and half the loaf to Juan, I put out of sight, *in toto*, the contents of the platter placed before me, and felt I had done my duty to myself and fared well. But that admirable landlord's resources were not exhausted, for in came some lamb chops. I felt I could eat no more, but out of curiosity tasted them. One mouthful settled the matter. I would eat the chops if they killed me. They were the very best ones I had ever tasted ; juicy, tender as butter, cooked to a nicety, piping hot. They were crumbed, fried to a light brown in sweet, fresh, olive oil, had been just touched with garlic, and were garnished with thin slices of crisp fried potatoes. A dish fit to set before a king. Truly, though that *posada* was a dingy, grimy, unfurnished stone barn, I have a great respect for its landlord. My only regret was that, being dripping wet, muddy, and tired, I was not in a proper state to enjoy such cooking. But there was more to come. Black coffee and *aquardiente*, excellent apples and grapes were served. For that most excellent feed for man and dog, with good, very good wine at discretion, and which I had punished heavily, I was only charged two-and-a-half *pesetas*, or, in plain English, two shillings and a penny !

By the time I had enjoyed coffee, dessert, and a pipe, the weather had cleared, and my wet garments being uncomforable and chilly, I was glad to try to warm up by taking the road again.

Soon it recommenced to rain ; so, when at three o'clock I arrived at the little mountain hamlet of Betelu, and saw rising up before me a lofty chain of steep mountains—the pass over which was evidently a high one—I determined to go no farther, and, good quarters or bad, to stop for the night at the little *posada* that fronted me.

CHAPTER VI.

DECEMBER 4, 1876.—Judging from what I have heretofore heard and seen, the Betelu *posada* was a thoroughly typical country inn of northern Spain, in unfrequented parts. The lower portion was barn, stable, poultry-house, and outbuildings all in one, and the usual stairs led to living-rooms above.

I walked in and up, and meeting no one, went into the kitchen. There a middle-aged woman sat sewing and cooking, while half-a-dozen, more or less, children played about her on the floor; and a very pretty girl of some sixteen years of age, kneeling before the fire, was feeding it with broken brushwood, and blowing it into a blaze with her breath. All answered my salutation with a chorus of "Welcome, your worship;" and on requesting to be shown a bedroom, I was ushered by the girl into an adjoining chamber—an attic—whose rough flooring had holes through it, affording a view into the

F

stable below, but containing two clean, comfortably-
appointed beds, and whose otherwise bare walls were
hung with coloured prints of virgins and martyrs most
hideous to behold.

Taking such a wash as the diminutive basin and tiny
water-jug permitted, I left my traps on an old worm-eaten
chest of drawers standing opposite one of the beds, returned to the kitchen, and stretched myself to dry at full
length on a bench that was close alongside the fire.

The fireplace in the kitchen of this *posada* must be
particularly described, it being also a typical one. Almost
in the middle of the room was a rough hearth, about four
feet square and a foot high, and composed of tiles, flat
stones, pieces of iron—anything that would not consume.
In its centre burned a fire of three sticks, laid star-
fashion, with a pile of blazing brushwood heaped on them.
Around stood, with different messes stewing in them, a
goodly number of pottery pipkins and utensils—in shapes
and patterns identical with the Roman ones in use before
Christ. A large wooden hood, supported by massive
rafters, caught and conducted such portion of the smoke
as did not circulate about the room to a hole in the roof
furnished with a rough louvre, through which it escaped,
and from a cross iron of the hood hung a stout chain,
terminating in a hook, by which was suspended a large
pot full of potatoes slowly simmering. In a corner stood a
primitive-looking *casserole* range, for cooking with charcoal
in little hollows. A few coarse, badly-constructed chairs,
with bottoms of raw hide, and an old chest, completed
the furniture.

There only seemed to be one man about the *posada* a tailor, working in a room on the other side of the kitchen from mine, who often came in to heat the lump of old iron which served him for a goose—I think it was the broken-off horn of an anvil—and who had almost always something pleasant to say. The children belonged to the *posadera*. The pretty girl was her cousin. It did not transpire whether my hostess was a widow or not, nor did anything reveal the status of the tailor, and I discreetly asked no questions.

At six o'clock a clean tablecloth was spread on the old chest of drawers in my room, a large white napkin furnished—one nearly twice as large as the towel—and a very fair dinner of several courses served, of which the best dish was an excellent *omelette soufflé*, a much better dinner, both as regards cooking and material, than I ever got in any English country inn. And the wine was a good sound Spanish burgundy. The only failure was in the *café noir*. It was wretched. However, the next morning's chocolate was as good as possible, and—which I had not expected in such a hole of a place—with it were served *azucarillos* (sweetmeats of flour, sugar, and rosewater). I had had an excellent night's rest, felt well refreshed, and my bill—wine, attendance, everything included—was but nine *reals*.

It rained no longer, but the mountain peaks were obscured by clouds, and a hard head-wind blew as I started up the pass that would take me over La Sierra de Aralar.

About a mile beyond the village of Betelu I passed

the bathing establishment of that name; a large, handsome building apparently capable of accommodating two to three hundred guests, but shut, for summer is the season for Betelu springs. The waters are thermal and sulphuric, and have considerable reputation.

Midday was passed when the summit was achieved, and the prospect, which had been bounded by steep faces of bare precipitous mountains on each side of the road for many miles, suddenly became a striking panorama of peaks, alps, and valleys; and perched on seemingly inaccessible ledges, nestled in sequestered hollows, stood either groups of quaint buildings, picturesque villages, or huge churches. Wherever two or three houses were gathered together, there certainly was to be seen a church, often bigger than all the houses of its parish put together. Where, in the name of common sense, did the money and labour come from to plant churches everywhere, and support their officiating priests? No wonder Spain is poor.

A few yards farther and a small brook appeared coming from my right out of a bed of rushes and osiers. I turned my head and looked back. The spring source of the stream up whose course I had been travelling was within pistol-shot. I regarded with a feeling of interest those two tiny rills. One of them went to the Bay of Biscay, whose blue waters I might never see again; the other was going the same course as myself, its bourne the Mediterranean. I stood on the comb of the divide—the meeting of the watersheds; before me lay the ancient kingdom of Navarre.

By eleven I arrived at Lecumberri, a village just like any of the other ones, and after despatching a good breakfast and enjoying a rest, pushed on again.

The general slope of the country proved but slight, compared with the sudden rise of the other side of the range; the view was open, the mountains well wooded, the fields larger and more frequent. Numerous mountain watercourses paid their tribute to and swelled the stream I was following, which soon became a little river; and dams, mills, and watercourses succeeded one another until, at half-past three of the afternoon, I arrived at the *hacienda* of Don Ramon A——, Las dos Hermanas.

Las dos Hermanas—or The Two Sisters—are a couple of sharp, narrow, but Bute-like ridges of bare granite, inaccessibly perpendicular, rising about five hundred feet higher than their base—spurs, almost detached, of adjacent mountain ranges, and barely far enough apart to leave a gateway sufficiently wide for road and river to run through; and on a little flat immediately above this singular cleft stood the dwelling, buildings, and furnaces of the Don.

The house was a neat, pretty villa, with a nice garden adjoining, and having a paved and enclosed yard, well furnished with shady trees, in its front. In this yard two immense and handsome mastiffs ran at large, but they evinced no hostility, evidently were the dogs of a hospitable house, for they contented themselves with a sniff at me and Juan, and then laid down in the shade of a tree, wagging their tails and watching us.

A servant-girl appeared in answer to a knock, and to her I handed the card of introduction that had been so

politely given to me at Tolosa, and my pasteboard, with
" E. P." (*en persona*) in its corner.   The young woman, who
evidently could not read, twisted the two cards all ways
with a bewildered air, stared at me as though I were a wild
beast, turned suddenly round, and without a word bolted
down the hall passage.   Almost directly, a middle-aged
man (who, I subsequently learned, was the *major-domo*,
and who, in dress and look, was the counterpart of a regular
West of England mine " captain ") came forward and bid
me welcome.   He told me Don Ramon was absent, but
would shortly return.   He then ushered me into a reception-room, and begged to know what refreshment I would
like to have prepared for me.   Assuring him I had breakfasted heartily and lately, and could eat nothing, he seemed
but half satisfied, and insisted, if I would not eat, I
must drink ; I therefore accepted a *petit verre* of French
cognac, which I sipped as we sat conversing.

It was nearly five when a carriage drove up, from which
descended four gentlemen, to whom I was presented by the
major-domo.   One of them—a man considerably above
six feet in height, and of powerful build, with hair and
beard *à l'Anglaise*, attired in a dark velvet shooting
jacket, " horsey " waistcoat of the same material, Bedford-
cord trousers tucked into wellington boots, a heavy-twilled
check linen shirt, with large turn-down collar, a loose
silk necktie round his throat, holding a wide-brimmed, low-
crowned gray felt hat in his hand, and sporting a handsome gold watch-chain and massive cuff-studs—stepped
forward and said :

" I am Ramon A——, your servant, and glad to see

you. This is your house ; I and mine are at your disposition." The other gentlemen were a government commissioner of railroads and two mining experts connected with iron and copper interests, and they had come to witness some experiments of a newly-discovered process for forging iron-ore which were that evening to be made in Don Ramon's furnace rooms.

After due introduction to his friends, the Don said if such things interested me, he should be glad of my company with them over his foundry, and he would promise to show me iron bars forged direct from the ore by the old Catalan process—the method used by him, and one identical in all particulars with that employed in England prior to the use of coals—in fact, as he believed, the most primitive way known ; then he would conduct me to his copper works, and finally I should see the experiments. I gladly consented. We took a little " nip" all round and descended.

The interior of the works, which were mostly underground, was picturesque in the extreme. The walls, built of rough-hewn unfaced stone, the dark passages, the huge smoke-stained beams supporting the vaulted roof, half in deep flickering shadow, half brightly illuminated by the ruddy glare and blaze of furnaces, were strikingly in keeping with, and fitting background for, the workmen— stout Basque mountaineers, black with grime, shiny with perspiration, and clothed only in coarse linen garments like scanty nightshirts without sleeves, and wearing the national *gorro* and the sandals of Scripture pictures—fitting gnomes for such a weird scene.

After witnessing the forging of a number of bars direct from the ore—without smelting—which I was assured were, as they lay, marketable as best quality iron, and, as I had seen, worked like lead, and were tough, malleable, and fine-grained as the best Swedish iron, I was taken to the copper rooms, and there saw basins of copper made from Rio Tinto ore. Then we proceeded to the ironworks, for all was ready for the experiments.

As it was getting late I began excusing myself, alleging that if I further delayed my departure I should not arrive at my stopping-place that night.

"You have arrived. Your stopping-place is here," said the Don. "There are five of us, without you. Well! where there is enough for five to eat, room for five to sleep, there is plenty for six. When I said 'This is your house,' I meant it."

So I stayed and saw the experiments, which, for my entertainer's sake, I gladly perceived were great successes. The new process saved time, fuel, and labour, and was therefore calculated to put money in his pocket.

At half-past seven we sat down to a most excellent repast ; and a large dish, heaped with trout, averaging ten inches in length, had irresistible attractions for me. I learned the river abounded with such fish, but that it was too late in the season for them to be catchable by rod and line; those before us had been taken that morning by the casting-net. The wine was choice, and pushed sharply round. After dinner and black coffee, cognac, little glasses, and cigars were placed on the table, and all smoked and drank neat brandy. The conversation then took a mining turn, and

happening to mention the Comstock Lode and Nevada
mines and works, I was assailed with questions concerning
them. Fortunately I was "well posted;" but though, purposely, being an unauthenticated stranger, and not wishing
my veracity to be doubted, I considerably understated the
yield of the Virginia City mines, the commissioner insisted I asserted impossibilities—must have had wrong
information given me; and, to prove it was so, went into
long calculations, to the great amusement of the company,
who said I must excuse him, it being well known that the
Spanish railway companies had driven him quite crazy.

"Would you believe it," said my entertainer; "the other
day an engine arrived without wheels—they had been stolen
en route, for there are very expert thieves in Spain—and
our lunatic commissioner actually attempted to prove
statistically that they had not been stolen ; that the engine
had started without wheels!"

This changed the conversation to the subject of Spanish
railway management, and a state of affairs and way of doing
business was revealed to me, that, had the commissioner
been really *non compos mentis*, would have fully accounted
for the "milk in the cocoanut," and that would drive any
public but a Spanish one to distraction.

By-and-by champagne was brought in, glasses filled,
and songs sung—and very well too. My new friends were
no mean proficients, and being old chums, and accustomed
to sing together in parts, rendered the airs with great
effect. Until then I had no idea how fine were the old
Basque songs, or, more correctly speaking, chants ; some of
them being perfectly charming. Then they astonished me,

by singing, in my honour, without words, for they did not know them, but excessively perfectly as to tune, "God save the Queen;" and I was fairly aghast when, refilling their glasses, and standing up, they roared out the rattling chorus of "Dixie." My host then reseating himself, and blowing out his cheeks, assuming a pompous deportment, and bringing the guests to order by tapping his glass with a spoon, delivered himself in this wise: "I am der Lor Mayor London," and continued in Spanish, for his English broke suddenly down: "Our right worshipful visitor will now make a speech in English. We, to our great loss, shall not understand a word he says, but we shall know what he means; and as we have never listened to an English speech, we wish to hear what it sounds like." So I turned the word-tap on, and myself loose, to loud applause.

Then the commissioner brewed punch. If he understands his country's railway system as well as he does punch-brewing, that extremely valuable official is a very Solomon of railwaydom. After punch, and more songs, we took a look below to see how the smelting progressed, for the Don's furnaces burn day and night, and at half-past six in the morning retired to bed.

Taking them both together, it was as heavy a day's and night's work as I ever creditably got through; but all arose at nine, and, thanks to the genuineness of the Don's tipple, none complained or looked seedy, and everybody eat heartily of the *déjeûner à la fourchette*, to which, at eleven o'clock, we all sat down. I had had but short time for sleep, but made the best of it, and reposing with all my

might, slept hard, if on a soft bed; indeed, I was most
comfortably quartered. While making my toilette in the
morning I also made a discovery. By the litter of the
room and toilette-table; by the initials on dressing-cases,
silver - mounted whips, and other nicknacks scattered
around; by the crest on studs and rings; it was plainly
evident that my host had bestowed me in his own chamber,
and, as I afterwards found, made his couch of a sofa in the
drawing-room.

Such was the reception, such the hospitality, given to
a wandering Englishman—an unknown stranger, meanly
dressed, tramping on foot—by the courtesy of a Basque
gentleman!

At breakfast Don Ramon strongly advised my taking
the train at the railway station, two miles off, as thence to
Pamplona was but a short way; while the station and
Pamplona being in the same valley, I should not, by so
doing, miss seeing any country, all of it being visible from
the ramparts of that city, while I should so be enabled to
arrive sufficiently early to hunt up quarters before night,
and, added he: "I have ordered my carriage to be at the
door for you in time to catch the half-past three P.M. train,
our only one, there being but one passenger train each way
daily. To be sure, we shall hardly have finished by that
time, but we will not hurry; no man is ever too late to
catch our trains."

All accompanied me to the door, and, as they wished
me God-speed, cordially shook me by the hand. I jumped
into a light comfortable chaise, followed by Juan—who
took to a carriage as though used to ride in one—and

behind a fast trotter, driven by a liveried servant, started.

As we passed between "The Two Sisters" I glanced back. In the road stood my recently-made friends, and a group of forgemen, looking after me. Jumping upon the carriage-seat, I swung my hat in the air, and shouted out the old war-cry of the Basque : "*Gu-bagaitue ba ala jaincoa !*" Up went the *gorros* with a yell of delight, and we had seen the last of each other.

The railway station was a heap of ruins. It had been burned by the Carlists, and not yet rebuilt ; a little temporary clapboard shed, like a large sentry-box, serving for the office. The train came slowly up. Being only an hour behind time, there was no necessity for hurry. After dawdling along a few miles I found myself arrived at the Pamplona station, but a good half mile from the nearest gateway through the city's fortifications. Why, excepting to benefit the 'bus interest, this is so, passes my comprehension. There is no engineering or other visible reason that the station should not be at the foot of the glacis. I was told it was for strategic reasons. Everything they do in this country that seems absurd and foolish is done for "strategic" or "fiscal" reasons. I am getting tired of those two words.

Small boys besieged me to carry my traps from the station ; so giving haversack to one, gun to another, and dog to a third, we made a procession, and marched into the city. In the Plaza de la Constitucion I deposited my plunder in a shop, delighted the boys with *cuartos* and *ochavos*, and leading Juan by his chain, who, subdued

I suppose by the city's strangeness, noise, and bustle, followed at heel in a submissive manner, commenced prospecting for a *casa de huespades*.

It was no easy matter to get housed in this old capital. Its population amounts in number to twenty-three thousand; its surrounding fortifications have prevented expansion; it has no extramural suburbs, excepting the faubourg of Rochapea, consisting only of a fine well-arranged and constructed public slaughter-house, a couple of agricultural implement manufactories, and some laundry establishments; it covers a comparatively small area, consequently it is like a beehive. Still, under ordinary circumstances, admittance into boarding-houses, or rather boarding-flats, is not difficult to obtain, for they are plentiful, and Spaniards understand close packing. Indeed, most families of limited means take boarders, I am told. At present, however, Pamplona is the head-quarters of the "Army of Occupation;" General Quesada and staff, and four thousand men and their officers, are quartered in it, and every hotel, lodging, and boarding-flat seemed full, and it was almost dark ere, at last, I obtained what I required—that is to say, as nearly so as it appeared possible to get under such circumstances.

CHAPTER VII.

DECEMBER 12, 1876.—In many respects my present quarters compare sufficiently unfavourably with those I had the good fortune to occupy at San Sebastian. My bedroom is small, almost destitute of conveniences, very dark, and by no means overmuch swept and garnished. The bed, however, I am glad to say, is scrupulously clean, and, though small, comfortable. I should certainly have declined such accommodation had I not been wearied looking for lodgings and finding none, every place full, and night approaching fast. I was shown my present rooms by a young *señorita*, who I now know as the eldest daughter of the house. She stated that the terms, including board, for each guest were three *pesetas* a day—no difference being made as to which of the couples of rooms they occupied—and added she was only too

sorry the pair of rooms untenanted were not the best. But
the dog was a difficulty. I must see her mamma about
him, said this fair maid. (By-the-bye she was a brilliant
brunette.) Would I wait till mamma came home ; she had
only gone to rosario ; the church was close at hand ; she
would be back in five minutes. "Will you walk into the
parlour," said the spi—— (no, I mean the *señorita*), "and
wait ? "

When the old woman appeared I would have certainly
bolted, but had come to the conclusion I must take such
quarters as I could get, or should find myself without any.
I did not like the looks of "mamma." If I knew anything
about physiognomy, and the deductions drawable from
personal appearance, the fare would be indifferent. There
was a look about her of careful shabbiness, cunning, and
sanctity that argued ill for the liberality of her *menu* and
the general comfort of her establishment. This highly-
respectable octopus immediately proceeded to verify my
hastily-formed opinion. She said a dog was much trouble
and ate a great deal ; but if I would keep mine in my bedroom, and pay for his food an extra *peseta* a day (equal to
paying a florin a day in London), I could stay. There was
nothing for it but to accept the inevitable ; so in her house
I stopped and still remain.

Hearing last Friday that in celebration of its being the
eve of *La Purisima concepcion de Nuestra Señora, La
Capitana-General de las Españas*, there would be a *gran
funcion* at the church of San Saturnino ; that "all the world"
would be there ; and that attendance would confer upon
every member of the congregation the reward of two

thousand four hundred and eighty days let off from purgatory which he or she could appropriate to his or her own personal and private use and benefit ; or, if so inclined, turn over to some departed soul in that uncomfortable region for theirs ; I determined not to neglect so favourable an opportunity, and so, in company with one of the daughters of the house to show the way, marched off, just as it was getting dark, to church.

San Saturnino—a Gothic church of the fourteenth century—proved, in many respects, an interesting building. Its south doorway is remarkable : on its right capital are illustrations of our Lord with His Cross, the Descent therefrom, the Resurrection, and the Descent into Hell ; on the left is the Annunciation, Salutation, Nativity, and Flight into Egypt ; the Crucifixion forming the canopy of the doorway. It is not a big church, but so arranged in its interior as to accommodate, for its size, the largest possible number of worshippers. I should judge a congregation of from six hundred to seven hundred persons would fill it comfortably full.

For the occasion the Virgin's shrine and image was as showy as draperies, gilding, gems, and wax candles could make it, and the floor of the church covered with people— about a thousand—all as closely jammed as they could stand or rather kneel, for all were on their marrow-bones on the hard stone pavement ; no chairs, no cushions, no mats ; for was I not in bigoted Navarra, where to worship comfortably would be sinful !—excepting for priests, who, I observed, had luxuriously-stuffed velvet couches or chairs to repose on between whiles. There were very few men present—perhaps a proportion of one for every twenty-five women. The latter were all dressed in complete black, with veils and *mantillas* on ; giving a strikingly funereal aspect to the body of the church. The men, without exception that I could see, were of the very lowest class. Some of these unfortunates were close to me. They were nasty, dirty, sandled bundles of brown rags ; wretches who had never voluntarily touched water since they had been baptised, except holy water ; walking pestilences, whose persons poisoned the atmosphere. The strongest incense could not disguise the smell. Feeling, as I had walked to church in a generous frame of mind, I had intended to turn those two thousand four hundred and eighty days over to the ill-used friend of my youth, old Guy Fawkes ; but after suffering the smell of those animated atrocities, and getting pains in my knees and back from remaining so long in a most unaccustomed posture—for all knelt upright, no sitting back on the heels—I determined to keep them for myself. I may not want them, but if I do, they will average things as against what I suffered ; otherwise, I am, to that extent, an injured and outraged individual for ever.

As I looked up at the beautiful image of the " Captain-General of the Spains," gazed on her lovely face and splendid raiment, and then on the dark mass of worshippers kneeling at her feet, the reflection was forced upon my mind, that I knew of but one religion, ancient or modern— Judaism—that with its lineal descendants and continuations, the churches of the Reformation, the beliefs of Mahometism, and the Mormon faith, is without a female deity. As I knelt I could almost have fancied myself a Pagan.

G

The following day I attended high mass at the cathedral and parish church of *St. Juan Bautista*, for the bishop was to officiate, the apostolic benediction would be conferred by proxy, and a huge indulgence granted to the congregation. How far the indulgence was to extend I did not concern myself. Had I not those two thousand four hundred and eighty days in hand? The large and handsome Gothic edifice was crammed. So closely, indeed, was it crowded that to kneel, or, when down, rise up again, was nearly impossible. The male attendance was proportionally much larger than it had been at *San Saturnino,* but of the same class. I doubt if in the multitude present there were twenty educated men. Almost all the males were the lowest of the low. Though I suffered in consequence, for the smell was dreadful, I was glad of it. Such fact plainly indicated that even in the very hotbed of Carlistism, even in the most priest-ridden part of Spain, the sceptre is departing from the hand of superstition, that the feet of clay are crumbling, that Spain's long night is drawing to an end, that the race between darkness and enlightenment has become a close one, that at last the schoolmaster has collared the sacerdote.

What this country now requires is an Oliver Cromwell, with plenty of earnest, truth-loving " croppies " behind him. That is the revolution wanted, not a succession of military conspiracies. When the day of his and their advent arrives, Spain will emerge from her long infancy, will become a nation of men and women, not of full-grown children. If it never comes, then, assuredly, she that was once the first will at the end be left the last of civilised peoples.

By-the-bye, the idea these Spaniards have of their

country's martial power is simply preposterous; for instance : the other day, the conversation having turned on
the Eastern Question, the remark was made that in a contest with Russia England could do nothing without help,
her military strength being so insignificant ; and I was
asked by an officer of high rank if I thought England
would offer Gibraltar to Spain to purchase her assistance
to save the British Empire in India ! As if the help of a
country unable to put down a beggarly one-horse nigger
insurrection in Cuba was worth purchasing, even for the
small cost of the value of the powder expended in a royal
salute !

The ceremonies of the *fiesta* of the " Patrona " of Spain
terminated with a discharge of fifteen guns at sunset.
Trumpets sounded all over the place. The church-bells
were clanged—that's the proper descriptive name for bell-
ringing in this country—all in honour of the " Queen of
Heaven, Captain General," &c., &c. Then everybody whose
duties, infirmities, or poverty (the ragged go to church
only, not to the promenade) did not keep them indoors,
paraded for a couple of hours round and round the spacious
arcaded *Plaza de la Constitucion,* and up and down the
tree-planted avenues of *La Taconera* and *Plazuela de
Valencia.* It was quite a crowd. I do not doubt half the
population and all the military not on duty were there—
ten thousand would be under the mark—so it was an
excellent opportunity to make observations.

Though doubtless in their best, yet only a few ladies, and
the military, were really well dressed, but all looked neat
and respectable. It was hard, though, to discern how the

male citizens were attired, for most of them—certainly all of
the better class—were enveloped in the national *capa*, and
that too though the temperature of the evening was milder
than it had been for some days, it being about as warm as
a South-Walean one at the end of June. But few men
wore "top" hats. "Billy-cocks" of all shapes were the prevailing coverings for the head. Amongst the women I
looked in vain for bonnets or hats ; I do not believe there
were any in the entire assemblage. All wore the high
comb, with long black veil falling behind, and the *mantilla*
(generally of lace)—a fashion giving even to the plainest a
certain air of grace and refinement. Not one of them but
was well gloved and shod ; and, excepting the fat and old,
all walked with grace. Still, though I saw many handsome,
some pretty, faces, the *señoras* did not, as far as beauty is
concerned, average with the cream of French beauty, the
Bayonnaise. To be sure, they had not the *en evidence*
"got-up" look Frenchwomen so often have, and their
dresses fit figures, not stays.

After dinner a number of *señoritas* came to visit the
daughters of the house, and a very pleasant *Tertula* was
enjoyed. Games of forfeits were played, and we otherwise
conducted ourselves like children. Our visitors were good-
looking girls, one of them a beauty. At parting the women
all kissed each other and shook hands with the men.
Heretofore I have been under the impression that hand-
shaking between the sexes was not considered correct in
Spain, but I am gradually being disabused of many notions
as to the *cosas de España* obtained from reading and
Spanish-American experience ; for instance, I thought the

women of the country had all very small feet, and smoked. As yet I have not found myself among a small-footed population. The boot, or shoe, worn by females, who do not go barefooted or shod with sandals, is generally a number four. I can only account for the fact that their feet do look smaller than my fair countrywomen's, by their not only being very symmetrically shaped, but very well *chaussée*, and that, as a general thing, the women here are much heavier built from the ankle up than are English-women ; for though, theoretically, Spanish females are supposed, like the bird of paradise of the ancients, not to have legs, the majority have very fine ones—at least the winds that blow have so credibly informed me. As for their smoking, not only have I never seen so much, or rather little, as a *cigarilla* between their lips, but have been assured by natives of all parts of Spain that no Spanish women smoke excepting returned *Cubanas*, *Majas*, and the class that in all countries does so. But I may yet arrive where *señoritas* have little feet, do not shake hands, and, notwithstanding what I hear, do smoke ; if so, will make a note of it.

While writing of the houses stopped at, if I restrict myself to descriptions only of quarters and commissariat, and neglect to give any of inmates and their ways, how can I hope to convey a just and lively idea of the most interesting feature of this trip—the characteristics of the people met with ? On the other hand, how avoid the impu-tation of a want of delicacy, the charge of betrayal of the confidence of domestic life, by being explicit ? However, it is quite certain these letters will not be translated into

Spanish ; therefore, that those written about will never know
what has been said ; and I shall take care to use such harmless and allowable deceptions and mystifications concerning
names, exact dates, and particular localities, as to, without
affecting the truth essential to worth of description, make
it impossible for any stray traveller over the road I have
gone before, who may have read these olive-oil-lamp lucu-
brations, to, from them, identify individuals.

The *Casa de Huespedes*, which is my temporary abode,
judging by what I hear, and by what I have seen of the
many boarding-houses that I have paid calls at, may be
considered a fair average specimen of the better class of
such places in this portion of Spain. We live on a flat, for
in this crowded city of many-storied dwellings it is almost
the universal custom so to do. Only a few houses owned
by nobility, or very wealthy people, are not arranged in
flats ; each flat in all essentials being a complete house to
itself, as indeed is customary in many towns in France,
with the difference that here *concierge* and *conciergerie* is
unknown, and the stairway being under nobody's especial
charge, and merely a highway common to all the flats, is
unlighted at night—consequently, then, as dark as a negro
chimney-sweep's face—is never cleaned, and generally smells
abominably—ours does. The door admitting from the
landing of our flat is, like all other "flat" doors, a stout,
strong one, well furnished with bolts and fastenings, and
has a knocker, and a little sliding metal grating through
which seekers for admission can be reconnoitred. The
rooms open one into the other, as little space as possible
being bestowed on passages. My bedroom door will not

shut by a good inch ; but it does not matter to me. The little dormitory between mine and the general sitting-room is not at all objectionably tenanted. My sleeping-room is seven feet wide by nine long. Its garniture consists of the following articles : the hereinbefore described bed, a piece of carpet three feet by eighteen inches, and an iron construction, like a spiderly umbrella-stand, supporting a basin and jug, said basin being exactly eight inches across and three deep, and the jug holding a pint and a half of water (places for soap, for tooth and nail brushes, mouth glass, &c. &c., exist not in this uncomplicated washstand ; perhaps such superfluities are considered unnecessary, or not known of here), a chair, a towel, and all things are enumerated.

A double-door of glass opens from my sleeping apart-ment to my private sitting-room, which latter is but little larger than the former, a foot more in length being all the difference. It is furnished with a table eighteen inches by thirty, two chairs, and a small looking-glass. In neither room is wardrobe, cupboard, or chest of drawers. I suppose a man is expected to keep his clothes in his trunks, or pile them in a heap on the floor in a corner. The floor is a waxed and polished one—that is to say, it once was. At the end of the room a double French window occupies the entire width of the chamber, and gives access to a narrow iron verandah that overhangs the street.

It is one of the good streets of the town that my sitting-room window opens on, one going directly to the chief Plaza of Pamplona. I have also measured this leading thoroughfare. It is eighteen feet wide from house-front to house-front ; carriage-way, pavements, gutters, all included. The houses are six stories high, the verandahs overhang considerably; as a consequence, my room, being on the first floor, is so overshadowed as to be always dark and gloomy.

The family consists of the old lady—principally of the old lady—of the old lady's husband, and of several daughters. I am afraid what has been written about "mamma" is not very gracious ; perhaps it will be as well to say no more about her. Of the husband nothing unpleasant can be said. He is a good-looking man, some ten years her junior ; was, until the late civil war, a professor of some eminence in a college ; then, being a Carlist of strong convictions, joined "Charles VII.," became in time a full colonel, was driven over the frontier, interned in France, returned after the pacification, and is now a man without occupation—a cultivated, sociable, kindly-disposed, agreeable gentleman. The daughters range in age from • fourteen to twenty-two, and excepting one, who when she gets old will be not unlike her mother, are fine, handsome, elegant girls.

The boarders besides myself are a captain and lieutenant of infantry, and a lieutenant of cavalry. These three are by no means as good style men as were those I associated with in San Sebastian. They talk " shop," appear only on rare occasions in mufti, and always eat their meals with regimental overcoat and regulation-cap on, giving as a reason its being so cold. It is about as cold as in England in September. The captain is the most formal of the three, and a quiet, well-mannered man ; but the other two are both very " barracky," one very much so.

Thus does he disport himself : We are seated round the table waiting for dinner, for he is always late for meals, sometimes keeps us half an hour. We are in hungry expectancy. Our only consolation is we can kill time chatting with the girls, who, though the family do not eat when we do, usually bring their sewing and sit at table, sandwiched between us, during our repast, " for company's sake."

The step of the " awful lieutenant " is heard on the stairs, and in comes the first course, overcooked or nearly cold, as the case may be.

As the late arrival swaggers along the passage he hauls an immense cigar out of a case, lights it, takes a whiff or two as he enters the room, salutes, flings himself into his seat, and, still smoking, helps himself to soup. He tastes the soup, says something facetious about it, lays down his cigar on a plate, reaches out his hand for an old guitar that " lives " in a corner convenient to his seat, and alternately tunes a string and swallows spoonfuls of soup.

Then, for awhile, doth he play and sing with all his might. The lieutenant plays very well, is a good *improvisore*, and composes most ridiculous couplets concerning the fare and the fair then and there present.

After that he gobbles up his soup, roars out " *autre cosa*," and goes on with his music, his smoking, and his eating.

If, in passing to fetch thread, scissors, or anything else they require, any of the girls come within his reach—and, of course, some of them are always wanting something—he catches hold of, and squeezes, or pinches them till they scream, and then mimics them till the room rings again.

He pelts "mamma" with bread when she remonstrates, calls her his dear cousin, and the girls his precious ones; and if he gets through dinner without breaking a plate or wineglass, upsetting a dish or the wine, he does well.

This gay *caballero* generally goes straight from table to the *café*, but if he remains is sure to start some game going; for instance, two evenings ago three *señoritas* came in after dinner to see the girls, and our lively warrior insisted on everybody's going into an adjacent room to dance. The infantry men, being on duty, were obliged to return to the citadel, and so excuse themselves; but he would not be denied by the rest, and drove us all before him like a flock of turkeys.

Throwing himself into a chair, sticking his lighted cigar between his teeth, he started a wild waltz, joining in, between whiffs, with snatches of peasant songs, and admirably mimicking the peasants' twang.

It was more than the girls could stand, and two of them jumping up commenced dancing opposite each other like mad, playing castanets with their fingers and thumbs. The infection spread like fire in a stackyard, and, immediately, as many couples as the room contained were setting to each other, or whirling round, dancing the national dance of Navarra, *La Jota.*

The room was a bedchamber, lighted with a single flickering candle, casting giant, shifting shadows; in one corner was the bed—a bed without the valance of concealment. Certainly it was a strikingly novel scene, and a queer performance to English eyes.

La Jota finished, the lieutenant flung down cigar and

guitar, and declared his determination to dance, in rotation, with every woman present ; and, one and all, the *señoritas* declaring in chorus they would not dance with him, this son of Mars, true to the military traditions of the sabre, stopped not to palaver, but gallantly charged the bevy, singled out the prettiest girl, and, *vi et armis*, and singing the tune, dashed into a gallop with his captive partner. After a few rounds he let her go, caught another, and so on, with them all. Waltzes, polkas, mazurkas, all well danced. He was really an accomplished partner. But the way his overcoat and sword (for he had never taken them off) swung round was perfectly dreadful. At last the skirts of his garment—I believe purposely—swept the candle from the place where it had been standing, and we were in darkness. Perhaps, also, the swinging sword may have hurt some *señorita*, for I heard a smothered scream ; then " Old Sanctimonious " appeared, interfered, read the Riot Act, stopped the ball, and dispersed the rioters.

It is amusing to watch the girls make eyes—beautiful ones too—at, and coquette with, that young fellow, especially the least pretty one, who is the most demonstrative. Either each of them thinks he is in love with her, or else, being Spanish girls, and handsome, they cannot help coquetting. That the mother, however, being an old huntress, and having so many daughters to settle, has her eye on the bold lieutenant with speculation in it, is quite plain to a close observer, and who knows ? a lover affair may be going on ; but, so far as he is concerned, I think not—*le lieutenant s'amuse.*

Apropos the girls bringing their sewing to table,

yesterday, during dinner-time, they were embroidering for themselves garments of "a dual form." Verily, different countries have different standards of the proprieties. Here these people are considered gentry, and, though not rich, would certainly if English be recognised as such in England; but then they would not make their income comfortably sufficient by taking boarders, and the girls would be as demure and quiet as the daughters of an English ex-college professor, or retired distinguished colonel, would there be. Besides, they would not then have Spanish vivacity, and the graceful gestures, flashing eyes, and modest assurance of " *Las Hermosas de Navarra.*" I, as a foreigner, often, no doubt, mistake natural graciousness of manner for coquetry; and worse, it has been explained to me that I have said and done things that quite outraged *les convenances*, while all the time I innocently thought I was behaving beautifully. From now out I shall bear in mind that I must judge conduct by the country's standard, and not by any preconceived one of my own, when estimating people and their actions, and be most careful and circumspect also in what I say and do, so as not to bring discredit on my country's breeding by conduct, there all right, here all wrong. I am, too, discovering that a multitude of small things are done in Spain in a reverse way from what obtains in England; by-and-by, I shall probably find out this rule extends to matters of greater importance. Last evening I took a hand at some round games of cards, and learned the custom of the country is to cut from the dealer, deal from the bottom, and against the course of the sun. Here the same noise is made to quiet a dog that we make to set him on. Here they clip the hair off the back and sides of horses and mules, and leave it on the legs. I bought some string whereby to suspend my dog-whistle—whip-cord was not procurable—and on " double-twisting " the same found it had been " flung " the opposite way from that I am used to. But I could give instances without end.

This morning the girls heard me whistling, " The Conspirators' Chorus," from "Madame Angot." They were quite pleased at my knowing the air, declared I was " *Buena Carlista*," and joined in with " rebel " words. On inquiry I find the tune is claimed as an old Basque air. Whether this is a delusion, the fact being that, chiming with a musical chord of the *Viscayan* soul, it has become so popular they think it native, or that it is *Viscayan*, and has been utilised by Lecocq, I cannot tell. But that, accidentally or otherwise, there is in its music the Basque " lilt " is without doubt.

CHAPTER VIII.

DECEMBER 16, 1876.—The old lady is right; "a dog is
a great deal of trouble" when he has to live in a house.
But it is to me, not to her, that Juan is one; for I have, the
first and last thing each morning and evening, to take him
for a walk; and to do so is sometimes very inconvenient;
when I am lazy or have "fish to fry." Besides, while
leading him along the streets, on my way to some open
space where he can be let loose, I am annoyed by numerous
curs who swarm in every street, and charge upon, or "dog,"
our steps. Fortunately, though well able to take care of
himself, he is not quarrelsome, and so big, and of such a
bold presence, these street dogs fear to close with him. I
am getting quite fond of Juan, for he is extremely affectionate to me, and really the most gentlemanly animal I
ever possessed; admirably clean in his habits, and never
makes the least noise in the house. I fear, though, he has
not much "point" about him, for when loose he runs after

and tries to catch every chicken and pigeon he sees ; and
has in no instance " set " or " drawn " on one. The weather,
too, is not now always pleasant to turn out in early and late,
for though not absolutely cold, it is sometimes quite chilly.
Latterly the sky has been generally overcast, and it has
threatened to rain all the time—occasionally done so—and
as fireplaces, excepting in kitchens, seem to be unknown
in this part of the world, a little cold goes a long way. I
have nowhere before witnessed such a continuation of heavy
threatening weather without rain, for what little has fallen
has been merely light showers. But I shall certainly stop
where I am until the sky clears. I have no intention, if
avoidable, to be caught travelling on foot in wet weather,
without change of raiment, and while here find no difficulty
in amusing myself.

The only drawback to my present quarters that I care
for is that, as compared with my happy experience at San
Sebastian, and *en route*, the commissariat of the house is not
good. To be sure (excluding the imposition for the dog), I
only pay three *pesetas* a day as against five at San Sebastian,
but here rents and provisions are so much cheaper than
there, that were it not for the town's being so extraordinarily
full, I could have extremely nice rooms, and the very best
of fare, at the price I am paying. Really, Spain is by far
the cheapest civilised country I have ever lived in.

Comparisons being odious are appropriate to my present
boarding. To begin : The morning chocolate, instead of
being made with milk, and accompanied with *azucarillos*,
finger biscuits, or milk rolls, as it ever heretofore has—yea,
even at the roadside *posadas*—is in this house made with

water, and with it only served three diminutive strips of crust, each about the size of your third finger, and evidently trimmings of the scraps left from the previous day's dinner. I have vainly tried to make "mamma" understand I want a better *desayuno.* Breakfast, nominally at twelve o'clock, but really at any time it suits the mistress's religious exercises, or the servants' convenience, is a hash-up of oddments; and I could often eat up myself all the choice portions of what is provided for the four of us. It is well cooked, but badly served, being generally half cold, while the quality of the raw material is far, very far, from being the best of the market, and after the meal no coffee is provided. My stand-bys are bread and wine : the former, as it always has been since I crossed the frontier, is excellent, and the latter good. I begin to doubt that there is any bad wine in Navarra ; were there, I am sure we should get it. The lady of the house is, however, very careful with "the ruddy." There is no liberal helping by the servant, and each time anyone takes any, the bottle is recorked by her. Six o'clock dinner, not often served till seven, is also comparatively indifferent, and excepting one of the courses, always exactly the same thing over and over again. Here it is ! First : soup made by boiling vermicelli, almost to a paste, in water with mutton bones, said bones being carefully extracted before serving. Secondly : a vegetable course; a dish of mixed together, chopped up, white cabbage, coarse white beans, and chunks of potato, boiled in water, with a suspicion of grease, and served nearer cold than hot. Thirdly : the old bones fished out of the soup. Now come the variations. The fourth course consists of either a dishful of boiled scraps of mutton, or of a piece of neck or shoulder; or of a portion of a month-old lamb—the entire animal being no larger than a hare. Afterwards follows the regular salad, naturally good, but ruined by being drowned in vinegar. This is all—no coffee—and where, oh where, in this land of fruit, is the dessert?

The way that woman has of watching each mouthful you take, and when everything has been devoured of spreading out her hands and exclaiming, "Well, gentlemen, I hope you have dined well?" as though we had been partaking of a sumptuous feast, and made gluttons of ourselves, is most amusing. I wonder if the careful old humbug really believes that deportment can impose on stomachs?

There is no excuse for failure in excellence of table. I have visited the markets and they are well supplied. Every English vegetable of all the year round is in the utmost profusion, and extremely fine in both quality and size; and besides, a multitude of vegetables we have not. In fruits, there are oranges, grapes, pears, apples, raisins, plums, walnuts, chestnuts, and divers others, all fine and plentiful. Poultry of all kinds abound. Eggs are there in thousands. Meat is good, abundant, and cheap. I certainly "gaited" the lady of the house rightly when I first set eyes on her. Nor is the fish-market a bad one for that of an inland town, as a sufficiency of sea-fish is daily brought by the train from the coast, but it is comparatively dear. The river here—the Arga—at present affords but little. Eels and dace are the most usual. Occasionally, however, trout are netted. When it is the fishing season the neighbourhood of Pamplona must be a piscatorial paradise; one cannot go far in any direction without seeing mountain-streams full of falls, rapids, eddies, and pools, everyone of them easily fishable, there being scarcely any trees on their banks, and all well stocked with trout in spite of cast and drag net, for there are but few places where rocky shelves, boulders, and ledges do not afford inaccessible harbours of refuge against nets.   Still, trout are captured by their means.   I saw a young girl in the market with a basketful for sale—a wide, deep basket, bigger than a bushel measure, and heaped full of trout ; none were under a pound, most of them four and five pounders, several seven and eight.   I never saw such another basket of trout in my life.   All of them were, however, out of condition, lately off their spawning beds.   What beauties they would have been had they been fat!   They had all been taken the evening before in a drag-net, close to town, just under the Rochapea curtain of the fortifications.

I am afraid I shall get no shooting here, for the wide rolling plain in which Pamplona is situated is now devoid of covert, and the mountains encircling it are too far off to go to shoot on and return the same day ; while amongst them are no places advisable to put up at—in fact, they are all very advisable to keep away from.   I am told that just after harvest the miles of stubble commencing at the base of the fortifications are alive with quails, and the vines full of hares and partridges; now, there being neither covert nor feed on the plain, hares and partridges are in the mountains, where there is plenty of both, and the quails at this season are in Africa.   There is one mountain, to be sure—the San Cristobel—that may be considered in the plain and not far off, but it has some little villages on its farther edge, several roads crossing it, and is so much travelled over and hunted as to be nearly devoid of game. I have tried it as much to see what Juan would do as in expectation of sport. The base of the San Cristobel is only about half a mile from the city wall, but to its top was a severe climb. The side of the mountain towards Pamplona is a precipitous face altogether too steep to beat.

I was an hour gaining the summit ridge, arriving there at the point where stand the remains of the Carlist battery established when the city was invested. I found the farther slope of the mountain covered with species of heather, tuft-grass, and strange-looking prickly plants, splendid laying ground, the covert being thick and about a foot high, but very fatiguing to walk over. Slipping Juan, away he went, careering over the ground like mad, and not paying the least attention to voice or whistle. By-and-by, accidentally, I think, for he had evinced no knowledge of their being there, he dashed right through the midst of a small covey of red-leg partridges, and away they went with him in full chase, till birds and dog were lost to sight over a spur of the mountain. Soon Juan came back, tearing along as though he had a tin can tied to his tail, and ran up a single bird. All efforts to control him proved abortive, so he was left to his own devices, and I proceeded quickly in the direction the birds had gone, hoping to find them for myself when he was a mile away, but the dog ranged too fast and thoroughly for that little scheme to succeed,

and galloped them up again quite out of range. Soon
after, I heard a shot fired on the other side of the comb
of the mountain, and off Juan tore in the direction the
sound had come, and trusting I was rid of him for some
little time, I made, at the double, for a copse of dwarf
oaks, half a mile off, towards which the birds last put up
had flown, hoping to arrive there before he could. Alas !
he was again one too many for me, and, for the third time,
flushed the partridges out of shot. Eventually I caught
my dog, put one of his forefeet in his collar, and started to
cast towards home, for dusk was approaching. On three
legs he, notwithstanding the thickness of the covert,
managed to charge around in a wonderful way. He is
certainly a most active, strong, determined devil of a dog.
However, we found no more game.

Juan's wildness I care nothing about. It is simply
indicative of " go " in him. I can break him of that. But
I fear there is neither " point " nor " set " about him, and
that to act the part of a mute spaniel, and perhaps retriever,
is all I can train him to. It may not prove so though. If
ever we get amongst plenty of birds he may take to pointing ; then all will be easy enough, and he will soon become
a splendid sporting dog.

There are charming walks all round this city, so I go a
few miles out into the country every day to see the views
and do a little dog-breaking. I have already completely
worn out a two-and-a-half *peseta* dog-whip, and my pupil is
only so far advanced as to "downcharge" at the uplifted hand,
but he will do it as far off as he can hear the whistle. At
the further expense of two or three more of these rubbishy

Spanish apologies for dog-whips I hope to finish his course of "competitive education." Slight corrections have no effect, he thinks you are playing with him.

The main roads leading from this city are most excellent, and would be a credit to any country : straight as practicable, broad, smooth, well graded, and thoroughly repaired ; mostly, also, planted with avenues of well-trimmed, shady trees. In many places are double rows of such, on each side one, overhanging a wide footway. All these roads are well furnished, at convenient distances apart, with handsome cut-stone seats and frequent drinking fountains—excellent arrangements for walkers in hot weather ; and for hot weather all the preparations of this country, even to the way the city is built, seem to have been made. Pamplona's streets are very narrow, her houses many storied. Porticoes, covered balconies, wide overhanging eaves are the general rule. There are not half-a-dozen streets in this city in which the sun's rays ever reach the pavement. In summer the result may be a refreshing coolness, a pleasant shade. Now it entails gloom and dampness. Step into one of these streets out of a sunlit *Plaza* or *Plazuela*, and it seems as though you had entered a cold cellar.

The drinking fountains just mentioned have generally fronts of dressed stone measuring two hundred square feet, and are carved in alto-relievo with the arms of Navarra and Spanish lions, the lions looking more like trimmed French poodles than the king of beasts. From the centre of these fronts protrude, for about a foot, stone spouts from which flow streams of pure water into long, deep

stone troughs, for animals to drink from ; and shady trees
and seats, for the comfort of wayfarers, are always close at
hand.

In my rambles not even one single " country house "
has fallen under my observation. Indeed, since leaving
the neighbourhood of San Sebastian I have not seen any,
for the numerous *casas solarias,* the country-seats of the
ancient grandees, I cannot reckon as such now, for to-day
they are the abode of peasants and their animals. I am
told the few titled families, and numerous rich ones, of this
vicinity live entirely in the city, and that it is not now the
custom, in this part of Spain, for people of means to have
country residences. This is the chief reason I have seen so
few " turn-outs," for Pamplona covering but a small area,
and there being no one to drive out to visit, not many
people keep carriages ; seven are all my landlady could
count up for me, and she knows all about everybody,
and there is not a cab in town. Probably the chronic
state of insecurity of Navarra is the reason why those
who are rich live but in cities, and by preference in a
fortified one.

There are many good private houses here. Amongst
the best are the residences of the *Duque de Alba,* the *Conde
de Espeleta,* and the *Conde de Guindulain*— three historic
names. They are old, massive stone buildings, having
wide *porte-cochères* and handsome interior court-yards.
Their lower windows are heavily ironed, and on their
fronts coats-of-arms are sculptured.

The scenery of this place is very charming, and from a
little distance Pamplona looks very well indeed. I wished

to get views of it as *souvenirs*, but though there are three photographic galleries here not a single picture of the city has been taken by any of the enterprising (?) " artists " who conduct them, so I have done what I could with my pencil and a sheet of paper, but it is impossible to render justice to such a scene without colour ; and, besides, I am not an artist.

I have been learning *La Jota*, song, tune, and dance, for all three go together. The music is very uncommon and pretty, full of accent and lilt. In the words of the song " it lifts the feet." Until lately *La Jota* used to be performed every Sunday evening in the *Plaza de la Constitucion*, hundreds of couples dancing and singing it to the accompaniment of a band, and the castanets played by themselves. Since, however, the " Army of Occupation " has had its head-quarters here this entertainment has had to be put an end to, for the populace get quite excited when indulging in their national dance ; and these people being *Carlista*, the performance generally ended by their falling foul of any soldiers in sight, and a general row, which conduct having led to several riots, public *Jotas* are now prohibited. I am sorry ; it would have been a most interesting sight to a foreigner.

I notice the women here, irrespective of class, have wretchedly bad teeth ; those of the younger girls are even and white, but seem to decay ere they reach the age of maturity. On the other hand the men's teeth are of average soundness. For some time this has been a puzzle to me. I presume the reason is some difference of habit or diet. The only ones I can discover is in the smoking and drinking.

Smoking I at once dismiss as an efficient cause, for there are no such smokers as the Spanish-Americans—women, as well as men, even small children, indulge in the weed, and they all have splendid teeth ; so I suspect the drinking-water used contains some chemical constituent conducive to caries of the teeth, which may easily be the case notwithstanding its clear, sparkling, tasteless qualities, for it is all obtained from springs, not out of the river. And for this reason do I think so : while I have not seen a Spanish woman touch wine, neither have I seen a man drink water. I have taken a lesson from observation ; out of respect for my teeth, and on the principle of " When in Rome, &c.," have carefully avoided drinking the less wholesome beverage. Indeed, for my part, I care not for " the juice of flints," or, if you like it better " the blood of the earth," though the Spanish proverb does say it, " *no enferma no adeuda no enviuda* " (neither makes sick, nor in debt, nor widowed). On the contrary, I incline more to agree with that other one which rather irreverently asserts, " *Mas vale vino maldito, que no agua benedita* " (Cursed bad wine is better than [even] holy water). Navarra wine is good enough a drink for me.

This is the first place I have stopped at where the night-cries are excessive to the point of annoyance. Here is no peace for the restless. The *Serenos* of Pamplona are very proud of their voices, and ambitiously strive to excel one another in the loud, long-drawn cadence of their chant, while the no less strong-lunged sentinel on the ramparts also does his best to murder sleep.

Los Serenos are the Spanish prototype and present

representative of the obsolete "Charleys" of Old England
—the night-watchmen to whose vigilance is entrusted the
safety of person and property after dark. They are here
mostly middle-aged men of respectable appearance and
staid demeanour, all clad in uniform of dark blue, ample
cloak, and glazed cap ; slow, sedate, dignified of deportment, terrible in appearance to small boys, but I doubt
their efficiency against criminals. They are equipped with
a long black staff, tipped with brass—of no earthly use—
and carry a light, like a stable-lanthorn, which serves to
render their slow, pompous progress visible from afar,
and prevents their seeing anything half-a-dozen yards off.
Their principal duty is to march along calling out at the
corner of every street on their beat the hour and half-hour,
and adding each time thereto a statement of the condition
of the weather. As one can hear them a dozen corners off,
their prolonged cry falls on the ear of a listener twenty-four
times every hour of the night. If you have the luck (?) to
live near where two beats meet, you will have the advantage (?) of your curiosity as to the state of the weather
being enlightened fifty times an hour, but as it is almost
always fine here the statement "*y se-re-no,*" prolonged in
an interminable drawl, commencing in a low bass, and
terminating in the highest falsetto note attainable, becomes
monotonous.

That "and serene" should be so nearly invariably the
night-watchman's announcement as to have given him his
appellation speaks volumes for the Spanish climate.

The cry of the "watchman on the walls" is simply
"Alert-o." But they take great pride in that "O"; set

it to music—make quite a complicated tune of it—with variations. The cry commences at the mainguard of the citadel every quarter of an hour, and seems almost continuous, for the sentinels are close together and numerous, and each waits patiently until his predecessor has done with his own particular " O," while the town, covering for its population a small area—the circle of the fortifications—is not large, and the "*Alerto*" of every sentinel is plainly to be heard by each of its inhabitants not fast asleep—trying for a restless invalid or fidgety character. I like it. It brings pleasant reminiscences of wild life. In my dreams I hear again the plaintive howl of the midnight wolf.

There is a fine large theatre here, but at present it is given up to a " renowned " troupe of " English " acrobats and gymnasts. I never heard of them in England. Their names are quite unknown to me. I do not care for such performances. I did not come to Spain to see my fellow-countrymen make exhibitions of themselves. I can do so at less trouble and expense. So I have carefully kept away. There is also a fine *Plaza de Toros* that will seat eight thousand persons; but July and August is the season, and it is now shut up. The *pelota* court is, however, in full swing. It is a very inferior one to that at San Sebastian.

I have met with a little book that purports to give an authentic and particular history and description of this ancient city and of its fortifications and neighbourhood, with some account of its blockade by, and "heroic" defence against, the Carlists. As Pamplona is an interesting and important place, I am going to translate, condense, and omit—principally omit—and, throwing in a few observations of my own, make the product serve for a portion of my next letter, by way of a desperate attempt to combine instruction and amusement—to, in fact, come Barlow over my readers.

CHAPTER IX.

DECEMBER 20, 1876.—Here goes for the translation, &c.
" Elevated one thousand two hundred and ninety-three
feet above the level of the sea, planted in the centre of the
province of Navarra, at the foot of the Pyrenees, and to the
south-west of the same, upon the left bank of the river Arga,
is situated the city of Pamplona, extending on the crown of
high ground which forms a platform whose centre the city
occupies." There! That is as nearly literal as possible,
and gives a fair specimen of the Spanish way of spreading
it out. Then it appears to be proved " beyond intelligent
controversy" that the city was founded by Tubal before
the dispersion at the building of the Tower of Babel, and,
consequently, that the Basque language, being the speech
introduced by those early settlers, is the original tongue of
paradise and the angels. Having then come to grief—
principally from age, I suppose—Pamplona had to be re-

built. This was done in less prehistoric times by Pompey, B.C. 68.

Conquered by Euric VIII., five hundred and thirty-four years after its first rebuilding ; by the French nearly one hundred years later ; regaining its independence, and being retaken by them under Charlemagne, who destroyed it again ; it was yet once more rebuilt by its indomitable inhabitants, fortified, and subsequently successfully defended both against the Moors in A.D. 907 and the Castillians in A.D. 1138, and it in consequence rejoices, " of legal and prescriptive right," in the titles of " *Muy noble, muy leal, y muy heroica* "—for in Spain cities as well as families bear titles.

Pamplona's encircling fortifications are an admirable example of Middle Age defensive work, and the city is considered one of the strongest in Europe. It is enclosed within an irregular rectangular quadrilateral, composed of eight redans and their connecting curtains, and of the citadel at the south-west corner.

The faces of the redans and curtains are of most unusual depth, and excepting where escalade is rendered impossible by the extreme height of the escarped river bluff, are covered by deep wide moats, and strengthened by semi-detached works, covered ways, lunettes, and ravelins. The five fronts of the fortifications are pierced by posterns, giving access to the moats, by sally-ports, and by the six strongly defended gateways by which the roads giving access to the country leave the town. The river Arga flows close under the north side of the fortifications, and is crossed by but one bridge—*La Magdalena*—which is swept by the guns of a battery on the walls, and covered by a

strong ravelin to its left.   The largest and most important
redan is on the south or opposite side from the river, and
is that of *La Reina*.

La Reina has in its interior a well-constructed crown-
work, which commands the country on that side, and whose
armament sweeps the glacis.   It also protects the powder
magazine in its rear, a most solid construction, of a capacity
of eighteen hundred hundredweight.   In times of peace
the powder is stored outside the walls in a magazine, built
in 1842, on the eminence of Ezcaba, which can hold
twenty-six hundred hundredweight.   The postern leading
to the moat on the right flank of this redan is known as
" The Gate of Death," for through it are led prisoners
sentenced to be shot in the moat.

It was on the right flank of *La Reina*, a little way back
off the face of the curtain, that an event happened, a
casualty occurred, which, in the results developed from it,
has done Spain more fatal damage than all her other cala-
mities put together.   An otherwise trifling incident which
was the first and potential cause of torture and death to her
best and noblest sons and daughters, which has done
Christianity more injury than Pagan and Infidel, from
whose effects the world is not yet free, which is still working evil in darkness, for there, defending the place, fell, in
1521, Ignacio Loyola, unfortunately for humanity, not killed,
but so sorely wounded that he lay recovering long enough
to conceive and mature his scheme of Jesuitry, that most
striking example of what " the cruelty, baseness, and
wickedness of the human mind can plan, and the folly,
credulity, and cowardice of mankind can tolerate."   Close by

stands the chapel of *San Ignacio,* founded in 1691, to commemorate the event, and in which may be seen badly-executed pictures illustrating it.

On the south-west of the *place d'armes,* between the fronts, *La Taconera* and *San Nicolas,* is the citadel, constructed in 1571, by order of Filipe II., under the able direction of Gorje Peleajo. It is a regular pentagon of six hundred and eighty yards of exterior sides fortified on Vauban's first system; and has two sets of re-entering flanks, half lunettes, and counterscarps to its exterior fronts; and five redans and corresponding curtains forming the remaining fronts. The side which looks towards the *Plaza,* called *De la Victoria y San Antonio,* has in its centre a gateway and drawbridges of communication with the city. In the fourth curtain is the gateway *Del Socorro,* which opens to the exterior and has three posterns in it communicating with the moat and covered ways, and with openings enfilading the walls that join the redans, Victoria, Santiago, and El Real. The citadel contains three barracks for infantry, capable of accommodating twelve hundred men; a small one for cavalry having a capacity for eighty men and sixty horses. Twelve small blocks of houses standing round the open square, and grouped in twos and fours, furnish quarters for chiefs and officers. A large building for an artillery park has spacious bombproofs to the right and left, and there is a good bombproof powder magazine, similar to the one in *La Reina,* capable of holding twenty-five hundred hundredweight of powder; also another underground bombproof, containing four ovens for baking bread in times of siege, a small engineer park, and a chapel. There are yet twelve more bombproof cellars, lying below the terreplein of the curtain, in which is the Socorro gateway, that can also serve for safe retreats for a portion of the garrison in case of necessity.

The gateways through the fortifications, giving ingress and egress to and from the citadel and the city of Pamplona, are strong stone buildings, pierced by arched tunnels wide enough for a waggon to traverse, and sixty feet in length, are each furnished with drawbridge crossing the moat, portcullis, and two strongly-ironed folding-doors. On each side of the tunnel are guard-rooms. These gateways are faced with smooth-wrought, fine-grained white stone, handsomely carved, and bear, immediately above their entrances, in alto-relievo, the arms and insignia of the kingdoms of Navarra and Aragon, the city arms, and the date 1666—that of their last restoration.

Pamplona owes much to her fortifications. She cannot, to be sure, claim to be a virgin city ; for, ere they were erected, Goth and French both took her ; but since, she has been inviolate, a most unapproachable—widow, let us say. Moor, Castillian, French, have tried to force her, but in vain ; even that rough and intrepid wooer of cities, the "Iron Duke," had to content himself with a blockade when he would fain have captured her ; lately Don Carlos attempted her for five months with a like result.

Round Pamplona lies a valley-plain of elliptical figure, whose largest diameter is from north to south, and least from east to west. It is surrounded by a cordon of mountains, seven Spanish leagues in circumference, and composed of the *Ezcaba*, the *San Miguel de Miravalles*, and the *El*

Perdon y Zanil ranges. Within this ellipse lay the sub-valleys of *Echauri, Aranguen, Egues,* and *Eloiz,* the towns of *Huarte* and *Villava,* and the hamlets of *Ansoan, Iza, Tosin, Sular,* and *Olza.* Beyond it is a wild stretch of mountainous country bounded by the *Cordilleras Cantabrica* and the *Sierras* of *Andia* and of *Monreal.* The valley of Pamplona is wonderfully productive and entirely under cultivation, principally of the vine and wheat. The hills and mountains are well wooded, and full of small, fertile, lateral valleys.

Pamplona consists of one thousand nine hundred and seventy houses, distributed in thirty-seven streets—for the chief part straight and narrow—and round eight *Plazas* and *Plazuelas,* the largest of which is that of *La Constitucion,* an imperfect square having three hundred and twenty yards of side. There is too a pretty public garden which also serves for promenading.

Though Pamplona's citizens are *Carlistas,* and at the outbreak of the late civil war the garrison of Pamplona was but a mere handful of men, the fortifications just described saved the city to King Alfonso from a *coup de main,* and its reduction had therefore to be attempted by blockade.

The investing force consisted of five "companies of Jesus," five sections of cavalry—viz. four of the 1st *Navarro,* and one of "*Los Alagoneses,*" and a reserve of ten companies of the 4th infantry of the line and two batteries of field artillery.

The defence of such an important place was entrusted to three hundred *Carabineros,* one hundred and fifty *Guardias Civiles,* four companies of the *Cadis* reserve, and one hundred and fifty artillerymen of the 3rd foot artillery, all under the command of the military governor, His Excellency Don Manuel Andia.

The Carlists cut the aqueduct that supplies the public fountains on which the inhabitants depend for water, entirely prevented them from procuring fuel, and almost completely barred the ingress of provisions from the 3rd September, 1874, till the Alfonsist army, forcing the pass of the Carrascal, five months after, raised a blockade that had nearly brought twenty-three thousand persons to starvation.

There! I think that is about enough of the "authentic and particular." *Adieu*, Barlow, *adieu!*

At last, there was a lift of the heavy curtain of clouds that for so long had canopied the earth, obscured the sky, and hidden the distant mountains, and I judged, while the evidently brewing storm was concentrating its forces, a few days of fine weather would intervene before it burst; so, believing my opportunity had come to make safely another stage of my journey, announced my intention to depart early the following morning.

It was really very gratifying to listen to the prettily-turned speeches of regret addressed to me by all. The lively lieutenant was especially demonstrative, and I was glad of it, for I had got to like him much. With all his cavalier ways, he had in the background a heap of sound sense and right feeling; besides, we had discovered a bond of union between us. As he wished me good-night for the last time, he gripped my hand and said, "Remember, wherever you may happen to be, if I am there, there you have a friend you can rely on." I liked those girls too—the youngest especially. She was a very nice child, clever, pretty, and engaging. She made me promise " never, never, never " to forget her and Pamplona.

The 20th was a lovely morning. The clouds, excepting an ominously heavy bank to the nor'-west, had vanished. The air was just cool enough to be bracing. I was congratulated by the Colonel on my luck. " You see," said he, " we are going to have splendid weather ; do not hurry away." I laughingly replied, " Deceive not yourself ; look at that black bank over yonder, to-day is the clear-up before the storm ; ere Sunday Pamplona will be white with snow. I am escaping—*à dios,*" and I ran downstairs under a volley of " *Via 'sted con dios* " from the entire family, my fellow-boarders, and the servants.

I had intended making an early start ; but, as usual, found it impossible to do so without leaving before any-one was up, which would have been considered most discourteous. The delusion that Spain is an early-rising country has vanished after the others.

It was nine A.M. when Juan and I passed through the *San Nicolas* gateway, crossed the drawbridge, and found our-selves in the open country. I turned and kissed my hand to Pamplona and " the girls I left behind me." The fool of a sentinel pacing the drawbridge thought the gesture was made to him and threw up his hand with an exclamation of astonishment, then remembering his manners—all men have manners in Spain—waved his adieux to the " mad Englishman." I am considered mad here because I walk when it is evident I can afford to ride.

Twenty-five minutes past ten found me at the Carlist-war-ruined hamlet of Noan, a quarter of a mile beyond which, on crossing a little ridge, a most charming view was sighted. Before me lay a long, narrow, shallow, winding valley, one mass of young wheat of a most brilliant green, a pretty stream bordered with tall poplars and willows meandering down its centre, and, crossing stream and valley, topping willows and poplars, a magnificent aqueduct, solidly built of hewn stone, but from its great height and graceful proportions looking light and airy. There were ninety-seven arches, and where they crossed the river, the lofty poplars fringing its banks failed by many feet to reach their curves. They could not have been much under seventy feet in height, and had a span of about half their altitude. I estimated the entire distance of aqueduct supported by them was but little short of half a mile. The towering, and apparently close at hand, Carrascal range — rough, precipitous, and bare — made a rugged, handsome background and contrast to the level verdure of the valley and symmetrical evenness of the aqueduct.

A peasant farmer, who was driving his little flock of goats and sheep along the road, on being questioned, said, " The Romans made the aqueduct to bring water to Pamplona." At the distance it was from me (being half a mile to the left of the road) the aqueduct looked as new as though built but a few years ; but, as we talked, I noticed that the line of caps to the " man-holes " of the " ditch "—a covered stone one running under ground—crossed the road to the front of me. Doubtless they were coeval with the archway; I could test his statement by their look of age on a close inspection.

"*Muy lejos*" (very far off) was the most definite information extractable from the farmer as to the whereabouts of the "ditchhead;" but far as eye could see the square, gray, tombstone-looking manhole caps were dotted, in a winding course, along and climbed the mountain sides to my right. Coming to where they crossed the road I sat down on one to rest, enjoy the prospect, and criticise it. In colour and weatherstain, in condition of surface and edges, those hewn blocks were in appearance identical with the neighbouring rocks *in situ*. So far as information derivable by sight warranted a conclusion, the masonry I sat on was as old as the mountains.

An hour-and-a-half's walk brought me abreast of Tiébas, a most ancient-looking mountain village, built on a spur of the Carrascals, and standing a few hundred yards to the left of, and some hundreds of feet above and commanding, my road, which there wound along through the narrowest portion of the pass that led from the elevated valley, in which is Pamplona, to the lower country beyond the Carrascals.

Close to the village, and occupying the entire top of a rocky mound, whose form is so regular as to convey an impression that it is partly artificially so, stand the remains of an old, a very old castle—in fact, the oldest-looking ruin I have yet seen in Spain. These mementoes of the days of chivalry and romance consist of portions of a square tower and two round encircling walls, one below the other. The tower is built of roughly-hewn freestone from the nearest mountain. Its walls are of great thickness, and the cement or mortar that was used in its construction of wonderful tenacity, for as time, and perhaps gunpowder, destroyed the building, the course of cleavage invariably crossed the blocks of stone and never followed the line of cement. A large gateway—the entrance to the castle court—has lost its right support, which, fallen to the ground, has crumbled away and become but a heap of grass-grown mould ; still the arch—an inverted U mutilated of the lower half of one side—hangs in the air carrying a superincumbent mass of masonry. Take away one of the supports of the Marble Arch, and how long will the " Iron Duke " and horse continue from their present conspicuous elevation to greatly astonish artistic foreigners?

From Tiébas onward the prospect was hemmed in and bounded by a mountain's side, and, close at hand, rolling hills, until *Venta de las Campanas* was reached ; at which place I stopped to breakfast.

Venta de las Campanas is not a village, but, as its name implies, a roadside tavern—the tavern of the bells. Of course there is a church near it—there is near every place. This one has a rather fine doorway, with a huge arch above it, rising nearly to the point of the gable, and a circular window pierced within, very similar in appearance to some of the church doorways in Pamplona. The *venta* proved a nice, clean, decent little inn, and there I enjoyed an excellent meal, quite a treat after my late fare. Juan, too, got a good " tuck out," and fifteen pence paid the entire bill, including excellent wine *ad lib.*, which, being thirsty, I spared not.

While waiting for breakfast to be cooked, a mule-cart

drove up, stopped, and its driver came in, saluted, and sat
down. On looking around he spied in a corner an old
guitar, and immediately seized upon it. The instrument
lacked two strings. "'Tis well," he exclaimed, "it matters
not, I am always prepared," and he forthwith produced
from the folds of his voluminous sash an old pocket-book,
containing more guitar-strings than anything else, found
and fitted those lacking, sat down, tuned up, and played
away. Though but a common waggoner the man was full
of music, and played some beautiful airs with charming
chords. Amongst them was an old friend, one last heard
thousands of miles off, years ago : "The Spanish Retreat."
I closed my eyes, and saw again the waving tree-ferns, the
feathery palms of other days, almost fancied I smelt once
more the night-blooming cereus's intoxicating perfume!
His music made the time of waiting seem but short.

Soon after leaving the *venta*, the edge or rim of the
plateau was reached, and the direction of the slope of the
sides of the mountain, on each hand, changed—pitching
from instead of towards Pamplona ; and at a turn of the
road, the prospect opened out to a splendid bird's-eye view
of valleys, ridges, and distant ranges ; the valleys studded
with detached Butes having table-land tops. One of these,
the nearest to the right, showed plainly three broad terraces,
scarped on its front, connected by wide, graded roads,
leading to its top, while the adjacent ridges had evidently
been once extensively entrenched. Undoubtedly I saw
before me the site of some ancient military camp, and no
small nor temporary one either. It was very like, but
larger, what have been pointed out to me in England as

remains of early British or Roman camps. The strongest
side of this fortified position faced towards Pamplona;
evidently, it was intended to accommodate an army of
protection, covering the country in its rear from raids
through the Carrascals from the north, as the Tiébas Castle
had been located for a defence of the pass against the
Moors from the south. The camp was perhaps Roman,
possibly Carthaginian. Hannibal's army may have rested
there—who can say?

A third of the country spread out before me was, as far
as the eye could discern, vineyards or wheatfields, the rest
a jumble of intermixed moorlike waste lands and scattered
mountain elevations, all covered with loose rocks, stunted
brush, and wild herbs; and appearing in most unlikely
places, were to be seen little villages, made conspicuous
only by the towers of churches and monasteries, the dingy
brownness of their prevailing hue matching so closely with
that of the surrounding ground as to render them otherwise
hardly discernible.

I entered Tafalla over the new stone-bridge, crossing
the river Cidacos. I call it the new bridge, though it looked
older than any I have ever seen in England, because there
close to it—alongside, but not parallel, as if the river had
when it was built run a slightly different course—was the
old abandoned bridge, still looking in its hoary age solid
enough for the traffic had the river been as unchangeable
as it.

Night had fallen, it was quite dark, and I hastened to
find food and quarters for myself and Juan.

CHAPTER X.

DECEMBER 22, 1876.—Tafalla appeared to be a town of some size and importance, as large as all the hamlets passed near in the course of my walk from Pamplona put together, but had about it a dirty, dismal, disreputable air.

I stepped up to the only decently-apparelled and respectable-looking person I saw, an infantry lieutenant, and made inquiry for a stopping-place. By him I was directed to the leading hotel, a large, rambling stone building, capable of accommodating a company of men, but seemingly uninhabited, no lights being visible, no sound issuing therefrom.

I entered the *Fonda*, and after groping my way up a pitch-dark stairway, wandering along a passage, opening half-a-dozen doors giving entrance to untenanted rooms, at last found my way into a large kitchen, and in it beheld

sitting on the hearth with a babe at the breast, and two
young children sprawling on the floor at her feet, the
mistress, two smartly-dressed girls cooking, and several
travellers or loafers warming themselves at the fire.   After
the usual salutations of the country had been given I made
my wants known, and was conducted by one of the maids
to a roomy, clean, and sufficiently-furnished bedchamber,
an astonishingly good one for such a dismal-looking house,
and there made a comfortable toilet, changed my walking
boots for the *alpargatas* I carried in my pocket, and then
returned and joined the group around the kitchen-fire.

My dinner was soon announced, and, following a
maid, I found it set out in a large, handsome, but scantily-
furnished room.   It was a very good dinner indeed, of
many courses, admirably cooked.   Its crowning glory was
a large plateful of lampreys nicely browned in the sweetest
of olive oil.   Oh, how good they were !   I ate them all.   I
dined in solitary grandeur all alone.   But I did not mind.
I was waited on by, I think, the most talkative, I am sure
the handsomest, servant-girl I ever saw.   This affable maid
told me lampreys were awfully dear, the most expensive
dish that could be served, their price being sevenpence
three-farthings a pound, but that they used to be much less
costly.

On my return to the kitchen I found a guitarist had
arrived and was playing merrily.   Pieces he executed
indifferently, but accompanied well enough, and having
a rich tenor voice, which though uncultivated was quite
under control, and a good *répertoire* of songs, was quite an
acquisition.

Before long the *Guitarrista* started a *Jota*, and everybody importuned me to dance; they should so much like
to see how I danced it. On explaining the *Jota* was not
an English dance, that I was English, consequently could
not, they were still unsatisfied, maintaining it was evident
I was no stranger to the ways of the country, and must,
therefore, know the national dance; so being unwilling to
appear churlish, or to give an impression that Englishmen were indifferent to oblige, I told them I would do
my little towards the entertainment of the evening, and
made my bow to the beauty who had waited on me at
dinner.

And she was a most decided beauty, her figure charming,
her face lovely in classical outline, in delicate brilliancy
of complexion, her large lustrous black eyes deadly at a
thousand yards. She had such elegant limbs, and, great
Cæsar—such feet! Where a peasant-girl got feet like hers
from passeth my understanding; short, high arched, small
heeled, muscular, symmetrical models!

The young woman played shy; so, seizing her by both
hands, gentle force was added to entreaty, she was landed
in the middle of the floor, and we started. It was a treat
to see the graceful, hearty agility with which that *Mozuela
hermosisama* danced; there was a grace, *chic*, and abandon
about her movements which was quite enchanting.

I believe it is a point of honour to dance down your
partner in the *Jota*, and mine tried her best to do so. But
my wind was too good, I was not on a pedestrian trip
for nothing, my training was too much for her; and though
with set teeth and flashing eyes she gamely continued till

her colour left and her breath failed, I still "kept the floor," winding up with a florid *pas seul* ere I sat down. "*El Inglés*" did not disgrace his nationality, as first in all athletics, and a hearty round of applause rewarded my exertions.

An old fellow next whom I seated myself declared he had always thought England a great country, and was now sure of it. Said he : "I'll tell you what we'll do. We'll marry the little Alfonzo to the Queen of England's daughter, if she has one. Then he will be King of Spain and England, Gibraltar will belong to both nations, and he will eat up Portugal and France for breakfast, and conquer the world at his leisure, for there is no fleet like the English, no armies like those of the Spains. *Viva Ingleterra y Los Españas !*"

This old man proved very talkative, and quite bored me with questions, but in return I managed to get a little information about Tafalla out of him : that it was a *Cabaza de Partido* (district capital), had a population of five thousand souls, was once a very rich place, but in decadence; that it could boast of the remains of an old palace, built for Charles the Noble, king of Navarra, of two Gothic churches, and of a celebrated hermitage famous as the scene of the assassination of Echevarri, Archbishop of Pamplona, by Don Nozen Pierres de Peralta, Grand Constable of Castile in 1469, and that taxation and the octroi was quickly sending it to "*El Demonio.*" As this respectable old gossip seemed read up in the history of his neighbourhood, I inquired about the builders of the splendid aqueduct-bridge, with whose beauty I had been so much taken. He told me the structure now standing was not erected by the ancients, but by a celebrated "modern" engineer, Don Ventura Rodriguez, who finished it in 1730, on the site of the original bridge, which he strove to replace as well in appearance as in utility. The ditch and its masonry were, he affirmed, undoubtedly Roman work.

Having learned incidentally from me that I intended walking to Tudela, this old gaffer most urgently advised my not attempting to do so alone, assuring me I had to cross a stretch of country having the worst reputation for robberies and murders in Spain—*Las Bardenas Reales de Navarra*—and strongly recommended my journeying in company with a *carretero* sitting opposite us, who, he informed me, though poor, was a man in whom the utmost confidence could be placed; and who, having come from Zaragoza with a load of figs, and sold them, would start back empty the next morning; adding, as further inducements, that I should be able to put my traps in the man's cart, that should it rain I could take shelter therein, that the mules would go no faster than I could walk, and returning to the old song that two persons might be safe when one would be in great danger. So I broached the matter, and as he seemed well pleased with the idea, it was arranged that we should travel together so long as it suited me, he fixing times of departure, halts, stations, &c.; ten o'clock the following morning, sharp, being the appointed hour at which to leave the *fonda*. That settled, and an early rise not being necessary, I sat up till late, amusing myself by listening to the songs sung, and watching the dancing, for the ice once broken, an alternate *Jota* and

Copla was the order of the night, and so the entertainment was kept up unflaggingly.

Talk about " fast girls of the period," why that *fonda* beauty of Tafalla could give any I have ever seen a distance. She was the rapidest two-footer it has ever been my fortune to encounter. Before parting, towards morning, she absolutely made me an offer of marriage ! No doubt it was in fun, to fool me, but it was done with the gravest, most sincere, and most serious air in the world. She said she had saved a little money besides her inheritance, and if I would take her and settle down, she and the money were ready. Upon my word, if I had been a young fellow of fortune, and " on the marry," I might have done far worse than taken her *au sérieux.* She knew enough, if necessary, to have stood over my cook, English or French as the case might be, and prevent her or him poisoning me by bad cookery, even if she had to show how it was done herself with her own pretty little hands. She was handsome and elegant enough to grace the head of any table, to make a sensation in every ball-room in Europe. Courtly manners, would have come to her as though by intuition ; they always do to women with well-bred hands and feet. I was really sorry as I reflected that in all human probability fate would throw her charms away on an ignorant, half-clad, half-barbarous Navarra labourer, with about the same appreciation for the beautiful as a jack-snipe has of a fine game of billiards ; *j ay de me !* but 'tis a badly mixed up world.

Before getting into bed I looked out of the window. The night was black dark, and a fitful wind sighed and moaned through the streets. At half-past twelve I heard the Serenos' cry, *Est las doce y media y nublado.* In half-an-hour, "It is one o'clock and raining." A gentle drizzle was falling. Soon a steady rattle on the window-panes showed the rain was coming down in earnest. Rapidly it increased to a regular deluge. The storm had come at last, and I fell asleep to the lullaby of a howling tempest.

A little before nine in the morning my proposed bride brought the *desayuno* to my bedside and awoke me. It was the old San Sebastian matin repast. There was the milk chocolate that a spoon could almost stand in, the *azucarillos* and the milk roll for which my soul had sighed in vain at Pamplona. The rain had ceased, but heavy clouds covered the sky, while the streets were deep in mud and slush. As I was to leave by ten, breakfast was out of the question, so I paid my bill—half-a-crown's worth of Spanish money—had an appropriate leave-taking with the beauty, and was ready. Not so the *carretero*, for his theoretical ten o'clock sharp proved to be, in fact, a quarter-past eleven, at which time we eventually did get under weigh.

From the very edge of the town extended a succession of fruit orchards, vineyards, and olive groves, through which stretched, till lost to sight, a wide, well-made road, bordered by walnut and other shady trees. The vineyards were full of pruners, the olive groves of pickers, equipped with poles, ladders, and baskets. The straight, broad, level highway seemed the capacious centre walk of a gigantic garden. The truth was apparent of the local proverb :

De Olite á Tafalla,
La Flor de Navarra.

Some two Spanish leagues south of Tafalla (there are twenty Spanish *leguas* to the geographical degree) lays Olite, the first place we arrived at. It is a quaint old walled village, with two picturesque churches, one in ruins, the other having a fine tower surmounted with a spire, the only church-spire I have as yet seen in Spain ; tower and spire most unique and original in design, and adding quite a novel feature to the landscape.

The ruins of a once very fine castle attracted my attention, and I ascertained they were the remains of a royal palace, built at the latter end of the fourteenth or beginning of the fifteenth century for Charles III. of Navarra. This castle is a grand old ruin, and inspection revealed that the carvings of one of the two churches were pre-eminently odd and remarkably clever. From this place to Tafalla there is believed to be a subterranean passage to the palace there, made also by *Don Carlos el Noble*—that is to say, is believed by the peasants ; I do not believe any such thing.

Beyond Olite, wheatfields, pastures, and stretches of wild land, supplanted the olive groves, and, to a great extent, the vineyards ; the face of the country became rolling, the distant prospect strongly accidented.

Arriving at the summit of an acclivity, I turned to take a look at the country I was leaving behind me. Though so recently travelled over it was unrecognisable. My prophecy to the Colonel had been speedily and thoroughly fulfilled. I gazed on a white world. That round Pamplona there was a foot in depth of snow was unquestionable. The mountains between me and there showed not spot or place uncovered. I had got out in time, but with none to spare. As the day grew older the wind steadily increased in force; and, being from the north-west, coming from snow-clouds, and over many and many a league of fallen snow, was bitterly cold. A chilling, drizzling rain began to fall, and I gladly took refuge in the covered cart; Juan following as though he were a waggoner's dog. He, too, was glad of partial shelter, and found it by trotting along between the wheels. As the day wore on I naturally got hungry, and asked where we were to stop for breakfast. "Oh, we can't stop," said the *carretero ;* "we had such a late start, it will be all the mules can do to get to Caparroso before dark, by continuous travelling ; I breakfasted at a friend's in Tafalla, and supposed you would at the inn, while waiting for me." Evidently I was in for nothing to eat until nightfall. However, an occasional short fast hurts nobody who is hardy, and I had made many a longer one before ; besides, being fortunately a smoker, I have always at command a meal of two courses : first, to take up my waistband a hole ; second, a pipe. But such a diet is too light and virtuous to be a satisfactory substitute for " cates and ale."

We passed through wretchedly poverty-stricken villages, each having, though, several large, solidly-built, cut-stone houses in them—" *casas solares* "—houses with *porte-cochère* and court-yard, and on whose front were sculptured coats-of-arms. On the newest-looking of these old mansions a date was plainly distinguishable; as compared with some of the carvings, its engraving looked like the work of yesterday ; the date was 1617. These houses, the shelter of peasants, living huddled with their fowls and goats, their cattle, donkeys, and fleas, had been the homes of belted knights of old, of the grandees of the kingdom of Navarra, of Christianity's advance-guard against the conquering Moor. I begin to differ from my San Sebastian friend, to cease to look upon Spain, through his spectacles, as the country of "to-morrow," and to consider it, on the contrary, as that of a long-passed, almost-forgotten yesterday.

Towards night the cold wind moderated, the rain ceased, and I gladly exchanged a cramped posture in a cart without springs for the free use of my limbs on the road.

We were within half a mile of Caparroso when I stopped to admire a very prettily-built, ecclesiastical-looking building, standing in a grove of trees a hundred yards to the right of our road. When the *carretero* came up he surprised me greatly by saying: "Ah! you seem to know where we are going to stop for the night. That is a better and much cheaper *posada* than any in the town yonder." I told him I had been thinking what a pretty church it was.

"It does look like a church, for you see it is a *santa*. The wing on this side is the part which is the *posada*. Almost all the *santas* in this country have a *posada* attachment."

I did not know what a *santa* meant—did not dare to ask. My *compagnon de voyage* might consider himself outraged if he discovered he was travelling with one who was, so evidently not a "*Cristiano*," as to be in ignorance on such a subject. However, ere night I found out. A *santa*, or *santo*, as the case may be, is a chapel of commemoration built over the spot where a ghost of the Virgin, or of some saintess or saint of renown has appeared, and which is opened for worship once a year, namely, on the anniversary of the appearance of the spectre ; on which occasion a special mass is performed, attended by such pilgrims as the holiness or other attractions of the spot has brought there. It is the harvest-day of the *santa posada*, for there the congregation eat, drink, and sleep—or rather, spend the night feasting, guitar-twanging, jota-dancing, singing, and, generally speaking, in what is called in colder and more puritan climes immorality.

On entering the *santa posada* I was glad to find its interior corresponded with its outward aspect. It was very clean, smelt pure and sweet, and had been freshly white-washed. In the kitchen was a trim old woman, cooking at a most unusually tidy hearth, who greeted the *carretero* as an old acquaintance, and, saying we must be hungry, im-mediately prepared a couple of *jicaras* of chocolate and presented them, as stays to our stomachs till a regular meal could be got ready. My hunger was too pressing, however, to be so easily satisfied ; I therefore begged a big slice of bread, toasted it on the wood coals, rubbed it with a lump of salt, saturated it with fresh olive oil, gave it a finishing warm up, and washing it down with a tumblerful of wine, felt more contented and better able to contemplate with equanimity the preparations of what would really and truly be my breakfast—my first meal that day, though it was long past sunset. The old woman gave us an excel-lent repast : soup, two courses of meat, several dishes of different vegetables, apples, roast and raw, dried grapes,

and roasted chestnuts, wine and bread without stint. I
had a most cheerful bedroom and comfortable bed, and
really felt more "at home" than I had done before in
Spain. In the morning we had the usual *desayuno*, we
carried away with us a big half-loaf of bread and several
slices of cold meat, to sustain us until we reached Valtierra,
our appointed place for breakfast, my dog had all he could
eat, and the entire charge for man and dog was one shilling
and tenpence halfpenny! I never was more comfortable in
any inn in any country; certainly have never been charged
so low a price for such entertainment.

We were to have made an early start, so as to arrive at
Tudela before dark—half-past five A.M. had been the appointed time. I woke at six, but I did not jump out of bed
and dress in frantic haste ; oh no, quite the contrary. I
carefully went to sleep again. Is not foreign travel to
make a man wise ? Does not experience make even fools
so ? Have I not already learned what fixing a time amounts
to in Spain ? At seven I was called by the pretty and
engaging granddaughter of the old woman, who brought
chocolate, etc. etc. to my bedside, and at half-past seven A.M.
we were on the road.

Just before arriving at Caparroso we crossed, in the
gray dawn of day, by a fine old bridge of eleven pointed
arches, a clear, sharp stream—the river Aragon, there
about the size of the Thames at Richmond. Its low right
bank extended back in grassy meadows, fertile orchards,
vineyards, and wheatfields. Directly in front of us its left
bank rose in frowning bluffs eight hundred feet in the air,
the precipitous and wall-like face of the table-land desert

" *Las Bardenas Reales de Navarra.*" These bluffs showed
a section composed of alternate strata of veined limestone,
gypsum, hard close-grained red cement, and barren gray
clay ; a huge natural scarp, cracked and seamed in fantastic
shapes by the shocks and wear of ages, breached and riven
by the eternal siege of time. On a wide terrace-like ledge,
a third of the way up the face of the bluffs, was perched
Caparroso and its church. A church and Caparroso, I
should have written, for the house of worship was by far
the more conspicuous of the two, being large enough to
hold, not only all the parishioners, but the greater number
of their dwellings as well. The disproportion in the size
and number of churches to the requirements of the population is, in this country, continually forcing itself on my
notice. It is Falstaff's suit of clothes for an infant in arms.
How insane of these people to build such churches. But
what they did they did well. Then architects were *not*
all dead, and builders were not yet invented.

As we left the town the *carretero* called to me to stop—
I was in advance—and, on coming up, addressed me as
follows :

"I pray your valiant worship to take heed of what I
am about to say. We are now entering a very bad country,
one in which there have been many murders. Load your
gun well. Put good caps on. Carry your weapon in your
hand ready to shoot. Call upon our Lady ✠ and Saint
Iago. Be watchful ! be brave !"

I am no stranger to the expression of fear on a man's
face. I looked in my companion's, and saw he was really
seriously apprehensive of danger. I suppose the man,

having sold his figs, had in his sash what, to him, seemed a large sum of money, and being aware that all Tafalla knew he was returning empty, and consequently had the price of his late load about his person, he considered himself a possibly-marked prey to be waylaid and assassinated So, assuring him my double-barrel was all right, and good for two robbers, and that I was not at all afraid, I cocked and shouldered it.

We were soon in very nearly as wild a looking country as can be seen anywhere. Arid stretches of broken table-land, furrowed with deep ravines, and gullies, studded with detached butes, crossed by ridges of bare rugged rock, formed foreground and middle distance. Beyond, bounding the prospect on every side, rose chains of fantastically-out-lined mountains ; those to the north sheeted with snow. Immediately in our front, far beyond Tudela and the Ebro, but cutting so sharply and distinctly against cloud and sky as to seem almost at hand, its peaks and domes showing where they pierced through the mountain's cap of clouds, brilliantly white with the first snows of winter, and fur-nishing an appropriate point of culminating interest and focus to the picture, the clustered summits of *La Sierra del Moncayo* towered six thousand feet above our level. A few scattered trees on a distant ridge to our left, apparently cedars, was all the timber in sight, and where the surface of the ground was not bare gray clay, rock, or gravel, it was but scantily clothed with a sprinkling of tough wire-grass, low shrubs of wormwood, oldman, and spine-plant. It was a portion of the wildest part of " The Great Desert of North America " over again. As I walked along, cocked gun in hand, " eye skinned and beard on shoulder," neither man, beast, nor habitation in sight, the old accustomed tinkle of the mule-bells ringing in my ear, I almost fancied myself back there again.

It would have been in thorough keeping with the accessories to have heard once more the war-whoop of the Hualipais, and the *swish* of their arrows.

CHAPTER XI.

DECEMBER 27, 1876.—Two hours' travelling on *Las Bar-denas Reales de Navarra,* in a southerly direction, most of the time at a trot, on which occasions I gladly run ahead or alongside the cart to warm myself, for a cold damp wind was blowing, gave us a few glimpses of better land— low-lying flats and strips of ground, affording scanty pickings on which were seen small flocks of goats and sheep, and their attendant guardians, men and dogs. Presently, in one of the roughest, deepest, wildest of ravines—a jagged rift, stretching miles to our right— appeared on an isolated, rocky bute, the gray ruins of a huge monastery. The world cannot furnish a more for-bidding site for habitation of man than where those ruins stand, but it was one well suited to the spirit of asceticism of the age when that old-time refuge for the weary, the disappointed, and—the idle, was founded. Certainly from its window-holes all creation looked accursed.

Towards the middle of the day we came in sight of a square building, standing on the summit of a hill in front of us. It was a *parador*—in plain English, a halting-place. There, my companion said, we could procure a drink, so we at once attacked our bread and meat, and, on arriving abreast of it, left the team to take care of themselves, ran in, and called for wine. We tossed off a couple of tumblerfuls each, and our thirst was quenched. It was most indifferent "Navarrino," but wonderfully cheap. Fancy being charged at a place of entertainment, out in a desert, where there was no opposition, five farthings for four tumblerfuls of pure, unadulterated, drinkable wine! An hour's farther march brought us to the upper edge of the bluff looking towards the wide valley of the Ebro, and the road turning into, and descending by, a winding ravine, we shortly debouched by its mouth into the verdant plain. It was a most charming change. The bluffs sheltered us from the bleak wind. A bright sun shone in an almost cloudless sky. Our climate was as instantaneously changed as though we had be entranslated to another zone. It was as one of England's balmiest of July days.

The valley—there some four miles wide—was a continued succession of fruitful verdure ; vine, olive, and wheat covered the ground. Two long bold curves of the river disclosed long vistas of river valley ; its opposite side, like the one we were travelling, being bounded by the precipitous bluffs of an elevated country, apparently similar in characteristics to the tract we had just traversed, and extending to the base of the Moncajo, which, seen through the warm haze, seemed to have receded by fifty miles.

And, sufficiently in our front for distance to lend its enchantments, lay Valtierra.

On a near approach this little town proved to be a walled but not fortified one; and as the main highway swung round its walls, we turned instead of going through it. Doubtlessly I lost little by so doing. The peep obtained, as we passed, through one of the gateways revealed narrow, ill-paved, squalid streets. But our so doing was a postponement of breakfast until we should arrive at the next town—Arguedas. This change of plan was necessitated, said the *carretero*, by our having made so late a start, for at Arguedas he hoped to buy a load of potatoes, and the meal being prepared while he loaded with them, no time would be lost.

A league's farther travel down the Ebro's valley brought us to our halting-place, which, though an insignificant town, has a more cared-for look about it than any seen since leaving Pamplona. It actually appears to be flourishing in a lazy sort of a way.

Leaving his cart, team, and me in the middle of the town, my companion of the road started off to hunt potatoes, and it was over an hour before I saw him again; then he informed me none were to be obtained, and that we had better drive without further delay to a *posada* and get our breakfasts. As we were about to start an old woman came up, and informing the *carretero* she had a friend who had plenty of potatoes for sale, carried him off yet again. A quarter of an hour elapsed and he came back. At last he had made his purchase; at length he was ready to proceed to the *posada*.

The little tavern we entered looked tidy enough ; and being very hungry, I ordered the best breakfast possible, and confidently expected a fair meal. But I continue to find that in both great and small, Spain is emphatically the land of surprises, and sometimes disappointments. That landlady's idea of a good breakfast was a compound mess of cut cabbage, sliced potatoes, chunks of bread, all boiled together in water, strained, and served with hot oil poured over it ; of a loaf of bread, and a goatskin bottle of indifferent wine. Such was " the best breakfast possible " affordable by that *posada*. However, hunger obligeth, and between us we " worried it down."

The little scheme for saving time, by loading whilst our breakfast was cooking, that had been propounded by the *carretero*, proved, like his early starts, a matter of romance; for when our late in the afternoon breakfast was despatched, he told me the potatoes he had purchased were in bulk, and had to be sacked and weighed, which it would take until after dark to do, so that we could go no farther that day. There being nothing interesting to inspect in the little town, I accompanied him to see the operation, by way of killing time. He led the way along some very narrow alley-like streets, to a dilapidated stone house, whose handsome façade, sculptured escutcheons, carved stairway, and general appearance, proclaimed it had been the residence of some noble of the past; and, in its ancient banqueting-hall, found five old women on their knees, or rather, sitting on their heels, sorting the potatoes that covered its stone floor. Evidently those mature females would never get the twenty big empty sacks waiting for the reception of the potatoes filled before nightfall, for they were taking the tubers up singly, rubbing off all shoots, and placing them deliberately in a basket, from which they were to be poured into the sacks. And they paused and had something to say over every potato. They talked more and did less than any *employées* working by the job that I have ever seen.

The potatoes were splendid ones—finer I never saw—sound, even in size, plump, and bright-skinned. They only cost, including the labour of sacking, at the rate of fivepence the stone of fourteen pounds.

On my return to the *posada*—I did not remain long at the potato-sorting—the hostess's mother, a white-haired wiry dame of sixty-seven years of age, was busy cooking our dinner. She lifted the lid of a stew-pan to put in some seasoning, and I noticed it contained the joints and pieces of some small animal, but not its head, and immediately had my suspicions. Thinking to ascertain the truth by a *ruse*, I rubbed my hands together, as if in satisfaction, and cheerfully exclaimed : "Ah! we are going to have stewed cat."

"Cat, indeed! It is a rabbit. Does your worship think I would cook a cat ?"

"Where is its head ?"

"Oh, I gave it to the dog. A rabbit's head is not worth cooking."

At dinner I found the animal I had seen in the pot was the *pièce de résistance*—and most resisting pieces its morsels were—of a wretched meal. It, and a mess like that had for breakfast, comprised the entirety.

The old woman had been very painstaking as to the

cooking of the animal; had stewed it for two hours and a half, seasoned it with some cloves of garlic first slightly boiled in oil, with salt and pepper; had added plenty of good olive oil. All to no purpose; it was tough as buckskin, flabby as cotton wool in texture, watery and insipid in taste—in short, unfit for food. Whether it were rabbit or cat I did not know, never shall know; but I did most certainly know it was miserable trash as I ever tried to eat. If it was a fair sample of cat, then no more cat do I want while I live. I tried to eat a piece of back, a leg, a shoulder; no go, and so generously presented the rejected pieces to Juan. He is not a dainty dog, eats potatoes, even eats cabbage. He sniffed, looked insulted, and retired.

During dinner a blind guitarist entered playing, led by a small boy, who accompanied with the triangle. When we had finished they supped on what was left of our dinner, including the pieces refused by my dog; probably poverty had educated their taste. They were poor strollers, but the blind man played very well, while the boy was as sharp a young monkey as ever followed the road. When they had eaten and smoked the *cigarros* I handed them, they commenced a *jota*, the sound of which soon attracted several persons in from the street, some of whom for fun begged and teased the old woman to dance. She, by way of a chaffing back-out, declared she would dance with nobody but the Englishman, thinking, no doubt, I could not dance the *jota*. So, to carry on the joke, I remarked I did not believe she meant what she said, that I was sure could I dance she would not. Then the ancient dame swore " by the Holy Virgin " she was no old fool to say a

thing and not do it. That oath delivered her into the hand
of the enemy, and, jumping up, I exclaimed, " I can dance
a *jota* with any *Navarrina* that wears *alpargatas ;* " and the
old girl, not to be beaten, faced me, and, to the great
delight of the company, we started. The plucky grandam
came to time in a wonderful way, but could not last, and
soon yielded the floor. Amongst the spectators was a fine,
fresh-looking, strapping peasant-wench, and, on my ante-
diluvian partner's retiring, I danced up to her, made my
bow, and she took the old woman's place. When the dance
was at its fastest, as an experiment, to see how it would go,
I took a leaf out of the Pamplona cavalryman's book, and
dexterously floored the lamp. It went very well. After
that all the girls in the room were ready to dance with
" *El Inglés.*" But I danced no more. The rest, however,
did, and I soon saw that, danced by peasants, the *jota*
is a very queer performance. I cannot give detail ; some
of the movements and gestures are neither produceable
before nor describable to a British public. And to say that
such are not intentionally grossly immodest would be to
state an unmitigated untruth. By-and-by the sharp boy
handed round his *gorro* for *limosna*. I had a pocketful of
Spanish coppers, *cuartos, ochavos, maravedies*, not much in
value, only about a shilling's worth, but many in number,
and I dropped them all in the cap. How the boy's eyes
sparkled ! I heartily wished the poor musician's could have
done so too.

I retired to bed, but not exactly to sleep. For the first
time in Spain my bed was a bad one ; the mattress of
chopped hay and straw, the sheets not too clean ; and,

worst of all, mine enemy was upon me. Queen Mab's lancers mustered their squadrons to the attack; a slower but not less formidable foe marched and countermarched upon my prostrate body, and in the morning I was a "speckled victim." So, after swallowing my little cup of chocolate, I gladly departed from that miserable *posada*.

As is often the case, extra bad fare and accommodation was, as a set-off, charged for at extra high rates, and my bill amounted to considerably more than double what it had been at the *santa* where everything was so good and comfortable.

Arguedas, though a little place, is a walled town; and as we approached close to the old arched gateway through which our road ran, an enchanting composition presented itself to my view. I beheld an ancient square tower—all that remained of extensive works the traces of which were discernible for one hundred and fifty yards, while the bluff behind was pierced with galleries—a tower, in size, shape, and proportions wonderfully like as old Norman castle's keep, or donjon. Its base was built of roughly-hewn stone, the corners of its three sides—the fourth had fallen and wasted to mould—and occasional cross-courses were stones rough as they had come out of the quarry, its filling was rubble. Beyond was a green, smiling river-valley; then brown rugged hills; in the far distance snow-capped mountains; overhead a bright blue sky; while, to complete the picture, to give it the interest of life and motion—oh, rare and happy chance!—down the road towards us came a squad of cavalry. The sun lit up their polished brazen helmets and the steel points of their lances, their accoutrements flashed in its rays; the ruby-and-yellow pennant of Spain fluttered from their lanceheads. Surely it was a picture of the Middle Ages, framed and set by that old-time archway. Had the cavalry been armoured knights, nothing in the surroundings would have been incongruous.

To behold that living picture was, alone, worth my journey to Spain.

Our road down the valley ran between the base of the bluffs and the *Acequia Molinar*—an irrigating ditch that, taking its waters from the combined streams of the rivers Aragon and Cidacos, some four leagues west of Caparroso, skirts the foot of the scarp of the Bardenas Reales, and renders fertile the left bank of the Ebro's valley for over fifty miles.

Soon after leaving Arguedas, the valley is so slightly above the level of the river that the soil becomes too cold and wet for vineyards or olive orchards; and a continuous meadow of marsh-grass, with frequent willow-breaks and beds of reeds, occupies it exclusively. This is the summer pasture of the fierce bulls of Tudela, famous in the annals of the arena of Madrid, Sevilla, and Barcelona. Ere long we passed a range of stone buildings. They were pointed out to me as being the head-quarter bull-farm of the neighbourhood; from there Tudela with its many towers was in sight.

By half-past ten I had crossed the bridge over the Ebro, passed through one of the gates of this city, and was arrived.

Immediately within Tudela's walls we were halted by the octroi officers, and, while they rummaged the cart, I

took advantage of the stoppage to wish *a dios* to my companion, for he was going on beyond Tudela before stopping
for his breakfast. He seemed sorry to part with me, and
it was with much difficulty I prevailed on him to accept a
propina. His last words as he pressed my hand were : " *A
dios*, brave sir, who I hope to meet again, if not on earth,
certainly in heaven." Just fancy a British carter delivering
himself of such a sentiment in such terms, and being diffi-
dent about accepting drink-money ! The people here are,
in their ways, as antique as their country, and sometimes I
can hardly realise I am not dreaming.

I should like to give a short *résumé* description of the
country I have been passing through ; but only to one who
knows the wild parts of North America would it be easy
for me to do so. To him I would say: Take a large portion of
the central Arizonan plateau, substitute chestnuts and oaks
for pines and *piñons*, living rivers for dried-up watercourses
and *arroyos ;* take a little of the best and most fertile part
of southern California, a large tract of country exactly like
that below the Lava-beds of the Black Cañon district, well
mixed with the Soda Lake country—and you have its physical
aspects. Put every available acre in wheat, vines, or olives ;
stick old, dirty, dilapidated stone villages, large churches,
monasteries, ancient ruins, fortifications of every epoch around
about, on mountain sides, on rocky pinnacles, in valley, plain,
and hollow ; add a few fortified cities having most of the
modern improvements ; place in the open country a scanty
population of half-clothed, ignorant, credulous, but well-fed
and industrious peasantry ; fill its walled towns till they
are like human bee-hives at swarming-time ; let the dress,

L

utensils, manners, and customs be those of twenty-five centuries, so mixed and blended, so inextricably confused together as to be unsortable—and you have the country and its inhabitants from San Sebastian to Tudela.

On parting with the friendly *carretero*, I at once commenced looking for quarters. They were very hard to get. I was hugely disgusted with this place on my first arrival. The inns were most unpromising in appearance, and the boarding-houses I enquired at, all full. There is a large garrison, part of the "Army of Occupation," here, and the officers have, of course, helped themselves to the best to be had in that line. I began to fear I should absolutely be unable to find a decent place to stop at, when a happy accident directed me to where I am staying, a house on the outskirts of, in fact almost without, the town ; a house cheerfully situated, with gardens in front, large yard and outbuildings behind. It is a basement and two storeys high, clean, tidy, and of genteel appearance.

This is a very private *Casa de Huespedes*, has neither sign nor card, and is not advertised. It is conducted and owned by a very amicable old fellow, and his much younger and not less agreeable wife ; people of some independent means, besides being the freeholders of the property they reside on. They are childless, but have adopted two orphan nieces, who are living with them. The table is excellent, better I almost think than at San Sebastian ; and I have a nice large room, fitted up as bedchamber and sitting-room combined, with a lovely view from my balcony. For these and other mercies I am to pay only a dollar a day. I am told it is a very extravagant price for Tudela, but that I am in what is considered the very best boarding-house in the place ; a house that had I been a Spaniard, or any kind of foreigner except English, I should not have been received in without good recommendations from responsible parties.

The work of the house is all done by one servant and the two nieces of the proprietor, with occasional help, principally consisting of scoldings, from the host and hostess. The domestic is almost as handsome as the Tafalla girl, and a daughter of poor but honest parents, like her of the nursery tale. She and the nieces treat each other on terms of great equality ; speak of one another to third parties as "*La Señorita Josefita*," "*La Señorita Colonetta*," "*La Señorita Tomasa*," as the case may be ; and when talking together *thee* and *thou* each other. As a major of dragoons, who is my fellow-boarder, said to me yesterday : "Classes are now (in Spain) confounded together in a manner that you, as an Englishman, can hardly understand. There is a practical democracy in the domestic circle like what I have read of in the backwoods of your Canada. And you must remember, in the country you are passing through there are no ladies and gentlemen by profession, as in all parts of your country. The native families of means and leisure are absentees, living in Madrid and the chief southern cities now, and at fashionable watering-places in summer, and leaving their estates habitually to the care of *administradors* and *major-domos*. They never go near them."

This officer is evidently an "upper ten" man. Besides having his orderly to attend to his wants, he keeps a *valet*

de chambre, wears most expensive linen and jewellery, and
dresses stylishly.   He is a well-read and informed man,
with a turn for philosophising; a thinker of a very
advanced school, and though professedly a Catholic, terribly
severe upon priestcraft.   In politics he is most liberal, and
has his eyes very wide open to the faults of his country.
He looks upon his enforced residence in this place in much
the same way as a guardsman would regard being quartered
in an inland town of Galway.   He is quite an Anglomaniac;
ranks " Sah-kay-s-pey-air-re," as he calls " the immortal
William," above Cervantes, and Darwin as the first *savant* in
Europe; and has been most courteous and politely attentive
to me.   There are two other boarders, but they seem to be
intermittent ones, coming and going in a most irregular
manner.   I think they are connected with the railway
interest.

Yesterday I took a look at the markets and priced
things, Tafalla being sufficiently well in the interior of
northern Spain to be a good place to average prices at.
But I must premise that everybody grumbles at the dear-
ness of the times; for instance, *La Josefita* tells me that
before the war partridges sold for fivepence apiece, now
they are worth one shilling and eightpence.   She says
other things have risen in proportion.

The market-place is a tumble-down old square, filled
with dilapidated sheds, but there is the same profusion of
fowl, flesh, fish, vegetables, and fruit I have always heretofore seen in Spanish markets.   These are present prices,
weights and money being brought as nearly as possible to
English equivalents : beef—best cuts—fivepence per pound;

mutton and lamb—best cuts—sixpence per pound; fresh
pork, sixpence-halfpenny per pound; chickens—there are
"spring chickens" all the year round here — from one
shilling and threepence to one and eightpence each;
turkeys—large ones, fattened by being crammed with
chestnuts and walnuts—twelve shillings each; eggs—fresh
laid—eightpence a dozen; ham, from tenpence to one
and threepence per pound; fish, the cheapest, fresh sardines, threepence-halfpenny a pound; the dearest, salmon,
half-a-crown a pound; chocolate, tenpence to five shillings
a pound, according to the confections mixed with it; olive
oil, threepence three-farthings per pound; milk, fivepence
per pint; wine, the very best, twopence-halfpenny the
pint (there are more vineyards than milch cows); best
loaf sugar, sixpence-halfpenny the pound; grapes, table,
one penny-farthing a pound (they are very dear now, for it
is nearly Christmas). Vegetables, not being sold by weight
or measure, excepting potatoes, I cannot well give their
price, but they are cheap beyond conception. Nor can I
give a list of them, not knowing the English names of the
chief kinds; indeed, not having seen them in England,
I do not know they have such. The fuel used here is olive-
wood, costing for dry seasoned twopence-farthing per quarter
of a hundredweight; it is splendid cooking-wood, making
a clear, intensely hot charcoal fire, with little smoke, and
that rather fragrant than otherwise. Servants' wages are
also very low, according to our standard. A really good
woman-cook—who is also a servant-of-all-work, no matter
how many other maids are kept, for here no such phrase
as "It is not my place" is known, nor would such an idea

be tolerated—gets six shillings and threepence per month. The very highest wages paid to any domestic is ten shillings a month. These prices account for a dollar a day commanding the very best of board and lodging. Agricultural labourers are paid one shilling and eightpence a day—a day meaning here all the time there is sufficient light to work by, excepting an hour at noon. At harvest time wages sometimes rise to half-a-crown a day for first-class hands. At all times the labourer has, out of his wages, to lodge and board himself and find his own "allowance," and they are the best contented, most cheerful peasantry I have ever seen.

CHAPTER XII.

Tudela—*La Plaza de la Constitucion*—A Curse in Stone—Extraordinary
Bridge—A sporting Excursion—Ancient Mound Fort—Christmas-Eve
Festivities—The National Dance of Navarra—Midnight Mass at *San
Nicolas*—Military Mass in *La Santa Maria*—A wonderful Piece of
Carving—A strict Catholic Fast—The Licorice Field of Spain—Esparto
Grass.

JANUARY 2, 1877.—I have been wandering about this
place taking items, but, having a mortal antipathy to
guides, and owning not a handbook, in a most desultory
and happy-go-lucky manner.

Tudela is a walled city overlooked by a citadel of
considerable strength, crowning an eminence to its north,
and also by a small fortified and entrenched tower—a toy-
like affair, pretty, but very weak, standing on a conical
detached hill to its south. It occupies the mouth of a little
valley, down which runs an insignificant stream—the
Quelles—and extends close to the right bank of the
Ebro, having a river wall. Tudela is almost enclosed by
the barren bluffs of a country similar in all respects to
Las Bardenas Reales de Navarra, and is situated at the
head of a wide opening of the valley of the Ebro—an
expanse of country seemingly a forest of olive-trees.

Though nestled under beetling cliffs, and but little

above the level of the river in times of flood, Tudela is
seven hundred and eighty feet above the sea. It claims
to be one of the oldest cities in Europe, to have had a
continuous existence since before the foundation of Rome.
The truth of that assertion being conceded to her, it is
certain she has put her time in to little advantage. To
be sure, due allowance must be made for the fact that
for over three hundred and fifty years the city has
been developing backwards. When Navarra was a kingdom, Tudela was the frontier town towards Castile, and
its chief entrepôt and export city; now she has no
importance.

I find myself greatly disappointed by Tudela. As seen
from a distance, her many and fine church-towers, the
broad, tree-shaded, avenue-like roads leading to it, the
forest of olives below, the grand bridge across the Ebro,
caused me to expect a handsome place. It proved a dirty,
dilapidated, squalid one. Its population of nine thousand
is crowded into a space that in England would only be
occupied by a third of that number. Its streets are narrow
passages between houses looking like dingy, uncared-
for prisons. There is not one thoroughly good dwelling-
house or shop in it, as we understand such things. I will
describe its *Plaza*, for, like all Spanish cities, the *Plaza* is
the best portion of the town.

La Plaza de la Constitucion is a square of two hundred
and seventy feet—three hundred and fifty yards' walk
round it—with five entrances thereto, three being deep
archways, or tunnels through houses, and the remaining
two open ways from narrow streets. The buildings

enclosing this square are massive stone structures, a basement and three storeys high, of uniform design, with overhanging roofs and two tiers of balconies. The basements
are now either stables, store-rooms, or cafés. Around the
Plaza is a pavement about as wide as that of Regent
Street. In its palmy days it was a handsome *Plaza*, and
the armorial bearings, sculptured on the houses, show the
style of people who then lived in them. Now it is as
disreputable in appearance, as dirty, as odoriferous as a
Chinese quarter of an American mining town. Paint,
plaster, mortar has crumbled and fallen from the walls of
the houses, their balcony railings are masses of rust, their
windows displays of dirty rags, and the crowd promenading
the pavement is in thorough keeping with the aspect of the
houses. I except, of course, the military stationed here,
the leading officials, and their respective families. In
uniform or mufti most of the officers are unmistakably
gentlemen, and their women-folk have all the air and
manner of thorough ladies.

I do not see much chance for any improvement in
Tudela. It is built up so closely, and so shut in by bluffs,
there is no room for new houses ; to pull down for the
purpose of rebuilding, or to repair when repairs are not
absolutely unavoidable, seems foreign to the genius of these
people ; and so, as unhappily the ancient architects who
built Tudela cursed her with houses that won't fall down,
she is bound to go from bad to worse, as she has done since
no man knows when, until she becomes unfit for a Christian,
yea, even a " *Cristiano veijo rancio,*" to live in.

The rest of the place, excepting a few decent houses in

the outskirts, the pretty terrace-walk by the side of the river wall, the fine bull-ring, and the eleven big churches and convents, is a labyrinth of many-storeyed dens.

The bridge over the Ebro merits a better description than I am likely to give. It was built by *El Rey Don Sancho Abarco de Navarro*, but at what date I cannot find out. When E. R. D. S. A. de N. "flourished," no man seems able to tell me. But we must not be too hard on these natives for their ignorance. How many Englishmen could tell off-hand, without reference to authorities, the date when the celebrated Danish king of England, whose name is spelt with a C or a K, as the case may be, sat down "by the sad sea waves," and did not exactly rule them ?

This fine bridge is four hundred odd yards in length (measured by pacing), and is composed of seventeen arches, eight of them acutely-pointed ones. Between the arches, on its upper side, are long sharply-pointed piers ; on its lower one, flat buttresses. It is built in a very singular manner. Its general direction crosses the river at a considerable angle to its course, with a view, according to the ancient fallacy, to its being less affected by the current ; and it is not straight, but has a bend, like a slightly-strung bow, the curve being up stream, presenting in effect an arch to the downward pressure of the current. Standing at one end of the bridge, persons crossing the river by it disappear from the spectator's view, round its curve, before they leave the bridge. At its farther end from the town is a *tête de pont*, loopholed for musketry, through the gateway of which the bridge is reached, and where a small force of soldiers is stationed.

In default of being able to procure a photograph, I have made a sketch of the town and bridge, but from one point of sight could not get in the head of the bridge on one side, nor the citadel on the other, and only ten of the arches ; while the Quelles river discharging itself into the Ebro just below the bridge, its mouth was hidden thereby. The snow-covered mountain in the background is the Moncayo.

Soon after I arrived here, one of my fellow-boarders, who is an ardent sportsman, invited me to accompany him to Castejon, situated a few miles up the valley of the Ebro, saying we might, if lucky, get partridges, woodcocks, hares, and rabbits. So we went. We did not get anything but a capital breakfast and dinner at the Castejon *fonda*, and a long tramp.

My friend had with him three well-broken dogs—a pointer, and two liver-coloured cockers, whose legs were exactly like dachshunds, and who worked splendidly. I put one of Juan's feet in his collar, and he charged around on three legs like a bear on hot irons. We saw two fine coveys of red-legs, but a couple of hundred yards off was as near as any of the dogs ever got to a bird of them. My companion fired a long shot at, and missed, a cock. I saw a hare, and the cockers set afoot lots of rabbits, but in such thick brush we could not get even snap-shots at them. My friend tells me the partridge-shooting in September, October, and March is excellent, but that between times there is no getting near them except accidentally. Cock-shooting is very uncertain here. Some days, in the season, you may find plenty, often, for weeks, none. Quails in August and September are tolerably thick. His diary for last year shows a bag of eight hundred and seventy-four, that of the previous year six hundred and fifty-three, all shot within an easy walk.

At Castejon I saw some interesting remains; the Ebro valley is there very wide, and a plain of wild grass, brush thickets, and willow brakes; and in its centre, close to the right bank of the river, appears a conical hill of several acres in extent, and some hundreds of feet in height. It is artificial—a mound. Not very far off are the excavations whence the soil was procured to raise it; and the Ebro, in one of its recent floods, having cut away a portion of the extraneous *débris* accumulated at its base, disclosed a surface reveted with stone-work. The hill is an ancient fort. It was its exact resemblance in size, relative position to the river, and form to some of the prehistoric mounds of the Mississippi valley that made me, an ignorant stranger, at a distance of a mile therefrom, ask my companion, to his great astonishment, What people are supposed to have constructed that artificial hill fort? I might just as well have demanded to be told who invented spoons.

This mound gives to the district its name, and the railway from Madrid to the north crosses the Ebro in sight of it by a splendid iron bridge seven hundred feet in length, standing on tubular piers, braced and guyed in the strongest way with iron cables. Alongside of the rails is a broad planked footway, over which we passed, our shooting-ground lying on the left bank of the Ebro.

At the Castejon railway station I had the pleasure of meeting some of my country-people, the first English tourists I had seen since entering Spain. It seemed quite strange to find myself talking, and being talked to, in English.

I must give an account—perhaps I ought rather say, make a confession—of how I spent Christmas Eve. A nephew of my landlady, who is a civil engineer at Zaragoza and cousin-in-law of the girls, came to spend his holiday-time here, to see his mother, who lives not far from us. He stopped in this house because his mother, who is a widow and very poor, had not room for him in hers. This young fellow invited his two cousins and our handsome *criada* to spend the evening at his mother's, to meet a lot of his friends, and enjoy some dancing and singing. He pressed me to go also, and being here to see all I can, I gladly accepted his invitation. The party was seventeen in number, all young people excepting the old mother, and more than half of them girls. The music, an old guitar, which everybody seemed able to play. The ball-room, a large, low-roofed attic with bare walls, and furnished with three beds, two chairs, an old trunk, a four-inch square looking-glass, and coloured prints of virgins. The refreshments, *aguardiente* and biscuits. We danced with our coats off, for it was hot, and *cigarros* in mouth, polkas, waltzes, mazurkas, and the *jota*, principally the *jota*. But as compared with the Arguedas folks, we danced the *jota* most decorously indeed.

The *jota* being a national dance, I must give some idea of it. It is danced in couples, each pair being quite independent of all the rest. The respective partners face each other, the guitar twangs, the spectators accompany with a whining, nasal, drawling refrain, and clapping of hands.

You put your arm round your partner's waist, balance for a
few bars, take a waltz round, stop, and give her a fling
round under your raised arm.   Then the two of you dance
backward and forward, across and back, whirl round
and *chasses*, and do some *Nautch-Wallah-ing*, accompanying yourselves with castanets, or snapping of fingers and
thumbs. The steps are a matter of your own particular
invention, the more *outré* the better.   And you repeat and
go on, till one of you gives out. The *chic* of the dance, the
pas d'excellence, is, when your partner whirls round and the
air extends her skirts, to dexterously entangle your foot in
and with a quick jerk kick them up as high as you can.
To a *vieux sauteur* and old dancer, the trick is easy
enough, and " I guess I rather astonished that crowd," as
our cousins over the big ferry say, judging by the way my
partners screamed and the lookers-on applauded when I
" fluttered the white."   Indeed my *élan* was considered a
credit to my country.   I was regarded a proof positive to
the contrary of the (absurdly wrong) popular belief of
Spain, that in society " Englishmen are, collectively
taken, a composition of reserve, haughtiness, shyness, and
stupidity."   I certainly did my best to disabuse all present
of such an idea.   This is the record of my exploits (?).   I
picked for a partner the prettiest woman in the room,
started with the steps of a regular " Hoosier breakdown,"
threw in touches of the Highland fling, the sailor's horn-
pipe, the Irish jig, all the little I know of the *can-can*, and
wound up with an Apache yell and caper that " brought
the house down."   Thenceforth I was " *Gefe*."

Now the queer part of all is, the assembled company,

though poor in estate, were all decent, respectable, and respected people ; the girls all modest, proper girls—girls of unsuspectable reputation, dancing to, with, and before their brothers. There yet lingers, I take it, a strong leaven of nature, in other words of the savage, in the ways of Navarra.

At twelve o'clock we adjourned to midnight mass in the pretty church of San Nicolas—choral service of course. I certainly was with a wild party. A lot of Scarborough "trippers" at a circus could hardly have behaved worse. They talked aloud, laughed, threw kisses, made fun of the service, and played practical jokes on each other. And this in "the most Christian country." After service we hurried back, ran upstairs, rushed into the room, and, ere the last could enter, those first in were dancing again. We broke up at four o'clock, and as we went home found the street full of fantastically-dressed mummers, some twanging guitars, others blowing horns, many singing, both in solos and in choruses.

By-the-bye, two of the women at our little *tertulia* were "awfully" handsome, and one of the two was our *criada*.

On the last day of the year I attended a military mass at Tudela's famous Gothic cathedral—*La Santa Maria*— a wonderful building, quite an architectural triumph, for though small for a mediæval cathedral, the genius of its architect enabled him to impart to its interior an effect of vastness and impressiveness quite out of proportion to its size. It most deservedly has the reputation of being one of the best specimens extant of Gothic art. It is said to date from A.D. 1135.

I thoroughly enjoyed the performance, for in the first place I got a comfortable seat, ensconcing myself with great effrontery in a stall in the choir ; secondly, and as a consequence, was not subjected to offensive smells, an occasional whiff of incense being the only appreciable odour ; thirdly, the music was excellent ; and lastly, the scene most picturesque and dramatically striking.

Santa Maria looked large and lofty ; its high and pointed arches light and elegant, its vistas full of perspective, its detail simple, chaste, and beautiful. In its centre the military occupied the entire space—artillery, cavalry, infantry. Their varied uniforms gave colour and brilliancy to the scene ; the large blue cloaks lined with crimson of the 5th Dragoons, their burnished steel morions, spiked, plumed, brass-mounted, and bright as looking-glass, were most effective. The music was exclusively military, and played by the band of the Estremadura Foot (15th Infantry). I am glad I heard that band ; doing so corrected an impression I had formed that Spanish military music is atrocious, for I have rarely heard a finer brass band. It was forty instruments strong, excessively well led, and executed a charming selection of operatic airs and a rattling schottische. The acoustic proportions of the cathedral must be very good, for I detected neither echo nor vibration ; indeed, had the music been in the open air and at some little distance off, it could not have sounded more melodiously. It really seemed as though mellowed by floating along the arched and groined roof and around the many pillars. The only time when the music was really noisy was at the elevation of the

Host, where brass, wood, and skin crashed forth Spain's national and royal air, the " Marcha Real."

After service I saw the soldiers march past. They went at their usual tremendous pace. If those fellows could only fight as well as they march, what invincible troops they would be. When the soldiers and following crowd had left the cathedral's front in solitude, I took a quiet look at its main porch, having been recommended to do so. It is a wonderful piece of carving ; there must be hundreds of figures, all in stone alto-relievo. On the left as you face the door are the blessed being led to heaven, I suppose, each by two saints. On the right, the wicked being tormented, very evidently, each by two devils. The " sheep " and saints are clothed. The " goats " and devils are male and female, *in puris naturalibus.* The torments are most varied and extraordinary, but quite indescribable. The intimate manner in which the grotesque, the cruel, and the obscene are blended, surpasses anything conceivable by the mind of man that is not cloistered monk. Sufficient to say, indecency bordering on insanity is there revealed in stone, has been the ornamentation of a cathedral church for over seven hundred years, and looks quite capable of remaining to make it remarkable for seven hundred more.

In the afternoon there was a general promenade of the inhabitants around the *paseo* adjoining the bull-ring, to the strains of another military band. It was not as good a one as I had heard in the cathedral, nor was there anything remarkable about the promenaders.

The past Christmas Day was one of the very few of my

M

life not celebrated by a Christmas dinner. In our house the powers that be are great "*Cristianos;*" here Christmas Day is a strict fast, *Bula* or no *Bula;* and so starving nature had to content itself with oyster soup, several kinds of fresh fish, excellent pastry, all the delicacies of the season in vegetables, the finest of fruits, and good wine. However, we made up for it on New Year's Day by a regular feast after high mass, which I attended at the cathedral. This time the music was not military, but the regular choir, a good organ, and a string and reed band. The singing and playing were really fine, and a credit to the musical ability of the city ; I had no idea the place could furnish as good. The attendance was numerous, and who can wonder ? Here high mass is the people's opera. They see a gorgeous spectacle, and hear good music, all for nothing; and have besides a pleasing feeling that they have performed a work of merit—knocked off so many purgatorial days. Duty and pleasure, religion and amusement, go hand-in-hand in sunny Spain.

The weather since my arrival here has been bright and clear, and the sun hot, but the snow on the mountains makes the wind cold. We have light white frosts almost every night, and as there are no stoves nor fireplaces in the houses of this country, excepting in the kitchens, I feel chilly much of the time ; and since an east wind commenced blowing, a few days ago, have been still more uncomfortable. However, the gardens do not seem to be affected; the pea plants are already so far advanced in growth as to be "sticked ;" the broad beans are knee high, and will soon be in blossom ; and we commonly have artichokes for dinner—not merely mature heads, as in England, requiring to be picked to pieces leaf by leaf, and having but a small portion of each leaf eatable, but young heads that you cut up with a knife and fork and eat entirely, and most delicious they are. But, indeed, they can never have any frost worth complaining about here, for Tudela is in the centre of the chief licorice field of Spain. It is here an indigenous plant, grows wild anywhere and everywhere. Large stacks of its roots stand just outside the city's walls, thatched and protected from the weather by coverings of reed-canes, for there is a company established in Tudela that buys up all they can get. The best roots are sent to England and the United States; the next quality to France and Russia; from the worst is manufactured stick licorice for Spanish consumption. This company must be making money hand over hand. They are paying but one shilling and eightpence per hundredweight delivered for roots, and last year they exported over forty thousand pounds sterling worth.

This place has also, from a wild product of nature, another source of revenue. Esparto-grass is brought in from the mountain-sides and valleys in September and October, and bought up and sent away by agents for paper mills, principally French ones.

Tudela ought to be prospering; but if she is, it is so slowly as to be quite unapparent.

CHAPTER XIII.

JANUARY 10, 1877.—I stayed longer than intended at
Tudela, being there laid by the heels ; a severe attack of
influenza and sore throat dry-docked me. The *señora*
wanted to call in a physician, the family *Medico de
Cabecera ;* but against such proposition was quoted the old
proverb of the country, " *El medico lleva la plata pero Dios
est que sana* "—the doctor carries off the money, but the
Lord cures—and I declined making his learnedship's acquaintance, except socially. My ailments gave me no
exclusive right of complaining, for everybody in the house
was suffering from the same indisposition. The east wind
seemed to have brought a regular epidemic of it. I, however, was hit the hardest ; possibly from being an unaccli-
mated foreigner. The remedy of the country for light
cases is to totally avoid wine, beer, and spirits, drinking
instead of them barley-water sweetened with licorice, to
take a long hot drink of mallow-flower tea (not the marsh-

mallow, but the smaller plant, the upland mallow) the last thing at night and first on the following morning, and to lie in bed till noon; a course I was put through, and which did me much good; I recommend its trial to so afflicted countrymen at home. Here the dried flowers of the mallow with which the tea is made are sold at every apothecary's shop. I found the decoction a fine sudorific and gentle soporific, the barley-water and licorice excellent for my throat.

While laid up at Tudela I studied my future course, and determined, so soon as it would be prudent to resume my tramp, to take the tow-path of the *Canal Imperial* from its commencement, a few miles below there, and follow it to Zaragoza; for, as it is one of the greatest irrigating canals in Spain, I wished to see it—its locks, bridges, and accessory works, and besides, should have a level road, for I was tired of climbing and descending; and, too, the scenery would be a change from that of mountains, through which my way had heretofore always been.

I found Tudela a convenient place to have a cold in, for there, when able to go out to take my daily afternoon's constitutional stroll on the sunny side of some shelter from the wind, I could anywhere outside the town walls pull licorice roots out of the ground, to chew as I walked along. I am sorry for the cause of my detention at Tudela, of course, but hardly so at having been detained, for I was, as an invalid, necessarily much indoors, and so obtained considerable insight into the social ways of Navarra.

My friend the Major is undoubtedly right. As he truly said, "In this country social relations are decidedly mixed."

Certainly, the *señoritas* of the house I have so recently left were most decided exemplars of his proposition. Except when "got up" for parade or a *tertulia*, on which occasions they were beautifully arrayed, they dressed like kitchen-maids, were regular Cinderellas, but nevertheless, with their hair in the latest Paris agony. One or other of them brought my early drink to my bedside and awoke me, as often as did the servant ; made no bones of coming into my room, slop-pail in hand, and doing the chamber work while I was present, and habitually, and as a matter of course, both freely interlarded their discourse with ejaculations and ex-pressions of the most objectionable character. Let us hope they did not realise their signification. They were words at whose English equivalents a scullery-maid of an English gentleman's establishment would stand aghast—expressions that no virtuous English woman ever uses.

And yet the *señoritas* in question belong to a most respectable rank of life, can and did behave in company in a most ladylike manner, will have independent fortunes at the death of their uncle, and have received the education of young ladies. For instance : the elder of the two, whom I am best acquainted and have most conversed with, is well up in geography and general history, has learned drawing, and " does heads " very nicely in crayons ; has a fair theo-retical and good practical knowledge of music—singing, and playing the guitar and piano very well—dances elegantly, and, excepting the expletives, talks charmingly. She has also learned French, and is a sufficiently good scholar of that language to enjoy a French novel ; but she speaks it in a way that no Frenchman could understand, pronouncing the

words as though they were Spanish ones, and grouping
them and pitching the emphasis all wrongly. She is
twenty-two years old, fair as a lily, with a fine delicate
colour in her cheeks; has beautiful, small, white, regular
teeth, golden hair, and bright large chestnut eyes. She is
full of life, grace, and vivacity, with a figure beyond praise.
And she does not paint—no, not even use powder, nor does
she dye, nor bleach, nor pinch—no, not even wear corsets ;
and she does not possess a tooth-brush ! Water, soap, and
nature do her beautifying. And she is besides an excellent cook and a slashing housemaid. Great Cæsar de
Bazan ! how our grandmothers would have admired such a
girl ! To be candid, I admired her not a little myself, and
doubtlessly should have done so more, but that there was a
much prettier girl—in fact, the handsomest I have seen in
Spain—an almost daily visitor at the house.

This fascinating girl was in the habit of coming in the
evenings with an aunt, a gay and lively young widow.
She is only sixteen years old, but quite a woman in development and *aplomb;* a high-coloured, brilliant-com-
plexioned brunette, with a true "*ojos arabes.*" She is
the best waltzer I ever put arm round ; so, though not a
dancing man, we used usually to take a spin together to
the music of the guitar and the clapping of hands. The
aunt (an old hunter, knows the crack of the whip) kept a
very sharp eye on the young woman, who, on her part, was
as demure, as "*tan formal,*" as possible in " dear auntie's "
presence, but far different when the widow was away ; then
she showed herself to be as wild as any unbroken filly who
ever took bit in teeth and bolted ; showed she had as much

of the world, the flesh, and the devil to the cubic inch as any she who lives. I liked that widowed aunt very well; she, too, is a good dancer, handsome, and *intriguante*, but I liked her best when she was not present and the niece was.

The Major is a great admirer of La Ysidra, and was not at all pleased at our "carryings-on." He said : " It is just like the women. She does not care a fig for the Englishman ; but because he is an Englishman, and the only one she has ever seen, she flings herself at his head in a most barefaced manner." Now the fact simply is, the girl naturally likes to be admired ; she is so extremely handsome it was impossible for me, and would be for any man of taste, to avoid showing admiration for her ; and of course she felt flattered and pleased, and, after the manner of Spanish women, showed her feelings. And, after all, she is but a child.

However, to all things there must come a termination ; so this morning, though the influenza and a feeling of weakness hung about me, the day being unusually fine, I determined to make a move ; and so, shouldering my gun and traps and whistling to Juan, at 8.45 A.M. I took up the line of march.

Adieu was bid to the Major in his room, he not being out of bed at that early (?) hour. He seemed really sorry to part with me, and said many handsome things about England and the English and myself, concluding with the assurance should anything occur to me while in Spain, should I require in any way the good offices of a friend, I must let him know, and to the extent of his power I could command him ; at all events, when my hazardous journey—

as he pleased to consider it—was terminated, I must write and tell him how it had fared with me. The rest of the household were also effusive in their farewells and good wishes.

As a travelling Englishman, and so, to a certain extent, a representative of my country—if an indifferent one—I had considered it a pleasing duty to create as favourable an impression as possible ; and the manner of those I was parting with plainly showed I had been fairly successful.

I started feeling seedy enough, but it was just the day to gain strength in. During the night a most pleasant change in the weather had taken place ; the horrid east wind had blown itself out and the lowering clouds away. It was replaced by a light balmy breeze from the south-west ; and excepting a few fleecy cloudlets hanging round Moncayo's summit peaks, the sky was one fair expanse of azure and the sunshine warm and brilliant.

For two miles the broad, well-kept *camino real*, or highway, ran straight through the olive forest, and then forked. I took the left prong, that leading to *El Bocal*, or the mouth of the Imperial Canal. We should have called the other, or lower end, the mouth ; but as Spanish ladies sit their horses on the " off " side, perhaps it is all right in Spain to call the upper end of a canal its mouth. It was a good road, planted with a double row of fine elms, but showed little sign of travel. The canal is not the highway it once was. No longer is it the great commercial artery of the country ; an occasional barge-load of wood, and the carriage of the grain harvested on its banks, is all the transport business it now does.

At 10.25 A.M. I passed the little village of Fontanas, and taking a footpath to the left, found myself in a few minutes at *El Bocal*, looking with interest and pleasure at one of the finest river-dams in the world—a dam over which, with a roar I had often heard at Tudela, the entire flood of the Ebro rushed in one unbroken flashing sheet. Truly the Imperial Canal is a splendid work—the most worthy as well as most lasting of its great projector, Charles V., King of the Spains and Emperor of Germany. It is a work that has redeemed nearly sixty thousand acres of land from sterility, and made them a marvel of rich fertility; a work that does, and will long continue to, repay the world for the losses and sufferings caused by his ambition.

From each side of the dam extends for a considerable distance a fine river-wall, and immediately above it, on the right bank of the river, is the entrance to the canal. But the flood-gates are gone; no more do boats emerge or enter there; and the water is admitted through a tunnel in the stone apron replacing them, by an iron apparatus regulating its flow.

Close to the edge of the bank of the Ebro, just below the canal-head, stands a wing of what was once *El Palacio del Bocal*, a finely-dressed stone building three storeys high. The rest of the palace is a heap of ruins, a "cave" of the bank having some years ago let it down with a run. Thence, for some distance, I found the canal's sides were of perpendicular cut-stone masonry, and eighty feet apart; the flow of the water between having a velocity of three miles an hour. Soon I arrived at the *Almacens*, or magazines—an extensive range of stone buildings, storehouses for goods conveyed on the canal, but almost all empty. In their front was a commodious stone landing-wharf with steps down to the water's edge, and a row of mooring-posts—hard stone posts wrought round and having carved knob-heads ; posts that have been in use for generations, perhaps since the canal was first used in A.D., 1528, and whose only sign of wear is their having become polished.

In the row of *almacens* stood a *posada*, and after there ordering my breakfast and disencumbering myself of my traps, I walked a few hundred yards to see an old "palace" of the emperor-king, standing close to the river, and behind the row of warehouses. It was not much of a palace. Nowadays it would not be a palace for a policeman ; but it was a curiosity, as showing what one of Europe's greatest potentates had built as a residence for himself. The building was in excellent repair, not that any care has been taken of or restoration done to it, but because it had been so solidly constructed as never to require repairs while it stands, and it will continue to stand so long as it is not meddled with. The palace is now used to store vegetables in. Just above it there is another dam across the Ebro, a more ancient one than at *El Bocal*, having a very wide " race " close to the bank, immediately in front of the palace. This dam once threw water into the walled moat that protected the royal residence ; but the moat's head has been filled with soil, its drawbridge replaced by a permanent plank footway ; it is now dry and protects nothing. Below, and quite close to the palace, is a handsome clump of six fine old mountain pines.

I made a rough rapid sketch of the place, just to show what was a palace to an emperor who made Europe tremble.

Outside the moat, and immediately opposite its bridge, is the old palace-garden—a long parallelogram enclosed by high stone walls, pierced at the west end by a fine wide entrance ; the gate being open I looked in. Up the centre of the garden is a gravel walk, on each side of which grows a row of old cypress-trees, leading to a large raised level grass-plot, surrounded with stone seats, looking wonderfully like a modern croquet-ground, but probably constructed for a bowling-green. The enclosure contains about one-and-a-half acres, and is utilised as a market-garden.

Two hundred yards farther up the river, and close to its banks, stands the palace *capilla*, a small chapel about the size of the lodge to an Englishman's park ; a square building, with a roof running to a sharp point. Unfortunately all the apertures of the *capilla* were fastened up, and I could not see its interior. Outside it was in no way remarkable. Opposite thereto, and in line with the walled garden, is a small open *plazuela*, or pleasure-ground, having gravelled walks, grass-plots, and flower-beds, furnished with stone-seats under spreading shade trees, and its centre ornamented with a now waterless stone fountain.

My breakfast was a poor affair. The *posada* was roomy and clean, and its appearance had indicated better things. Charge : six *reals*.

Soon after one o'clock I resumed my tramp, taking the tow-path. Crossing the canal a little below the *almacens*

Palace of Charles

is a bridge of modern construction ; it has stone piers and a wooden span, and is only remarkable as an example of bridge-building without knowledge of the true principles of so doing ; some day it will unexpectedly take " a header " into the water. It afforded an opportunity to again measure the width of the canal, which was found to be still the same—eighty feet. The tow-path was a fine level, broad, waggon-road, but grass-grown, clearly showing that the traffic was but slight. Alongside of it, as also on the farther bank of the canal, ran a wide continuous strip of timber, consisting principally of elms. The remains of old stumps showed these plantations were ancient, but the standing trees are mostly young. After walking a couple of miles I came to a moored canal-barge—the first seen. It was a very old one to be still in use. Alongside stood its team of two mules and a horse, eating a bait of barley and chopped straw, mixed, from off a spread-out old rawhide, while the crew of half-a-dozen Aragones were loading their craft with firewood, that had been chopped in the plantation close at hand. The boat was very different from an English canal-barge, being built almost ship fashion, with a round bottom and keel, and was nearly the size of a Thames collier. It had no deck nor cabin, and a most prodigious rudder. I never before saw such a rudder.

Two hours more brought me opposite the village of Ribaforado and to the Ribaforado bridge ; the former evidently a place of insignificant size and paltry appearance, standing on a barren knoll, which comes so close to the canal as to make its south bank for some distance a high precipitous cliff. The latter is the finest canal bridge I have ever beheld; why such a structure was built to lead to so wretched a hamlet I cannot conceive. It is a brick bridge, with keystone, facings, and foundations of cut-stone, and its single span springs across not only the eighty feet broad canal but also the wide tow-path; a beautiful arch, the half of a true oval, whose width is its major diameter, and whose crown is forty feet above the level of the water. The approaches are two steep grades, at right angles to the bridge, and so parallel to the canal's course, which lead up to and down from its traverse; an extraordinary arrangement, presenting two right-angled turns to the inexpert teamster, so giving him in crossing one bridge two fine chances for a grand smash. The pitch of its traverse is very great; the slopes, too, coming together very acutely— indeed, the bridge's parapet-walls make quite a sharp angle in its centre. The gable-like profile thus caused contrasts strongly with the beautiful sweeping curve of the arch; and the combination of angle and oval, as seen when descending or going up the canal, presents to the beholder a very striking and pleasing effect.

Just below this remarkable bridge, I was passed by the barge seen before; its team was trotting, all hands were singing, and it went merrily by. Still farther on was another bridge; that leading to Cortis and Mallén, two towns to the south of me. It was very similar to the Ribaforado bridge, excepting in having two small arches on each side of the main one.

As the sun approached the edge of the horizon, the church tower and roofs of Novillas came in view, apparently about a mile from the canal's course, and between it and the river. It was time for me to seek a resting-place for the night ; and the canal evidently making a sweep to the right, while the little town was some distance to the left of my direct front, I attempted a cut off across the fields, got entangled amongst irrigating ditches, and, nothwithstanding several successful water jumps, lost both time and distance by so doing.

Novillas proved to be a small place, with a big church standing immediately on the right bank of the Ebro ; a decent-looking little town, cleaner than most of the villages I had seen, and I confidently looked to finding a comfortable *posada*, especially as I had been positively assured of there being such. There had been two ; but travel, and travellers, had become scarce and infrequent. Novillas no longer had an inn.

I sought a lodging-house, and found one—the only one in the place. It was a little general store; grain and vegetables, groceries and hardware, sausages and haberdashery, were there exposed for sale. The *Amo*—Spanish equivalent for the French *Bourgeois* and American *Boss*—said he could provide me with supper and breakfast, but not a bedroom to myself, only a bed in a chamber where others slept, but that they were *personas regular*—only such were permitted to sleep in his house ; so making the best of the inevitable, I answered, "All right," stacked arms, refreshed myself with a tumblerful of wine, lit my pipe, and waited for the seven o'clock meal ; taking post on a brick bench, covered with sheepskins, built under the hood of the fireplace, and where I was soon joined by an infantry sergeant and some peasants, who dropped in, and took seats next and opposite me. The sergeant proved to be the non-commissioned officer in command of the little garrison of twenty-five men billeted in the village, and one of the *personas regular* who lodged in the house.

Supper was plentiful in quantity, but in quality neither choice nor luxuriant. I was the only person favoured with a plate and tumbler, though all had clean napkins; the rest helped themselves direct out of the several dishes with wooden spoons, and drank their wine by tilting the bottle containing it, at arm's length off, above their open mouths, and pouring a thin stream down their throats. The wine was not to my taste, being sweet and fruity. My dog, as always, was an object of general admiration; his size, beauty, and manners were greatly praised. "Oh!" said one of the peasants, "if it were only now the latter end of summer, what sport you could have with your dog and gun." Then I learned the country below me was, from the canal to the Ebro, and for many miles down, one vast grain field, which in the summer is full of quail, and that immediately after harvest an ordinarily good shot can confidently back himself to bag fifty birds every day he goes out.

On retiring for the night, I found the bedchamber was a little room, with a curtained-off alcove containing a bed —the sergeant's. Two more beds stood immediately in front of the partitioning curtain of the alcove, and pretty close together, for the room was very small. One was to be my resting-place, the other a couch for the third *persona regular.* This apartment's only window was in

the wall of the alcove, and consisted but of an eight-inch
square hole, closed by a tightly-fitting wooden shutter;
and its floor, as here seems to be the usual way in country
places, was a cement one. Bed, sheets, floor, everything
was clean; but when I looked up at the rafters a dreadful
suspicion crossed my mind. Those rafters were dry-rotted
and worm-eaten, until it was a standing miracle the roof
did not fall in. If that ancient woodwork was not un-
pleasantly tenanted it would be most extraordinary. My
prophetic apprehensions were soon realised. And though
the " regular persons " who, for the nonce, were my room
mates, did not disturb my sleep by snoring, they certainly
did audibly scratch. And so did I, too, for " Norfolk
Howards" ranged, reared, and ravished until the dawn of
day, and I arose in the morning, when called by the *amo*
at eight o'clock, if rested, certainly not refreshed. He left
me a dim and smoking lamp to dress by, for the tightly-
shuttered window-hole in the curtained alcove admitted no
ray of light, and but that my watch told me differently, so
dark was the room it might have been midnight. Down
stairs my chocolate was ready waiting for me. I paid the
modest bill of eight *reals*, and serene in mind, but decidedly
irritated in body, pursued my way.

The road struck the canal in about a mile, at a point
where it was crossed by another bridge, this time a modern
one, much after the same pattern as that immediately below
the *El Bocal almacens*. Close to it lay the barge that had
passed me the evening before. The crew recognised and
bid me " Good days," and " Go with God," in a cordial and
hearty manner; and from them I learned that the boundary
of Navarra was just behind me, and that I was in Aragon.

CHAPTER XIV.

A Contrast of Fertility with Sterility—Multitudes of Birds—Gallar—Comfortable Tavern—Admirable Engineering—Primitive Husbandry—Pedrola—A cross Mariatornas—A Dragoness of Propriety—In bad Company—A dark Reception—Preparations for a Way-Lay—Horrible Thought—A lonesome Walk—Alagon.

JANUARY 11, 1877.—The weather of my first day in Aragon was simply superb ; though in midwinter the temperature was as one of summer's finest, and a bright sun, and balmy invigorating breeze, soon raised my drooping spirits and insect-depressed soul.

The general features of the country I was passing through continued much the same as the day before, but the elm plantations being replaced with single rows of tall poplars, I therefore had a more continuous and open view of the landscape. On the opposite side of the canal stretched from its bank a vast expanse of brown, barren-looking country right up to the foot of the snow-capped *sierra* bounding the horizon. On the side I was, an almost continuous wheatfield, brilliantly green, and but occasionally broken by small vineyards and little olive groves, reached from the edge of the tow-path to the banks of the Ebro. Beyond, on the river's farther side, bare, arid, and

forbidding, rose the bluffs of the *Bardenas*—very incarna-
tions of wild sterility—perpendicular precipices, table-
topped peaks, barren gorges, ridge on ridge, range after
range, a chaos of dreary desolation.

The cornfields were alive with larks. They were there
in thousands, in such quantities assembled, that I suspect
the valley of the Ebro is the chosen wintering-place of the
migratory larks of North-Western Europe. Indeed, so
numerous were they, and so tame, that Juan became at
last tired of chasing, and got to look on the birds as
matters of course, unworthy of his attention, and so taking
no further notice of them, galloped wildly about in an
apparently purposeless way, unless for diversion and exercise. On coming to a low-lying part of the valley, where
for a stretch of about one thousand acres the wheat-land
was replaced with swampy growths of reed-canes, rushes,
and sedge-grasses, Juan flushed a snipe, but far out of shot.
Soon, the level of the valley rising a few feet, it was again
a wheatfield. As the day grew older the temperature rose,
it became oppressively warm, and my great-coat an almost
unbearable nuisance, though it was rolled up, and slung
knapsack fashion at my back ; for, as saith the country's
proverb, " *En largo camino paja pesa* "—on a long road a
straw is heavy.

The breeze had died away, not a cloud was to be seen,
the sun's rays were scorching hot, and the motionless air
resounded with the song of birds. Besides the hovering
larks, goldfinches, linnets, and many feathered songsters,
whose names I knew not, whose plumages were strange to
me, filled my ear with melody. Had not the tall poplars

been leafless, it would, indeed, have seemed summer come again.

I put up a covey of red-leg partridges, close to the canal. They had probably come to drink. My slung overcoat prevented the handling of my gun quickly enough to put in a shot, and they got away unscathed. Soon after that indefatigable ranger, Juan, took it into his head to cross the canal and beat the uncultivated wildlands on its farther side—a gravelly sandy waste, sparsely covered with stunted heather plants, sagebrush, oldman, rosemary, and wire-grass; and ere long galloped up another fine covey of birds, and pursued them till lost to sight beyond a rise of ground.

While following the canal, I saw numerous streams leaving it through stone culverts, passing under the tow-path, having well-constructed flood-gates governed by winches, and alongside each of which stood a square, pointed-roofed cottage—dwellings for water-bailiffs and section men—and all built much after the same pattern as the *capilla* of the emperor-king's palace near the *almacens*. These streams are from half a mile to two miles apart, and generally discharge two cubic feet of water at a rapid flow. They are the feeders for the irrigating ditches to which the plain between canal and river owes its fertility. I also passed two flour-mills, whose wheels were turned by still larger streams, also furnished by water from the canal. Not having seen any augmentation to its volume from confluents, its width remaining the same, and its current not slackening, the conclusion was inevitable that the upper course of the Imperial Canal is very deep,

and that it gradually shoals, and thus provision has been
made whereby, without a lessening of the traffic capabilities
its width affords, a sufficiency of the essential of fertility is
furnished to the valley.

Noon was passed, when Gallar was arrived at, a town
standing immediately below the left bank of the canal, of
some size, having two large churches, but of a poverty-
struck appearance, with a semi-abandoned look about it.
The town lay much lower than the tow-path; lower even
than the bottom of the canal. In fact, the difference in
level between it and the river-plain had become considerable, for the canal had been without locks, and so engineered
as to wind along the edge or face of the low bluff that
bounded the south side of the valley of the Ebro, with no
more fall than sufficed to maintain the current, while the
plain had fallen rapidly. Close to the canal stood a fine
large flour-mill, storehouse, and residence—quite a handsome range of buildings, enclosing an ornamental well-
kept *patio*. They, and it, had an unmistakable air of prosperity. Alongside of the storehouse was a long flight of
stone steps. Descending them, crossing by an old stone
bridge, the race from the mill, and traversing a narrow alley
way, I found myself in the *plaza* of the town—a dirty,
untidy, irregular square—and opposite a rambling old
posada of most uninviting presence. Inquiry of a passer-
by if there were no other inn elicited the answer: "Yes,
and a better one, which stands just outside the town, and
close to the canal." Thither I bent my steps, and was glad
to find truth had been told in the matter. It was a much
better inn—a clean, respectable-looking roadside house,

close to a fine bridge over the canal. A smart *Aragonesa* invited me to enter, took my orders, and ushered me into a tidy, cheerful room ; that is, it would have been cheerful, but its walls were covered with an unusual number of far from unusually atrocious ecclesiastical outrages on fine art, hideously conceived and abominably executed—coloured prints of martyrs in torment and most impossible virgins. In due time a capital breakfast was set before me, the chief feature of which was an excellent dish of eels stewed in wine. The salad was well compounded and crisp, the lamb cutlets delicious, the eggs fresh-laid, the wine to my taste, and I refreshed myself and Juan without stint. For this good repast for man and dog I was only charged, inclusive, six *reals*, and departed feeling all the better for my short rest and long commons, and well contented with the world and myself. I even forgave the designers and makers of those awful pictures, for, as Sancho Panza told his ass, *Todos los duelos con pan son buenos.*"

On the near buttress of the bridge that stood by the inn was a water-gauge, showing the canal's depth close to the bank. It was a chance for accurate and reliable information—a thing not always procurable in Spain ; and though I nearly slipped headlong down the steep bank into the canal on availing myself of the opportunity, succeeded in ascertaining that it was eight feet six inches from the water's level to the bottom.

Soon after leaving Gallar, the low bluff on whose edge the canal had heretofore ran rose into steep, but not high hills of barren gray clay, interstratified with layers of red cement, and coarse gravelly boulder-bands, having almost

perpendicular faces towards the valley; and the course of
the canal became very tortuous, as it wound along, scarped
most of the way out of the face of these cliffs, the tow-path
being entirely made-ground, reveted in many places on its
lower side with solid masonry, and several small lateral
valleys were crossed by embankments carrying canal and
road, some of them forty feet high, and faced with rubble
masonry, whose cement was harder even than the stones
it held together. The embankments were pierced with
central archways to permit a discharge of the waters of
the valleys, and through several of them sharp streams
were flowing. A breast-high parapet of rubble and cement
protected the tow-path wherever it traversed these combined aqua- and via- ducts. The lateral valleys afforded
no vista of view, for they were invariably closed, within
half a mile of the canal, by the wall of barren bluff, being,
indeed, merely recesses in the general front presented by
the upland to the plain. The engineering of this part of
the Imperial Canal is admirable, and the work, oftentimes
very heavy, has been most conscientiously and thoroughly
performed. Nothing short of a convulsion of nature can
break the canal.

In the course of the afternoon several ploughs were seen
at work, all alike in construction, and most primitive in
appearance. This is how they are made: the "beam" is
a pole, twelve to fourteen feet long, at an acute angle to
one end of which is fixed a shorter one, which serves
instead of "stilts;" opposite this, and nearly at right
angles to the long-pole, is another still shorter, sharp-
pointed, and sometimes tipped with a piece of iron; this

last stick is "coulter" and "share" combined. The plough
teams were mules, in pairs, and the method of harnessing
curious. Two mules were attached together by a yoke,
like what is used for oxen in England, only the "bows"
were replaced by four straight sticks padded with half-
collar, and in the centre ring of the yoke hung the traction
end of the long pole of the plough, kept in its place by
a wooden peg—no traces. The mules were driven entirely
by the voice. Adjurations and anathemas seemed quite
efficient substitutes for reins and whips; and a light head-
stall without blinkers was all the leather on them.

At four o'clock the town of Pedrola was sighted, lying
half a mile to the left of the canal; and having learned
from a shepherd—the only man met on my road in the
whole course of the day—that it contained a *posada* at
which accommodation could be obtained, the tow-path was
left and the town made for, for I had gone far enough for
one day, and the heat and weight of my traps had quite
tired me. A little footpath, leading through gardens and
small olive orchards, was taken, and their flourishing look
and the imposing appearance of the town—at a distance—
led me to hope it was a thriving prosperous place. Pedrola
proved the most rambling, tumble-down, dirty, disreputable
rookery yet seen in Spain, and its inhabitants looked like
swarms of beggars and cut-throats. With difficulty the
posada was found — a woebegone old building, whose
ground-floor was a big stable, cart-shed, and lumber-hole,
all in one, with a corner boarded off for a kitchen. Above,
and just below the eaves, was a row of small holes in the
front wall of the building, possibly windows for any apart-

ments the upper storey might be partitioned into. However, I had been so often already deceived by appearances in this country that I was not discouraged, and asked a woman in the kitchen for supper and a bed.

" You must ask the *amo*."

" Where is he ? "

" At the café."

" When will he return ? "

" Whenever he thinks fit, perhaps soon, perhaps not before morning."

Evidently " Mariatornas" was in a very bad temper, no satisfactory answers were to be expected from her. I sat down to wait, rest, and smoke a pipe, then started out to hunt up the café. I found it, a low dark room full of a bandit-looking crowd of herdsmen, labourers, and loafers. There were about forty of them. Involuntarily I thought of the " Forty Thieves." Take the stage ruffians of a melodrama, make them as dirty as possible, give them each a long knife and a four days' beard, half fill them with ardent spirit, and, so far as personal appearance goes, you will have fair representatives of the customers of that café ! Behind a filthy counter stood the presiding goddess, ·
a large, handsome, but bloated brunette. I learned the *posadero* was not there. He had just left, and, unknowingly, I must have passed him, so I retraced my steps. At the *posada* I found the landlord arrived. I could get no accommodation. He told me there were no provisions, no rooms in his inn—the upper portion of the building was only a lumber-loft, but there was a lodging-house in town, the *Casa Lorenza ;* there I could get a bed and meals.

It was with much difficulty the Lorenza house was found, a comparatively clean-looking little cottage in a narrow street. I knocked, and the door was opened by an old woman. "Could I get lodgings for the night?" "Was I a single man—alone?" "Yes." "Then I could not." And it was explained to me that the old woman was a lone widow and had but one bedroom in her house, a double-bedded one; she slept in one of the beds and let the other to "families;" a single man could not be admitted. I tried to persuade that very mature female she would be in no danger—indeed, she was old and ugly enough to rely confidently on her virtue—but it was no go. *La Casa Lorenza* was like Cæsar's wife. While talking to this ancient dragoness of propriety, a cloaked and sandalled individual, much the worse for drink, stepped up and volunteered to find quarters for me, and, as a last resource, I followed him. My conductor led me to several forbidding-looking dens, but none of them had an unoccupied bed, and he proposed to try the café. There we met with no better success, and to show my consideration for the trouble he had taken, I called for two *copas* of *aguardiente*, and took a drink with him. The liquor was excellent, and to my amazement only cost one farthing a glass. Then my self-constituted friend called for wine, and insisted on my taking a tumbler with him. While we were being served he volubly detailed to the assembled crowd my position, winding up with a declaration that he was quite willing to share his own private bed with me, adding we could take home a bottle of *aguardiente* and some bread and eggs, and make a night of it; he was not afraid, a man who had a licence to carry arms, and could afford to keep a dog, must be both respectable and rich. This recklessly courageous and liberal chevalier in sandals was very dirty ; unmistakable signs showed that "the familiar friend to man" harboured in his clothes, sported over his person. He was an insect preserve, and he was most decidedly drunk. I declined, therefore, his proffered hospitality with many thanks, assuring him nothing would induce me to incommode such a high-toned gentleman ; and making my escape with difficulty from his tipsy importunities, sallied forth and started for the next town. I was very tired, very hungry, and it was getting dark, but there seemed nothing else for it.

While passing the last house of Pedrola, on my way out of town, I spied the first respectable-looking person I had seen in it, stopped him, stated my case, and asked if he could direct me to any place to stay at. He said : "In the town—no, but a little way out of it—yes ; on the high road, the other side of the canal, is a new *posada*, there you may possibly get what you require." Hope dawned again, and crossing the Pedrola bridge I soon arrived at my last chance, and found the "new *posada*" was a barn-like building, daubed with mud, shut for the night, and showing no light. I knocked long and loudly. At last the upper portion of the halved door opened, and a voice asked who was there and what was wanted.

"A traveller requiring admittance."

"Have you your regular papers ?"

"Yes."

"Have you a licence to carry your gun ?"

" I have."

" Then come in."

The lower half of the door swung back and I stepped
into utter darkness, so obscure was it that neither anyone
nor anything was visible. I was bid to "Go up," and
stumbling against a stairway, groped my way to a loft used
as a kitchen, and by the dim light from the embers of a
sagebrush fire, perceived an old woman and young girl
squatted back on their heels, one on either side of it
warming their hands. I asked to be shown my bed, and
to have supper prepared for me. The old woman looked
me in the face, with as much amazement depicted on
hers, as though I had asked for the golden apples of the
Hesperides.

" Bed! our bed is the only one. Everybody sleeps in
the mule quarters, in the straw. As for supper, you are
too late for that. There is nothing to eat on the premises.
If you must have a bed and supper you will have to go to
Alagon. I do not expect you can get a bed in Pedrola.
I am sure you cannot here, nor anything to eat either."

" How far is Alagon ? "

" Two leagues—*largas.*"

In plain English, I was eight miles from my supper and
bed.

Was the tow-path of the canal or the road the shortest
way? The road—the canal was half as long again. I
wished the old woman and girl a very good night, and
" went with God."

As the door of the *posada nueva* was bolted behind
me, the last string of the cork to my champagne-bottled

patience was cut, only my mother-tongue seemed adequate to express the sentiments of the occasion, and, for the first time, Juan heard me speak in English. I do not think that sagacious dog was favourably impressed with the language, for he tucked his tail and looked scared. I was much, very much dissatisfied. Eight miles farther to go, carrying weight, is no joke when a man has made his day's march under a hot sun; besides, I was very hungry, and therefore, my nationality asserting itself was, under such circumstances, cross.

While tramping along, it forcibly occurred to me that I was on the very portion of my route where my friend the San Sebastian banker had earnestly cautioned me on no account to travel the road after dark, nor let strangers know what way I was going; and it was pitch dark, and all the ugly-looking customers in Pedrola knew I had started for Alagon. I pulled up and prepared for possible contingencies. Not that I cared. It would, in my then frame of mind, have done me good to have had an encounter, been a vent to my feelings to turn my double-barrel loose and try the effect, on some of the denizens of that inhospitable atrocity of a town I had left behind me, of a couple of charges of "buck and ball," for I had drawn my partridge-shot out of, and dropped into, each barrel a loosely-fitting bullet and three buckshot, and carefully "chambered" them with snipe-shot, the most effective and certain load for night-work a gun can have. Not that I seriously apprehended molestation. I had little doubt but that the hard-looking cases I had seen at the café were, in reality, honest peasants, and, like the people of the *posada nueva,*

more afraid of *malas gente* than I was ; that they were, at
worst, smugglers in peace, *guerrilleros* in times of civil war.
What I really feared, though, was the possibility of losing
my unknown way in the dark, and either arriving practically nowhere, or getting to Alagon when every house was
shut up, no one about, and unable to discover the *posada*, or
—horrible thought—find Alagon as deficient in accommodation for wandering strangers as the town just left ; for a
town Pedrola certainly is, having not only its two large
churches and *Plaza*, but a population of, I should judge,
from a thousand to fifteen hundred souls ; for I was beginning to lose faith in Spanish statements to wayfarers, and
becoming half a believer in what my friends at San Sebastian and Pamplona had told me, when they said the region
I had entered was unfit for any decent man to travel
through, excepting in the regular way.

The sky had become thickly overcast. Not a star
showed a ray of light. It was dark as a closed grave. A
strong cold wind blew directly from the snow-peaks of the
Moncayo. Before me, in the direction of Zaragoza, probably beyond that place, strong vivid flashes of lightning
almost continuously illumined the heavens. A downpour
of rain seemed likely to make my circumstances still more
disagreeable. The road showed dimly white when the far-
off lightnings played, and I pushed on rapidly. Still I
could not discern my way with sufficient certainty to avoid
running occasionally into the heaps of stones placed at
intervals along the sides of the road, stumbling over the
ruts in the middle, and stubbing my toes against the half-
embedded cobbles with which, in places, they had been

mended (?). More than once I was nearly down. No doubt, being tired, I went too near the ground.

The road soon diverged to the right, and after a short rise, seemed to be crossing an upland plain. It was very straight, with neither hedge nor fence of any kind, nor, so far as the light diffused from the distant flashes enabled me to judge, was there even a single tree near; it seemed to be traversing a waste. In fact, for an hour and a half, the faint indications of a road before me, surrounding darkness or gleaming lightning was all I could discern, for Juan had trotted on ahead. Truly it was a lonesome walk.

A long gradual descent, a bridge presumably across the canal, a short sharp declivity, and I was in a totally different country. On each hand was timber—olives most likely— shade-trees nearly met overhead. The continued gurgle of running water informed me I was near irrigating ditches, and at last I found myself amongst houses. I had been walking at the best pace I could go for over two hours; without doubt I was in Alagon. Not a soul was to be seen, not a light showed. It was close to nine o'olock, and I listened for the cry of the *sereno*. No sound came. I gave ten minutes' grace. The stillness remained unbroken. So, concluding the town was of insufficient wealth and import- ance to employ any guardians of the night, I started on a voyage of discovery.

CHAPTER XV.

JANUARY 12, 1877.—Walking slowly down the centre of the chief street of Alagon, the glimmer of a light streaming through a crack in the door of an unprepossessing-looking house was spied. Advancing and knocking boldly, the door was immediately opened without question, and I looked in on a room lighted by the blaze of a brushwood fire, around which sat a semicircle of men, women, and children, who all stared with evident astonishment at me ; doubtlessly they had supposed it had been some expected neighbour, for I think it was a social gathering I beheld. Announcing myself as a traveller in search of the *posada*, who wished to learn the way thereto, a young man got up and offered to be my guide, saying as a stranger, ignorant of the nomenclature of the streets of the town, directions would be of no use to me. After passing along some short, narrow, irregularly laid-out alley-ways, between dilapidated overhanging old houses, we came to a small

Plaza, and pointing to an open doorway, through which came a flood of light, my guide said : " Sir, there is the *posada—a dios*," and left me so suddenly, I had neither time to offer a *propina*, nor even thank him.

The open entrance led immediately into the kitchen of the *posada*, into which I walked. A goodly fire was cheerfully burning under the wide hood, and on the benches round it reclined several picturesque Aragonese peasants, while the *ama* and two *criadas* sat on the brick hearth, she knitting socks, they spinning yarn, like Arcadian shepherdesses, with their fingers and a distaff. The spinning-wheel of our grandmothers is a modern (?) invention seemingly, not yet known in Aragon's rural parts.

Greatly to the wearied traveller's satisfaction, I learned my wants could be supplied, and was immediately shown upstairs into a large bedroom, having two big alcoves, each with a double bed in it, and informed I would have it and them all to myself.

After making a comfortable toilet, for which there were all necessary appliances, I descended to my unconscionably late dinner with a ravening appetite. It was an indifferent though sufficient meal that I sat down to ; want of notice and the time of night were, however, reasonable excuses for all shortcomings, but for the first time in Spain food was placed before me without a clean napkin being furnished.

The meal finished, the natives seated round the fire were joined, who immediately assailed me with innumerable questions. The Yankees have a world-wide reputation for inquisitiveness ; as compared with the peasantry of

o

Northern Spain they are, I take it, a very reserved people. But here the stranger is questioned, not for the sake of asking, but for the pleasure of listening to what he has got to tell, for to a non-reading community a traveller is as a newspaper, sometimes as a novel, and the farther the distance whence he comes the more interesting is he. Some of the questions asked about England and the English are absolutely amazing. I verily believe several of my audience were so ignorant and confiding, that had a chapter out of the "Arabian Nights" been recited to them by me, with an assurance the venue was in Great Britain, and myself one of the actors therein, they would have seen nothing incredible in my statements. And it must be remembered that a people brought up from infancy to believe implicitly all the ancient and modern Catholic miracles, religious fairy-tales, and necromantic monkish legends, have credulity and love of the marvellous strongly developed in them. And they are also a stay-at-home people; the man amongst them who has made a few smuggling trips across the Pyrenees is a sort of Marco Polo in their imagination; none of these people seated round the fire with me had, for instance, ever been in Navarra, though that province is but a good day's march off, and they almost talked of *El Reino de Navarra* as of a foreign country. They, simple souls, seemed to think I had made an extraordinary journey, and prophesied I should never get to Barcelona—"It is too far off."

Ere long the ubiquitous guitar was produced. One of the men proved a good player, and after favouring the company with a few airs, started "*La jota Aragonesa,*" which, of course, I was pestered to dance ; and though, from the difference in rhythm of the music from that of the Navarra *jotas*, I suspected the dance too differed, more or less, I thought it better to risk dancing wrongly than disoblige by not dancing at all ; so, being well refreshed by supper, the good wine, and warm fire, rose up, bowed to one of the maids, and handed her to the middle of the room, with a delighted grin across her broad *Aragonesa* face.

That girl's style of dancing is easily conceivable by anyone who has ever seen a heifer frisk about a pasture, the two performances being identical, and I was not sorry when she said "*Gracias*," and we sat down. By the time we had concluded, the sound of *La jota* had half filled the large room with lads and lasses, the floor was immediately taken by as many couples as could find space to dance in, and a *baile* was improvised. Some of the dancing was very good indeed, and there was a commendable absence of the objectionable ; unlike the Arguedas saturnalia, there were no flagrant improprieties perpetrated. Amongst the company were many good-looking men and women and one really handsome girl. With her I danced a *jota*, to acquire the *Aragonesa* style, and a waltz, for the pleasure of doing so, for she was an elegantly-made girl and waltzed remarkably well.

On retiring, I found my bed most comfortable, its linen white as snow, and no insects troubled the repose of the tired-out wanderer.

The peasants in the *posada* of Alagon were distinctly different in appearance from the Navarros, as markedly so as English from German bucolics; in fact, immediately upon crossing the line I noticed a change of type. These Aragonese are, both men and women, fuller-chested, heavier limbed, broader in the face, squarer-jawed, and their dress also is different and more picturesque. The men are mostly attired in this fashion: A short-waisted jacket, sometimes frogged, and slashed in the sleeves; a low-cut very open waistcoat, plentifully garnished with pearl buttons; cotton shirt, with very wide turn-down collar— generally a checkered or striped one—and no neck-tie; knee-breeches, usually of black velveteen, very wide, not reaching the knee, and open halfway up the thigh, the ribbons to tie them hanging unfastened. Below, and through the slash of the knee-breeches, shows a pair of loose white linen drawers, tied by a draw-string just below the knee, and met by woollen stockings without feet; no hats, and the hair cut Newgate fashion; a coloured kerchief folded narrow tied round the head; and on the otherwise bare feet, sandals. The sash completes the costume, and is almost a garment; very wide and long, blue or red in colour; it is wound many times round the waist, and reaches from the middle of the ribs to con-siderably below the hip-joints. It is a sort of universal pocket and travelling-bag; money, smoking apparatus, knife, provisions, string, anything and everything that has to be carried is, if possible, stowed away in the folds of the sash. A striped blanket, or rather scarf, in size and shape not unlike a Scotch plaid, is, when out of doors, thrown around their shoulders in all kinds of fantastic ways.

The skirts of the women are fully six inches shorter

than those worn by the *Guipuzcoanas* or *Navarranas*, and all wear numerous ones, each of a different colour and of a trifling less length than that immediately below it, the outer or uppermost one being finely and closely kilted for several inches below its waistband. The waist of the bodice is very long, as long indeed as it is possible to be worn, and the women of Aragon either lace very tightly or are naturally extremely small-waisted, perhaps both. Many of them wear a small shawl, which in shape, size, and manner of being put on exactly resembles those worn by Welsh market-women. They, too, tie a kerchief round the head as the universal out-door covering, but in many and diverse fashions, but do not cut their hair short. Stockings with feet and low-cut light shoes complete the list of their visible array.

Their feet are generally smallish, well-arched and plump. The prevailing complexion of both sexes is the florid-brunette ; but the dark-sallow is numerous, and the red-Celtic not scarce.

In the morning, ere departing, I took a look round the town. The only remarkable object was the tower of its church. Dome-shaped, and covered with a chequerwork of white, pink, and green tiles, it had a fantastic and Tartar appearance. My way led through a succession of gardens, olive groves, and cornfields ; these last had all been artificially brought to an exact, slightly-tilted level, or rather series of levels, each below one of its neighbouring enclosures, and every level surrounded with low earth-banks. They were, in short, catch-water fields, and a system of ditches enabled them to be flooded. Some were so, and looked like small square lakes. Irrigation had, at immense cost of labour, been brought to perfection. Several large ranges of white buildings, having high chimneys, were probably factories or mills, and in the distance could be seen houses whose appearance suggested country seats —probably a nearer view would have resolved them into farmhouses and stablings. Fine trees bordered the wide road on each side, and cottages were frequent.

Before I had gone far, two *guardias civiles* appeared and stopped me. They saluted and asked if I had a licence to carry arms. Replying that I had, I was about to produce and show it, when they said I need not trouble myself, my word was sufficient, and again saluting, passed on. I have frequently met members of this corps, always in couples and on foot, and have invariably been politely treated by them.

The *guardias civiles*, actually the rural police of Spain, are a government force of about seven thousand men, scattered in small posts all over the kingdom, and to their vigilance and activity is due the security of the roads ; for though at no place numerous, considering the extent of the beat patrolled, their appearance is at any time and anywhere on the cards; and being invested with authority to kill if they think necessary, and having a great reputation for bravery, decision, and determination, they are held in much dread by the evil-disposed. They must be a picked body of men, for all I have seen were tall, handsome, well-built fellows. And their serviceable and picturesque uniform sets them off to great advantage. A cocked hat, in form much like a French gendarme's but more elegant in shape,

mounted with wide white braid ; a blue frock-coat, with red
and white facings, and white cord shoulder-knots ; yellow
belts, carrying pouch and side-arms ; their nether limbs
clothed in dark blue pantaloons, and leggings of dark
chocolate-coloured cloth, reaching halfway up the thigh,
and fastened with a row of buttons all the way up on the
outside ; and good walking high shoes, is their costume.
Their long blue military cloak is generally rolled tightly
up and carried *en bandoulière*, their breech-loading carbine
slung across their back, their hands encased in clean white
cotton gloves. All are close-shaved, except a fierce-looking
heavy moustache. Taking them altogether, they are the
most stylish police force I have ever seen.

At eleven o'clock I reached Casetas, the first place I
have seen in Spain at all resembling in appearance an
English village. It possessed "a green," well covered with
a verdant close-growing sod, around which stood neat,
modern-looking cottages ; and a clean, tidy roadside tavern,
presented itself to my sight. I entered, gave the usual
salutation, and asked for breakfast in the *patois* of the
locality—I had picked up the words the night before in
the Alagon *posada*. Being told my worship should have
his breakfast cooked immediately, and shown into a room
that served for kitchen and parlour, I mounted the raised
hearth, and, stretching myself on the brickwork bench
under the fire's hood, took a survey. The room was a
pattern of cleanliness ; its whitewashed walls and ceiling
were without a stain ; the tile-floor well swept ; pots, pans,
and other cooking and table utensils—scalded, scoured, and
burnished—were hanging around or racked in profusion.

On the hearth glowed a cheerful bed of red coals—rosemary-bush charcoal—that diffused a grateful warmth and fragrant odour.

On her knees, just below me, was a good-looking peasant lassie, cooking my meal. She had very white, regular, and sound teeth, coal-black eyes, and, I thought, most unnecessarily short petticoats. The young woman—she seemed to be about four-and-twenty years of age—paid a high compliment to my assumption of the appearance and manner of a better-class native. Looking up with a smile, she said: "How is your brother?" "Very well, thank you," I replied with a laugh. The laugh puzzled her. She looked hard at me and asked: "Are you not of the mountains? A brother of Don Miguel of Tabuenca?" No, I was not; did not even know Don Miguel. That was very strange, we were as like as two eggs. Then she chattered on that she had an aunt and cousins in Tabuenca whom she visited often; that she knew the Señor Don Miguel very well. He was a great friend of hers. And she again showed her pretty teeth. And so she rattled away, talking and laughing as she cooked.

My breakfast deserves description : a bowl of strong excellent soup, a dish of black pudding spiced and seasoned with fine herbs and *piñon* nuts, pieces of fresh pork and sliced potatoes nicely browned in olive oil, lamb cutlets and greens, a well-mixed salad, cheese and olives, bread at discretion, and a bottle of excellent wine. After thoroughly satisfying myself, the remains and half a loaf of bread made a fine mess for Juan. The entire charge for all which was tenpence! On this trip I have so often been charged much more for very indifferent fare, that the conclusion is inevitable—as a stranger and pilgrim—I have, three times out of four, been overcharged from twenty to fifty per cent. But though I have often felt sure I was being imposed on I have never said so. Really, as compared with English charges, the most exorbitant bill ever presented to me has seemed ridiculously small; and on the line I have taken travellers are so evidently scarce, that if these unfortunate *posaderos* do not impose on foreigners who on earth are they to impose on?

Notwithstanding the lavish display of utensils in the kitchen parlour of the Casetas inn, I had eaten with a wooden spoon and fork; indeed, I have seen no other table weapons since entering Aragon. As always, they were made of boxwood; the spoon very shallow, the fork —six-pronged—quite blunt, and the prongs close to each other. Practically, the two instruments are but very wide chopsticks. But, for a white man, I can handle chopsticks very fairly, and therefore have not been inconvenienced. I am told that in Aragon, only in first-class hotels, fashionable restaurants, and the houses of the very rich, are metal forks and spoons to be seen.

Soon after leaving Casetas, the handsome towers and domes of Zaragoza's famous churches appeared above the tops of the olive-groves surrounding that town, but it took me a two-and-a-half hours' walking to reach the city. As I neared it, the roads were deep in mud. The edge of the storm, whose lightnings had given me glimpses of my way when walking to Alagon the night before, had reached there.

I had a letter of introduction from a Tudela acquaintance to a family at Zaragoza, with whom he was closely related and often lived. It had been explained to me that they did not take inmates, but, as his friend, they would make an exception in my favour, and gladly put his room and the entire house at my disposition. So I walked straight to the place, and there received so effusive and warm a welcome that, at once, I felt myself established "as one of the family."

CHAPTER XVI.

El Pilar—Al Fresco Peasant Ball—Fine Canal Locks—Remarkable Wine—
Licorice Works—A splendid View—Waterworks better than Redoubts—
A Theatrical Entertainment—A *legitimate* Speculation—The Cathedral
of *El Seu*—A *Gran Baile*—Riotous Proceedings.

JANUARY 25, 1877.—The city of Zaragoza pleases me
much. It is by far the most considerable town I have
yet visited in this country, and has about it an air of
prosperous, progressive activity, quite refreshing and
absolutely novel, after my late experiences.

Sunday I attended high mass at one of the show
churches, "El Pilar," and was greatly struck with its
unique beauty, for in appearance it is totally different
from any Spanish church I have seen, and is in a certain
sense handsomer than any of them. In architecture, lighting, and ornamentation, it is a temple ; but, though a place
of worship, hardly a church. Full of marble sculpture,
decorative painting, and gilding ; well ventilated, light,
airy, almost gay. The fine sacred music floating through
it seemed almost out of place ; the airs of an Italian opera
would have sounded more in keeping with the surroundings.
The congregation—a for the most part well-dressed and

respectable one—was continually changing. Streams of people, coming and going, passing and repassing, paying their devotions first at one beautiful shrine then at another, fills it with life and motion. The most frequented shrine was a very fine picture of the Virgin and Child, hung around with votive offerings, chiefly modelled in wax— some being as large as life—of hands, arms, breasts, and legs; legs, however, being more numerous than all the others taken together. More of the visitors to this shrine were sightseers than worshippers.

In the afternoon I went to a public dance in the bull-ring of the *Plaza de Toros*—a peasant ball only to be seen on Sundays—for I wished to see the interior of the ring, which is closed on week-days, and also a public peasant dance. Admittance was obtainable by all persons "decently attired," on payment of one *real*.

The Zaragoza bull-ring is a large circular building, not unlike in form of construction the old Roman amphitheatre, and much larger than the cursory glance I gave its exterior had led me to suppose; indeed, on pacing across it I was surprised by its dimensions. The circular, well-gravelled and swept arena, was three hundred feet across. Around were ten tiers of stone seats, rising one above the other; then two storeys of *palcos* or boxes, comfortably arranged with wooden seats, each storey consisting of one hundred and four boxes. It was evident over ten thousand spectators could be comfortably seated. In the centre of the arena was a circle sixty yards across, temporarily railed off for dancers, and two bands, a regimental and a citizen one, alternately played from two raised platforms. Both bands were strong in numbers, and played well, keeping and marking the time extremely so. The dancers were all of the peasant class, and clothed in their holiday dresses, but, though picturesquely arrayed, and of good figures, were as a general thing very plain in the face. The way those people acquitted themselves was astonishing—valses, polkas, mazurkas were danced with an agility, grace, and precision far superior to anything of the kind I have seen in France. Indeed, the worst dancing of these common peasants was better than the best English ball-room performances, and I was well pleased by the general propriety of conduct observed. Whether such decorum was entirely due to the presence of police, *polizones*, not *guardias civiles*, or that the Aragones are more "proper" than the Navarras, I do not venture to decide. The ball concluded with a *jota Aragonesa*, some of the dancing in which was quite equal to the ballet-dancing of London theatres.

For this dance the ring filled with couples, and the scene was most gay and animated. Try and fancy the Hodges and Bettys of one of our rural districts dancing all the fashionable dances of the day with easy elegance, agile grace, and neat precision—if you can !

Fine well-kept roads lead from Zaragoza in all directions ; and as, accompanied by Juan, my faithful and affectionate friend, companion, and guard, I take my daily constitutional, most charming views and fresh objects of interest continually present themselves. The other day I walked out to see the canal-locks, about three miles from town. They are two in number, and like everything connected with the Imperial Canal, well designed and constructed. The first is one hundred and forty feet long, by thirty wide, with a drop of thirty feet; the second of similar dimensions, but only having a drop of half the first. These figures are approximations, for I had no means of making actual measurements.

Just above the upper lock is the finest flour-mill I have seen anywhere, except the "Lick" mill in California. The miller politely showed me over it. The water power being furnished by the canal without stint, and the fall close on forty-five feet, its capacity is very considerable ; but, at the time, only twelve pairs of stones were running ; for at present it hardly pays to convert grain into flour, wheat being now worth forty-eight to forty-nine *pesetas* per one hundred and thirty-eight and a half kilogrammes, while the best flour only fetches thirty-six, and second best thirty-four, *pesetas* per one hundred kilogrammes. But this is unusual and temporary, and the market will soon right itself.

After showing me over the place, the miller took me into a handsomely-furnished sitting-room, and produced a bottle of wine for my opinion. It was quite different from any I have tasted in this country, and more of a cordial than a wine, in colour a bright garnet, very sparkling and clear ; but I should not like it as a drink, for it is slightly sweet and strongly alcoholic. It had been made on the premises, from grapes off a hill-side in sight from the window, situated above the level of irrigation just beyond the canal. The wine was a perfectly pure one, had been nine years in the wood, and a few months in bottle. It had been made for, and never off the premises of, the miller, so he could vouch for its integrity ; nor was there a single drop of it in the market. On taking a second glass I liked it better. It was decidedly a very fine wine. A third glass I declined ; it really was too strong to drink much of.

A mile beyond the flour-mill is an artificial guano manufactory, and to it I was taken by the miller to see what he considered a splendid mastiff. The dog was a big, clumsy, cross-bred brute, and I was much more interested in the factory. The guano is made from the flesh of horses, mules, and asses, dried, pounded, and mixed with the dust of their calcined bones, and has a great reputation. Certainly if its rank as a fertiliser is at all proportionate to its rankness of smell, it is hard to surpass.

Below, and not far from where I tasted the wine, is another flour-mill, run also by water from the canal It, too, was a large and handsome white stone building, but smaller than the other.

Returning to town by a different route, my way ran past a licorice-mill. I entered it, and introduced myself to its manager. He proved to be also its proprietor ; and on my expressing a wish to see the process, kindly made himself my cicerone, showing and explaining everything connected with his fabric, from the chopping up and sorting of the roots to the final casting of the juice into oblong boxes, containing two hundred and sixty pounds each of cake licorice. Under the porticoes of the large *patio*, or interior courtyard of the building, were squatted on the ground about a hundred women, young and old, at work cutting the roots into convenient lengths by chopping them on blocks with small hatchets, sorting by size and quality, and clearing from the soil adhering to them. All were singing, chatting, or laughing. In one side of the building, mules were turning huge stone rollers that bruised the chopped roots into pulp, the apparatus much resembling that used for crushing silver-ore in Mexico. Afterwards the pulped roots were macerated by steam, the resulting syrup being concentrated by boiling. The owner of the works was a young and most intelligent man, and extremely polite and friendly; a great admirer of all things English, and a student of our language. But though by hard study he had advanced so far as to have, with the assistance of a dictionary, translated very creditably "Oliver Twist" and "Hide and Seek," he could not speak intelligibly; for there being no one living in Zaragoza who can talk English, he was in utter ignorance of how the words of the language sound; neither, of course, could he understand me when I spoke to him in my own language.

Still nearer home I passed a potato-mill—a manufactory of starch, desiccated potatoes, potato flour, &c. &c., near which I obtained a splendid view. Rising above a foreground of dark green olive-trees appeared the towers, domes, and buildings of Zaragoza; beyond, a rugged, broken, desolate stretch of chaotic hills and ridges of gravel, gray clay, and cement; then, forty miles off, the Sierra of Alcubierre, dark blue and indistinct from warm haze, and showing no detail; above, brilliantly white with dazzling snow, the summits of the Sierra de Guara, distant seventy miles; while to the north-east—in which direction there stretched to the horizon an apparent desert of broken

mesa—rose sharply and distinctly defined against a cloudless sky, the glittering peaks of the *Maladetta* mountains of the Pyrenees—more than a hundred miles away.

The day was a remarkably fine one, clear and brilliant, showing detail with a distinctness and reducing distance in a manner unknown to an English climate. I was so delighted with this view, that I went back the following morning to take a sketch of it. Alas! I could make no approach towards doing it justice. It was a view at once too panoramic in extent, too minute in its lovely details, and too charming in its gradations of tint and variety of colour to be more than hinted at within the limits of the four corners of a sheet of drawing-paper, and by the simple use of black and white; I was obliged to content myself with a most inadequate sketch of the centre of the town and country immediately back of it.

The following day I took a different road from town, and when about a mile and a half out, saw at work on the summit of a hill dominating the city, some hundreds of men and about fifty carts and horses, making excavations and moving soil. I supposed they were making fortifications, but was glad to find they were doing nothing so foolish. The work in progress was the construction of three large reservoirs, from which, by mains and pipes, to supply the houses of Zaragoza with water. Truly it is encouraging to see in progress a work of public utility in a country whose constructive energy has so long been exclusively devoted to, and monopolised by, military engineering. Waterworks are better for Spain than redoubts.

On my return I looked in at the foundry and ironworks

p

of Don Martin Rodon *et Hermano*, situate close to the little bridge over the Huerva, and a little without the *Santa Engracia* city gate, for I wished to renew my acquaintance with the young fellow at whose mother's house I had spent Christmas Eve in Tudela. He was quite glad to see and show me over the works. They were extensive and busy. I noticed the best turning-lathe in the machine-shop was branded " Edgar Allen, Sheffield." One for old England !

There are three theatres here. I have been to a performance at the principal one. The building is much after the same style as the San Sebastian theatre, but smaller. Like it, the ventilation, temperature, and lighting left nothing to be desired. There was a house of about seven hundred people, principally occupying the stalls and dress-circle. Military men, *en grande tenue*, and *en paisano*, with their ladies, were very numerous, and the most stylish in appearance of the audience ; but all the occupiers of stalls and boxes had the air and manner of the *beau monde*, much more so than I had expected to see in a provincial capital. The first piece was a political comedy—a hit at crises. The audience seemed to appreciate the points highly, but not being versed in Spanish politics, the allusions were lost on me, and I found it stupid enough. There were five actors and three actresses. The men were very fair artists, the women rather " sticky," one especially so—her corsets seemed to be preying on her mind. Afterwards came a spectacular ballet, " The Daughter of Fire." It was excessively well put on. Scenery and dresses were most artistic and beautiful ; nor was there the remotest approach either to tawdriness or vulgarity about the performance, while, as

was to be looked for in Spain, the dancing was admirable.
A *bailador*, two *primera bailarinas*, and forty *danzarinas*
constituted the *corps de ballet*. One of the *bailarinas* danced
as well as any "first lady" I have had the pleasure of
criticising of late years. But what pleased me most was
the general goodness of the corps, all of whom could,
and did, dance well, with grace, ease, precision, and becoming naturalness ; in striking contrast to the *en évidence*
drilled and awkward ungainliness of an average London
troupe. The "display" too was decidedly good. No
"broom-sticks," no "beef to the heels," no padding, no big
feet, no flat feet. Why does not some enterprising manager
import an entire ballet troupe from Spain, and give the
cockneys a chance to see, *en masse*, dancing and shape that
is really elegant? He would certainly make a financial
success, for the *exhibition* would be sure to draw, and their
salaries be undoubtedly low ; evidently so, for the best
places in the theatre—the fauteuil stalls (*butacas*)—were
only half-a-crown, the others proportionally cheap ; so
though the attendance was good, there could not have been
over seventy-five pounds in the house ; and out of this had
to be paid a good orchestra of a leader and thirty-eight
performers, and a prompter, eight actors and actresses, forty-
three dancers, numerous supernumeraries, all splendidly
dressed, and besides that, handsome scenery, gas, rent,
and contingent expenses ; and the management is making
money !

Sunday I went to high mass at the metropolitan church
—the "Seu"—the archbishop officiating. The cathedral
was the greatest possible contrast to the "Pilar." It

seemed the very type and exemplar of the mediæval
cathedral—solemn, impressive, obscure ; too obscure, for it
is full of work of the highest merit—sculpture, carvings,
paintings—a very mausoleum of art. Really lofty, its
groined roof, supported by pillars and pointed arches,
seems, in the dim light, still farther off than it really is.
Indeed, on entrance, I thought the cathedral narrow for its
height and length. It was only when I noticed how trifling
a relative space the knots of kneeling worshippers occupied,
and counted the numbers in some of the nearest of them,
that I commenced to realise my mistake. Of course I
could not pace the distance, but estimating by the eye,
counting the squares of the marble inlaid floor between the
rows of pillars, and multiplying by the average size of the
squares, I presumed the width of the cathedral is at least
two hundred and fifty feet, but this is possibly much within
the mark. The organ was a very fair one, and the chanting
and playing good.

There being a ball every Sunday night in one of the
minor theatres, and wanting to see all phases of Spanish
life that I could, I went after dinner, notwithstanding I had
been warned there would be nothing worth seeing ; but I
was like the young girl, who being told that love was all
folly, wished to see the foolishness of it. As far as I could
learn from my informant, these Sunday balls were only
frequented by the Zaragoza species of the genus Cad, and
the females who were to be expected at a ball where the
entrance fee was but a matter of two *reals ;* that, in short,
they were " Fivepenny Argyles."

The " *Gran baile* "—as the advertising posters called it—

was announced to last from eight o'clock in the evening to
two o'clock of the next morning; and at half-past nine I
looked in. The dancing-floor was one hundred feet by
sixty in dimensions, around which were five rows of seats,
and on the stage was a brass band of twelve performers,
executing a waltz. I say "executing" *avec intention;* for
though they kept excellent time, the instruments were
brassy in tone, and out of tune, and the music (?) was
atrocious. About sixty couples were footing it. As I had
observed at the peasant-ball at the *Plaza de Toros*, the men,
as a usual thing, danced better than the women; why, I
cannot say. Perhaps the voluminous petticoats of the
females lessened the apparent grace of their movements.

The best male dancers were, I noticed, waltzing with
each other. By-and-by a policeman came in and went
round the dancing-floor, stopping and separating all the
male couples. The inference was plain. Here the authorities do not consider it proper for men to dance with each
other in public. That policeman had a lively time of it.
While discussing the matter with some loudly-expostulating
couple at one end of the room, half-a-dozen others would
start at the opposite one, and on his going in pursuit of
them, as many more would commence at the place he had
just left. Evidently they were "devilling him;" he rushed
out and brought in another representative of the proprieties. But by then the number of dancers in the
building had increased, and the last state of affairs was
worse than the first; so he fetched two more, and the four,
stationing themselves one in each corner of the floor,
effectually enforced their prohibition.

The malefactors seemed disgusted and retired. Ere long I noticed several of them had returned, and were dancing with very queer-looking ladies. A sudden rush and dive of the four policemen revealed the true state of the case. The queer ladies were the remainder of the sinners against decorum, who, during their temporary retirement, had wrapped their own and their partners' cloaks around their waists, their scarf-shawls around their shoulders, their coloured neckties round their heads, and so attempted to circumnavigate the vigilance of authority.

These "riotous proceedings" were the only breaches of strict conduct. The dancing was proper, amounting to stateliness. Indeed, considering who and what the men and women were, the assumption of dignity with which they danced was almost ludicrous. There was none of that "romping to music," which I have sometimes seen even in "good society." The only thing a fastidious spectator could object to was the unconscious displays of the very few peasant-girls in the room, whose extremely short skirts were most emphatically unadapted to the whirling waltz, especially as they were not prepared for the occasion, after the manner of ballet-girls. Taken as a whole, the *gran baile* was a slow affair. I soon had enough of it, and left for home. Perhaps things went faster after midnight.

CHAPTER XVII.

JANUARY 24, 1877.—Zaragoza can boast of many agreeable promenades, or, as they are called, *paseos*, but the *paseo par excellence*, that of *La Santa Engracia*, is by far the finest I have seen this side the Pyrenees. It is a well-gravelled, smooth walk, hedged and planted with trees, one hundred feet broad, nearly half a mile long, and having cut-stone seats and gas-lamps at short distances apart, for its entire length. It terminates, at one end, by the well-built *Plaza de la Constitucion*, in whose middle stands the chief city fountain, a large, richly-carved stone basin, having in its centre a bold, well-executed figure of Neptune, round which are grouped four dolphins, from whose mouths flow copious streams of clear, sparkling water. At its other end it is bounded by a set of light, graceful, ornamental gates, railings, and stone pillars— *La Puerta de Santa Engracia*—through which is seen a charming expanse of olive groves, fine houses and their grounds, and the distant *Sierra de Algairen*, the hand-somely-planted, well-kept road beyond serving for a continuation of the promenade. Immediately without the low hedges, bounding on each side *El Paseo de Santa Engracia*, and running parallel thereto, are wide carriage-ways, pavements, and houses. The buildings to the right, going down, are principally cafés as to their ground-floors, private dwellings above stairs, a lofty continuous colonnade covering the pavement. They terminate by the *Teatro de Novadades*, succeeded by an open planted square, and the building used for the *Exposicion Aragonesa*. The houses to the left have, like the others, handsome white stone fronts, and are all private residences, excepting a few very elegant clubs and cafés, and the middle building, the handsomest of all, which is the college convent of the sisters of *Jeruselen*. This row terminates with the official residence and offices of the Captain-General of the Province; the striking tower, entrance-porch, and broken archways of the ruined convent of *Santa Engracia*, a beautiful building of the richest Gothic style of the fifteenth century and almost totally destroyed by "Napoleon's barbarians" in 1808, and by a boulevard. Towards its farther end the *paseo* widens into a large circle, in the middle of which stands a well-executed statue of Pignatelli, the able engineer who completed the works on the Imperial Canal, here always spoken of by his familiar surname of "*El Moro.*"

Spaniards being great *flâneurs*, the *Santa Engracia paseo* is a regular afternoon resort. On Sundays it is quite crowded. Then not only does a population of sixty-eight thousand turn out in force, but the country round about sends in its contingent of visitors and holiday-makers. It is a motley throng ; all grades are represented, from the sandalled shepherd in jacket of sheepskin, and greasy, well-worn, and patched knee-breeches, his ragged blanket swinging from his shoulders, to the elegant citizen dandy and gorgeous military swell ; from the short-skirted village maiden in garments of many colours, to the long-trailed lady of fashion. Zaragoza has as much wealth and enterprise as all the other towns seen since the frontier was crossed taken collectively, consequently on its public promenade there is a great display of good clothes—indeed, the number of really well-dressed, stylish-looking men and women one sees here is remarkable. I join in a promenade, and make observations and reflections. I count the number of women wearing bonnets in an hour's walk—sixteen. These bonnet-wearing belles are well got-up stylish women, under the escort of genteel men ; but their appearance is not, as they fondly fancy, improved by their Paris *coiffure*—quite the contrary. Amongst the elegant head-dresses of lace veils and mantillas, the bonnets, though as pretty ones as the centre of French taste ever sent forth, look flaunting, vulgar, almost barbarous. Amongst the best-dressed men, the overcoat to a great extent supplants the *capa* or Spanish cloak, much to the advantage of their appearance.

The more I see of the *capa* the less I like it. It can be put on so as to confer a look of elegance, but, as generally worn, gives a round-shouldered, almost hump-backed appearance. Usually its long folds impede their wearer's legs, make them shuffle and shamble, or, from preventing the natural balancing swing of the arms, causes a roll in their walk. Even the few men in ulsters—for that garment has invaded the peninsula—look smarter than the majority of those wearing the cloak. A dressing-gown even of frieze gives an old-womanish look, but most of the men *en capa* seem as though they had some ancient females' petticoats tied round their necks.

The number of beautifully-dressed and pretty children is remarkable. Altogether the variety of costume is very pleasing to the eye. Not only are the local ones to be seen, but mingled amongst them those of Navarra, Catalonia, and the Basque provinces, mountaineers and plainsmen. The military are in force, in mufti and regimentals, the latter adding greatly, by their variety, elegance, and showiness, to the general effect. Staff, lancers, dragoons, engineers, artillery, infantry, white, blue, pink, scarlet, green, gold, silver, and steel, make an evershifting kaleidoscope of colour and brilliancy. A sprinkling of tall, handsome *guardias civiles*, looking as though they might have just stepped off the boards of an opera-house, give quite a scenic air to the gathering, while the all-black *curas* in their ample cloaks, almost touching the ground, and wide shovel hats, serve as excellent foils and contrasts. Truly Spain is the land of the picturesque, as well as of the dance and song. A few well-horsed and appointed carriages, *fairly* filled, drive up and down. Some extremely handsomely-mounted, good-form men, dressed, gloved, and spurred *à l'Anglaise*, and whose horse-trappings are quite English, show off themselves and nags to the promenading *señoritas.* It is midwinter, not a cloud is to be seen, the sky is a brilliant blue, the air soft and balmy !

El Puente de Zaragoza is a very fine example of bridge-building in stone, considering it was constructed over four hundred and forty years ago, strong and massive, for the Ebro is liable to immense floods, yet withal light and elegant in appearance, but it looks also very quaint and queer. It has seven lofty arches, and six pairs of piers. The piers on the bridge's upper side are all sharp wedges ; of those on its lower, four are half octagons, and the other two are large, square, three-storied houses, whose entrance-doors are accessible from the water by flights of stone steps, and which communicate with the footway of the bridge by trap-doors. No doubt these houses were designed to serve for the shelter and accommodation of a bridge garrison. The length of this bridge, without including approaches, is eight hundred and twenty-five feet ; its width, excluding the deep semicircular recesses above the piers, thirty-six feet. It is very hog-backed, has a thick parapet, and up and down the river therefrom extend along each bank for considerable distances, deep, strong, river walls, having, at intervals, flights of stone steps descending to landing-places.

A little below the bridge, on the river's farther side, are the ruins of a large convent. Above it, on the city side, *El Pilar,* and from it is obtainable towards the south-west a lovely view of winding river and champaign country, backed in the far distance by the snow-clad *Sierra de Moncayo,* looking almost as near as it does from Tudela. The

four half-octagon piers appear much more modern than do
the two that are houses, as though they were restorations
of, or rather substitutes for, the original ones.   I have
made inquiry about the matter, but, as usual, the stereotyped, and quite unnecessary to impart, piece of information, that "God knows," and the absurd counter-question,
"Who knows?" is all the satisfaction obtainable by an
inquiring mind.   Probably, however, though Spaniards here
do not know, there may be plenty of my countrymen at
home who do.

The foundation of the bridge is continuous stonework,
and over it, between the piers, the Ebro rushes and boils as
if over a dam.   Four well-sculptured stone lions couchant
guard the approaches to the bridge, and lines of nets,
hanging up to dry, give evidence that fish are to be got out
of the river.

On my return from amusing myself by inspecting this
interesting bridge, and feeding my appetite for the beautiful
in nature by gazing on the views up and down the river, I,
just before reaching the *Plaza del Seu*, passed a pair of
large oak doors, standing partly open.   Peeping in, I saw
what I supposed to be the interior of a church, and, "no
man forbidding," entered.   I found myself within a large
square edifice, whose lofty, arched, and sculptured roof was
supported by twenty-four beautiful columns, whose walls
were covered with coats-of-arms — the imperial ones of
Charles V., Emperor of Germany, &c. &c., being the
most conspicuous—with paintings, and with old banners.
At one end was a raised daïs, and the whole floor was
littered with canvases, paint-pots, brushes, and scantlings;

while draughtsmen, painters, and carpenters were at work on all sides. On inquiry, I learned I was in the ancient *Hôtel de Ville*, and that, for the nonce, it was being utilised as a studio for scene-painting for the theatre. It was a beautiful interior, quite equal to some of Spain's famous churches.

I was so pleased with the reward obtained for curiosity, that for the rest of the way to my quarters I peered into every open entrance, hoping to obtain a sight of another good interior, and not in vain. Entering a wide *porte-cochère*, I stood in an unroofed courtyard, enclosed by a double portico, resting on pillars, with wide overhanging eaves of elaborately-carved woodwork. Pillars, porticoes, walls, were a mass of sculpture, the labours of Hercules, and bust-portraits of ancient Spanish kings being the most conspicuous ; but nude human figures of all sexes, human and other monsters, and demons, were not lacking. The wear of the lower portions of the hard stone pillars, and the whole style of the building, showed its extreme antiquity. But the newness of some portions of the sculpture puzzled me, until I noticed a scroll with an inscription setting forth that *La Casa Infanta* had been restored in 1871 by the direction of the Liberal Monarchical Club of Zaragoza. A close scrutiny satisfied me the work of restoration had been committed to able hands, and conscientiously and artistically done. It also forced on my notice that there was not only a great lack of fig-leaves, but a realistic completeness of detail that the nineteenth century considers quite superfluous. I suspect some monk of old had a hand in the designing of those figures.

From a sportsman of this city I have learned a fact concerning the migratory quail of Western Europe, which upsets my previously-conceived opinion. I have heretofore believed that the birds in question bred in Africa. He tells me the Ebro's valley, between the Imperial Canal and the river, is one of their great breeding-grounds. The old birds arrive in April, and immediately go to nest, in that immense wheatfield. After harvest, in the end of July, the young birds are strong on the wing and very fat. Then the sport is excellent, the bag to a good shot, who has well-broken dogs, being only a question of quick loading and walking.

I am disgusted to find I have burdened and troubled myself with gun, sporting equipment, and dog, to make the trip at the very worst time of the year for shooting, indeed when there is none. But it is not my fault; I tried to get full and reliable information on the subject in England, and could not. As a result, I have journeyed through a country which, in the proper season, abounds with game, prepared for shooting, and have not bagged fur or feather.

I am again bothered by the copper coins. In Tudela, a *peseta* was a silver piece of forty *cuartos;* here it is reckoned as worth thirty and a half, for, while there a *doscuarto* meant five of the new *centimos*, here a *cuarto* piece means one of the now legally obsolete *cuartos* of Old Castile, by which coin, however, these shopkeepers persist in computing prices. As to some of my countrymen, who ought to know better, so the decimal system is, to these provincials, foolishness.

During the last few days the temperature has become rather chilly. In the early mornings there have been dense river-fogs, and though the afternoons and evenings have been bright and clear, the natives are all shivering and grumbling. Here they warm their rooms by large braziers, full of red-hot charcoal sprinkled over with ashes, and placed in wooden frames having wire-gauze screens over them. These are put under the tables of the dining-rooms, and anywhere in the sleeping-chambers. Doors and windows are closely fastened up ; and why people are not asphyxiated I do not know—they ought to be. The fuel used for cooking is the branches and roots of rosemary plants—an endless supply of which is growing wild all over the uplands. It is brought into town on jackasses, long strings of which beasts of burden, loaded until they look like perambulating brush-piles, can be seen any day on the roads leading to town, or in the market-places. This shrub is now in bloom, and the plants look quite pretty.

The other day I made inquiry of an official whom I have become acquainted with, what they meant at the " new *posada*" near Pedrola, by asking me if I had regular papers, and learned from him, that though the foreign passport system is here abolished, the interior one is in full force ; for instance, said he, " Did I wish to go by rail, or otherwise to Madrid, or elsewhere, I ought to be furnished with papers—a passport or permit." These " papers " vary in price from a few coppers, for leave to make a short journey, to as many dollars for a permit good for a year and all Spain. The *visa* of the Spanish Consulate in London on my Foreign Office passport is, I find, equivalent to a permit of the latter class, so I am all right. But, knowing that a passport was not required by an English-man to enter Spain, and not being aware before of this internal police regulation, I might have easily run myself into a difficulty, and been "run in " by authority—for lack of "papers," found myself arrested, in some out-of-the-way village, by country officials who were stupid, obstinate, and zealous. And may all Spain's thousand saints defend me from zealous village authorities, of all and every country and place.

Last Tuesday being *St. Ildefonso's* day, a saint who by a stretch of official ingenuity is considered the king's tutelar, all Zaragoza was *en fête*. The balconies of the House of Deputies, those of the Captain-General, and of every other public building, were covered with crimson velvet embroi-dered with gold lace, and in every direction fluttered and waved yellow draperies and banners. After breakfast there was a march out and review of the troops of the garrison, which everybody, dressed in their best, went to see—a remarkably well-attired and behaved crowd. And the ubiquitous, sandalled, ragged-blanketed, crop-haired *arrieros, labradors, pastors,* and *andrajosos*—all picturesque-ness and dirt, but quiet and inoffensive in behaviour—served but to enhance, by strong contrast, the handsomeness of the numerous really elegant toilettes of both sexes.

The show of female beauty was far beyond what I have seen here on the Sunday promenades ; doubtlessly the class in which it is mostly to be found are, as a rule, not Sunday promenaders. Seated in carriages, standing in balconies, walking up and down—escorted by their attendant *caballeros* or propriety *dueñas*—were more pretty women than I have yet beheld before in Spain, all taken together. Amongst them were many blue-eyed beauties ; and, handsomest of all, a tall, full-chested, queenly, golden-haired blonde, who takes rank amongst the dozen most beautiful women I have seen anywhere. I begin to think I must add beauty to dance, song, and picturesqueness in my list of what is most remarkable in Spain. Small—very small—feet were plentiful ; and the percentage of little, elegantly-shaped, well-gloved hands was marvellous.

There was a very respectable turn-out of troops. I walked down the review line. Without including intervals, it was considerably over a mile long. I timed the march past ; even at the extraordinary pace Spanish soldiers go at it lasted forty minutes. Nearly all arms were represented —the engineers with iron sections of pontoon bridges, boats on trucks drawn by mules, and portable forges ; horse artillery—to be accurately descriptive, it should be mule artillery—with guns and ammunition carts ; a four-gun battery of mountain rifle-cannon — guns, carriages, ammunition, equipments, all on pack mules ; foot artillery, infantry, cavalry, and mounted *guardias civiles;* a brilliant, staff, several generals. I was more than ever struck with the varied and real elegance of Spanish uniforms. On or off the stage I have not seen them equalled. The mounted *guardias civiles* were the most plainly attired of the horse-men, but looked extremely well. Big good-looking fellows, arrayed in patent-leather jack-boots, snowy-white breeches, double-breasted tail-coats—dark blue, with crimson breasts and silver buttons, crimson collars, coat-tails turned back

Q

with crimson, and having a crown and lion embroidered in silver on them ; cocked hats, heavily braided with white, and having a crimson badge in front ; white gauntleted gloves, long steel spurs, sabre and carbine, and splendidly horsed. The staff seemed all colours. Even the long ostrich plumes of their head-gear were dyed of many hues —gold and silver, lace, ribbons, orders, covered them. They were a gilt, silvered, and jewelled rainbow. The bands—numerous and respectively strong—played very well.

The number of handsome men amongst the officers was remarkable, and many, who were "on the show off," displayed horsemanship that would have made their fortunes in a circus. The mules were big, heavy, serviceable animals, ranging from fifteen-and-a-half to nearly seventeen hands high ; and weighing, I should suppose, from nine to thirteen hundred pounds each. Taking them altogether, they were almost as fine a lot of mules as though they belonged to the United States transport service.

This review was, as a spectacle, very striking and effective. I have never seen so fine a show made by the same number of troops, and I have been in the way to see a great deal in that line. But, however, an army must be good for something ; and if the Spanish one has not greatly improved in fighting qualities since the days of the Peninsular War — which the skirmishing, dodging, and running-away performances, called collectively, "The late civil war," and its Cuban fiascos, would lead one to doubt —it ought to be ornamental in peace.

I have received so much polite attention and courtesy

from Spanish military men, that it seems ungrateful in me
to make such a remark as the foregoing; but I fear there
is more truth than sarcasm about it. And after all, pageantry
ought to be the only use for an army in Spain. No foreign
power wants, or, if her external affairs are conducted
rationally, is ever likely to make war on this country; and
if Spain's upper classes would cease being conspirators, the
people—hardworking, frugal, patient, given more to dance
and song than thinking, a people of "*vuelta mañana*"
(to-morrow will do)—would give no employment to the
military. Unfortunately, as it now is, the short cut to
power and wealth in Spain is a successful treason; and the
individual ambition and energy, that in England conduces
to general prosperity, makes Spain the arena of interminable
revolution. It will be a most happy time for this country
when the day comes, that to participate in a conspiracy will
be to take a short and sure cut to the gallows.

In the evening the public buildings were illuminated.
The *Casa de Deputacion* appeared to the best advantage.
The gas lamps and jets arranged around its windows, along
its balconies, and under its eaves, gave to its white front a
look of alabaster, lit up the crimson and golden hangings,
and brought out in strong relief against their dark shadows
the sculptured figures of the façade; and the motto in large
letters, " Vive Alfonso XII.," showed at all events official
loyalty.

CHAPTER XVIII.

JANUARY 27, 1877.—Early on the morning of yesterday I walked forth from Zaragoza, bound for Lerida across *Los Monégros*—a tract of country I had been solemnly warned against attempting to traverse on foot or alone. I was told it is a most uninteresting stretch, quite unworthy of being visited ; that settlements are very far apart ; that it is a retreat, or refuge, for banditti, and that I ought positively to go from Zaragoza to Lerida by rail, viâ Monegon, so turning instead of crossing *Los Monégros*. But I started out to walk from the Bay of Biscay to the Mediterranean, and am going to do so—" A wilfu' chiel mun gang her ain gait," even if it brings him to grief. So, being totally averse to making any considerable gap in my pedestrian trip, I again urged on my three to four miles an hour " mad career," quitting Zaragoza by the *Puerta del Duque de la Victoria*, situated immediately to the left of the old and interesting church of San Michael, whose sculptured porch—over which, under a colossal scallop-shell, is an heroic-sized figure of his saintship in single combat with a most extraordinary-looking devil—is well worth a passing glance.

The city gate of the Duke of Victory is a fine Tuscan porch with three sets of handsome iron gates, connected by railings marked Henry Russell, London, 1860 (wonder if they were paid for in Spanish bonds?), and when through them I found myself on the *camino real* to El Burgo, a hamlet near which I had been informed there was a good ferry across the Ebro—for thence my route would be north of that river.

Traversing by a stone bridge the little stream *La Huerra*, my course led past two large flour-mills, a grove of olives, and then a fine railway station, once locally believed to be the finest in Spain. This station consists principally of a range of imposing-looking buildings forming three sides of a quintagon, the enclosed space being elegantly laid out as an ornamental garden, with a handsome fountain in its centre. The cost of this station is said to have been so great as to have made its construction the proximate cause of a stoppage in that of the line, which, starting out with the grand title, " Line of Zaragoza and the Mediterranean," and having, on paper, branches to almost everywhere in Spain, has stopped at *Fuente del Ebro*, at a distance from its commencement of but thirty-eight kilometres, where, judging by the present financial prospects of the company, it will continue to stop *sine die*. In the meantime the buildings, nearly all uninhabited, are going rapidly to the bad for want of care and repairs ; already the place had acquired a dilapidated appearance.

Two hours' walk from this huge commencement of a small ending brought me to El Burgo. I had traversed vineyards, olive orchards, and gardens ; crossed several small bridges, passed a most tastefully-laid-out and handsomely-monumented hospital cemetery, and inspected the ruined towers and walls of what I took to be a huge monastery, two sides of whose encircling outer square of walls were still standing. They were of solid masonry, twenty-five feet high, and strengthened at short intervals by round towers, of which I counted seven on one side, fifteen on the other.

I took the El Burgo route, for I wished to see the present termination of the Imperial Canal, its mouth, and because it was a shorter one than that which, crossing the Ebro by the *Puente de Zaragoza*, led round by the town of Alfajarin.

Arrived at El Burgo, I found it an insignificant village, with nothing remarkable to distinguish it from many just such others I have seen. I also discovered that the Imperial Canal has no mouth ; that, as a canal, its waters do not rejoin the Ebro. Pignatilli, the engineer, who had the completion of this great enterprise committed to his charge, died ere his plans were executed, and then and there the work stopped. Below El Burgo the canal, as such, ceases, and becomes a system of irrigating streams.

The village appearing to be some half mile from the banks of the Ebro, I inquired of a peasant I met in its one street the way to the ferry. He said the ferryman was, at that time of day, most probably not at the river's side, but in his house, and kindly volunteered to take me to it. He was right. The ferryman was found sitting in his cottage over the embers of a wood fire, smoking *cigarrillas*, and drinking out of a goatskin *botella*, which, the usual salutations having passed, he handed round. I have been already long enough in Aragon to learn the accomplishment of drinking in the style that is the custom of the country; so raising the *botella* at arm's length, opening widely my mouth, I directed a thin stream into it, and poured a continuous flow down my throat, until thirst was quenched ; nor did I disgrace myself by wasting a drop of the appreciated fluid. I have assiduously practised the trick for conformity's sake, and always with good wine for my own.

When I made my wish to be ferried across the river known, the ferryman politely but positively refused to stir, alleging the wind was too strong to make the attempt. It certainly was blowing hard. It had been a lovely, balmy morning when I set out, but though cloudless, and not cold, the force of the wind had been steadily increasing, and was still. doing so. It was blowing harder and harder every minute. But I thought of the excellent ferry I had seen at El Bocal, judged the one at El Burgo would certainly be as good, and suspected the ferryman before me was simply lazy and hated to leave his comfortable seat, tobacco, and wine, to go to work ; so I stoutly insisted. Getting up, he remarked, with a shrug of the shoulders : " What must be must. One cannot hasten or postpone his destiny. Every man must march when the drum beats for him." So, calling a boy to accompany us, and throwing a long coil of light rope over his shoulders, the ferryman led the way.

Arrived at the river, I must say I did not like the prospect. The stream was at least twice as broad as at Zaragoza, full of gravel and shingle banks and of shoals, between and over which rushed sharp currents and rough rapids ; and the wind, then blowing a stiff gale, lashed the water into miniature waves with broken crests. Nor was the look of the ferry-boat reassuring. I had altogether too rashly taken it for granted that the only ferry across the Ebro, connecting the high-road from Zaragoza on the south of the river with the Lerida route, was of course one for waggons and carriages. The means of crossing was simply a very rickety flat-bottomed skiff. But I felt sure the man and boy would not risk real danger. At all events, it would not do for me to be the one to propose turning back, so preparations were at once commenced.

The object of bringing the coil of rope soon became evident, one end of it was attached to the stem of the skiff, the other looped round the shoulders of the man, who started walking up stream. Taking one of the long poles that lay on the skiff's bottom (there were no oars), the boy, keeping alongside, braced the skiff's bows outward, and so it was towed along to get an offing. I took notice, not at all to my satisfaction, that that boatman did not know enough to tie his tow-rope so as to draw with advantage. As a consequence, the line of traction being diagonally against him, and the stream strong, the boy's strength was overtaxed, and the skiff continually grounded ashore. Lending a hand, sometimes to the lad, then at the tow-rope, we proceeded half a mile up the river, and then all three getting in, the ferryman commenced poling across.

I crouched down—there were no seats—and held Juan by the collar, fearing he might, by putting his paws on one of the gunwales, upset us, for the crank skiff was totally unfit for rough water. About a third across was a long shingle shoal, whose hog's back showed, in places, just above water. On arriving at its commencement the ferryman kicked off his *alpargatas*, took the rope in his hands, jumped overboard and commenced towing again, the boy poling on the shallow side.

Before we had gone far the current became like a millrace. The wind was with it; together they were too much for the crew. The ferryman's progress stopped; he began to lose ground; the shingle slipped beneath his feet. He alternately prayed and cursed, as he lunged against the stream. Then the boat began to swing outwards. The ferryman gave a cry of despair. If he left hold of the rope we should leave him like a rocket, and never be able to get to him again. If he did not, then would he be dragged into deep water and infallibly drowned. No swimmer could have made the shore caught in those cross currents and that rough water. In either case we should, in all probability, ground broadside on some shoal, be rolled over and fare likewise.

Of two dangers I chose the lesser; and, shouting to the boy to hold down the dog, who was frantically excited, I snatched his pole from him, and dropped the lower end of it on the deep side—the one to which the boat was swinging. To my amazement the twenty-feet pole only cleared the surface some three feet. Putting my shoulder to its upper end, and throwing my weight and strength against it—after the manner of bargemen—I essayed to stop the outward swerve of the skiff.

It steadied—stopped.

The ferryman took fresh courage and wind ; and, inch by inch, he pulling, I pushing, we gained headway ; and after a quarter of an hour's desperate work the rapid was passed, and we were in slacker water. Then jumping in the skiff, the ferryman recommenced shoving, and I, resigning my pole to the boy, again took charge of Juan, much to the lad's relief of mind, for he seemed in mortal terror of the dog, who, indeed, looked wild enough, and had more than once tried hard to get away from him, and growled and showed his teeth in a very menacing manner. Ere long we were in dead water, had only the wind and waves to contend against, and at last reached the bank in safety. On jumping ashore I looked at my watch. We had taken an hour and ten minutes to make the crossing.

It was simply idiotic of the ferryman, knowing, as he must have, the strength of the currents and the difficulties to be contended with, to attempt that crossing with a gale blowing down stream. But what could be expected of a boatman (?) who fastens a tow-rope to the stem of a craft ? Besides, like all lower-class Spaniards, he was a fatalist, and that always counts for something. Had I not been deceived by the waves disguising the rapidity of the current, certainly I would never have risked the crossing. As it was, we had had a close enough shave of turning the Ebro, so far as we three were concerned, into the Styx. I could not, after such a passage, offer the trifle that the legal fare amounted to. If anything, I went to the other extreme, judging by the look of grateful astonishment and hearty *"gracias"* of the ferryman. But my excessive payment was, after all, but a sort of "candle to the Virgin for safe deliverance."

My expectation was to be met at the river's side by a Zaragoza acquaintance; but no one was in sight excepting the ferryman and his boy. The gentleman I refer to is a licorice speculator, who had a gang of hands somewhere in the neighbourhood of the ferry's north landing, digging and stacking licorice-roots. These men he had gone to look after a short time prior to my leaving Zaragoza; and, ere doing so, had invited me, if I would content myself with camp fare, to breakfast with him when *en route*, saying he would be on the look-out for me at the landing. I inquired of the ferryman where the licorice camp was. He did not know. There was one somewhere, up or down the river, he said, and added immediately: "God knows! who knows? May your worship go with God." Then waving an adieu, he and boy lay down under a bush growing by the river's bank to smoke and snooze.

Walking on a few yards to the top of a little knoll, I reconnoitred. I was in a wide river-bottom, a sandy, hillocky waste of sage-brush thickets, scattered growths of willows, wild rosemary, and rushy hollows. The small town of Alfajarin and hamlet of Noallen, backed by mountains and hazy from distance, and a few far-off farmhouses, were the only habitations in sight.

Taking a direction diagonally from and down the river, in a line that would lead me on my journey's way, I started to find, if possible, my friend's camp, or if not, to gain the road to Lerida. Juan, jumping a rabbit, dashed after him, and, three feet from the narrow path I had taken, was lost to sight in the dense sage-brush. I whistled and called to no purpose; he was to windward, and it is no use whistling against a gale. I waited for my dog's return till patience ceased to be a virtue; besides, I had no time to waste, I was "burning daylight," so again proceeding on my way, ascending every little rise of ground to look around for the whereabouts of my friend's camp and my lost dog. Before an hour had elapsed I spied patches of dug ground, where licorice-roots had been extracted, midway between me and the river to my right, and worked my way to them through the brush and reed-beds.

Arrived thereat, I found places where the soil had been quite recently turned up. I was all right, it was only a case of tracking, and in a few minutes "I ran in the trail" to my friend's camp, a small cabin in a hollow surrounded on three sides by tall reed-canes. I entered the door and was greeted with a shout of welcome. I had not been met at the river's side, my friend having been sure a crossing in such a gale down stream was impossible. The little cabin was full of labourers taking their "nooning." Breakfast was finished, but a meal for me was immediately set cooking, and, *en attendant*, my host and I started out to hunt for Juan. After going a short way we heard him, at intervals between the furious gusts of wind, howling dismally in the distance. We ran up on a knoll, caught occasional glimpses of the dog making wide circles to get my trail, which, soon striking, he, ere long, reached us at a tearing gallop, and seemed ready to devour me with delight.

After breakfast, my friend accompanied me about a mile to show the way to a foot-bridge across a wide irri-gating ditch, its only crossing for several miles, and point-ing out the best way to proceed thence, bade me a final *a dios.* After traversing ploughed fields, alkaline flats, and sand barrens, the *camino real* was regained at the entrance to the hamlet seen from the Ebro's bank, and from there the road wound along the sides of gray-clay hills (the bluffs forming the enclosing rim to the river's valley). These hills were quite bare of vegetation, look-ing, consequently, extremely forbidding ; nor was the aspect of the valley much better, such wheat as there was being short, scattered thinly over the ground, and sickly in colour.

At half-past three was passed, a mile to the right, the little town of Villafranca de Ebro, looking very picturesque and striking, lit up by the rays of the declining sun, that brought sharply out the detail of the towers of its Gothic church, and brightened and gilt the pointed gables of its houses ; and soon after five the end of my day's journey was reached—the small town of Osera, situated immediately on the bank and in a big bend of the Ebro.

Osera has two *posadas*, both much of a muchness. I walked into one with the least forbidding exterior, and was glad to perceive that, for an inn in an Aragonesa country town, it was within rather clean than otherwise. A bed and supper were at my service, so I sat down in the entrance passage, lit my pipe, and chatted with the host, a burly peasant proprietor, and his handsome wife. By-and-by the little son of the house, a child of ten years old, entered, satchel on back, on his return from school. This small boy literally "kissed hands," beginning with me as the stranger present, and consequently the first in honour, and ending with his youngest sister, a baby just able to toddle. It was the first time I had seen this old Spanish custom practised, and as the little fellow was of a pleasing countenance, and his hands and face clean, I did not mind the performance.

Supper was set out for me at the same table and time as for the family; but a more sumptuous, or rather less frugal, repast was furnished me than they were content with. A mess of cabbage and potatoes (the latter having been first boiled soft in water), stewed in olive-oil and water, and seasoned with little morsels of garlic fried in oil prior to being put with the cabbages and potatoes, salt, pepper, and red chillies; fried eggs and a sausage—a very hard one; a salad, no napkin, wine at discretion, but too fruity and sweet for my taste, is a full, true, and particular account of what was set before me.

My bedroom was clean, as also the bedding, the washing apparatus hardly worth mentioning, the chamber furnished principally with martyrs and virgins. I was one, a martyr of course, but only to a limited extent, for I was armed against the midnight tormentors. At Zaragoza I had purchased from a chemist a quarter of a pound of insecticide, and the Christian prevailed against the wild beasts.

On coming down in the morning, only the eldest daughter, a girl of twelve years old, seemed to be stirring. I requested to have my chocolate. She ran off, but soon returned with a lump in her hand, and asked, " Would I prefer to eat it raw, and wash it down with a drink of *aguardiente,* or have it cooked ? From which I infer that to breakfast on a lump of raw chocolate and a " go down " of still rawer spirits, is a not unusual Aragonesa meal. But I cared not to try such, so the little maid had to blow up a fire with the bellows and her mouth, which latter she seemed to prefer using to the former, and to cook me my *iicara* of chocolate after the ordinary fashion. At leaving, the little lass told me my bill was ten *reals* (two shillings), and seemed quite astonished at receiving a gratuity, kissed it, crossed herself, and ran upstairs flourishing the small silver coin over her head, evidently intending to show it in triumph. It was, perhaps, the first bit of *plata* she had ever had to call her own.

CHAPTER XIX.

JANUARY 29, 1877.—The little town of Osera was left on one of the most lovely mornings that ever broke, and as, there, the Ebro and the road along which my route ran parted at right angles, I took my last look at a river I shall probably not see again ; one I certainly shall never again give another as good a chance to drown me. Soon I found myself amidst barren, desert-looking hills ; but they were not altogether as worthless as they appeared ; the gray sage and brownish-green wire-grass growing sparsely on them was sufficiently nutritious and plentiful to afford sustenance to flocks of goats and sheep, of which I saw several. The road itself was, if possible, harder than it had been the evening before. It looked as though it had never been rained on, and the gray clay, parched by hot sun, swept by moistureless wind, was like cast-iron to one's feet. When, at half-past eleven, I arrived at the first habitation come to on the road, I was almost footsore.

The house was a *posada*, and, on passing through its open portal, I stood in a huge stone stable, occupied only by a young woman sitting on the floor, knitting. She looked surprised at seeing me and Juan come in, and asked what I wanted.

"Some breakfast."

"For how many?"

"Only for one."

"What would your worship like? Whatever your worship wishes for shall be cooked."

"What is there in the house?"

"Everything!"

"Then cook everything, for I am hungry!"

The young woman got up, and inviting me to follow, led the way into the combined kitchen and living-room. This apartment was neither more nor less than a gigantic chimney, and in shape and proportions exactly like a champagne bottle, without a bottom, placed on the ground, entered by one small door, and having no other aperture excepting its mouth. It was flagged; a fire burned, or rather smudged, in its centre, and round three sides of it were wooden benches. Of course, this queer interior was almost dark, the light through the little doorway and the few rays able to struggle through the smoke down the funnel chimney, being all the illumination. It was darkness revealed, and the smoke of perhaps two centuries had blackened everything to the uttermost. When sufficiently accustomed to the darkness to see clearly, I took note of the other occupants of the room, if such it can be called. On one of the benches sat a man of about forty years

R

of age—a "good devil" sort of fellow—and very close to
him reclined, in a most *dégagé* attitude, a sister of the
woman who had brought me into this inhabited smoke-
bottle. The relationship of the two females was apparent
at a glance, and both were young and very good-looking.
The man was probably the landlord. The women were
too old to be his daughters, certainly were not his sisters,
nor, I am sure, was either of them his wife. Perhaps they
were his nieces, but, if so, he permitted himself to indulge
in a licence of expression and conduct that was highly
reprehensible in an uncle.

Soon "everything in the house" was cooked, and my
meal set down before me, literally so, for there being no
table in the establishment, an old smoke-blackened cooking-
pot in which water was being boiled was placed on the floor
in front of me, its lid taken off, and a plate substituted
therefor, containing the "everything in the house," that is
to say, a repetition of my previous night's supper minus
the vegetables. A loaf of dark, hard, sour, most indifferent
bread was put on the bare floor beside me, and a wooden
fork furnished. "*Vaya!*" exclaimed the good-looking
wench who had been officiating as cook, as she spread
out her hands palms upwards, and I fell to work.

For the first time in Spain I had to ask for wine at
a meal, and then, instead of having a bottle placed before
me, was asked how much did I want. The wine proved
poor for this country, but was the best thing provided,
and I and Juan contented ourselves with what we could
get.

These people were civil, but rude and rough in manner;

indeed, I have observed a gradual change for the worse in the manners and customs of the peasantry since leaving the land of the "honest" smugglers. My bill was as moderate as the quality of the fare. As to quantity, my big dog and I had not stinted ourselves. It was three *reals*. Sevenpence-halfpenny, including wine of course, of which I had drunk about a pint and a half, is not a ruinous price for a full meal for man and dog. In conversation with the "good devil," I learned that the country I had traversed that morning was "a great grazing range." One man, the richest in the district, ran on it a herd of twelve hundred head.

"Of cattle?"

"No, goats."

The wind, which had been gradually rising, was, when I started again, blowing "great guns;" fortunately in my back, still it was most disagreeable. As I proceeded along, the hills on both sides became a rolling plain, and large fields of young, sickly-looking wheat appeared in every direction; but scarcely any habitations, those that were in sight being so small, and so closely resembling in colour the bare ground, as to be quite inconspicuous. The gray-clay soil showed occasional horizontal bands of sulphide of lime, and several rude lime-kilns appeared at intervals. Towards evening the town of Bujaraloz appeared in the distance. It stood in the middle of a wide depression on the general level of the country, looking verdant with wheat, and close thereto lay a small lake, of perhaps fifty acres in extent. Bujaraloz was to be my stopping-place for the night. By five o'clock I arrived there, and was glad to do so, for the desperately hard ground, the heat—the sun had shone fiercely forth part of the day—and the strong wind, had fatigued me much.

The one *posada* of Bujaraloz was a dirty affair—a very dirty one, and the best meal it could afford me simply wretched. White beans boiled with a little grease in water, bread like that I had had for breakfast, and, boiled together, some cabbage and salt cod—a vile mess. Again I had to ask for wine. Again no napkin was to be had.

After supper, on taking my seat under the hood over the fire, in the dirty den which served for living-room and kitchen, I was immediately accosted in French, and welcomed as a countryman, by two individuals, who I afterwards ascertained to be itinerant French knife-grinders, who, like myself, were for the night guests of the inn. The accent of my answer proved, doubtless, the truth of my statement, that I was English, but my knife-grinding friends seemed not a whit less pleased at finding a person with whom they could converse in a language not understood by the natives, for though they had ground knives, razors, and scissors in Spain for ten years, and spoke Spanish like natives, it evidently did them good—before the face of the people of the country, and without being understood by them—to abuse the ways of the *posadas* of Aragon, and the rough, uncouth behaviour of its peasantry and inn-keepers. "Ah," they said, "we are in a country of savages. It is not like beautiful France!"

I got a better room and bed than I had expected ; both were large and clean. The window-holes were spacious, and the washing apparatus, if limited, sufficient. Of other

furniture there was none. On preparing for bed I discovered why my feet ached, and felt so hot and sore. They
were covered with deep blood-blisters. I was disgusted, for
the stations between me and Lerida were far apart from
one another, and should my feet give out, it would seriously
inconvenience me. Of course there was but one thing for
it, to open my penknife and run the blade through the
blisters—experience had long since taught me that—and,
trusting to be able to resume my march next morning, I
turned in and slept soundly. I had intended an early start,
but, as usual, was frustrated in my endeavour to do so. On
asking for my chocolate in the morning, I was informed the
cook had gone to early matins, and I must wait till she
returned from church. "She will be back in a little
moment," said the landlord—a big, lazy-looking lout, who
was making his *desayuno* on a crust of wretched bread, and
aguardiente, which he drank by "word of mouth" out of
a bottle. The "little moment" proved to be over an
hour.

Truly a trip in Spain is an education in patience. To
waste an hour of the cool of early morn, waiting for an
eggcupful of chocolate and a little thin slice of bread, is
decidedly aggravating. But grumbling on a journey only
annoys the grumbler ; besides, I had not come to Spain to
grumble. I can, did while at home, and will again
when I return, grumble in my own country against its
climate, its cooking, the way the women walk, and, generally speaking, against everything that travel shows England
does not excel in. Is it not my natural inheritance and
birthright, as a Briton, to grumble at everything British

that does not suit me? Yea, I will even, if so inclined, grumble at the income-tax. So with a bland smile, looking, in fact, rather pleased than otherwise, I paid my bill of eight *reals*, handed a small gratuity to the chambermaid, with a parting compliment; and the host, after a preliminary suck at the bottle (his breakfast was evidently to last, at intervals, all day), wishing me to "Go with God," I replied, with a polite wave of the hand, "and you remain with him," and departed.

The morning was simply superb, balmy as spring, not a cloud in the air; the lightest of white frosts melting on the ground; a suspicion of a breeze from the south, just enough for the air not to be stagnant; a ghost of a mist rising on the low grounds; larks singing all round, the goat-bells of distant flocks ringing in the air. I took a good long gaze all round me. The old-time village I had just left, standing by its deep-blue little lake, bathed in the warm haze, distorted into quaint grotesqueness by the vapours stealing from the water's surface, made a sweetly-pretty picture. As I stood there a goatherd passed with a small flock. I inquired if there were any fish in the lake. "Fish! why the lake is so salt and alkaline it is not drinkable for man. It is hardly fit for my goats. The town is supplied by wells, and the water of them is bad," was the answer I received.

The *pastor* and his flock were just disappearing in a hollow to the right, when, to my amazement, I observed three wolves trotting, in Indian file, across the road, just in front. They were, I take it, a female and two males, and looked about the size of large colleys, and very gaunt;

but, being too far off for shot to be effective—about one hundred yards—I did not fire. Juan, too, saw them, but did not appear inclined to cultivate their acquaintance.

The wolves gave the finishing touch to, and were the most appropriate living accessories of, the landscape.

A gradual rise of half a mile's length, a steep acclivity of a couple of hundred yards, took me out of the table-land basin, in whose centre I had left Bujaraloz, up to, and on, a higher level of country, and immediately my view became widely extended. I had a sea's horizon. Around me stretched a broken, accidented plain of small, isolated, perpendicularly-sided, flat-topped hills, with intervening wide, shallow valleys and basins. To my right rose above the horizon what seemed a line of pale blue clouds, drifting into the clear sky, but which I knew to be the far-away *Sierras de Cucalon y San Just*, whose nearest peaks were sixty miles off. And to my left, more than one hundred miles distant, but looking within an easy day's ride, so sharply defined, so brilliantly white, did they glisten in the morning sun, stretched in a long continuous chain of serrated peaks the Pyrenees. Oh, how cold they looked! one immense unbroken sheet of virgin snow.

The prospect, though extensive to vastness, and having many of the elements of the sublime, struck the mind with a sentiment of barrenness and solitude. But for the broad, hard, well-kept highway, I could have fancied myself back again once more on New Mexico's wild plains. The table-topped, precipitous-faced hills were the same as these. The Pyrenees looked exactly like the *Sierra Madre*. The warm, moistureless, clear air, the brilliant sky, were similar;

so, too, was the general hue of everything, and the apparent absence of human habitation.

On looking for details, however, it became at once evident I was in a land of industry, that the expanse around me had to a great extent been conquered by man's hand from the curse of sterility, and converted into a huge granary. The light green tint which covered extensive stretches was given by young wheat; much of the barren-looking portion was ploughed and harrowed ground ; nor were small, low, widely-scattered-apart houses wanting ; but so exactly did the brownish-gray bricks of which they were constructed match in colour with their surroundings, that only after being closely looked for, did they strike the eye. I have since learned that the country I was looking over is, when it does rain in due season, the greatest wheat-field of Spain, but that not few are the years wherein no propitious moisture falls. Then there is no harvest. The young wheat scorches and withers on the ground, and the whole region is indeed a desert.

At nine o'clock I came to a large engraved stone. It marked the north-western boundary of the province of Zaragoza ; another step and I was in that of Huesca.

At half-past ten I reached the little town of Peñalba, and being very hungry, and finding it could boast of a *posada*, repaired to it, and obtained breakfast. It was a very poor meal, like unto, and scarce better than, the one eaten the day previous. The inn resembled much in appearance what one would suppose a highwayman's boosing-ken was like in the time of Dick Turpin. Had it been a decent one, I should have halted for the day, as my poor feet were troubling me ; but the next town being but two hours farther on, I continued my way, hoping there to find more prepossessing accommodation.

Soon after leaving Peñalba, I got amongst small, broken, stony hills, quite devoid of soil, wheat patches disappeared, and for some miles I seemed truly to be traversing a complete waste. Emerging from this forbidding tract, I came to a more level and productive district, and at two o'clock got to the town of Candásnos.

This place at once favourably impressed me by its appearance. A tall, round, white stone chimney, and steam stack, from which issued puffs of steam, was a harbinger and sign of progress. Candásnos is a very little town, but many of its houses are new, and most of its old ones recently whitewashed. I had not seen whitewashed outer walls for many a long league, certainly had not seen clean whitewash since leaving Zaragoza. A short way in town stood a neat trim-looking barrack for the *guardia civil*, and in its porch, chatting and laughing with a lot of girls, sat two members of the corps.

Next to the building having the tall chimney and steam stack was a largish better-class house, the best-looking in the town ; and of the elderly blue-eyed man, who sat in its entrance hall, I inquired where I should find the *posada*. His answer pleased me. "This is the *posada*. You must not pass here without eating and resting. Please enter." And, rising up, he relieved me of my gun and haversack, led me into a clean if bare sitting-room, and asked what would I like to refresh myself with until supper time. It was the first occasion in this country of Spain on which a landlord had received me otherwise than as though I was a nuisance, come to disturb him from his lazy repose, but who, from the nature of his calling, had by him to be tolerated.

I took a glass of *aguardiente*, gladly disencumbered my feet of my walking-boots, and slipped them into my *alpargatas*. Then this attentive old landlord suggested that the sunshine in front of the house made that the pleasantest place to rest, and taking a chair out for me, set it against the wall, and told me to make myself comfortable.

While enjoying repose, warmth, and a *cigarro*, two disreputable-looking individuals, whose dress and physiognomy proclaimed them Frenchmen, came up to and asked me in villainous Spanish if I could understand French. Answering in the affirmative, they told me in that language that I beheld before me two *misérables*, who were in a hard plight —strangers in a country whose language they could not speak, and therefore unable to make their wants known, without money and hungry. Volubly the two Frenchmen commenced then to explain the circumstances that had brought this unhappy state of things to pass. But I cut them short, not being given to believe tales told in such cases, nor wishful to encourage lying by affording opportunity to practise doing so to me, and said their state called for assistance under any circumstances, and then handed them at once all the coin I could conveniently spare. They thanked me with vehement expressions of gratitude and departed.

These two made the number of Frenchmen I have

assisted since I came to Spain three. The first one, I have since ascertained, was a rascal, a swindler, and a thief. These, I had little doubt, were poor devils of deserters; but it was quite possible they were escaped *galériens*.

From me they went straight to the barracks of the *guardia civil*, showed some papers to the two *guardias civiles* in the porch, had quite a confab with, and accompanied by one of them, passed out of sight down the street and round a corner. Before long one of the guardians of order came to the *posada* to ask for my papers. Of him I inquired what sort of chaps the Frenchmen were. He told me that, according to their passport and account of themselves, they were travelling paupers, professing to be on their way to Barcelona in search of work there at their trade of machinists; failing to do which they would leave the country by any ship they could get passage in for their labour. That they had a pass from the civil governor of the province, and a requisition on the *alcaldes* of the towns on their route to give them "the usual assistance." He further told me that in Spain able-bodied pauper foreigners never had any difficulty in getting such papers, provided nothing was known against them, the authorities being glad to pass them on, and get rid of such trash out of the country. "But," said he, "they will keep hungry on the allowance they'll get, for we do not encourage that class of men; and if they leave their designated route, or fail to report themselves to us at every station on it, they'll pretty soon find themselves in prison as rogues and vagabonds. There are lots of such Frenchmen on this route, and more of them than like it in gaol."

Seeing a man go past the front of the *posada*, wearing boots, and sporting a hat on his head, and so evidently one of Candásnos's most superior citizens, I suspected immediately he was the owner or manager of the steam flour-mill, for such I had ascertained the tall-chimneyed building to be ; and inquiry proving this to be so, I watched for his return, and when the opportunity presented itself asked permission to look over his mill, a request that was most politely complied with. Though the day was Sunday, it was in full work. Its engine, an upright cylinder, having the minimum possible amount of gearing, and very direct action, was running a pair of large stones, and doing excellent work. Engine and machinery had been made at Barcelona. The enterprise was only just started, but its proprietor said he had every prospect of making a great success. I hazarded the observation he must have plenty of grain to grind, if it was necessary to run on Sundays. " Indeed," said he, " I have to run when I can get my hands to work. They won't do anything on saints' days, of which there are more, as you know, than there are Sundays, and they'd as soon work as not on the Lord's days. Anyway, that's the priest's business, not mine."

CHAPTER XX.

JANUARY 30, 1877.—The Sunday evening spent at Candásnos was being celebrated by the burning of huge bonfires in its narrow and only street; the day being one of those Sundays specially appointed whereon to pray souls out of purgatory.

Within a distance of sixty yards I counted seven of these tangible reminders of the flames of futurity, each, however, a centre of mirth and revelry; I doubt if anyone there thought of "the great majority." Our blazing pile, the one in front of the *posada*, was not the least of them. Round each were congregated men, women, and children yelling, laughing, and romping; but though Sunday is a great dancing-day in Spain, not a note of the guitar was to be heard. In fact, since leaving Zaragoza I have not even so much as seen one. Possibly, "according to the eternal fitness of things," the guitar, the vine, and the olive go together, and I have no right to expect to hear its twang in a country which only produces wheat.

Supper was a great improvement on my late meals.
Bedroom and bed clean and comfortable. The little cup
of chocolate served promptly in the morning. I felt well
rested and refreshed, paid ten *reals*, and got a comparatively
early start.

At half-past ten o'clock I arrived abreast of a small
roadside settlement, every house of which excepting one was
either a total ruin or nearly such. In their day they had
been residences of people of quality, testified by the stone
armorial sculptures over their broken porches. The one
unruined and inhabited building proved to be a *venta*, and
was my chance for a breakfast. Traversing a wide hall,
cheerful with the sunshine that poured through a large
open double doorway, I entered one of the dark dens
that in the country dwellings of Aragon seem always
to serve for kitchen and parlour, and there perceived
seated on a wooden bench, drinking wine and munching
dry bread, my two vagabond acquaintances of the day
before. They sat regaling themselves with the two
cheapest refreshments of the country, and trying to converse with the only other occupant of the room, a clean,
tidy old woman, seated on the floor opposite them
spinning.

After exchanging salutations, I turned to this spinster,
or old wife, as the case might be, and asked if I could have
breakfast ; and she answering, " Certainly," and proceeding
at once to cooking, I confidently supposed a meal was about
to be prepared for me, and so, to while away the time of
waiting, entered into conversation with the two Frenchmen.

These apostles of " the dignity of labour " soon introduced what was evidently their favourite topic, "the rights of man," launching into a denunciation of "the tyranny of capital," and kindred grievances; evidently they were Socialists, possibly Communists, perhaps Internationalists. One of them showed me his "pass," on the back of which the authorities had from time to time endorsed the several amounts of "relief" given to him, and the dates when. The *guardia civil* was right. The Frenchmen would "keep hungry" on "the usual assistance." A *real* per day seemed what was considered enough for subsistence—a ha'p'orth of wine and two pennyworths of bread, I suppose.

They told me that even their poverty-struck appearance had not prevented them being waylaid in the "bad country" we were in. And one of them narrated that on leaving Peñalba, he and his companion were suddenly pinioned from behind, menaced with knives, stripped, and searched for money. Having but a few *sous*, they were kicked and beaten by the disappointed robbers, and soundy abused for travelling without sufficient money to pay for "the right of the road." However, the few *sous* were not taken from them, which the Frenchmen considered very strange. I did not. To take them would have been, commercially speaking, to take a loss. Absolution for highway robbery would have cost more. And Spanish thieves are all devout Catholics!

Possibly the tale I had just heard was altogether a coinage of its narrator; but it might have been true, the Frenchman gave no other indication of being a romancer, and I was surprised to find, as our conversation continued, how well informed he and his comrade were on questions of political economy, and in the modern history of England as well as of their native country.

Presently the old woman took the eatables off the fire, and carried them out of the kitchen ; and I looked for her return to announce that breakfast was served in the hall. I waited till patience became a vice, and then went to look after her ; she was sitting in the sunlight engaged as when I first saw her, spinning, and asked what did I want. " My breakfast," I exclaimed with emphasis ; " where have you put it ; I am hungry and in a hurry to be gone." " Oh, you never ordered your breakfast," she quietly replied. " I and my family have just eaten ours ; you could have eaten with us. You only asked could you have breakfast. Now you will have to wait till I cook again, and take what you can get ; but I will give you a *home*-made sausage—made of *killed* meat, not of goats and pigs who have *died* like those at most places—and some new-laid eggs, and a salad." And she returned to the kitchen and her cooking. It was provoking, but could not be helped.

I had had enough of the political economists, and sat down in the sunny hall to console myself with a *cigarrilla*. While smoking, a very superior looking mule-waggon drove up, and a middle-aged man of most respectable appearance, and a very pretty, showily-dressed young woman alighted therefrom and entered. The *señor* saluted, and took a seat in the hall. The *señora*, or *señorita*, as she might happen to be, produced a large hand-bag from under a wrap, and disappeared into the kitchen ; to which retreat I, too, soon repaired, to look after my breakfast and the *old* woman, of course. I found my breakfast was nearly

ready, and the newly-arrived traveller, with her gown
pinned back, her skirts and sleeves tucked well up, getting
her and companion's (the *señor's*) breakfast ; for she was
cooking what had been the contents of her hand-bag.

The meals were ready almost simultaneously, and then,
by the two women, set out on the hall-table, upon a clean
white cloth, which was furnished by the young one, who
fetched it out of the mule-waggon, and all three of us sat
down to eat together, having mutually invited one another
to partake of our respective dishes ; I being the clear gainer
by the arrangement, for my new acquaintances had been
well furnished with raw material, and *la señorita*—for she
was not a married woman—was a good as well as a lively
cook.

After we had eaten a few mouthfuls, the *señor* turned
towards and with a most unexceptional accent addressed
me in excellent French ; and after a few complimentary
remarks touching the pleasure of meeting me, &c., he asked
what department I belonged to.

I am continually annoyed by being taken for a Frenchman, not that I consider such mistake a bad compliment,
per se, but I find in Spain the French are most cordially
hated by all degrees of people ; and as, *per contra*, English
are liked, it is annoying, to say the least of it, to be so
misjudged. In this instance I have no doubt I got even
with my unintentional aggravator, for I replied : " Sir, I
am not a countryman of yours, but an Englishman." He
hastened to explain that neither was he French, but a
Spaniard ; adding he, however, supposed few Spaniards
spoke French with such an accent as he did, for he had

enjoyed unusual advantages in acquiring that language, having "passed his class" in France, and also been a traveller, on commission, in that country for six years. He now lived in Zaragoza with his daughter—pointing to the pretty girl beside me—and was an itinerant merchant, also a collector of old coins; and, too, picked up, when possible, pictures of merit for a Paris house. On his present trip he had obtained over three hundred coins, chiefly Roman, and would show me some choice gold ones if I wished. Of course I did. After inspecting them we talked of art in general, and his amount of knowledge on the subject quite surprised me. Our opinions concerning many things coinciding, we were naturally mutually pleased with and impressed by the discernment of each other; and on separating from him, this "itinerant merchant" professed great regret that our ways lay in opposite directions, as had they been similar, he would have been delighted to offer me a seat in his conveyance, so as to be enabled to enjoy the pleasure of my society—a flattering speech that his pretty daughter added a still more gratifying remark to.

Soon after leaving this best *venta* seen since leaving Zaragoza, the country commenced to fall rapidly, and became very broken. All the hillsides and steep grounds were either bare of vegetation or sparsely covered with desert plants. The flats and hollows, however, were green with a much more thriving growth of young wheat than I had before seen since quitting the valley of the Ebro. This thriving condition they owed to their immediate vicinity to steep adjacent acclivities and numerous higher-lying gullies, and to the thorough arrangements which had been made to intercept, catch, concentrate together, and distribute over them every available drop of rain that fell above their level. Indeed, since entering on *Los Monégros*, I noticed with admiration the extensive system of so doing everywhere apparent. Each gully, every washout, all depressions in the ground, were invariably dammed by stone walls, sometimes slight and rough in construction ; at others, in places where torrents—when it did rain—might be expected, of good solid masonry. As a consequence, the land between these stone dams had, in time, from deposit and wear, become quite level, and small ditches served to convey and spread the surplus water running over from one level to another. In short, *Los Monégros*, once a barren waste, apparently a foredoomed desert, has, by the industry of ages, and thanks to the catch-rain arrangements, for the introduction of which Spain owes an eternal debt of gratitude to the Moors, been made a series of scattered wheatfields, some, indeed, little if any larger than billiard-tables, but many of them square miles in extent. The smallness of some of the cultivated spots of ground, lying below the short watersheds, was quite a remarkable feature in the landscape. No matter how small it were, every piece of ground on which it was possible to concentrate the rain-fall seemed to have been seized upon to grow wheat.

The day was lovely as one of England's finest summer ones, larks were singing all round, a flock of plover wheeled and whistled in the air ; the view, though totally lacking the charms of wood and water, and, excepting the birds, seemingly untenanted, was unique and interesting, and but for the state of my feet I should have greatly enjoyed my walk.

As evening was closing in, on rounding a hill, I came in sight of Fraga, the last town in Huesca. It looked large and important, is the *cabeza* of a very large *partido*, and I trusted there to once more find a good inn and the comforts of life.

When I first came in view of Fraga it was still some miles off, but, lying far below me, seemed quite near. Soon the road commenced descending rapidly, winding serpentwise round and along steep hillsides. A splendidly engineered and completed road, having fine ample-sized cut-stone culverts crossing under it wherever necessary, to carry off the wash from gullies, and a continuous stone parapet, breast-high in places, on its perpendicular side. Below ran the Cinca, a river whose head-springs lay behind the Mont Perdu of the Pyrenees, making verdant with its waters a wide valley covered with olives, figs, pomegranates, and vines, and on the steep slope of its opposite side, rising house over house, street above street, the town and its dismantled and ruinous old castle, while, far as eye could see up and down the deep chasm through the table-land which constitutes the valley of the Cinca, a continuous level of rich, luxuriant verdure presented itself to view. Only by the leaflessness of vines and fig-trees could I realise that it was not summer time. An avenue-like road across this Eden of a valley led me to the bridge over the river—a trestle-work, two hundred and eighty yards in length, but only one-third that distance was water, the rest being river shingle, then dry, but, when the Pyrenean snows should melt, to be swept over by a raging torrent.

The street-way between the houses of the town fronting the water and the river's wall was crowded with children, women, and idlers, for the day was the *fiesta* of *San Francisco de Salis.* Their general appearance was forbidding enough, all were dirty and uncouth. I inquired for the best *posada*, and was sent to a large, dilapidated, filthy building near the river's bank. I entered and asked of an untidy but be-ribboned and bedizened young woman, met in the horse-passage, if I could have a room and meals. She did not know ; I must ask the landlord. Where was he ? Did not know again. It was a *fiesta* night; he might not come home till morning.

Starting forth, I searched for another and, I hoped, a better inn. Surely, thought I, in so large a place, the centre and market of so fruitful a valley, the second town in importance and population of the province of Huesca, there must be such.

I wandered about the miserable, stony, steep, uneven streets of Fraga, and saw only hovels and dens. The least bad-looking house I saw was a saddler's shop. I asked the man behind the counter to be directed to a respectable inn—the best. The saddler, evidently from his accent and appearance not a native citizen, directed me to the one I came from.

" But," said I, " it is a beastly hole."

" I know it is," he replied, " but it is the best. None other is fit for a pig."

I told him what the maid had said.

"Never you mind what she told you," he answered. "All she wanted was to drive you away, so as not to have the trouble of making your bed. You go back, and take up your quarters there. You can do no better." So I went.

I entered the kitchen and living-room, sat down on a bench close to the hearth and took items. The room (?) was a funnel chimney, partitioned from the mule quarters by a dirty smoke-dried matting, and lit by a dismal old oil lamp. On the bench round the embers of a fire lolled several men and children, and a dirty slovenly "old fatty" was cooking some sort of a mess in the hot ashes. With much difficulty, and after considerable delay, I procured a supper. Such an apology! One egg, fried with a small hard villainous sausage. I thought of what the clean, tidy old woman of the *venta* had said about *posada* sausages, and I had my suspicions—very strong suspicions. A small loaf of the worst bread I have yet tasted in Spain, and a glass of poor wine, comprises the total of all I could get for self and dog. What a meal! It was served on a bare filthy table. A dirty wooden spoon was the only table utensil. I did not linger over that feast (?).

It was getting chilly, and I rejoined the group around the fire to warm and smoke. In person, in language, in manners, they were the most dirty, uncivilised, rough people I ever sat under a roof with. My remarks to them were either unanswered or replied to by a grunt, nor to one another were they more courteous. There was but one good-looking person present—a young mother with an infant in her lap ; she was quite pretty, had really refined regular feaures, but otherwise was as bad as the rest.

Her baby requiring washing, the operation was performed publicly in the following and, to me, novel manner : This madonna-faced female took her infant by one ankle, raised the young child up, and giving it a good shake, reversed all its clothes ; baby yelling like mad all the time. The old cook then held handy to her reach, and half full of water, the glass I had drunk out of at supper, and the mother, dipping therein the corner of a dirty apron, gave baby a smear all over with it, wiped it dry with her petticoat, and the ablution was completed. Then she rolled her brat up in numerous dirty wraps, and put it to sleep on an old sheepskin in a corner !

I had had enough and to spare of such society, and asked to be shown my room. The one redeeming feature of the chamber I was led to consisted in its not being dirty —at least, not very. It was about eight feet square and had no window, excepting a hole four inches by three in dimensions, situated close to the ceiling and opening into a dark passage. A truckle-bed was all the furniture and appurtenances it contained. In appearance it was a condemned cell in fact, a "demned" sell to offer to a white man as a bedroom. Of course this black-hole was equally dark by day or night, so every time I awoke I had to strike a light and consult my watch to ascertain it it were yet morning ; and at last discovering it was, I lit the dismal oil lamp that had been left with me and dressed. Of course I could not wash, and I knew it would be futile to ask for a basin, towel, and water, let alone soap. I do not believe there were such things in the house. Everybody in it had old dirt on their hands and face. The extensive (?) ablutions of the baby the night before were probably as heavy a wash as is ever made in the best *posada* of that city of the province of Huesca, which stands in rank next to its capital, a city of four thousand souls. I had to wait nearly an hour for my chocolate, the lump with which it was made having to be fetched from a shop, there being none in the house, and the girl doubtlessly availing herself of her errand to enjoy a gossip. I gladly quitted the vile place. Fraga is not fit for a white man and a Christian to visit.

CHAPTER XXI.

FEBRUARY 1, 1877.—Climbing up the steep road that,
winding up bare gray cliffs to the broken table-land above,
led from Fraga and out of the deep valley of the Cinca,
though depressed at starting by recent uncomfortable experiences, my spirits were soon rallied and invigorated by
a balmy tonic morning air, and consoled by the reflection
it was the last day of my pilgrimage across *Los Monégros*.
It was another most charming morning. I was on the
home-stretch for Lerida—there I would rest and enjoy
myself; so when my feet, warming to their work, ceased to
hurt, I was once more the jolly wanderer.

The top of the ascent was nearly achieved, when, being
hailed from below and looking back, I perceived a farmer-
like man striving to overtake me. On his so doing, he
saluted most respectfully and apologised for calling out
to me, alleging as excuse he had considerable money on
him, so did not like to risk travelling alone, and knew he

could do no better than journey in the company of the
inspector of roads, especially as he noticed my worship
carried a gun. I told him I was not the inspector of
roads, but an Englishman travelling for pleasure. "Ah!"
said he, "that is just as good so far as protection goes, and
better so far as obtaining information does, for I love
greatly to hear of foreign countries, especially of England."
And forthwith I found myself, figuratively speaking, witness-
boxed. My inquisitive friend seemed a very intelligent
individual. He was not of Aragon, and gave that portion
of the ancient kingdom we were in a very bad name ; said
it was the worst portion of the Spains; that Fraga was "*un
posoalbanal*" (sink-hole), and its people —— (an unwritable
and untranslatable word). I cordially agreed with him.
This good man showed me several short cuts across table-
topped hills, from whose flat summits splendid views of the
Pyrenees and mountain chains of Northern Huesca presented themselves, and round whose bases wound the well-
graded waggon-road to Lerida, for the general level of the
country was again falling.

After going three miles in company, my companion left
me, the house he was going to being close at hand, and I
had not long parted from him when I was overhauled
by a regular tramp and his "doxy." These illustrious
individuals were not at all proud stuck-up people, and
without the slightest encouragement insisted on accommodating their pace to mine, whether I loitered or pushed
on, and in talking to me. The man spoke excellent
Castellano, without any detectable local accent; and accepting the inevitable, I fell into conversation with him. This

vagabond told me he had served in the war twenty years ago; had been once attached to an English contingent; spent a few weeks in England, having gone there as an officer's servant, but could only speak a few words of that country's language, which he immediately fired off for my benefit, but with an accent that rendered them almost unintelligible.

The day became distressingly hot. We were traversing an almost barren alkali plain; the few attempts at agriculture were, for the season at least, manifest failures. The appearance of the country surrounding us was simply wretched; the hot acrid alkaline dust got into my boots, through my socks. My feet commenced to give me "the devil," and I was unhappy.

On leaving this uninviting stretch of country by a long hill, we passed near its summit the boundary line between Aragon and Catalonia, and his trampship informed me I was arrived in a more civilised region than the one we had just left. A little farther on and we came to a *venta*. The tramp, with the air of a grave courtier, invited me to enter, and repose and refresh myself with him. I was quite tired, very hungry, and complied with his request. The woman, who was companion and *señora* to this beggarly *caballero á pié*, produced out of a dirty, dusty, and travel-stained canvas sack she had been carrying over her shoulder, a stale *tortilla* and some bread, and proceeded to warm the former in the hot ashes of the hearth; and he called in a lordly way for a bottle of wine, which with difficulty I prevailed upon him to allow me to pay for. It cost twopence. With the warmed-up *tortilla*, the woman brought to the table whereat her companion and I were seated, a clean plate for me, and the two insisting I should help myself, I did so, and being hungry, found it excellent; the bread, however, was indifferent.

Whilst we were eating, two mounted *guardias civiles* rode up, entered, and asked for our papers.

These functionaries looked sharply and, I thought, suspiciously enough from me to my companions and back again. They were puzzled to see such a strangely-assorted trio; indeed, I felt myself to be in queer company. The raggedest, most sinister-looking, sturdy beggar of England would have, in personal appearance, compared favourably with the man. As to the woman, she was in all respects a fit and appropriate mate for him; and, as usual with such females, was " as women wish to be who love their lords." Their and my papers being, however, *en règle*, the two *guardias* could only wonder and pass on.

Having concluded our slight repast, we three, still in company, proceeded on our way.

Before arriving at the little town of Alcarraz, where I purposed to get a regular breakfast and take a good rest, I made a determined attempt to escape from the tramps. They had been polite, after their fashion, and hospitable, but I did not want to enter a town in such disreputable company; and they showing symptoms of fatigue, and lagging on the way, I pretended to be in a hurry, and wishing them *a dios*, put on a killing spurt. It was rough on my blistered feet, but I went ahead at a pace the tired tramps could not live at, and soon was at a safe distance ahead.

Alcarraz, though but a little place, showed signs of much improvement on the towns I had lately passed ; and, in it, I directly found a clean, respectable *venta*, and—the second encountered in Spain—civil, *empressé* landlord. He, too, took gun and traps from, and gave his guest a hearty and polite greeting. This commendable host was smoking a very good cigar, and after conducting me into a clean dining-room, handing a chair, and requesting my worship to be seated, produced another from a case, and offered it with an air and manner rendering refusal impossible. It would assist, as he said, to pass the time comfortably while breakfast was being prepared.

My *déjûner à la fourchette* at Alcarraz's little *venta* was a very fair meal, properly appointed, well served, and its accompanying wine excellent ; and, after my late unfortunate experience in the commissarial line, I enjoyed it thoroughly. Then I fed my dog, took a good rest, another smoke, paid the modest and, considering my entertainment, extremely reasonable bill of fifteen pence, and then pushed on for Lerida.

Soon the two fortified hills, ancient Gothic cathedral tower, and closely-packed houses of that provincial capital were in sight ; the district of ill-repute—*Los Moncgrons*—was passed, and the view changed in character.

A charming panorama was before me. Through its foreground wound the many bends and curves of a beautiful river—the Segre—whose upper portion, skirting the foot of the Pyrenean mountains of *La Cerdana*, coursing down the valley north of the *Sierra del Cadi*, was fed by the snows of the *Col de la Percha* in Roussillon—a river that is a French tribute to Spain. Irrigated by its fertilising waters, extended for miles a level tract of vineyards, olives, and almonds, gardens and nurseries, dotted with houses and clumps of shade-trees. Beyond, were the *Llanos del Urgel*, a vast plain strongly accentuated with detached ridges, small table-mountains, and sharp peaks ; looking, generally speaking, from its gray-brown colour, to be a desert tract ; but evidently, in truth, only partially such, as proved by there being no less than five towns of considerable size in sight ere distance rendered more invisible. On the horizon were the blue mountains of *La Llena* and Montserrat, and through a gap in the hills to the north was obtainable a peep of the snow-clad Pyrenees. Above was a sky of cloudless blue. A warm sunset glow brightened and illumined the entire picture.

Twilight was approaching as I walked into Lerida, and no time was to be lost in finding quarters.

I walked along a street facing the river Segre, prospecting for a promising resting-place, and had not gone far when a well-built, clean, comfort-suggesting, large-windowed cheerful-looking *fonda* — it was no *posada*, no *venta*— claimed my notice. On its wide balcony, three attractive and elegantly-attired girls and two young officers were chatting together, mutually entertaining each other. If I went farther I might fare worse. I entered the courtyard —clean as any gentleman's—passed through the large open door of the house, and stood in a spacious stall. A trim, well-built, *très-élancée*, smart waiting-maid appeared, and asked if I required a room. I did.

"Then please follow me, and I will show your worship to one."

She led the way up a wide, easy flight of steps, across a long, tastefully-decorated upper hall—whose French windows opened to the balcony so agreeably occupied, and into as comfortably-furnished a bed-chamber as any single man need wish for; told me the hours of meals, the charge per day, and, on my expressing satisfaction with the room, inquired what I would like to take before dinner-time should arrive. I told her a large jug of hot water. The girl stared with astonishment, for something to eat and drink was her idea of my requirements. I explained: "Not to drink, but to wash with; I do not want to spoil my appetite for dinner." She brought it and left me.

With the expenditure of much soap—of which, by-the-bye, there was a tablet of excellent quality on the washstand-table—and personal exertion I got rid of the real estate I had accumulated while journeying from Zaragoza, dressed the blisters on my feet with tobacco, and felt comfortable. Once again I was in a civilised house, and, being in Spain, felt sure of good company, good living, and an absence of insect tormentors. I had "fallen on my feet." I would stop where I was until they were well.

Juan stretched himself on the carpet of striped crimson and yellow matting covering the waxed oaken floor, evidently satisfied. He knew the quarters were good as well as I did, that once more we were in clover. The dog was as footsore as his master, as glad to come to an anchor. That long road of iron hardness, the penetrating alkaline dust, the hot sun, the long *journadas*, the poor and scanty fare that had so often been our portion had, too, told on him.

A few days at mine inn has proved I made a lucky hit when entering it. The table is both profusely liberal and extremely choice ; the cooking excellent ; and I profess to know something of that fine art, both theoretically and practically, having turned my attention to it as one of those things everybody ought to understand.

My only dissatisfaction as regards the living is with the wine, which is a Bordeaux. Being infinitely dearer than the native wine, it is of course more fashionable, and, therefore, I suppose our hostess, who naturally from her sex is a better judge of fashion than wine, thinks her house ought to give such to its guests. In my opinion, as compared to what I have been lately drinking, it is most inferior. I shall have to go through a course of English beer before I can again take proper pleasure in Bordeaux. Neither do the almonds suit my taste, for, as always in this country, they are quite spoiled ; but I do not mind that. The custom here is to slowly roast them, a process which entirely dissipates the essential flavour, and substitutes therefor that of roasted wood ; in fact, they become no better than so many acorns which have been similarly treated. The reason alleged for this barbarity is, so doing renders the almonds less un-wholesome. I say, what is the use of being at the trouble of making anything wholesome, if at the same time you render it not worth eating ?

The cook here, a white-garmented individual wearing the cap of his order, tells me he has served " with approba-

tion " in French, Italian, and English houses, and I have
no doubt he has. We have held several arguments
together touching the relative merits and demerits of
French and Spanish cooking ; for, to elicit opinion, and in
consequence of natural contrariness, I, as usual, espoused
the opposition. But I am a badly defeated individual.
The *chef* maintained that the French were good " dis-
guisers," but totally failed as " developers," and that to be
able to develop natural flavours, not to destroy, obliterate,
or confuse them, proved the *artiste*.   " Eat of twenty French
dishes," said he, "and if you look not at the carte I defy
you to tell what they profess to be made of, for every true
flavour is so overlaid with that of foreign sauces that the
several dishes cease to be mutton, beef, venison, and are
simply messes. Did not the famous cook of the Duc
Decazes serve up an ancient pair of his master's hunting-
boots, which an assembled tableful of guests pronounced to
be excellent eating ; and is not such feat (?) recorded by
them as a triumph of culinary skill ?   I say doing so proves
a state of hopeless misdirection of talent.   If *I* as a *Spanish*
cook had directed the cooking of those old boots, I would
have brought out their true flavour so strongly that no man
living could eat of them.   In a word, French cooks spoil
good victuals, but make trash eatable. *We* make good
raw material divine, and leave trash to the dogs."

This learned cook was too many guns for me ; I limbered
up, and left him master of the situation—did not propose to
make practical disproof of his ability to serve up old boots
in such a manner that I could not eat them.

The *chef* is the only indoor male domestic, the rest of

the house servants—waiters, or rather waitresses, included
—being clean, neat, smart, and attentive girls.

The guests of the *fonda* are a very pleasant lot, but
not numerous. About twenty generally sit down to dinner,
most of them transients ; but there is a little party at the
upper end of the table of *habitués*, some of whom have
been in the house over a year. They are quite friendly and
jocose together, and amongst them I have succeeded in
getting myself placed, and have already fraternised with
several and got on good terms with all. The principal
individuals of this coterie are the Medical Director of the
provincial military hospital, the District Colonel of *guardias
civiles*, a major of engineers, two subalterns of infantry, and
the Director-General of the telegraph department for the
province ; a married couple, rather stylish people, are here
too. The husband is so lover-like in his attentions as to
provoke smiles from the rest of the company. Did not
the "great expectations" of the lady forbid the idea, it
might be supposed the couple were passing their honeymoon.

With the colonel is a young lady, his daughter, I
presume, who is extremely pretty. She is here supposed
to be of the English type of beauty. And I am continually
asked if this is not so. National pride forbids me to say :
her complexion is of a too delicate hothouse fineness, her
hands and feet altogether too small for any critical Englishman to take her for his countrywoman, otherwise she is
quite English in appearance.

The three girls I saw on the balcony are the daughters
of the house, the eldest being hostess and manageress—a
great charge for so young a woman, but the *fonda* could
not be better conducted. The father is the proprietor of

the *fonda*, and a widower, old, and takes no further trouble. The family are rich for their position, owning, besides this property, an estate near Barcelona paying a large rental, but I suppose the *fonda* is too profitable to be given up. These girls appear to be well educated, talk French fluently, play the piano—one of them with great taste and execution—and are quite ladies in language and behaviour.

In the *señoritas'* sitting-room there is a nightly reunion of the privileged ; the colonel and the " English beauty," the telegraph and medical chiefs, the three officers, various visiting *señoritas*—friends of the girls—the daughters of the house, and, in spite of all protestations, explanations, and travel-damaged *tenue*, the so-called " milor " comprise the gathering. And, as one of the girls said the other evening, " We talk about everything we understand and everything we do not, and oftenest about the latter."

One of the young infantry officers here sings and plays nicely. He is Andalusian, and has been very polite to me. Our acquaintance began at table. Sitting opposite at the mid-day breakfast, he heard me remark to my right-hand neighbour, with whom I had entered into conversation, that I should much like to see the interior of the citadel and the old cathedral enclosed within the fortifications. Addressing me across the table, he volunteered to obtain for me from the Military Governor permission to do so, and get the keys of the cathedral doors from their custodian ; adding, that being off duty all the remainder of the day, he placed his time entirely at my disposal, if I felt inclined to accept his company and guidance. Of course I was " delighted," and we went accordingly.

CHAPTER XXII.

FEBRUARY 7, 1877.—Lerida's citadel is a fortified eminence immediately behind and dominating the town. The situation is one of great natural strength, for the hill is an isolated one, not commanded from anywhere, not large in its base, and carrying its size well up, being, indeed, unscalably perpendicular almost everywhere. Its height is close on three hundred feet, and the only practicable approach is over three drawbridges, each with its accompanying strong arched gateway and portcullis, on all which the fire from several redoubts, curtains, covered ways, and a long " serpent " can be converged. The outer gateway and its defences are the most modern of the works, and were finished in 1708.

The ancient cathedral stands within the most interior line of defence, crowning the highest part of the hill's summit, and close to the right-angled edge of the perpendicular side thereof facing the river, and has a reputation

of being the oldest, handsomest, most original in design, and strictly pure specimen of Gothic architecture in Spain, some say in Europe. Certainly, so far as I have seen, this is so, and if there be one surpassing it in all these qualities I sincerely hope some day to behold it. Its proportions, sculptured figures, tracery in stone, entrance porches, supporting arches, are all of exceeding merit.

In an elaborately and richly-carved recess to the left of the altar in the chief chapel lay a life-sized figure of a reclining ecclesiastic, as fine a thing of the kind as I ever saw. An accompanying inscription was beyond my deciphering power ; that it was in monkish Latin, all the letters capitals, no divisions between the words, and the date obliterated by age, was the extent of my discoveries. Fortunately I was more successful with an inscription the lieutenant called my attention to, situated on the right side of the choir, which, unless I am greatly deceived, sets forth that the foundation-stone of the cathedral was laid in 1203 in the presence of King Pedro II.

We ascended the winding stairway, enclosed in the octagon tower, by two hundred and thirty-four steps. Though deeply worn, they averaged ten inches in height in front, certainly they must be two inches thicker behind, thus giving the tower an altitude of between two hundred and thirty and two hundred and forty feet to its belfry floor, beyond which are no steps. The view we obtained thence was very fine and extended, quite bird's-eye so far as Lerida is concerned, and panoramic as to the rest—plains, mountains, rivers, and towns.

Then we noticed the bells and ancient clockwork, quite

curiosities from age and quaint construction. At four of the corners of the parapet round the belfry were the remains of watch-fire gratings, from which, doubtless, many a signal blazed forth during the first three or four hundred years of the cathedral's existence.

Descending the corkscrew stairway, we made our way to what was once the palace of the archbishop—a large oblong building, coeval with the cathedral. It is now used as a military storehouse and quarters. Everything in it was in soldierlike order and condition, excepting the instruments in the band-room. Thinking the opportunity a good one to learn the reason that the musical instruments of Spanish regimental bands are so generally dirty, I asked why those before us were in such a state. "I do not know," replied the lieutenant, "but will find out." He called up a man and asked him. The answer seemed strange to me.

"We are only musicians, not mechanics; if we took our instruments to pieces to clean them properly we could never put them together again; only an instrument-maker could do that."

I wonder what an English bandmaster would think if such a reason were given by one of his musicians for a cornet being disgracefully dirty?

The stores visited, we lighted *cigarros* and made the tour of the fortifications, of which I can give no description, merely remarking that now I know them, I should still less like to lead a "forlorn hope" to attempt their capture than I probably should had I remained in a state of ignorance of their strength.

We returned to our *fonda* by the public promenade, for it was the fashionable hour to take a stroll, and, as my companion said : " We can see the beauties of Lerida as we go along."

Walking by the side of my elegantly-attired acquaintance of that morning's making, I could not help mentally inquiring how many *young* British officers would volunteer themselves as cicerone to show the lion of the place and their garrison (for the cathedral is now a barrack) to an unintroduced foreigner, dressed in clothes hardly respectable from the wear and stains of such a trip as I am making, whose face was sunburnt and weatherbeaten, and who would afterwards allow himself to be seen by all the fashionables of the place, walking in familiar converse with him on the public promenade ? I fear not many. But I presume a Spanish officer and gentleman, however youthful, considers his rank and position too assured, too unquestionable, for him to fear misconstructions.

After resting awhile, the lieutenant proposed our doing the places of worship now in use, and we accordingly proceeded to the parish church of San Lorenzo, being the one ranking next in age and merit to the old cathedral. This edifice stands on a lesser eminence than the fortified hill, just in its front, and not far therefrom ; and a priest told me : " It was built in the latter part of the thirteenth century, so is now something over six hundred years old."

Thence we strolled to the new cathedral—an edifice constructed by order of the king when the old one became a barrack of the fortress in 1707. It is considered a very sacred building, for in its sacristy are deposited our Saviour's swaddling-clothes (*credat Judæus*). This new cathedral is decidedly, for a Spanish church, ugly. Built in the poorest, baldest possible style ; an attempt at, and failure in achievement of, being classic. Its interior is profusely gilt, and full of most indifferently-conceived and worse-executed images and figures. Then we took an outside view of the archiepiscopal palace, a still more modern structure and a fine range of buildings. There were more churches to see, but I had had enough of that kind of entertainment for one day ; besides, it was almost dinner-time.

Last Friday being that of *La Purificacion de Nuestra Señora*, a masked ball in celebration and commemoration of that event was given by the " Society of Arts and Belles-Lettres of Lerida." It is an annual affair, and *the* ball of the place. I was honoured by an invitation, and would have gladly gone—wishing, as a matter of course, to see a Spanish masked ball "of society"—but could not procure a fitting costume on so short a notice ; and, though pressed to go as I was, did not think it would be in good taste to do so, and, therefore, most determinedly declined. However, the colonel and girls insisted I should at least accompany them to see the rooms and decorations, declaring they would go before the company would arrive, so that I might look at everything at my convenience.

The hall of the society was a good-shaped but very small ball-room, having only a capacity for eight quadrille sets to dance at a time. It was most tastefully decorated ; and ante-rooms were numerous, and well supplied with toilet, &c., arrangements. After taking a look, we all went up a flight of stairs to inspect the society's " art collection " in a room above the hall. There were about fifty pictures hung on its walls ; the best being some very fair copies of works of Rubens and Murillo. The remainder consisted of copies, in oil, of well-known chromos, a few original—very original—landscapes, and some creditable pencil sketches. On the table were set a few academy busts and figures, and several albums filled with identically the same pictures that in England are affixed on handkerchief, glove, and sweet-meat boxes! If the society's *belles-lettres* are not superior to their *beaux arts*, there is room for advance in both branches.

Saturday was the *Fiesta* of *San Blas*—a martyr-bishop who still works miracles by curing, in some way not clearly explained to me, sore throats ; I wish he would cure my blistered feet. The proper way here to observe this church festival is to go on a picnic ; and, therefore, the roads lead-ing out of town were thronged with people, baskets on arm ; and on all sides groups were to be seen seated on the ground eating and drinking. A Spanish town of nearly twenty thousand souls can, for such a purpose, turn out a goodly number of devotees.

The picnickers were small tradesfolk, servants, and working people ; but, promenading the roads as lookers-on, were a large majority of the fashionables of Lerida—chiefly military and official people, got up in the latest style, mira-culously gloved and booted. Amongst them a hand or foot of average British proportions was not to be seen. In fact, since leaving Navarra I have observed the extremities of the upper classes getting smaller and still more small, and am beginning to believe that, excepting the labourers,

Spaniards are truly a small and handsome handed and footed people.

In the afternoon I witnessed the first street squabble I have seen in Spain. Two middle-aged peasants, quite sober I think, exchanged a few hard words, and then, more like Britons than Frenchmen, instead of venting their feelings in violent gesticulations and noisy clamour, they pitched into one another. But they fought just like children. The combat was soon over. A cavalryman who happened to be passing called on them to desist, and to enforce his order promptly drew his sabre and most impartially belaboured the peacebreakers with the flat of it—a rough-and-ready policing that quickly brought the combatants to order.

Lerida, though the capital, and in all respects chief town of one of Spain's largest provinces, is quite the reverse of being a handsome city. It has not one really good street or *plaza*. Its public buildings are ugly and mean, its shops small, dowdy, and uninviting ; but the place shows signs of progress. It is spreading, and every addition is after a modern and more civilised fashion. Ere long the town will have at least one fine thoroughfare, and not only are its streets lit with gas, but also many of its shops and dwelling-houses. Lerida is also clean and devoid of foul smells—two excellences rare enough in many of the Spanish towns I have seen.

The fine river fronting its chief street, and the expanse of country beyond, afford a most pleasing prospect to the eye ; and the weather whilst I have been here has impressed me with the idea that its climate is superb. But I am told it is not always so, winds from the Pyrenees bringing cold and fogs. This time last year, I am informed, water froze in the bedroom jugs, and for twenty days the sun was obscured either by fog or clouds. However, I have everywhere heard this season is an exceptionally fine one.

Just across the bridge over the Segre lies the city's chief promenade—a miniature Tuileries gardens, five hundred yards long by seventy yards in breadth. It is tastefully planted and arranged in flower-beds, in shrubbery, in gravel-walks, &c., and well furnished with shade-trees. Beyond, and close thereto, are the *Campos Elyseos*, a sort of botanical garden and place of respectable gaiety. It contains a summer theatre, large dancing-floor, shady groves and avenues; and there, during the season, a regimental band plays on two evenings of each week, and numerous and frequent *bals champêtres*, theatrical performances, &c., &c., are patronised by all classes. I am told that from early spring until late in the autumn, the *Campos Elyseos* is a very paradise of flowers; now, both it and the promenade are almost flowerless, untidy, and forlorn.

The stone bridge connecting these *paseos* with town boasts of great antiquity, that is to say its site, as such, does. The present structure stands upon foundations laid before Christ by the Romans. And it is related on authority "not to be disputed" that, just below where it stands, Herodias and the fascinating *bailarina*, her daughter, while showing off on the light fantastic, on the ice, to an admiring audience crowding the ancient bridge, broke through and perished, and, strange to relate, the ice closing over their bodies, cut off the head of her whose feet had danced off St. John's, and the unhappy head continued the step and figure of the dance, *la jota*, until exorcised by the "Catholic parish priest!"

The present bridge over the Segre is two hundred yards in length, and has seen better days—shows signs of much adversity. Of its four standing arches no two are of the same age, shape, or size, and I think even the oldest is not original, but a repair of a catastrophe. The river is subject to tremendous and destructive freshets. Not many years ago an unusually heavy flood brought down the half of the bridge nearest town. The gap has been replaced by a lattice-work iron structure, which, it is believed, allowing the water to pass through it, will stand the pressure. I doubt it—think it will leave its supports.

There is more money in this dilapidated old capital of Lerida than appearance indicates. For instance, there are here a great many men whose private incomes range from eight hundred to twelve hundred pounds a year—considerable sums in so cheap a country as Spain ; but none of them keep a carriage nor even saddle-nags ; they live in houses whose outsides are neglected, dirty, and untidy to the last degree ; hang their washing to dry over the railings of the front balconies of their residences, and on strings tied across the windows facing the streets ; do not entertain, and, except that their manners and tables are good, and their dress extravagantly so, live like the rest of the community and hoard their money. Andalusians, Aragonese, Castillians, all agree in telling me, except for personal show and pageantry, that it absolutely hurts a Catalan to part with even the smallest coin ; that they are more "cannie" than Scotch, more "close" than Yankees,

The telegraph department chief is extremely attentive and kind ; asks me out to walk with him each afternoon, and shows and explains everything of interest. He is Andalusian, and by all odds the best-informed man on scientific topics as well as general subjects I have yet met in Spain. He says I must not judge "the Spains" by what I have seen; that I have passed through the worst part of the peninsula, and its most uncouth inhabitants. I take the statement as I do the country's nuts—with a considerable amount of salt—for I have discovered there is a terribly strong sectional feeling pervading the minds of even the most enlightened Spaniards.

It appears to me this is, socially and politically, a country of five Irelands, each discontented with the central authority, no matter what party wields it, and cordially hating and despising the other four. I see evidences of this being so every day, and have all the time. While at a convivial party, when in Guipuzcoa, being towards the small hours called on for a toast, I had given " *Viva España ;* " to my mortification and surprise, the filled and half-raised glasses were, without exception, set down on the table, and the host, rising to his feet, addressed me thus : " Much appreciated sir, it is from no disrespect to you that all present refuse to drink the toast you have, doubtlessly intending a compliment, favoured us by proposing. Kindly substitute for ' España ' ' Guipuzcoa,' and the sentiment will be received with enthusiasm, but no true Basques will drink ' *Viva España,*' far sooner would they drink ' *C——jo al España.*'"

My usual morning ramble, to exercise my dog, is along

the banks of the Segre, and I daily admire the simplicity and effectiveness of the only floating flour-mill I have ever seen, and which, being situate opposite where I usually terminate my walk, I sit, and contemplate, while resting.

It consists of two barges, sixteen feet apart, but decked together with strong timbers, "Castalia steamship" fashion. On one of the barges is a wooden house—the mill; between them is the motive power—an undershot wheel, of fourteen feet diameter and twenty floats making seven revolutions per minute. These Siamese-twin barges are moored by iron cables close to the bank of the river, in a rapid, and at an angle to and catching the course of its stream. It is the cheapest constant power I have yet met with. The mill has been steadily going, night and day, since 1863, consuming only a trifle of lubricating oil, requiring but slight repairs, wanting no trained engineer, no refittings of expensive gearing, and having no boiler to prime or burst.

There are plenty of rivers in England with, in places, sharp enough currents to run such machines. Why are they not so utilised?

The dress of the Catalan peasant differs but slightly from that of the Aragonese, but that little suffices to invest it with a totally different aspect. It is, in the case of the men, simply a change of headgear, and an addition of short gaiters, covering the calf of the leg, of brown leather. The provincial (they call it national) head-dress is of red-cloth, shaped almost exactly as is, and looking just like, an old English nightcap of preposterous size; the very counterpart of the stage's traditional smuggler's cap. But, all things being comparative, instead of giving the wearers a lawless look, in my eyes, now used to the handkerchief brow-bound, bare-crowned Aragonese, they look to be as much like quiet, civilised people, as those appear to resemble half-wild savages. The costume of the women is also more modernised. The petticoats are again long and less voluminous, and the waists of a reasonable shape and size.

My friend the telegraph chief took me yesterday to see the public cemetery, which is about half a mile out of town, and on the opposite side of the Segre, and obtained my admittance. It is a very beautiful one, and, though typical as regards this country, very different from anything of the kind to be seen in Great Britain. The Lerida cemetery is a square enclosure of several acres in extent, divided by gravel-walks, bordered by tall cypress-trees, and dotted with many extremely handsome monuments, and not a few of great antiquity. There certainly was not a single unsightly one, nor any of my chief aversion—tombstones. The cemetery grounds are enclosed by a continuous building of white stone pierced by four gateways, each one of which is in the centre of a side. Along this boundary building runs on the inside a wide covered pavement, whose roof is supported on arches—cloisters in fact—while it (the building) consists of four tiers of small niches, or receptacles, for coffins; above-ground vaults they might be described as.

The mode of burying is to place the coffin in a niche and brick it up a foot back from the flush of the wall. In the space left a memorial marble, or more frequently a metal frame, having a glass door, is cemented. In the latter case the frame contains wreaths, inscription scrolls, and ribbons, flowers, little wax saints, &c., &c., invariably artistically arranged. Many of the most recent ones contain photographic portraits of the departed, as they appeared in the flesh, handsomely mounted and framed. In the centre of the side of the range, facing the main gateway, is a very pretty mortuary chapel, and in it I observed three ladies and a little girl on their knees, before the shrine, praying. On each side of the principal cemetery grounds are large annexes, where those who like to be really buried can have their wishes gratified by being put underground. In them were some monuments, but not many. Evidently the niches with the pretty fronts were preferred.

CHAPTER XXIII.

Preparations for the Carnival—Playing the Fool—The Carnival Procession—
"Seeing the Folly of it "—The *Bal Masqué*—Midnight Ceremonies—The
Devil takes "Pau Pi "—Tender Farewells—Departure from Lerida—
Spanish Peasantry—On the Way—A badly-matched Pair.

FEBRUARY 15, 1877.—The Thursday before Carnival
Sunday was a preparatory *fiesta ;* and at eleven o'clock a
cavalcade of maskers formed in front of our hotel, headed
by a band of music and a triumphal car, bearing a boy
dressed up as a goddess of something or other, and thence
made a peregrination of the town, collecting money as they
went, towards defraying the expenses of the approaching
carnival. It was a well-got-up procession, if small. The
fantastically-dressed and masked musicians were regimental bands, and made very good music. The triumphal
car was a cart belonging to our *fonda*, and had been
decorated in the yard.

The carnival is to be unusually well observed this year,
and considerable money has been already placed in the
hands of the committee of ceremonies, who have the direction of affairs. The weather promises to be all that can be
desired ; the only fear is, that the pedestrians will find it too

U

hot for comfort, midday being now as warm as it ever gets
to be in England's summer, while wasps and butterflies are
already numerous.

The inhabitants of Lerida seem especially fond of having
architectural designs and landscape scenery painted on
the outside of their houses.   The designs are generally very
good, and their execution admirable, but unfortunately,
from economical motives, the vehicle used is distemper.
At home a week would obliterate them. Here they last for
years, but soon acquire a dirty, washed-out look, and being
never touched up, render a building's appearance worse
than if no attempt at mural decoration had been made.

The chief of the telegraph department has been my
great companion here, and our daily walks together are
invariably prolonged into the country, for he is a great
lover of the picturesque and nature.   About the beauties of
Andalusia he is most enthusiastic; says I have not seen
Spain's show district, and promises me much pleasure if
ever I am tempted to visit his country. Our stroll generally
winds up with a seat in the *Campos Elyseos*, and a *cigarro*,
whose flavour is rather helped than otherwise by the perfume
from beds of narcissi in full flower, over which flit and
dart numberless sphinx convolvuli.   And this is early
February !

I had intended a full, true, particular, and detailed
account of carnival time as spent in the ancient city of
Lerida, but have been (for once in a while, let us say) so
busy playing the fool, that I have taken no notes whatever ;
while masks and ankles, *bromas* and intrigue, music and
wine, noise and folly, are so mixed and muddled up together

in my brain that I find my recollection of incidents a complete maze. And perhaps it is as well, for I cannot tell of my own foolishness without revealing that of others ; and to do the first would be *une bétise*, the last not the fair thing.

The grand procession on Carnival Sunday was extremely good, and the dresses of the maskers as nearly correct as possible—some of them very expensive—and the characters well sustained. It was twenty-five minutes in passing our balcony, which, by-the-way, was subjected to an almost continual bombardment of comfits, flowers, and sweetmeats —a tribute to the youth and beauty collected there, which latter was considerable. The order of procession was as follows :

Four Soldiers and a mounted Commander (time of Charles V.).
Giants (dance of cudgels).
Dwarfs.
Impostors (a numerous group).
Students of Folly, directed by their respective Masters.
Band of Trumpeters.
Infantry with Chief and Standard (time of Charles V.).
Cavalry Escort (time of Charles V.).
Allegorical Cars and Groups, representing the different Towns of the Province.
Representation of Lerida.
. Band.
Mounted group of Chinese.
„   „   Indians.
„   „   Greeks.
„   „   Romans (ancient).
„   „   Turks (very ferocious).
„   „   Persians.
„   „   Africans.
„   „   Arabs.

Allegorical cars of " Gambling," " Heroes," " Quacks," &c. &c.
Grand car of *Los Graciós Pau Pi.*
Mariners and Jockeys.
Band.
Flying Guard of Honour, with carriages of Maskers.
Infantry.
Cavalry.

I was told many of the masqueraders had spent for the occasion over fifty pounds in their equipment, and the procession was admirably mounted. I have since learned the cavalry chargers, the officers' private nags, in fact, all the best horses in the country, were in it. After the procession had made the tour of the principal streets it disbanded, and the individuals and equipages of which it had been composed were merged in the throng of masqueraders, crowding every square, street, and alley of the city, which indeed was also full to overflow of the peasantry from the surrounding country.

I was told that at carnival time everybody would be in the streets, grotesquely masked and disguised, and behaving like lunatics. It is perfectly true.

In the evening there was a grand public ball, but as there were to be several more such I did not go, preferring to wander about the city all night, " seeing the folly of it," and seeking adventures. I did not find them difficult to meet with. I was also honoured by an invitation to a mask and fancy dress ball at the *Casino de Artesanos*, but the streets, &c. &c., had an irresistible fascination. A fancy dress assembly of *comme il faut* people would have been a very tame affair compared to the fun, fast and furious, the intrigue and *consumación* of a Spanish city on

the night of Carnival Sunday. Neither did I see the fireworks announced to take place in the evening, for the
appointed time for them was when I was better engaged—
eating a most excellent dinner.

Monday night I went to one of the *gran bailes de trajes.*
We were a party of twelve—six *caballeros* and as many
señoras, paired off, of course. Our ladies were most
thoroughly disguised and closely masked, but withal very
handsomely attired. So well, indeed, were they disguised
that, on assembling ere starting out, they were not able
to recognise each other, so, after much fun from mutual
mistakes, they all unmasked to have an inspection of each
other. A *broma,* or pass-word, was then fixed on, so that
each individual of the party should be able to recognise
any of the others, for it would not have done to trust to
knowing each other's costume in a dense crowd wherein
there might be many more almost identical ones.

The ball was in full swing when we arrived, and a most
terrible jam it was. A pavilion had been temporarily
erected on the *plaza* for a ball-room—a light frame and
canvas building calculated to provide dancing room for six
hundred ; but as there were nearly fifteen hundred present,
dancing was a farce, consisting merely of jumping up and
down in one place with your arms round your partner, and
being well squeezed ; however, most of them seemed to
like it. The din was deafening. All were talking in that
piercing falsetto which is considered the correct way to disguise the voice, laughing, or singing. So loud was the
noise, it was but occasionally the sound of a large brass
band, playing on a raised platform, could be heard with

sufficient distinctness for it to be possible to distinguish what dance was being played. But what did it matter, a man can jump up and down, and be squeezed, and squeeze, to any tune, or for that matter to no tune at all. Of course, we got separated, and had the greatest possible difficulty to get together again ; and, in a good-natured way, made as much mischief as possible, persecuting other couples and standing fire ourselves. None of our ladies were discovered, but two of us were—two of the *militaires*. My fair .companion penetrated the disguise of some of her intimates and their companions, and putting me up to saying several things to them, caused considerable consternation. In fact, our party became at last such objects of interest as to render retreat in subdivisions a strategic necessity. Ultimately we all rendezvoused, in the small hours, at a club café, had a jolly supper, and went home in a body, finding the streets as we passed along lively with other returning maskers.

This saturnalia continued with unabated ardour for three days, and though there was plenty of drinking I saw nobody intoxicated. As a result there was no quarrelling, no bad language, in fact, there was not even any rudeness. Everybody was jolly; nobody had a headache. The wind-up was a midnight torchlight procession, pretty much the same as the inaugural one in organisation, but very different in pictorial effect, for it was a burlesque funeral. The grand car of *Los Graciós Pau Pi* was changed into a hearse, on which reclined the effigy of his Grace. The band of students of folly and their respective masters had become robed priests and bishops, bearing immense lighted

tapers, but some of whom were furnished with a hoof, or
tail, or pair of horns, that accidentally on purpose revealed
themselves. All the mummers wore crape. The bands
played solemn music, the sham priests chanted a parody
requiem, all the mounted men carried flaming flambleaux,
and the cars and carriages were illuminated with red and
blue Bengal lights.

The long procession filed down the narrow main street of
Lerida, between the lofty, many-storeyed, and balconied
houses, every window, every balcony, even the very housetops, a dense mass of spectators, all dressed and masked
in fantastic gorgeousness. Over the scene flashed and
played the cross-lights and shadows from the moving
torches ; the chant filled the air with solemn dirge ; the
roll of the muffled drums made fitting accompaniment.
It was a combination of the funeral and the grotesque,
only I suspect to be seen in Spain since the general advent
of modernism in Europe.

Arrived at the chief *plaza* the procession halts, a mock
funeral oration is said over the dead "*Pau Pi*," and the
lights are extinguished. Immediately, the devil and a band
of demons rush out of the crowd, seize on his body and flee
away, pursued by everybody, yelling, screaming, and cheer-
ing. Of course the devils are ultimately overtaken, dispersed ; the sham corpse rescued from their clutches, and
interred in a hole previously prepared for him. The carnival
of 1877 is dead and buried, a thing of the past. No more
such feast, frolic, and folly until—the next time.

On the 14th there was quite a gathering in the ladies'
reception-room, assembled to make my last evening gay

and pleasant, for on the morrow I had fixed my start. It was late, very late, before the last adieu was said that night. Many had been the pretty speeches made; not a few the mutual promises to write. Something had been spoken about "a year and a day." In fact the half-serious, half-joking farewells were made that the circumstances of the case, the recent frolic, the day itself (the 14th of February), and the claims of beauty called for. Besides, when people do not really expect to meet again, they, of course, make the most of the situation—unless they are in earnest, in which case generally (I am told) they miss making their points.

I achieved a tolerably early start—for Spain—from this most pleasant of *fondas;* that is to say, I got away in time to be at the post-office by eight o'clock—the advertised time for opening the delivery office—for I expected letters. I had to wait over an hour before the official appeared, lounging lazily along the street playing with the office-key and smoking a *papeleta.* I have long bottled my feelings about the administration of the postal department of this country. It is infamously conducted; but what can be expected when the entire concern is run, not for the public benefit, but for the private one of political adventurers, who are rewarded for assisting conspiracies by appointments in a service wherein they know plundering is never found out; *ai de me España!* While waiting, an acquaintance seeing me came up and chatted. Like everybody else here, he seemed to think I have been wonderfully lucky in getting through the trip from Zaragoza in safety, and repeated with great confidence the oft-made statement that a band of ten robbers (a product of the late civil war) infested the district I had lately traversed, living by depredations on all and sundry who they might catch ; and assured me, as many had before, that my double-barrel and big dog would have been no protection from them, they being all armed with Remington breech-loading carbines, and desperate and determined criminals, who, in the wild thinly-peopled track in which they ranged and harboured, had long evaded or defied the *guardias civiles*. Allowing sufficiently for Spanish romancing, I am inclined to believe there is some truth, some substratum of fact to this general belief. Quite possibly the two Frenchmen were " stuck up " by this very gang, and I have had a lucky escape. However, it is quite refreshing to hear of past dangers ; heretofore they have invariably been promised me, as experiences to come.

It was a lovely balmy morning, the sky a cloudless blue, a warm haze mellowing the distant mountains. My way led across an extensive plain, strongly accentuated by detached, flat-topped, steep-sided hills, and small, peaked, and pointed mountains, and seamed by miniature valleys. In many places rows of almond-trees bordered the road, masses of bloom, and looking extremely beautiful. Irrigating ditches abounded, and the wheatfields were a brilliant green.

I passed several old women and panniered donkeys gathering weeds : the donkeys after their usual way, the old women with short bill-hooks, with which they cut the weeds off close to the ground, and then crammed them into the panniers. Thinking the weeds might be " greens," and that by asking I might get a wrinkle, I inquired of one of these ancient females why she collected them. "For rabbits," she replied. "We all keep rabbits, and get their food for nothing, as you see, and so do our donkeys get theirs too." So much, thought I, for so-called Spanish laziness and thoughtlessness for the morrow. Would to heaven the old women of rural England were as lazy and thoughtless in the donkey and rabbit line. Rabbit stew or pie two or three times a week would surely be better, and, all things considered, cheaper than the occasional-snared hare, while the donkey would cost less and be far more useful than a lurcher. However, in Spain there is no work-house to pauperise and demoralise the peasantry. Here, to be thrifty or starve is the alternative, and as none care to go hungry to sleep and to breakfast on expectation, all are thrifty. So here there is no poor rate, no wages squandered in drunken "sprees," and none of the necessarily attendant crime. The peasantry of this country, so far as I have seen of them, are, as a mass, better fed, better clothed, better conducted, more intelligent, honest, sober, and self-respectful, and far more happy than their compeers in old England ; and were it not that they are degraded and warped by superstitious influences, that purposely make and keep them tools for all wickedness, they might be the first peasantry of Europe.

At the little town of Bell-lloch, only remarkable, so far as I observed, as having l's enough in its name to beat any average Welsh town, I breakfasted, for it was close upon noon when I arrived there. Fried bacon and sausage, a herb omelette, and bread and wine at discretion, was the repast. There was plenty to spare for me and Juan ; the meal was cleanly served, and the inclusive charge ten-pence.

Beyond this town of four l's, the ground became more diversified, even hilly; then followed a true plain, sur-rounded with far-away blue hills and mountains, and, to my left, glimpses of the white Pyrenees.

A dip of the road into a large broken valley, laying considerably below the general level of the country, brought me amongst seeming hills again ; and on a large detached one to my right stood an old church, in build so exactly a Welsh one as to be a real surprise to me. It was certainly strikingly different from any Spanish church edifice I have ever seen.

A chance presenting itself to make a considerable cut off, and at the same time exchange the hard high road for a pleasant footpath, the opportunity was not neglected. This path took me through a fine grove of poplars, alive with starlings, singing and chattering ; and Juan, who as usual was ranging at a swinging gallop far and near, put up a brace of redlegs. They rose from the centre of a nearly bare fallow, some two hundred yards ahead of him.

Soon after three o'clock the small town of Mollrusa was reached. It stood on the bank of a considerable-sized but nearly dry watercourse, the stream having been diverted for irrigating purposes. A comfortable clean *posada* was soon found, having a wide sunny verandah to sit in. A good-sized bedroom, sufficiently furnished, was assigned me, and clean towels and fresh water brought. Clearly I was in a more civilised country than *Los Monégros*. On the dressing-table were two books, and taking them with me, I stepped forth through the open window on the verandah, and there sat down to amuse myself. I expected nothing else but to find I had chanced upon some lives of saints, that being the class of books my experience had taught me to expect. But I was wrong. On looking at their respective titles they proved to be a very badly-matched pair; one was called (I translate) " History of the future—a treatise upon the Imperialism of the Grand Monarch, and the triumphs of the CATHOLIC Church unto the end of the world, according to the most celebrated ancient and modern prophecies —dedicated to *Don Carlos de Borbon y de Este.*" I read a considerable portion of this interesting (?) work. Its author took much the same line, and handled his subject in precisely the same manner, as a certain well-known British nonconformist preacher does to explain, amplify, and reveal (?) the Book of Revelation; and, from it, forecast the future. But as Liberalism was the "Scarlet Lady," and the Protestant Church one of the worst of the " Beasts," the conclusions come out differently from those of the B. N. P.'s, though I must confess the Spaniard's reasoning was quite as close and conclusive, and his style far more dignified and lofty than his British compeer's, while his phrasing was most impressive and appropriate. The other book was an excellent Spanish translation of Volney's " Ruins of Empires." To alternately read a little of each book was a mental drinking of hot grogs and eating of ice-creams.

While reading, a sweet perfume from time to time was wafted past me. It proceeded from a lot of pinks in full flower, growing in the open air ; and near them flourished some fine cacti, the first I have yet seen in this country.

My supper was not bad. Soup, stewed rabbit, lamb chops and fried potatoes, partridge and sprouts, almonds, raisins, and olives, bread and wine.

To-morrow's march will be a long one. To-day's was short. So I have rested myself well, and written up my notes.

CHAPTER XXIV.

FEBRUARY 17, 1877.—Wishing to make an early start from Mollrusa, not only on account of the length of the march before me, but because the midday hours are now so very hot as not to be fit to walk during, for one who is burdened with his little all, I explained the matter to the hostess, and ordered chocolate precisely at seven.

"Certainly; any time your worship likes," was the prompt reply.

At seven sharp I was ready and in the kitchen. Nobody else was there. No fire was lit. I clapped hands —the country's substitute for bell-ringing—stamped, blew my dog-whistle, and hallooed until I was tired. More than once I had half a mind to wait no longer. If no one would get up, even to receive payment of the bill, was I bound to lose the cool of the morning?

It was thirty-five minutes past seven when, at last, a servant-girl made her appearance, not quite half-dressed,

and rubbing her eyes. Did my worship want chocolate ?
No, not at that time of day. Could not wait an hour for
an eggshell full of chocolate. Wanted to pay the bill and
be off. Away went this nearly "adorned the most"
beauty, flying upstairs to ask her mistress how much there
was to pay. I sat down and solemnly lit a pipe, believing
thoroughly there would be plenty of time to finish it in ere
she again appeared. And there was ; not that she took
the opportunity to finish her toilette. No such thing. On
reappearance she had, if possible, more loose ends to her
than before. Goodness knows the bill was moderate
enough—one shilling and eightpence, all told !

An hour's walk brought me to the little village of
Golnez, where, at a *ventorrillo*, I obtained for three halfpence a glass of *aguardiente* and small loaf of bread, the
latter to divide with Juan as a "stop-gap," to be eaten as
we walked along. A few miles farther was Bellpug, a little
town by which coursed a fine irrigating head of water from
the right, while just beyond, upon a serrated eminence,
stood a most picturesque old monastery, whose three
galleried and pointed-arched cloisters gave it a most
imposing appearance.

Bellpug, though very small, is yet a walled town, and
its old gateways are handsome arches ; the one by which I
left being remarkable for having in a recess over its key-
stone a very quaint picture of Christ and Roman soldiers,
while just beyond stands a handsomely-proportioned
monolith cross, about twenty feet high, and of evident
antiquity. In Cataluna these old crosses seem to abound,
many of them carved and of singular merit. In the town's

centre stands an old Gothic church, with a fine octagon tower. A couple of miles farther on my way there appeared by the roadside what seemed to be an unusually large league-stone. It proved instead to be a memorial one, but in commemoration of what I could not determine, for so old was the inscription thereon that it had become illegible ; only the date, 1608, was decipherable. A niche, countersunk in its upper portion, a foot deep, contained a stone crucifix, whose Christ was most admirably carved ; one leg, however, had crumbled to powder. Over the opening was an iron grating, almost eaten up with rust.

The general features of the scenery remained much the same as the day before, the only novel one being a small tract of swamp-land, patched here and there with beds of rushes. On it were several flocks of lapwings, which afforded sport and exercise to Juan, who pursued them with eagerness. Half-past eleven found me standing on a stone bridge, over a large irrigating canal, whose waters flowed from my left—*El Cañal de Urgel.*

It was high time to find a place to breakfast at, and seeing a cottage of unusually neat appearance, a little way off, and close to the banks of the canal, I started for it, to prospect for a meal. A young woman, with a beautiful set of teeth and two babies, was sitting on the ground in front of the cottage ; and, in answer to my queries, replied there was no meat in her house, but if I would be satisfied with a herb omelette, and bread and wine, she would gladly accommodate me. How many eggs were put in that omelette I know not, but I do know that thereon I and Juan made, with the assistance of a small loaf of bread, a hearty breakfast, and both of us were sharp set ; nor on my part did I spare the wine, for it was good, and I hot and thirsty. The charge was ninepence-halfpenny ! With great simplicity, this handsome young mother asked me if the silver coin I tendered her was good, for, she added, " It is very seldom I see silver money, not often enough to know much about it." I mention this as an instance of the fact, that to these peasants other money than copper is a rarity, and as showing their great unsophistication.

After refreshing the inner man I took a long rest in the warm sunshine, greatly enjoying it, my pipe, and the lovely view. Larks were soaring and singing in hundreds ; goldfinches were everywhere. The air rung with melody ; and, though but the middle of February, the perfume of a garden full of flowers added its subtle charm, while the busy bee hummed and flitted around !

It was close on four o'clock as I approached the town of Tarrage ; a long straggling place lying between two moderately-sized hills, the one to the right crowned by a modern fort—or old one furbished up—the other, surrounded by high loopholed-walls, while, in the centre of the *plaza* stood a nearly new stone blockhouse, round, and pierced for musketry. Evidently Tarrage had not meant to be captured by any of Don Carlos's flying columns. On a far-off eminence appeared the extensive ruins of a square tower, topping an entrenched, scarped, and terraced hill, and looking in its shape and surroundings very Moorish.

The only noticeable building I saw in Tarrage was a church, much like the one of Bellpug, but a little beyond the town I came upon a lovely cemetery. This garden of the dead was in general design like unto the Lerida cemetery, but much smaller and older looking. The arches of its colonnades were very sharply pointed, the banded columns extremely light—in fact, the architecture was quite Byzantine. It was full of flowers and old monuments, and its gateway really most handsome. On a grass plot between the highway and the entrance to this charming resting-place for the weary departed, stood, on a wide octagon stone base, a most beautiful cross ; its shaft, a very slender octagon monolith, over twenty feet high, the surmounting cross a large florid one, carved in the richest possible way. The handsomest thing of the kind I have yet seen in stone. One arm of the cross was gone. The inscription on the pedestal was so worn away that it was only determinable that there had been one. Evidently the cross was very old.

There was a fine background to cemetery and cross—three ranges of mountains. The farthest off—the snowy Pyrenees—showed sharply clear against a cloudless sky, while the base of the nearest was so indistinct with warm haze as almost to be invisible. Broken, irregular foothills, flat stretches, numerous wash-outs and gullies, near and far groves and clumps of trees occupied the intervening space. It was a beautiful view, and in all respects strikingly reminding of California. The day had become blazing hot. I sat down on a grassy bank, and long enjoyed the lovely prospect.

The next halting-place—Ceverra—I arrived at soon after five in the evening, and entered the gateway through its surrounding wall with the fag-end of a procession, for

the place was *en fête*. Immense and most tasteful bouquets
of paper flowers, lamps covered and decorated with many-
coloured muslin, flags, were everywhere ; the narrow
streets of the little town were so many rainbows ; the
many balconies and open windows all occupied by spectators dressed in their best, and the streets full of bands of
music and processions.

Making my way to the chief *fonda*, I entered, engaged
a room and seat at table, and without loss of time took my
stand on the balcony to observe the scene. A respect-
ably-dressed man standing by me, who I have since ascertained was the landlord, and on whose breast glittered a
decoration, kindly explained the affair to me.

The city was celebrating the repulse of the *Carlistas*,
two years ago. The *fiesta* had been officially established
as an annual celebration of that "great" event, and many
who had been prominent on the occasion had received a
decorative medal, he amongst them, and my informant
lightly touched his breast and bowed. One morning six
hundred Carlists made an unexpected dash at the place,
and two hundred got inside the gate and established
themselves in the nearest houses on each side of it before
opposition could be made. Then, twenty-four regulars,
forty volunteers, and four peasants armed with shot guns,
hastily threw a barricade across the end of the street,
manned it, and not only stopped the enemy's advance,
but kept up so lively a fire on the gateway as to deter the
four hundred Carlists without from entering to support
their van, and thus gave the *alcalde* and other authorities
time to sound the alarm bells and summon all able-bodied

citizens to turn out in defence of their homes. Into cellars, holes, and corners, into any and every place where safety might be sought went the valiant citizens, leaving the gallant sixty-eight at the barricade and the six hundred Carlists to fight it out. The four hundred outside, having a natural reluctance to be killed, fell back, so those in the houses, finding themselves abandoned, and thinking from the uproar in town that the citizens were organising and their position untenable, saw fit to advance backwards. On emerging into the street they were charged from the barricade and driven pell-mell through the gateway they had entered at, losing forty-two prisoners; while the casualties to the assailing defenders was but six volunteers, three regulars, and two out of the four peasants, these last falling outside the town gate, one killed on the spot, the other dying in a couple of hours. The repulse of the " Carlist army " by the " brave and loyal city of Ceverra " was one of the " events " of the late war.

Truly, while not noticing much for which they might be justly proud, these people often make monstrous mountains of minute molehills.

When night fell all the lamps were lit, the illumination being excessively effective. The narrow streets, overhanging roofs, projecting balconies, dark shadows, gleaming many-coloured lights, and moving figures, presented a scene of strange beauty mingled with grotesqueness. A party of vocal serenaders, who, with an attendant crowd, were promenading the streets, halted in front of the *fonda*, and, very well led, sung in score some stirring Catalunan airs. As I sat in the balcony, almost near enough to the fair occupiers of that of the opposite house to shake hands with them, and looked up and down the street and on the picturesquely-dressed crowd below, the spectacle quite realised my idea of the Spain of romance.

Later on, municipal fireworks were exhibited from a platform in front of the ancient university of Cataluna. They were far better than I expected; indeed, quite tasteful, and numerous exclamations of astonished delight from an admiring crowd testified to their appreciation of the display.

Every available spot from which a view could be obtained was occupied, the jam in the streets being excessive, somewhere between four and five thousand men, women, children, and soldiers—for the town is now strongly garrisoned—were wedged in a mass; but there was no pushing, no elbowing, no pocket-picking, and nobody intoxicated, nor did I hear a rude word uttered! The *grande finale* showed a portrait of the king, surrounded with flashing lights. It was the officially prepared moment for a display of loyalty, but there was none. Though the *chef-d'œuvre* of the performance, not even an exclamation of wonder or delight was indulged in by any of the audience excepting children. No notice whatever was taken of the portrait of " the little Alfonso." Royalty is not popular in Cataluna. Its people are Republican almost to a man. During the time the fireworks were playing a regimental band gave us good martial music, and on its marching away, the people dispersed either to cafés or their several homes. The *fiesta* was over.

I was regaled with good fare, and had a most comfortable

room. My bill was but one shilling and eightpence-half-penny ; and, having for once succeeded in getting my chocolate in good time, at half-past seven the following morning I was again *en route.*

The old university building demanded my attention before leaving Ceverra, for it was once a famous seat of learning. It is now utilised as a barrack for troops, serving to maintain the present military despotism called the Spanish constitutional government—*Toga cedit arma.* I should have liked to view its interior, but a sentinel barred the way. This university was founded by Philip V. in 1717, when it became the virtual successor of the old Lerida university. It is a quadrangular pile of buildings enclosing a large courtyard, entered through a very handsome porch gateway. The edifice has a front of one hundred and fifty-five yards, and looks scholastic and imposing.

As I left Ceverra a thick white fog enveloped everything. The road, a ramp round a hill-side, wound off to the right and disappeared, while a deep valley seemed to lay below me. As a narrow but well-worn foot-path descended the steep slope to my left, I suspected it was a cut off, and, chancing it, followed down the almost perpendicular declivity, and before long struck a returning curve of the high road. Soon the fog lifted and I found myself in a valley, winding amongst low hills along whose centre my road ran.

The hills confined the view considerably ; but every turn disclosed a fresh and interesting scene, and my walk was most enjoyable. Many a hill top was crowned by an old church or ruined tower. Numerous were the pretty villages scattered around, and several Roman cement mills were passed. Wheatfields, vineyards, olive groves, almond orchards occupied the entire valley, and up the furrows on the hillsides climbed tongues and strips of deciduous oaks, ilex and corks.

As I progressed the hills gradually closed in, becoming, too, more mountainous in character ; and, ere long, pines— the first seen since leaving the divide between Guipuzcoa and Navarra—replaced the oaks. By-and-by, though my road descended rapidly all the way, I found myself once again amongst mountain scenery. To my right was a deep, perpendicular-sided gorge, along whose centre coursed a mountain stream. The pines had become timber; the road a scarped ramp. It was very like a bit of the wildest of Welsh mountain scenery. But the deep blue hue of the heavens, and a flock of about thirty magpies chattering on some bushes, stamped it with a foreign look.

I had intended to breakfast at a little town called Pana-dilla, but missed, or rather overshot the place, not knowing it lay some distance off the road up a hillside to the left. But coming soon after midday to a roadside house, I entered, and asked if I could have breakfast there.

It was not a *posada ;* but an old man, who seemed its master, said, " Yes, certainly ; the family are going to eat directly, you can join us." So we all four sat down : the old man, his daughter (a good-looking girl of eighteen or so), a young man (a labourer), and myself. The first course was an old friend, a dish I had not seen for years ; pumpkins sliced, French beans, and macaroni, stewed together in olive-oil and water, and highly seasoned. It was very good.

Then a herb omelette. Bread and wine as usual. Charge, for man and dog, sevenpence-halfpenny. A pleasant siesta in the warm sun and fragrant air occupied the time till two o'clock, and I departed.

Still wilder and more mountainous became the way.

More magpies, also more partridges. Indeed, all the afternoon Juan was finding birds, but they were excessively wary, always rising at great distances before him, and then flying straight across from the mountain side we were on to that beyond the opposite edge of the valley.

I passed through two little villages — clean-looking groups of houses, more civilised in appearance than I had seen for some time. The influence of the not far-off sea-port, full of English, American, and French enterprise and capital, was beginning to show itself.

Every hour that I walked my surroundings were more picturesque ; the country passed through becoming quite Swiss in appearance, and my road continually crossing and recrossing by stepping-stones a wide brawling stream, flowing down a deep, wooded, and lovely ravine. At last a turn in the road gave a peep at a most strange-looking ruined castle. It was perched on the summit of a rock that in dimensions was a hill, and immediately beneath, around an old gray church, nestled a snug cluster of cottages, while still farther below, through a gap in the tufted pines, showed a curve of the highway I was following. If amongst those buildings I could find accommodation, then there would I pass the night, for it was getting late, and I had gone far enough.

FEBRUARY 18, 1877.—Close beside the road, just below
the little village, under the ruin-crowned rock, I found a
decent-looking *venta*, and gladly learned that there a room
and meals were to be had. Immediately opposite stood a
casa del cura and its attendant private chapel, and as I
sat in the porch of the *venta*, smoking, sipping *aguardiente*
and water, and resting, I observed the *cura*, a fat jolly-
looking priest, crossing the road towards the village church.
Seizing so good an opportunity to make inquiry about the
ruin, I accosted him, and, after the usual politenesses of
the country had passed between us, asked about it. It had
been a Moorish stronghold of great importance, built to
command the pass I had just travelled down.

In the course of the evening several teamsters stopped
at the *venta ;* with them I sat down to an indifferent
supper, and afterwards, round a blazing fire of pine
branches and cones, to chat. These men were very
respectful and civil to me, but, only speaking Catalan,

which is quite as different from Spanish as the broadest
Yorkshire or Cornish is from the Queen's English, conversation on my part was much like the Scotch shepherd's
definition of metaphysics : " He who listens understands
not what he that speaks means, and he who speaks does
not quite understand what himself says."

The room and bed furnished for my accommodation was
quite clean, but the house was an old one, and midnight
marauders attempted to rob me of sleep. However, with
the expenditure of considerable powder, and some vigorous
sallies, I kept them more or less at bay.

In the morning I succeeded once more in getting an
early start, for the energetic old woman who kept the
posada was stirring before break of day, attending to the
wants of the *carreteros*. Paying the modest bill of one
shilling and threepence, and astonishing the old woman
with a gratuity to which she was evidently quite unaccustomed, I departed, just as the dawn was gathering strength.

The grade of the road still continued to fall sharply.
Soon the hills opened right and left; a wide, wild view
of mountains and valleys came in sight, and conspicuous
above all, right in front, rose an isolated, jagged mountain,
all points, pinnacles, and pillars—Montserrat. There
could be no question about it; it was the wildest, most
striking mountain I have seen in Spain, and startlingly
like, in its profile against the sky, to "Granite Mountain,"
in central Arizona. That it too was one of nature's granite
monuments seemed certain, though how such could be,
considering the geological characteristics of the country,
puzzled me greatly.

At eight o'clock I came to a pretty little *santa,* and peeping in, observed before a shrine that was all gilding, flowers, and wax images, some women and children on their knees praying. One of the former having, doubtless, filthy lucre in her heart, on getting a glance of me arose hastily, crossed herself with almost startling rapidity, and leaving the service she was engaged on for that of Mammon, approached and asked if I wanted anything, adding, she kept the little *venta* in front, and had the best of *aguardiente* and other things. I did want something, for I was hot and dusty, so I tried the *aguardiente,* purchased a loaf of bread for self and dog, consumed a *cigarrilla,* tried another little drink, made a present to the Image, paid a few coppers, and started on my way refreshed, the business-like devotee returning within the *santa* presumably to finish her prayers.

The gorge to my right deepened, widened, opened into a wild broken valley, and in its centre I beheld the considerable town of Igualada, whereat I arrived soon after ten o'clock:

Repairing to a house to which I had been recommended by the old *señor,* father to the *señoras* of my Lerida *fonda,* I entered, and soon found myself quite at home, for its master and mistress, on my mentioning who had recommended me to their care, vied with each other in attentions.

I found Igualada a town of some manufacturing and business importance, and of considerable industry. It has a population of nearly sixteen thousand souls, and there daily arrive and depart three stage-coaches, well-horsed,

and from six to eight sixteen-mule freight waggons, plying
from and to Barcelona. Of course Igualada is a walled
town. It also is defended, or rather kept in subjugation,
by two small towers situated on a flat-topped eminence to
its south—new, I think—and also by a strong garrison.

This town can boast of one tolerably good and fairly
wide street ; some quaint little *plazas*, and several factories,
these last-mentioned being clustered together on the banks
of a river—when there is water in it—and for the rest, the
usual complement of rookeries and cut-throat-looking
alleys, called in Spain streets. There are also well-
constructed gasworks, but owing to " political questions "
—what on earth politics have to do with it, a benighted
Englishman could not be made to understand—the town
remains in nightly darkness, for gas is not supplied.
Perhaps the Ultramontane party, now rapidly gaining
strength under the Alfonso cabal, consider gas as having
dangerous political tendencies. The manufacture of
cottons, of cloth, velveteens, Roman cement, and iron
founding, are the chief industries. Churches, of course,
are numerous. There are eleven, including the hospital
chapel. I looked at and into the chief places of worship,
but saw nothing of unusual interest about any of them,
excepting La Paroquia, and not much there, only seven
hideous and grotesque human monsters, each protruding
horizontally as many feet or more beyond its eaves, and
serving as rain-water spouts. These figures were of all
sexes, nude, and I think some monk of old had a hand in
their horrible designing. In the same church there was,
however, in one of the recessed and railed-off shrines,

a large picture that, from what I could see of it, may be a fine old master; but in this country the ecclesiastical powers that be have a most provoking way of railing-off church pictures, so that a fair inspection of them is impossible. Igualada in many respects is a better town than Lerida, compared to which it looks new. Few of the houses appear to be over two hundred years old, while a great many are comparatively modern, say fifty years of age. The factories are quite things of to-day. I was comfortably and well housed and fed while in Igualada, and charged but three shillings and fourpence for a capital dinner, excellent supper, good room, luxurious bed, no insects, and my morning chocolate and *azucarillo;* and after despatching the last, started for the monastery of Montserrat, the mountain of that name in full view looking quite close, as if but an hour's walk off.

It was a bright clear morning, and though early, being but half-past seven o'clock, quite warm. My road soon commenced to climb the mountain, and the views were lovely. By a quarter to ten I had reached the little village of Castelloni, and seeing that thence the acclivity became quite steep, and being besides hot and thirsty, I regaled myself with the *copa de aguardiente* and following glass of cold-water, that experience had by then taught me was so refreshing and safe a drink. My road then became a mountain ramp, winding as it climbed among rocks and pinnacles; while huge laurestinas in full flower, boxwoods higher than a man's head, pines, hollies—in fact, a wilderness of trees and shrubs—covered every portion of the mountain's side.

Seeing a practical way whereby some steep climbing would enable me to effect a considerable cut off in the winding road, I left the highway, and plunged into the covert, catching, as I did so, a glimpse of two *guardias civiles* and a peasant, rounding one of the curves of the road directly above, but certainly had, at the time, no idea they also had seen me. I was mistaken. I had barely gone twenty yards when, emerging into sight on crossing a narrow opening in the thicket, I was stopped by a loud and imperative "*Alto!*" Looking round, I perceived, some thirty paces to my left, the *guardias civiles* and their companion. They had seen, and, scrambling down the mountain's side, aimed at intercepting me; but, miscalculating time and distance, or headed off by thick brushwood, had not succeeded in doing so. The *guardias civiles* stood with their carbines "ported," and called upon me to lay my gun down and come to them. Thinking it no greater distance for them to travel than it was for me, not wishing to lose ground, not indeed caring a straw about making their personal acquaintance, I did nothing of the kind, but, resting haversack and double-barrel against a rock, commenced coolly rolling a cigarette and staring at them.

Immediately one of the guardians of the road advanced upon me, doing so exactly as a sportsman walks up to his dogs when on a dead point, and holding his cocked carbine as a pigeon-shooter does his gun, when the string is about to be pulled; the other, placing the peasant in his front to cover himself, brought his weapon to the "charge." Evidently I was an object of suspicion, if not of apprehension.

When the advancing *guardia* got near enough to perceive I was grinning with hardly-suppressed mirth, and very evidently a peaceable pilgrim, he threw his carbine into the hollow of his arm, saluted, and politely demanded my papers. I drew my pocket-book, and was about to produce my " Derby," when, with a wave of the hand, the *guardia* stopped me, saying : " Let not your worship trouble yourself ; I see you are a pious pilgrim to the sanctuary of our Lady of Montserrat—go with God."

While he spoke, I observed more closely the apparent peasant, and it struck me his attitude was that of a man handcuffed. I asked : " Who have you got there ? " The reply showed that the tales of my Lerida friends were not devoid of foundation. " A robber captured this very morning, and, please our Lady, we will get the rest of the gang when this fellow is made to confess."

" 'Tis well, my friend—go you with God," I answered, and we went our several ways. So at last, after wandering hundreds of miles alone on foot and through the wildest places of Northern Spain, I have met the real live Spanish bandit ; but alas ! for the interest of my story, without his weapons and companions, a manacled and helpless prisoner, though probably therefore greatly to the advantage of my personal comfort, and to the preservation of my travelling personal estate. I have seen " the robber of the mountain," and am not his.

By the middle of the day I got to *Horno del Velio*, a most romantically-situated church, parsonage, and *posada*. This establishment for the benefit of souls and bodies stands on a spur of the Montserrat mountain, whence, beyond a wild chaos of hills, valleys, and broken mountains, is obtainable an imposing sight of the snow-clad Pyrenees. The church was quite small ; the *posada* not much of a building. But there was a fine large walled water-tank— a preserve for fish to fast on, and to supply water for irrigation—a considerable garden, and the place, as a whole, looked very pretty. My arrival was almost simultaneous with that of the passenger-carrying mail-cart from Igualada to Monistrol, a town on the farther side of the mountain. In it, besides the driver, were two travellers, and with them I sat down to breakfast on soup, bacon, omelet, and bread and wine.

The priest of the Church of *Horno del Velio* was in the room, and talked most affably to me all the time. Probably from my having uncovered myself to him on entering, which the others did not do, and because I was walking to the monastery, he took me for a Catholic pilgrim. I told him of the robber. "Ah !" he exclaimed with a start of interest, "what was he like ? How was he dressed ?" I described him as accurately as the opportunity for observation had permitted me to notice.

" He is not the chief, only one of the gang."

" Then there is a band of robbers in these parts ? "

" I fear I must confess such is the truth. It is a great scandal to our holy mountain, especially as they occasionally harbour in the ruined hermitages during winter, and I hoped it was their leader who had been taken."

The priest then asked me in Latin if I spoke that language, when, though I replied in the same tongue, he continued the conversation in Spanish—greatly to my satisfaction, for my colloquial Latin would have soon broken down—saying : " So I supposed, and I perceive you belong to the well-instructed class of Englishmen. Pray tell me what has been the general effect of Lord Ripon's conversion, and is the truth about Queen Victoria beginning to leak out ? "

" What truth ? " I asked, knowing well enough the rumour to which he alluded, for the assertion that England's Queen had become a Catholic had often before been most confidently made to me, even by ignorant peasants.

" Her conversion," said the priest ; "you know she has for some time been reconciled to Mother Church."

" Nobody has heard of such a thing in England."

" Openly, of course not. There are reasons of state for great discretion, but all good Catholics here know it is so ; and I had supposed so great a fact could not be entirely concealed from the faithful there."

Clearly it was no use arguing the point, for, admittedly, I could not speak with authority, and the priest believed himself in a position to do so. I therefore turned the conversation by making inquiries about our Lady's sanctuary of Montserrat.

It was very hot when I resumed the ascent, and quite a relief to find myself, from time to time, in the cool shadow of overhanging rocks, or in one of the many re-entering curves of the tortuous road that was in shade ; but though the oppressive warmth and continuous ascent combined to fatigue me, my walk was most enjoyable. The fine scenery, continually changing, the extraordinary diversity and luxuriance of the vegetation, above and below me, the beautiful

Y

and various wild flowers, the hum of bee, and buzz of winged insects, united to make it enchanting. Greeves and blackbirds were very numerous, and Juan flushed out of the thick covert of the mountain's side many redleg partridges.

At a quarter to four o'clock I came to a handsome granite pillar in which was countersunk a white marble slab, charged with an artistically-cut bas-relief representation of the mountain, and *Ntra. Sra. De Montserrat*, with an inscription, setting forth that the monument was erected in commemoration of a miracle performed on that spot by the "Virgin of Montserrat," on the 5th May, 1862, attested by—and then followed the names of five Dons and Doñas. And this is the latter part of the nineteenth century !

Half an hour's further walk, and, on turning a sharp curve of the road, I suddenly found myself close to the monastery, and beside another memorial pillar. On it I read, inscribed in *Castellano :* " Here became immovable the Saint Image in 880." Like as had the image, nine hundred and ninety-seven years ago, I too had reached a resting-place.

CHAPTER XXVI.

FEBRUARY 21, 1877.—For three days have I been the inmate of a monastic institution, and fain would I here remain, at least for some little time longer, for I am in love—fairly enamoured of this beautiful, this most charming mountain. But I cannot stay, alas! To-morrow I must go. To Montserrat all pilgrims—and every visitor is presumably one—are cordially welcome, and entitled to free quarters—not rations—but only for four nights; then, the rules of the place—unchangeable, like the laws of Medes and Persians—command you to pass on.

I am now sitting in my dormitory, trying to straighten out the tangled web of confused and mixed-up impressions. Lovely views, ruined hermitages, sacred chapels, holy tanks and springs, wonderful caverns, beetling crags, towering pinnacles, the varied beauty of more than eight hundred different kinds of trees, shrubs, and plants—matted and mingled in luxuriant profusion on mountain side, in dark ravine, on summit levels — are all blended together in a brain muddled with listening to innumerable tales and legends of wonders, miracles, and apparitions, while the everlasting melody of chant and *Ave Maria* ring in my ears. Here, where for close on a thousand years prayer, praise, and adoration has ascended to the female divinity of modern belief—here, where seems mingled with every breath one draws the monkish lore of ten centuries, it is not easy to write an intelligible account of what is seen and heard.

It is a pleasant little chamber I am in ; a small room of a range of buildings devoted to pilgrims, being No. 1 of the *Aposentos Sta. Teresa de Jesus.* The institution has considerably over a thousand apartments fitted up to accommodate visitors, and the Directory is building more, for during the summer and autumn months not only is every bed occupied, but all the numerous villages at the foot of the mountain are filled to overflowing; and everyone giving to the " Queen of Montserrat," according to their means or inclination, the more that come the better for her coffers. From the best data I can get, I have made a rough estimate of the present income accruing from these voluntary contributions, and cannot set the total at a less sum than fifteen thousand pounds a year, and am told it is sometimes double that amount.

There are other sources of revenue — the sale of rosaries, model images, blessed measures in ribbon of different dimensions of the Virgin, and other pious remembrances, all of most trifling intrinsic value, but charged for at a sufficiently high rate. Not the least of

these is the *Almacen,* or warehouse; a place whereat
nearly everything can be bought, even tobacco—a Government monopoly—which, too, is a post-office, a stage-
office, and a posting-house, all to the profit of the
monastery.

The arrangements are all very convenient. To me, as
a lone bachelor, only a single room is assigned, and I
have to get my meals at the restaurant-café, but were I
en famille, a range of rooms would be provided, having
attached thereto a well-found kitchen and chambers for
my servants. At the *Almacen* I should purchase—at a
sufficient profit to "our Lady"—provisions of all kinds
and fuel, and obtain the use of bedding, linen, and all things
necessary, and so live comfortably, indeed luxuriously,
if my purse and inclination permitted and prompted
me to do so. At the café I fare sufficiently well, but find
it dear, as compared with everywhere else. If, however,
as its host tells me, he has to pay a heavy percentage for
rent and as thank-offerings to the shrine, there is good
reason for such being the case.

I have the cleanest of rooms, the whitest of bed linen,
and am well looked after by an old monk—who is my
chambermaid.

The evening of arrival was agreeably spent, wandering
around the immediate precincts of the place, and examining
and admiring the remains of the old monastery, destroyed
by the French in 1812; when, after pillaging the place,
with a completeness long practice had perfected the
Napoleonic soldiers in, they, on the 31st July, buried so
many barrels of powder in its foundations, that the

explosion, when fired, was heard at a distance of twenty-four miles.

I attended evening devotions in the new church—a building of imposing appearance and size, most solidly built—and was well pleased with the choral service. Montserrat is celebrated for its school of church music, and choir, organ, and instrumental performance was the best of the kind I have heard in Spain. The monks had fine bass voices, the boys lovely sopranos, and the effect of the alternate verse and response was really fine.

Early in the morning of my first day, I started for the top of Montserrat. I was alone. In the season, guides are numerous. Now none are here, for visitors are rare. On my arrival I was the solitary one. But guides are not much in my line. There were sure to be beaten paths to every place of interest. An old mountaineer could not get puzzled, let alone lost, in so small a range. At 7.40 A.M. I arrived at the first hermitage, a ruined stone cabin on a jutting rocky shelf, with its holy spring and tank beside it. Thence the ascent was so steep that occasionally, like the first of Montserrat's Christian *solitaires* —the Friar Juan Garin—I had to go "on all-fours, like a cat;" occasionally, too, the way led along narrow ridges, or between perpendicular wall and sheer precipice—no road for giddy heads or uncertain feet—but I pressed boldly onward, and near noon found myself arrived among the summit peaks, immediately behind the monastery.

Out of breath, tired and hot, I sat down to rest. I was on a narrow sharp comb, or ridge, between two sugar-loaf-shaped pinnacles of conglomerate rock; by my side flowered a fine aloe and some cacti ; two jay-birds screamed, scolded, and chattered at me ; maiden-hair ferns, and pretty little blue, yellow, and crimson flowers grew on every coign of vantage, peeped from every crevice ; a balmy soft breeze fanned my cheek. I was over four thousand feet up in the air, and a striking and splendid view was spread before me. I gazed on it with peculiar interest, for to me its main feature was the Mediterranean. The end of my long tramp was in full view !

I stood up and gazed around. What a panorama ! To the north, the snow-capped Pyrenees ; to the south, the shining sea ; between, mountains and valleys, hills and dales, isolated peaks and spreading plains, winding rivers, cities, towns, and villages were laid out like a map. I could see the mountains of Valencia and of Aragon, the peaks and summits of far-off Majorca and Minorca.

There was another ruined hermitage close by me ; to it I repaired, and at its " holy tank " quenched my thirst. Then—for I was getting hungry—by a different path I returned to the monastery to get my late breakfast.

At the restaurant-table sat another visitor. The waiter informed me, in a very audible aside, that he was my countryman. The stranger proved to be an Austrian tourist, but spoke tolerable English. He was well dressed and shod for his work, and furnished with a light and conveniently-arranged knapsack.

During our meal together we became quite sociable, and he informed me he was a great tourist, spending a considerable portion of each year travelling about, that he had " done " nearly all Europe, but that this was his first visit to Spain. " Thus far I am well pleased with the country," he went on to say, " and this mountain strikes me as being most interesting and unique." So expressing my satisfaction at hearing Montserrat was attractive to him, I indulged a hope to have the pleasure of his company rambling over it.

" Oh, I am going directly I have finished dinner. I never stay long in a place ; all I care for is to see it. I can read up all the particulars by-and-by ; that's the way I always do," was his answer.

" Out of some handbook ? "

" Well, yes, generally. And I always carry the one of the country with me ; see here, for instance."

And he produced, out of his knapsack, the two volumes of Murray's " Handbook for Spain."

" This is the best on this country, the others are nowhere ; but it bothers me sometimes, because the bulk of it was written so long ago. I used to wonder why Murray did not bring out a new one, but I see now it would not pay. Too few tourists come to Spain. I daresay they lost money on this one."

As he rose to leave, I offered to go with him a short distance on his road to keep him company.

" Very glad," said he, " but I am not alone. I got a guide in the village of Collbato, at the foot of the other side of the mountain. A first-rate fellow, showed me all the caves, hermitages, and so forth, that were not too far off our road ; but we have had a misunderstanding about his pay. I thought I had engaged him for so much for the day : he says the tariff of the mountain is by the trip, so I shall have to pay him again to take me to Monistrol, where I am to catch the train to Barcelona."

Monistrol was in full view of where we stood, with a plain unmistakable carriage-road, running all the way to it, down the mountain-side. Why on earth anyone but a blind man should take a guide I did not comprehend. This " great tourist " thought differently, however. " I never," said he, " go without a guide anywhere in a strange country; it would be so terrible to get lost." And when I told him I had come from the Bay of Biscay, alone all the way, and never was in Spain before, his countenance plainly showed it was only out of politeness he did not express his entire disbelief of the statement.

Went to evening service again. It is so charming to sit in the dim light, listen to the " angelic voices," look at the " celestial lights," and fancy oneself a spectator of the *Invencion de la Santa Imágen* on this very spot a thousand years ago, and afterwards to burn incense to the goddess Nicotina, on the monastery's terrace, and think the view still more lovely by moonlight than by day. By-the-bye, I have discovered the Mediterranean can be plainly seen from the terrace when there are no low-lying clouds intervening.

Yesterday morning I arose at seven, and, as usual, glanced, the first thing, out of my window to judge the coming weather. It was easy to judge the past; everything was mantled with virgin snow, nor was the storm quite over; flakes were floating thickly about, falling, rising, going this way, going that; in fact, we were in the snow-cloud, for the peaks opposite—behind the

Cueva de Garin—were above it, standing clear against a brilliantly blue sky, while below us lay a white fleecy sea of tumbling cloud-billows, through which, in places, pierced mountain-summits like so many rocky islands of a ghostly sea. It was a dreamland ; vague, mysterious, beautiful, and ever-changing, pierced and rent by gleams of rainbow-tinted light. All at once the snowflakes commenced whirling upwards in fantastic spiral columns, swirls, and streams with astonishing rapidity, and dissipating as they reached the upper stratum of air. The storm was over ; the entire view came out sharp, clear, and defined ; the heavens were cloudless ; the sun shone bright and warm.

While dressing, a robin-redbreast hopped on my window-sill, the first I have seen this winter and in Spain. He seemed like a messenger from home.

The snow disappeared with magical rapidity, for, when I emerged from the *Sta. Teresa de Jesus* building to cross over to the restaurant for my morning chocolate, it had vanished. The snow-storm was as though it had been a vision.

All the morning I wandered about the mountain, visiting caves, hermitages, chapels, gazing at the lovely views, gathering wild flowers, thoroughly enjoying myself; then, as before, returned to a late breakfast.

More company—three persons. This time one of them was really and truly my countryman. He was the cicerone of the party, and an old resident in Spain. The other two, a Belgian nobleman and bride on their wedding tour. They had come to "do" the monastery—in a carriage and pair ; see what was to be seen—out of the window of the vehicle; after breakfast they would look around for a couple of hours, drive on to Monistrol, and then take the train home. It was a long way to come to spend so short a time; perhaps they too intended to read up "all about it," and persuade themselves they had seen it all. After breakfast we raced round, and glanced at as many things as the time permitted, and I persuaded the party to go as far as Garin's cave. His statue was much admired, and the bride greatly interested by the short sketch of the Garin legend I gave her. They were pleasant people. She was beautifully dressed, but more appropriately to the *Bois de Boulogne* than a rough mountain; and though graceful, active, and lithesome, her absurdly high-heeled Polish boots made her glad enough to accept a hand along the narrow, steep, and rocky trails. All three were greatly taken by Juan's handsome appearance, good behaviour, and winning ways, and caressed him much; he is certainly a most attractive dog.

My countryman is, I find, an old resident of Barcelona, connected with the diplomacy, and acquainted with all the leading officials. He has given me a most cordial invitation to call at his home, which I shall most certainly do, for I like his style.

This morning, having yet much to see, and knowing my time here is drawing to a close, I took my breakfast with me, and have spent the entire day rambling over the mountains, seeing all I could of the nine wonderful caverns, the thirteen hermitages, the six chapels; a heavy day's work, for most of these places of pilgrimage are perched upon apparently inaccessible peaks. In fact, I have been making a chamois of myself, for had I gone to them by the usual trails, they could not have been visited in twice the time. All are interesting spots, having connected with them legends and tales of hermits, of bandits, of military operations, Carlist occupations, and supernatural appearances. I feel strongly tempted to break through my rule, not to let my letters be after the guide-book fashion, and to give a particular account of them all—but I won't.

To-day I was favoured with an exceptional sight. One of the eagles of the mountain sailed close below me, and lighted on a jutting ledge. I could have dropped him with a revolver. He was a very large and beautiful specimen. Mine host of the restaurant says eagles are now very rare. He has only once seen one in twelve years.

I wrote just now I would avoid the guide-book dodge, but must give a short general description of the mountain. *La Montaña de Montserrat* is situated about twenty-four miles north-east of Barcelona, in a bee-line; an isolated mountain, springing from its base almost perpendicularly into the air. According to the Spanish author, Florey, " None can say whether it is a castle of towers and bulwarks, a bouquet of mountains, or a single mountain in the form of such." And he is right. Montserrat is one huge block of conglomerate, split in its upper portions into a multitude of tower-shaped pinnacles, having numerous benches, and seamed with dark ravines. Its circumference is about fourteen miles, its height three thousand nine hundred and ninety-three feet—at least those are the figures given by the *Presbitero* Amettler, a celebrated naturalist of the community of Montserrat, who took his measurements from a

rock lying in the centre of the Llobregat, a river washing the foot of the mountain, and situated just in front of the peak of *La Santa Maria.* Close to the highest point of the mountain are the remains of the *Ermita de S. Jerónimo,* which for three years was a *Carlista* military look-out during the late civil war. The monastery is a few feet below halfway up the mountain in perpendicular elevation. *La Sierra de Montserrat* is a botanist's paradise. The monks say there is a specimen of every plant in the world growing somewhere or other on it. Of course this is not quite true, but there is a most astonishing variety of them. To the geologist, from its strange forms, the extraordinary fact of being where it is, its large and peculiar caverns, its uniqueness, this mountain must always be full of charm. To the admirer of natural beauty, to the lover of monastic lore, to the " pious pilgrim," Montserrat is truly a mountain of delight.

CHAPTER XXVII.

FEBRUARY 21, 1877, Midnight.—Here the central point of attraction, the very *raison d'être* of the whole concern, the ancient source of almost fabulous wealth, the present cause of prosperity, is *La Santa Imágen de la Virgen de Montserrat*. It therefore requires description. The sacred image is barely two feet in height, and is a representation, in wood, of a middle-aged female seated on a chair, and supporting on her knees a wooden infant. Mother and child are quite black, not with age, evidently they were always so. Traces of gold show that their hair was once gilt. To an unbiassed eye the group looks like an unartistic representation of an African mother and her little one. However, that the image is the most correct and authentic likeness extant is, from the standpoint of a Spanish Catholic, not possible to doubt, for it was, according to "incontestable" evidence, the handiwork of St. Luke, who executed it from sittings vouchsafed to him at Jerusalem by the Virgin herself.

The local guide-book says: "The image of *Maria de Mont-serrat* beams with such an expression of superiority, piety, and sweetness, that it is difficult to resist the impression that it appeals to our very soul." When I read these words I was amazed, and went back to have another look, for it had seemed to me the Madonna's black face was forbidding ugly. I remain of the same opinion still, but admit that the figure is most gorgeously arrayed and tinselled.

This illustrious work of St. Luke was brought to Spain by the " Prince of the Church, St. Peter," given in charge of *San Eterro*, the first bishop of Barcelona, and became that city's " object of adoration in times of calamity and source of consolation ; " and at last in the fourth century, the bishop *San Severo*, and the miraculous lady of Barcelona, *Santa Eulalia*, with the consent of *San Paciano*, who guarded this sacred treasure in the Church of the Saints *Justo* and *Pastor*, it was exposed for present and future veneration, over the chief altar of Barcelona's then cathedral. There for over three hundred years the " Jerusalemitish image of Mary " remained the pride and glory of Cataluna.

Then came the Arabs, and made things unpleasant, all round, for the pious Goths. These latter worthies greatly feared the infidels would have but scant respect for their dark divinity, and when Barcelona, after a gallant defence of three years, feared falling under the power of the Saracen, her citizens determined their beloved image should be placed beyond the reach of possible indignities. So on May 10, 718, Eurigonio, captain of the Goths, governor of the city, &c., and Peter, the bishop of Barcelona, with a strong escort, carried this " Pearl of the Apostle " to the most secret recesses of the mountain of Montserrat, and hid it with diligent caution in a cave, closing the entrance thereof so that no man should ever find it. Now for one hundred and seventy-two years did the image remain hidden from the pious adoration of the faithful, and though its memory was vividly preserved, none knew where it had been concealed; when in 810, the Moors having been driven out of the country adjacent to Montserrat, and the true faith restored, the following extraordinary sequence of events occurred.

Some good little boys of the village of Olesa, who herded their parents' flocks at the foot of Montserrat, observed one Sunday at dusk on a ledge of its eastern slope a bright light, like unto a multitude of burning candles, which issued out of the mountain's side and illuminated the darkness. While gazing with astonishment at this prodigy, the boys plainly heard harmonious strains of celestial music floating in the air. Thinking no doubt these manifestations were for their special and private benefit, these knowing young urchins said nothing to nobody, but the following evening repaired to the same spot, hoping to be again entertained ; but there was no performance. Nothing daunted, they kept on repairing, and on the following Sunday, at the same hour, lo ! and behold ! the lights and band as before.

Having enjoyed the "celestial lights" and "angelic voices," many succeeding Sundays, these wonderfully reticent and discreet juveniles at last thought fit to inform their respective papas and mammas about it ; and, ere long, the wondrous tale reached the parish priest. He started out to satisfy himself, and for five consecutive Sunday nights, with his own eyes and ears, had it fully confirmed. Then he marched off and told his bishop, to wit, Gottomaro, first bishop—after the expulsion of the Moors therefrom—of the parishes of Manressa and Vich. Forthwith Gottomaro assembled all the clergy of his diocese, and all the persons of note in the neighbourhood, before which distinguished audience the lights and music played with great briliancy and execution. Then Bishop Gottomaro, sending some agile young mountaineers to scale the height to the very place, a great discovery was made. The lights retired unto a small opening in the rock, and being followed, a cave was entered, in whose centre lay, clothed in garments of striped silk, the lost image ; which miraculously showed its joy at being recovered, by exuding " a most fragrant smell." Immediately the bishop, the clergy of the diocese, the notabilities of the neighbourhood, the good little boys, and all and sundry, climbed up to and entered the cave, prostrated themselves before and adored the image, all smelling the sweet perfume. And the day following a devout procession was organised, to bear to the Cathedral of Manressa the recovered " Moreneta, Queen of Montserrat."

The route to Manressa from this cave of lights, music, sweet smells, and silk-clothed image, was then a trail across the mountain, and on the procession's arrival at the place where now the monastery stands, a halt was made, for to there is a long steep climb, and the processionists doubtless had had about enough of it ; certainly the image

had, for when, after resting awhile, its bearers attempted
to lift it from the ground, it was found to be immovable.
" Human force was incapable of separating it from its
resting-place."

So the bishop knew it was the will of the image to
have there erected a chapel worthy of its sanctity, wherein
it might be worshipped for all time.

That "The Image" was a first-rate judge of a site for
a monastery, no one who has visited this charming spot
will doubt. Indeed I question if the world can show one
more admirably suited, in every respect, for being a point
of pilgrimage. But the idea was not original. Already
did a halo of sanctity rest on the spot. Already was a
convent being erected close at hand, one commemorative
of even more astonishing events. Which occurrences,
being also vouched for by "unimpeachable authority,"
and well illustrative of Spanish credulity, I must also
relate. It is a long story, but shall be cut very short. It
is frankly minute in details. Most of them shall be left
out, for obvious reasons.

Friar Juan Garin, a Goth of noble blood, was born in
Valencia. Filled with " sacred ardour," he separated
himself from the delights of the world, retired to the
solitude of Montserrat, and there made his bed of hardest
rocks ; living solely on the wild herbs of the mountains.
He put in his spare time musing and meditating on the
wickedness of other men and his own sanctity, until "his
soul attained to the purity of a seraph." To so great
a height, indeed, did he rise in celestial consideration,
that when he made his annual visits to the sepulchres of

the apostles, at Rome, the bells of all the places of worship on his route rung out, "of their own accord," joy peals as he passed.

Juan Garin's proceedings had for a long time been very trying to the devil. He could stand much, but those confounded bells beat him. He could not stand the nuisance of all the bells from Montserrat to Rome and back again, making the row only Catholic bells can make, as an annual infliction, so he conspired against this annoying friar.

Transforming himself into an angel of light, Satan visited Juan Garin, told him he was engaged on a penance, and solicited the favour of becoming his disciple in sackcloth, much, no doubt, to the holy man's private satisfaction. It must be very gratifying to a hermit to have an "angel of light" for his first disciple.

At the same time "*se entró Satanás en el cuerpo de Requilda*" (daughter of Wilfredo II., Count of Barcelona) "*y maltratándola horriblemente.*" The afflicted father sent for all the priests of known piety and wisdom to exorcise the demon, when *Satanás* declared, with malicious intention, he would only desist from his outrageous proceedings at the command of one Friar Juan Garin, and not only that, but vowed he would come back to the unfortunate girl, and do worse, whenever she should leave the friar's protecting presence.

The count, therefore, informed himself of the whereabouts of this said Garin, conducted the fair Requilda to his retreat, recounted what had occurred, and left her to his pious ministrations.

The counsels of the disguised devil and Requilda's charms were too much for Juan Garin's morality, and he committed a crime that by old English law was punished with death, and now is by penal servitude ; after which, fearing the consequences thereof, he murdered his unhappy victim and buried her body in the ground.

Then the devil flew away, satisfied he had stopped those horrid bells.

Left to himself, Garin became a prey to remorse, hastened to Rome, confessed with tears his crimes to the Pope, and was sentenced by him to do penance. Juan Garin was bid to return and abide in a cave in Montserrat, close to the grave of Requilda, "crawling on all-fours like a cat," and without looking at the heavens, and to keep on all-fours and to hold his tongue until further advised by a tender infant. This did he, and in time, his clothes falling off him and his body becoming covered with hair, he looked more like some wild beast than a human being.

Several years had passed, when one day two of the count's huntsmen, while looking for game, encountered a strange beast (our unfortunate friar), captured him, chained him, carried him in triumph to Barcelona, and presented him to the count their master. Forthwith he, for whom the bells of Christendom had been wont to ring of their own accord, was attached to a balustrade of the hall-stairs of the Count of Barcelona's palace, an object of wonder and curiosity, and, no doubt, often well kicked by the footman for getting in the way, when his serenity deigned to carry up the letters, the coals, or a tray.

Seven years after the murder of Requilda, a son was born

to the Count of Barcelona, who, without loss of time, celebrated the joyful event by giving a *soirée*, attended by the
rank, fashion, and beauty of Barcelona. To them the heir
was exhibited ; and after he had been duly admired, the
strange beast was brought in for their further entertainment,
that he might amuse them with his antics. Immediately
on the entrance of the remarkable curiosity, the newly-born
babe opened his mouth, and with a loud voice, plainly
cried : " Rise, Friar Juan Garin, Heaven has pardoned you."
Instantly Juan Garin stood upright before the whole assembly ; he confessed all things to the count, craved for,
and received his pardon.

I expect the rank, fashion, and beauty of Barcelona was
considerably shocked. No doubt, had such a *dénouement*
been at all suspected, the "strange beast" would certainly
have had some clothes put on him.

With the friar to point out his daughter's place of burial,
the count proceeded to Montserrat, to disinter the remains
of poor Requilda, and give them Christian burial. When,
however, the grave was opened, Requilda was found to be
alive and well, but showing the mark of her strangulation
in the form of a red circle round her neck. Recognising
the hand of the Virgin in her preservation, she expressed a
desire that the count, her father, would found a convent on
the spot, of which she would be Lady Superioress, Garin
undertaking the post of *major domo* and *servidor* to the
nuns, " in which occupation he died in the odour of sanctity."

The cave of Garin, his abode during his penitence, is
not far in an air line from the monastery of Montserrat,
within pistol-shot in fact. It is situated under an over-

hanging ledge of rock, in front of, and about one hundred feet higher than it. But it is a quarter of an hour's walk therefrom, owing to the steepness of the mountain, and to the fact that it lies on the other side of a deep ravine.

The cave is not a commodious dwelling-place, only high enough for a small boy to stand upright in ; is not much longer than a man stretched on the ground at full length, and about half as deep. It is now closed with an open iron railing, and in it can be seen an old cross, a cruse of water, and a full-sized representation, in marble, of the notorious friar, reposing on the ground, contemplating the cross and telling his beads.

This piece of sculpture is a work of great merit. Garin appears of a noble countenance, and his hands are admirably done. But there is a still more extraordinary relic in the cave—the veritable skull of Juan Garin himself. As with my own eyes I beheld the skull of a man who had been dead nearly a thousand years, and perceived it was still ungnawn by mice or insects, unstained by the elements, the water in the cruse hard by not yet evaporated, I found no difficulty at all about believing the entire history ; for, of course, to suspect the holy fathers of furnishing fresh "original" skulls and water from time to time would be most outrageous.

CHAPTER XXVIII.

FEBRUARY 25, 1877.—Thursday, the 22nd February, early on a bright morning, having completed the time of pilgrimage, paid my restaurant bill, and delivered into the hands of the monk presiding at the *Almacen* my votive offering to " The Pearl of Cataluna," " Jewel of the Mountain," and " Queen of Montserrat," &c. &c. &c., I slung my haversack and gun, and started to rejoin the world of work, reality, and disbelief in the plain below.

I had not slept much the night before, for though physically tired from a long day's mountain scrambling, I had been so mentally awakened by all I had seen and heard, that sleep was an impossibility until a few hours' writing had exhausted restlessness, then I slept with all my might for a couple of hours, and a few breaths of that potent tonic, the fresh mountain air of early morn, having made me feel bright and vigorous, I bustled round and succeeded in getting a pretty good start, it being but

7.50 A.M. when, by the mule trail to Collbato, I left the monastery.

Certainly a mountain road on the descent has many advantages over a climbing one. It is easier; a man faces the views as he travels, and he feels more certain he has not taken a wrong fork of the road, for he has continual glimpses of its turns and winds below him.

The gravel being very sharp, I went at a rattling pace, being wishful to make distance ere the day got hot; and at 9.45 A.M. reached the foot of the mountain.

The plain was occupied by vineyards, olives, and almonds; very sandy and dusty, and by no means interesting after the mountain. A little over half an hour's walk brought me to the village of Collbato. There I refreshed myself with a *copa de aguardiente* and a long drink of cool water, and pushed on along an awfully bad, rocky, stony trail, until by eleven o'clock I struck the high road from Igualada to Barcelona—the road I had left to my right four days before, when, turning north-east, I commenced the ascent of the mountain I had recently come down.

For some distance the fields were fenced with aloe hedges, the first seen since leaving Central America; they looked strange and yet familiar. The way soon wound amongst red clay hills, when the aloes became of larger size, and the road ankle-deep in fine dust. Near noon the town of Esparagueva was reached. At its entrance stood a fine monolithic cross, round whose capital were sculptured scenes from the legend of the Queen of Montserrat, and which was further ornamented (?) with a stone skull—Garin's, I suppose. In the one long street of the town was a rather fine church—St. Eulala—over the porch of which appeared an image of her saintship.

A good-sized and very clean *posada* furnished an excellent breakfast-dinner for me and Juan for a consideration of one shilling and tenpence-halfpenny. And we continued on our way, passing, as the town was left, a large circular basin, in whose centre played a fountain of pure water. Juan seized the opportunity to take a plunge and cool himself. I should have liked to do so also, for it was very hot.

Soon after two in the afternoon, the Barcelona and Igualada diligence tore past me. There were ten fine large mules to it; they were turning a corner, on a sharp descent, at full gallop, and I looked for an upset. They passed in such a cloud of red dust, and so fast, I but just managed to count the number of pairs of mules, and see it was full of passengers.

At four o'clock I arrived at the small town of Martorell. I crossed the river Noya, on whose bank stands Igualada as well as Martorell, by a timber foot-bridge one hundred and forty-three yards long. Just above were the shore piers of a new stone bridge now in course of construction; still beyond were those of the old bridge that was washed away by a big flood six years ago. At the time I passed along, the river Noya was a small clear stream that would not wash a crane's feet away from under her.

Martorell was prospected pretty well for a *posada* to stop at—not thinking any I saw very inviting. At the least discouraging-looking I put up, though it was quite evident that bad was the best. Having two hours to spare before

dinner-time, I strolled off to see the famous "Devil's
Bridge" over the Llobregat. I came to the river's banks
at a curve some little distance below the bridge, and had a
fine view thereof. It is a most striking structure. Evidently
it had furnished the model for the bridges over the Imperial
Canal I had so much admired and wondered at. It has
four arches. Three of them are insignificant land arches.
The chief, or central span, is so large, so lofty, so light, and
so bold in its lines, as to at once rivet the attention. But,
excepting for its extraordinarily peaked gable-end appearance, the bridge did not look to me antique, for the joints
of the bricks it seemed built of appeared quite sharp and
fresh. Indeed, perceiving I could count the courses of the
bricks from where I stood, I did so, to enable me to judge
the bridge's dimensions.

After duly admiring this fine work from a distance, I
sought my way to it to make a close inspection. Then I
found I was a deluded individual. The bridge was not
brickwork. I had mistaken for bricks blocks of red stone,
like bricks, indeed, in shape and colour, but big enough for
gravestones. I paced the bridge, re-counted the masonry,
measured some of the stones to get an average, and
arrived at an approximation of the bridge's dimensions.
The central arch is a very acutely-pointed semi-ellipse,
whose apex is about seventy-six feet above the ordinary
level of the river, and of a span of not less than one
hundred and thirty feet. The length of the half of the
bridge's roadway which is on the side where there is one
land arch is seventy yards; on the other sixty-eight.
Width of roadway between the approaches four yards; of

the approaches, seven yards. This bridge is so pointed in the centre, so sharp in the rise and fall of its roadway as to be quite unfit for vehicles to traverse ; nor had it been intended for such purpose, as immediately above the key-stone of the central arch is a stone lodge, through which the roadway becomes but a narrow passage, for on each side are stone seats. In the wall of this lodge are two in-scribed tablets. One sets forth : " This bridge was built five hundred and thirty-five years after the foundation of Rome, by ANIBAL, CAPITAN CARTAGINES, who also erected the triumphal arch in honour of his father, AMILCAR." The other states : " This triumph of antiquity, being in danger of destruction, was repaired by order of Carlos III., A.D. 1768."

The triumphal arch mentioned in the inscription still stands. It is composed of massive blocks of concrete, and looks quite able to stand for another two thousand and ninety-four years. The bridge's foundations are of bossage masonry, and rest on a bed-rock of slate, which crops out, and forms the river's banks as well as bed.

I think this grand old bridge is, on some accounts, the best worth-seeing object I have beheld in Spain, as an historical curiosity, as a monument of the past, as a spe-cimen of the engineering skill of the ancients, and as being associated with the entire history of the country ; built by the Carthaginians, used by the Romans, fought over by the Goths, partly rebuilt by the Moors, repaired by the moderns. If all bridges could speak, how few of them could tell such a history as this one.

Accommodation and fare at the *posada* much below

average ; bill as much above, to square things, I suppose ;
fleas plentiful and intrepid ; morning cloudy and chilly ;
but the blazing vine-faggot fire in the kitchen very pleasant
to toast oneself over, while being kept half an hour waiting
for chocolate, for it was nearly half-past eight before I
obtained it and started from Martorell.

The road ran parallel to, and not far from the Llobregat's right bank ; and many charming views of river-bends,
backed by picturesque and broken hills, presented themselves. Before I had travelled far I overtook a bright,
intelligent boy, of twelve years of age ; and, slackening my
pace to his, we walked together conversing, for he spoke
good *Castellano*, which he had learned at public school.
The lad carried a biggish satchel on his back, and proved
to be a post-boy. He told me his beat took him a good
half day to walk over, delivering and collecting letters, &c.,
and that his pay was only at the rate of fourpence-half-
penny a day, while he had to clothe, board, and lodge himself ; but, added he : " It is better than nothing, and when I
get big they will give me more ; and as I live at home it
costs me nothing, and I give my wages to mother, and I
have my half day to go to school."

I think that boy will get on if he is not too good to live.

At 9.40 the sun broke with a grand " effect " through
the clouds, and illuminated a broad river-reach.

I noticed continually that little towers crowned all
commanding eminences on the line of hills beyond the
river, and it puzzled me to divine their origin and use. The
little postman explained they were old semaphore stations,
built long long ago, to notify by signs, from Barcelona to

the interior, any appearance of an enemy's fleet ; and that they had been used again in the war, under protection of *Alfonsista* troops, when the *Carlistas* cut the wires of the electric telegraph. 'Twas a sharp twelve-year-old of a boy. He also informed me the Llobregat was full of large eels and huge sturgeons, besides lots of little fish.

At eleven o'clock I was abreast of a large, handsome-looking square castle, on the opposite side of the river, crowning a big rock on the top of a small hill, and dominating a village.

My little cicerone said the Carlists tried to take it several times, but could not, for it had been well garrisoned. Just below I saw a fine dam across the river, to make the head for an irrigating canal, and also furnish power to some large factories situated a short distance below where it struck the left bank of the river, and surrounded with high handsome trees. Soon after I sighted a beautiful stone bridge of fifteen fine arches. It had a very slight spring, and was evidently quite modern. The post-boy told me it was the *Molins del Rey Puente*, that I had to cross it, and would enter the town at its other end. Then he left me, his route turning off to the right.

I found the "Mills of the King Bridge" extremely well built, wide, and furnished with broad flagged pavements for pedestrians. It is four hundred and fifty feet long, and a creditable piece of work for any country and any age ; but that it will last as long as has the "Devil's Bridge," erected by the Carthaginian captain, is doubtful.

Midday had arrived when I reached the town of *San Felin de Llobregat*, and seeing it was a place of some size, having a long, wide, chief street, and many side ones, expected no trouble in finding a good house to breakfast at; but neither hotel nor restaurant could I discover, though I made inquiries of several persons, until at length I came across a regular poor man's eating-house. However, I was getting impatient, so entered and risked the accommodation. Nor did my personal appearance forbid the presumption that a poor man's eating-house was my appropriate place. To confess the truth, scrambling up rocky places on hands and knees, forcing my way through thorny thickets, making short cuts while exploring the mountain of Montserrat, had put the finishing-touch to the wear and tear my garments had sustained between the two seas; and the dust arising from a road over ankle-deep in powdered soil, uniting with the perspiration caused by walking in a blazing sun, had coated my face and hands with a mask of dirt, and plastered my hair with a pomatum of thin mud. The only thing respectable about me was my handsome gun and *distingué* dog. I looked a dirty, ragged, almost shoeless tramp.

Walking through a long sitting-room—which had once been whitewashed, and whose only furniture was a narrow table on trestles, nearly as long as the chamber, two benches of charity-school pattern, and a coloured and badly fly-insulted print of "Her Majesty Queen of Montserrat," and empty of occupants—I pushed open a door and entered a very clean, tidy little kitchen, whose large open French window led to a pretty garden.

A fat old woman, looking as clean and trim as a prize dairy-maid, was busy cooking in this culinary boudoir, making soup, and a small girl-child sitting near was trying to say her alphabet. " Oh, ho ! " thought I, " this will do," and immediately made myself agreeable to the old woman, and explained that I wanted a good meal and had the wherewithal to pay for it.

" Let your worship be content. Your worship shall eat plenty with satisfaction," was the promising speech she made me.

And this much-appreciated old soul was as good as her word, for while, after a thorough brushing of clothes, I with the assistance of a large snowy-white towel, a big piece of soap, and a bucket of water, made an *al fresco* toilette amongst the flowers of the pretty back garden, she busied herself in preparations for my inner comfort. Soon a spotless cloth covered a little deal table, standing near the window, on it was set out a bottle of good Tarragona, a roll of such bread as is hardly seen out of Spain, the necessary tools for eating with, and my first course—a plateful of excellent clear bread-soup. Then came lamb cutlets, nicely crumbed, cooked in olive oil, and just pointed with garlic—so good !—afterwards omelette of eggs, finely-chopped ham, and herbs, followed by—crisply-fried in oil—fresh sardines, and a wind-up of cheese resembling gruyère, olives and dried fruits, and then a " grace " of *aguardiente.* The fragments that remained made an amply-sufficient breakfast for Juan; we were both well rested and refreshed. The bill was but one shilling and tenpence ; the old woman was delighted by a small gratuity, for which she solemnly and elaborately blessed me, then we pushed on.

Villages, manufacturing establishments, residences, became more and more closely clustered together, and after an interesting walk of about twelve miles, principally down the vine-covered valley of the Llobregat, I found myself between continuous houses. I was in a street. I had reached Barcelona.

Barcelona being a big place, the second capital of Spain, having a population of one hundred and ninety thousand souls, I had a considerable way to go ere I at length arrived at the locality of the good hotels. I repaired to the reputed best, and presented a striking contrast in personal appearance to the white-tied, white-waistcoated, swallow-tailed, patent-leather-slippered varlet who, standing at its doorway, with evident difficulty realised that I purposed to become a guest. However, as they had done before, my dog and gun vouched for my respectability, and I was admitted with sufficient bows and scrapes, and shown into an undeniably good room.

It was too late in the day to visit a tailor, but I could improve my comfort by obtaining such ready-made things as one can wear, so I beat up the shops.

My feet being nearly on the ground for lack of sole-leather, a bootmaker's was first entered. Spain has a just reputation for eminence in her Crispins, who consider themselves, and perhaps truly, to be the best shoemakers in Europe, so I had no difficulty in astonishing my lower extremities by getting them into a stylish pair of promenade boots. The shoemaker was quite as much astonished by those I took off, at which I left him intently gazing. I have never inquired after them; never entered the shop

since. Perhaps those old familiar friends are on exhibition
as curiosities. Certainly the remains of a pair of "half-
scotched" ankle-jack English shooting-boots are such in
smart-footed Barcelona. Then a glover, a hatter, and a
gentleman's outfitter supplied the rest.

I found a first-class bath-house, revelled in a most luxurious hot bath and cold plunge, and arrayed myself in my
fresh underclothing. I then went to a hairdresser's and
was groomed. After all that, I suspect I looked more
queer than before. Then indeed I had been *en suite*, a
seedy, dirty, ragged tramper—now much mixed. Was I
not as well dressed as any man, excepting my coat, my
waistcoat, my trousers? Was I not a most disreputably-
attired individual, excepting my modish hat, neat boots,
irreproachable linen, handsome scarf and pin, Estaban
Comella light kids? verily I was an incongruous *mélange*.
A good many people grinned at me as I strolled along. I
grinned at myself, too, whenever I beheld my reflection on
the plate-glass of some shop-front. So the first thing next
morning I took steps towards completing my metamorphosis.

Whilst at Lerida, I had noticed that a Barcelonian,
who was a fellow-guest at mine *fonda*, was an unquestionably well-attired man. Of him I had inquired the address
of a first-class tailor. "Go to mine," said he; "I will give
you a card, saying I have recommended him for your
custom, and request his best endeavours, and he will, I
feel sure, give you satisfaction." Armed with this document, I repaired to the *Plaza Real* (a *Palais Royal* in a
smaller and prettier pattern), soon found the place, and
introduced myself.

It was not a shop. A flight of handsome white marble steps led to a suite of elegantly-furnished rooms, all mirrors, gilding, and damask; the easy-chairs, sofas, and window hangings were of blue satin, the wood-work ebony, the floors waxed and polished oak. One of the partners waited on me; and, while showing patterns, talked of the topics of the day like an educated man of the world.

There was nothing of the tradesman in his manner or discourse. He spoke French perfectly and English tolerably well. I ordered what I wanted, and was promised my garments in a week.

"The trousers we will try on, for the rest a fit is a certainty," said he on parting.

It strikes me that if living is absurdly cheap in Spain, clothes are not. The charge for what I had ordered was about the same as Bond Street would have made; but, as it afterwards proved, cut, materials, and workmanship were quite equal to Bond Street's best, there was no cause for grumbling.

After breakfast I set out to hunt for a *Casa de Huespedes.* Not that I was discontented with my hotel as such, for it was a very good one; and considering its rank—being one of the best in the largest town of Spain, except Madrid—and that it was patronised by all foreigners of distinction, and the native magnates and nobility, not a dear one; its inclusive charge being but eight shillings a day. But in a large cosmopolitan hotel of a capital city, a man is more or less isolated and alone. I have not come to Spain to retire on my individual dignity or natural exclusiveness, but to make as many acquaintances as possible, as many intimacies as advisable and practicable, therefore a *Casa de Huespedes* is the place for me ; and besides, I had been recommended to an excellent one. The young officer at Lerida, who so politely obtained for me permission to see, and was the companion and guide of my visit to, the citadel and ancient Gothic cathedral of that city, gave me a note to the landlady of a house he always stopped at when in Barcelona, which he said was most comfortable, and where I was sure to meet good company, chiefly military men. I soon found the place. There was just room for one more. I immediately secured my quarters, and here I am. I have a comfortable bedroom, the usual meals— and very excellent ones—a latch-key, plenty of feed for Juan, good wine *ad libitum*, and pleasant company. The house is in a central position and good street. All for the very moderate price, as compared with other countries, of fourteen reals per day—not quite three shillings. Of a truth, as I said before, Spain is really a wonderfully cheap country.

We are eight in number, that is to say, an aide-de-camp to the Captain-General and Military Governor of the province, two artillery captains, two advocates; an old Spaniard, who having made a large fortune in Spanish America, spends each winter in Spain ; a Cubaña, who is here for political reasons, and " *El Inglés.*" And we are as friendly together as though old comrades.

CHAPTER XXIX.

MARCH 3, 1877.—I have now spent considerable time in this city, and been well pleased. The weather has been delightful, for Barcelona can boast of an average winter temperature warmer and more equable than Naples ; the place unusually gay, for the king had been visiting it. There are numerous objects of interest—antiquarian, architectural, historical, and military—to be seen ; and last, but not least, as a source of pleasure, I have had the good fortune to make some most charming acquaintances.

Barcelona is another of the cities fabled to have been founded by Hercules, and is really of considerable antiquity. It has existed, with varied fortunes, one thousand one hundred and twelve years ; has been a Carthaginian, a Roman, a Gothic, a Moorish, a sovereign independent, and a Spanish city. Here, on his triumphant return, was the intrepid discoverer of a new world received by the king and queen, at whose feet he laid an empire. In the Middle Ages it was the ruling maritime power of the Mediterranean. It is now Spain's first mercantile port. As Barcelona is increasing daily in size, population, and wealth, with astonishing rapidity, the boast of its inhabitants that it will eventually surpass Liverpool in commerce, Manchester in industry, New York in luxury and opulence, does not appear wholly chimerical ; certainly the newest portion of the city (*La Ronda*, and beyond) reminds me, by its width of streets, height and style of house-frontages, and general flourishing and growing appearance, more of first-class American towns than any other place I have seen this side "the mackerel pond." Her fine port, her geographical position, the energy and business qualifications of the Cataluñans insure Barcelona's prosperity in spite of every obstacle that a Government, hopelessly ignorant of the very rudiments of political economy, and Past-masters in the arts of grasping, extortion, and petty annoyance, can invent to bar her advancement. No wonder her citizens, the shrewdest people in Spain, are disaffected and turbulent under an infliction of combined folly and tyranny.

As the royal visit has been the chief event during my stay here, it merits first mention. Its publicly announced object was, "that his Majesty wishes to open the Industrial Exposition of Cataluña, about to be held in the building just completed for the exhibition, and to confer personally with the *savants*, local authorities, and leading citizens, with a view to ascertain how the arts, industries, and commerce of the place can be best advanced." This stereotyped form of speech has, whenever repeated to me, been invariably accompanied with the slight closing of one eye, or the waving to and fro of the raised index finger of the right hand before the nose—national expressions whose significance is unmistakable.

The general belief here is, that the visit was merely a portion of a programme of a pleasure trip having three objects : to divert the young king, to try and make him less unpopular, and to distract his attention from certain schemes supposed to be in course of incubation at Madrid.

On the day appointed for the august event the king did not arrive, and I learnt at dinner it was unknown precisely when he would ; that the exact time of his advent would be kept secret, for a conspiracy to kill or capture him had been discovered, several arrests made, and that much uneasiness was felt by those in authority. More closing of eyes and wagging of forefingers. The arrests were actual facts, but public opinion is that the only plot was one hatched in the brains of the authorities themselves, to enlist sympathy and excite interest for the boyish king, by pretending he had been the object of secret machinations ; if so, it ignominiously failed. These Catalans do not care a *maravedi* what happens to "the little Alfonso." In fact, whether he remains or not, the people do not seem to concern themselves. Experience has taught that it practically matters little to them what set of conspirators rule the country, for as they say here, it is but a case of "*Los misimos perros, con nuevos cuellos*"—the same dogs with new collars. However, some day there will be a revolution that will change things pretty effectually. The enlightened intelligence of the nation will rise against rascality in high places on the one hand, and demagogism on the other.

Those who dream that patriotism is dead in Spain will then have a rough awakening.

Great preparations had been made for the king's reception. The landing at the end of the *Rambla de Santa Monica* was the site of a pavilion of evergreens, profusely decorated and lively with pennants and streamers. The long approach thereto was bordered with trees transplanted for the occasion, alternated with flagstaffs, all gold and ruby— the national colours—and bearing aloft their respective flags of many devices. All over the town, windows and balconies had been draped in ruby velvet cloth with gold fringes. Paint, gilding, and upholstery had done their best, and in a manner only practicable in a climate on which dependence can be placed, as for a whole week decorations had been exposed to the weather, or in progress of completion, that were most expensive, and which a single shower would totally ruin.

At last the king did come. Yesterday, as I was dressing, word was brought that the escorting fleet was in sight, steaming straight for the harbour. Hastily I finished my toilet, and hurried down to the *Muralla de Mar*, to secure a coign of vantage. Close to the landing-steps, just without the enclosure surrounding the pavilion, were numerous huge blocks of building-stone, remains of those carted there some time since to repair the sea-wall. On these stones I had previously cast the eye of speculation, and straightway made for them. They were already in possession of spectators, but spying room on the highest for one more, I succeeded by a short run and good jump in securing a first-rate point of observation.

Soon after nine the magnificent war-steamers *Numancia* and *Vitoria* entered the harbour, the *Numancia* flying the royal standard. Instantly the heavy artillery of *Monjuich* opened in salutation, the guns of the *Fortaleza de Las Atarazanas* followed suit, and the *Numancia* and *Vitoria* turned loose their monster armament in reply. Then the military bands on board the vessels, those stationed on the platforms near the landing, that of the awaiting escort of mounted *guardias civiles*, and dragoons, crashed forth the " Marcha Real," an anthem only played in the king's presence, and at the elevation of the Host. And through clouds of smoke and a din indescribable, the young Alfonso took his seat in the stern of the *Numancia's* barge, and was rowed across the harbour. As he did so a numerous *cortège* of handsomely-horsed carriages, filled with gorgeously-apparelled magnates and officials, drove down the *Rambla*, headed by gold and ruby heralds, trumpets in hand. Every street converging on the route was a sea of heads, every window and balcony crammed, the very housetops black with people.

Of course, as soon as his Majesty set foot on shore he had to suffer from the modern phase of the king's evil —to wit, to listen to an address, and Spanish addresses are not mild forms of the disease. There is more six-syllabled grandiloquence in them that entereth into the imagination of the most gushing body of English alder-men and councillors, even when assisted by the prosiest and most verbose of town clerks.

After a short and, I suppose, suitable reply—I did not hear it, nor (L.D.) the address—the king mounted his carriage. Immediately the troops presented arms, the escort closed up, the rest of the carriages filled, the heralds blew a fanfare, and the progress commenced.

As his carriage started, the young king stood up for a second, and lifting his hat completely off, bowed right and left most graciously and gracefully. I looked for a deafening roar of responsive applause. There was a faint official cheer from the occupiers of the carriages behind, considerable waving of ladies' handkerchiefs and fans, but otherwise profound silence. And what looked even worse, not a hat, not a cap was raised to answer their king's salute ; and this in Spain, where not to answer a beggar's salutation is to insult him. I turned to my fellow-occupier of the building block, and asked him what it meant, why the people did not cheer their king? He was a stout, good-looking Catalan peasant ; in appearance, thanks to his national costume, a *beau-idéal* "Red." His velveteen slashed kneebreeches, short jacket, broad sash, crimson Phrygian cap, made him look most melodramatically such. His answer was as "Red" as was his cap. "C——jo the king and his *p*——*a* of a mother." And this not *sotto voce*, but aloud, and accompanied by the placing of the right elbow in the palm of the left hand, and shaking aloft of the right fist, a gesture which could be seen farther than he was heard, and was understood by all there—a gesture whose meaning it is impossible even to hint at in print. I felt very sorry for the young king. He looked gallant and bold. It was very disheartening.

At breakfast, I learned his Majesty was being entertained at the *Casa Consistorales*, in the *Plaza de la*

Constitucion, and thither I shortly repaired to see him leave
on his temporary return to his ship.   There was a dense
crowd filling all available space in the *Plaza*, and the
heads of the streets leading therefrom.   It was a polite
and obliging crowd, and though there was such a crush
that several ladies had to be taken home in a fainting condition, and only succeeded in emerging from the throng
through the strenuous efforts of their escorts and the
guardias civiles, a man accustomed to London mobs found
little difficulty in working his way up to the edge of the
main guard, that held the entrance porch of the building
in which the king was being regaled.   In fact, I got my
heels upon a projecting basement string-course, and so,
my head raised above the general level of the crowd, and
braced firmly against the wall by its pressure, I securely
and advantageously surveyed the scene.

Immediately in front of the *Casa Consistorales*, a clear
space was held by a close line of cavalry, who with serried
rank pressed back the people.   In this space was the
king's carriage and his escort of dragoons.   The escort held
their carbines butt on thigh, finger on scroll-guard, and at
full cock ; every balcony, every window, every house-top,
was a mass of heads.   Soon the king appeared, entered his
carriage and drove off.   As he did so, a perfect snowstorm
of fluttering handkerchiefs, waved by fair *señoras* covered
the front of every house, and a soprano cry of " *Viva le
Rey*" was audible.   But the feminine cheer was drowned in
hisses, which grew louder and more aggressive as the king
drove on, and which were freely " shotted " with derisive
whistles.

The king's reception was the engrossing topic at dinner-time, and was considered as very ominous. Bets that there would be an attempt on his person before the visit was over were freely offered—no takers.

I learned that his Majesty's unpopularity was not only because the Alfonsist party have only official friends in Cataluna, but that the young monarch himself is personally obnoxious to the Catalans.

Then was told to me a terrible story, and I was assured, " all decent Catalans consider Spanish personal honour has been nationally disgraced and degraded through the royal complicity therein."

I submitted that it could not be true—must be a calumny of the king's enemies.

" Not a bit of it," said in chorus my informants. And one of them added : " The whole world knows it. It is a matter of public notoriety ; and though only those in the colonel's chamber know, to a certainty, whose was the fatal hand, yet everybody does who, to get the old colonel out of the way while his wife and daughter were visited, ordered him on the distant duty, from which he so unexpectedly returned to meet his death."

Not only did I hear all this at dinner, stated too with direct and circumstantial evidence, in language much more to the point, and with details not repeatable, but afterwards in the streets. And though, on account of the extreme youth of Alfonso, the notorious old *roué* the *D—— de C.* is execrated as the misleader of his sovereign in this as in many other shady scrapes, everybody had a fling at the king about it, and some had at the ladies too, saying it was a disgrace that he should be so favourably received by them, but that they always do like a man that is a scoundrel where they are concerned. I believe the majority of the women have never heard the particulars of this court scandal ; certainly fathers, husbands, or brothers would not be likely to impart them. I think the young ladies are cordial in their reception of Alfonso because he is a rather good-looking young man, with an elegant figure and fine eyes, single, and a king, and has besides a reputation for general gallantry—quite sufficient causes for female admiration.

At night the public buildings were illuminated—brilliantly illuminated—and with a taste and elegance I was not prepared for. In artistic effects for official rejoicings I have heretofore believed the French to be pre-eminent ; I now award the palm to Spain ; certainly the midnight torchlight procession was the finest thing of the kind I have ever seen.

Through a friend's interest, I got a place on a balcony overlooking the *Rambla del Centro*, down which the procession moved. The *Ramblas* are a continuous boulevard running through the centre of the city, north and south. They consist of a wide gravel walk, bordered by two rows of fine large trees, whose branches, now bare of leaves, nearly inarch it ; of carriage-ways, one on each side, then of the pavements and the houses. The entire width of the *Ramblas* varies from sixty to one hundred feet, for though all run continuously in direction, they are not of the same wideness. Up the *Ramblas* I had a vista of about a mile in length, down which I could see the gleam of the advancing torches. Along the roadways, on each side, rode the cavalry—lancers, dragoons, *guardias civiles*— each trooper bearing aloft a blazing flambeau. In the centre, under the trees, illuminating the trunks, lighting up the delicate tracery of branch and spray against the darkness of the sky, tramped along infantry, artillery, marines, mariners, officials, all carrying flaming lights— white lights, blue lights, red lights. At intervals were the regimental bands playing martial strains.

After the head of the procession had well passed, I looked up and down the long boulevard. It was a rainbow blaze of moving lights and shadows, a stream of glitter and colour, while from it up to heaven rolled through the lit-up overhanging branches clouds of blue smoke and blended music. A scene not soon to be forgotten.

To-day his Majesty held a levee and visited the chief manufactories. At the levee he was very affable, addressed many of the consuls in their native tongue, apparently speaking English, French, and German with equal facility as *Castellano*, and, in short, displayed himself to good advantage. In the evening he attended a performance of Verdi's new opera " Aïda," at the *Gran Teatro de Liceo*. This theatre is one of the finest opera-houses in Europe, it being, as I am informed on excellent authority, the same size and built on the same lines as *La Scala* at Milan.

A good Italian opera company is nearly always in Barcelona, and the house is never thin, though it can seat four thousand persons and stand two thousand more ; for Spaniards love opera. The hours are reasonable—seven to ten o'clock—the charges moderate : boxes, sixteen shillings and eightpence; stalls, half-a-crown; general entrance, fifteenpence. The house is well ventilated, comfortable, and temperate, the entertainment always good, and so numbers of the citizens of all grades and their families can and do go regularly each and every night there is a *funcion* without injury to health or purse, and greatly to their satisfaction, and not, as the majority of the same classes in London would, rarely or never.

But if opera is plentiful in Barcelona, kings are scarce, so on this occasion seats were simply fabulously high-priced in theory, and not obtainable in fact; at least not so for those who had not engaged them long in advance. However, in this country authority is more potent even than coin, so, having a good friend inside the official rope, I was not left out in the cold.

The *palcos*, the *butacas* were crammed with the beauty and fashion of Barcelona, the cheaper portions of the house full of soldiers and their sweethearts; and uniforms, official costumes, orders, everywhere and all over, showed that the house was full of "the king's party," and when he entered there was an ovation. The whole audience rose to their feet. The play was stopped. The house rung with cheers. Evidently, when they choose, these Spaniards can be as demonstrative as Frenchmen, as loud in their acclaims as Britons.

"Aïda" was extremely well rendered and mounted; but the manager had unusual facilities. All the assistance the military could afford had been placed at his disposal. As a consequence, the march scene was superb. The bands were regimental ones, in gorgeous properties; the trumpeters, bandmasters, the triumphant army and their prisoners, real drilled soldiers of the line, brilliant in stage braveries, seemingly endless in numbers, and marching and wheeling as if on parade, not slouching about absurdly and confusedly like a lot of supers. It was very fine. The singing, too, was of excellent average; the whole thing very good indeed.

There were very few loiterers outside the theatre to see his Majesty drive off surrounded by his guard. Those who were gave him a hiss or two. I did hear, too, that a stone was thrown at him, but did not see it, and hope it was a false statement; but there might have been, it was a dark night. As on Friday the king returned to his ship, the people say he is afraid to sleep ashore.

CHAPTER XXX.

MARCH 10, 1877.—Eleven o'clock last Sunday morning, after his Majesty King Alfonso should have attended high mass, was the appointed time for him to open and inaugurate the *Exposicion Industrial;* a ceremony all the world wished to witness, but all the world could not, because admittance was only permitted to those who were provided with tickets. Of such were two kinds, pink and white ; the number of pink tickets quite limited, and except to expositors and head officials almost unattainable. They admitted at ten o'clock. The white tickets admitted at one o'clock, after the opening ceremonies. They were numerous, and not hard to obtain by anyone who was *comme il faut*, having been placed for general distribution in the hands of all the leading citizens whose discretion could be thoroughly depended on. Thanks to the kind consideration of the gentleman whose acquaintance I made at Montserrat, when he was there with the

Belgian nobleman and bride, I was the distinguished possessor of the honour of a pink ticket, and, armed with it, made my way to the chief entrance at eleven o'clock sharp.

El Palais del Exposicion is a fine, large, handsome building, and the ample open space forming its frontage was, excepting a lane held by mounted *guardias civiles* for the royal *cortège* to drive through, covered with lines of handsomely-appointed carriages and an extremely well-dressed crowd.

My experience in this country having been that Spaniards are always behindhand, I had taken things coolly, and, as I said before, only arrived at the time appointed for the king to do so. Just as I was passing the guard at the entrance I heard a cheer, a cry of *" El Rey ! El Rey !"* and the guard falling back, right and left, I remained solitarily conspicuous standing on the steps, and in the middle of the grand entrance. Being of a retiring disposition and not accustomed to receive kings, I incontinently took "a header" through the close sentry line, and had barely got out of the way when, in a cloud of dust, and surrounded by a brilliant escort, the king's carriage dashed up to the spot. He was greeted with acclamation, the band struck up the "Marcha Real," a gold-laced, bestarred, and ribboned reception committee advanced to meet him, he entered, and the ceremonies began. Alas! I did not, for the grand entrance closed behind his Majesty, and left me without disconsolate. But I remembered the sayings of the country, *" Cuando una puerta se cierra, otra se abre,"* and *" Quien no cansa alcanza"*—" When one door shuts

another opens," and "He who strives arrives." So a side
door and a little persuasion were tried with entire success,
excepting that the crowd within prevented my approaching
his Majesty sufficiently closely to hear what was said, or
clearly note what was being done in his immediate vicinity.

I have since learned that King Alfonso has the excellent quality of being punctual, and has repeatedly stated he
will teach his *entourage* and the public to be so too if he has
to go where appointed without the one, and disappoint the
other by leaving before they arrive. In the forcible and
unstudied vernacular of the Great West I say, " Bully for
Alfonso ! "

The opening ceremony finished, the king made a
progress through the building, to see and to be seen ;
principally to be seen I take it. Then, with the chief
swells, royalty retired to a refreshment-room to eat his
breakfast. Immediately the doorways to the sacred spot
were taken in charge by strong bodies of *guardias civiles*,
and it became impossible for common mortals to " see
the animals fed." After breakfast the king departed,
closely surrounded with officials and *guardias civiles*.
Indeed, so well was he guarded, that the lately-admitted
white-ticket holders could not get even a glimpse of his
Majesty.

The Industrial Exhibition was extremely creditable to
Cataluña in general and Barcelona in particular. The
variety of products, the excellent finish of workmanship,
the high artistic development occasionally displayed, were
most gratifying to a lover of progress in arts and manu-
factures, and to me as astonishing as pleasing, for I had

no idea that in many things Spain held such a foremost rank.

In the afternoon there was a review. It was to take place in the *Pasco de Gracia* (five spacious avenues of fine trees) and along *La Ronda*, and again was I in luck. A foreign diplomatist asked me to a capital luncheon, graced by some charming ladies, and with them I afterwards shared a balcony overlooking the line of review.

There were between four and five thousand troops of all arms in line, not a large force, but of excellent raw material, admirably uniformed and equipped, and officered in lavish proportion. Those in sight of our balcony were drawn up along the opposite side of the street, our side being kept by a sentry line. Soon the king, on horseback and closely followed by the captain-general and a brilliant staff, rode past. He went very fast, riding beautifully, and with his hat raised a few inches from his head in a prolonged salute. As he galloped by our corner he got a hearty cheer. His face beamed with smiles. He checked his horse into a slow trot, bowed right and left, and dashed off again, getting, as he did so, another *viva*, louder than the first.

The king returned slowly to the saluting-point, and the march past began, the troops farthest off taking the van, and the others as they passed wheeling into column behind. The infantry went by our balcony in open order, with a front of eight, going at their usual terrific pace. They carried their breechloaders slung crosswise behind' and swung their hands across and back from right to left in front of them, as they marched, hands going left when left foot led, right when right foot led. I have since tried that way of marching, when out for a brisk walk, and am inclined to approve of it. The cavalry passed in close order and four abreast. They were very well mounted. The dragoons had their carbines in slings, and sabres drawn. The mountain artillery—on muleback—attracted much attention, deservedly, for the animals were splendid ones, and the entire equipment ingenious, compact, and serviceable.

The review over, I went to a little dinner with some more friends, and then to the *Teatro Principál* to see a *Sainete*, with my fellow-boarder, the aide-de-camp.

The theatre was a fine large house, very well filled, the playing good enough, and the dancing admirable, especially the *Baile*. I will back two first-class Andalusian performers, male and female, against the world for grace and go in dancing. They can posture better than Nautch-Wallahs, outskip the French, and are never scraggy.

By-the-bye, I owe this said gallant officer quite a debt of gratitude for the results of his kind attentions to me, for, thanks to him, I have been able to see much that was interesting, which otherwise I might not.

The captain may be most emphatically described as a gay boy. To him is known the entire *arcana* of Spanish town life. His position here, for he is a favourite, and oft companion of his chief — the captain-general of the province—his means, his address and personal appearance, give him the *entrée* everywhere. Therefore has he proved a most excellent guide, philosopher, and friend to a foreign stranger whose keenness for information concerning the

manners and customs of the natives is, like that of an
entomologist for strange beetles, quite reckless; and so
it has come to pass I have been willing to go, and there
made welcome, where without the introduction of an *habitué*
I could not have obtained admission, and have seen the
most exclusive phase of a social problem that in its more
common and open manifestations has, more or less unavoid-
ably, been almost continually under notice during my walk
here from San Sebastian.

But this is a matter fit, both as regards its facts and
conclusions, for philosophical disquisition, and not apropos
in narrative letters; sufficient to say, therefore, in this
country, where *all* women are sober, a reflecting observer
behind the curtain of propriety must indisputably conclude
that nine-tenths of what are at home considered the necessarily attendant evils of transgression, and nearly all its
repulsiveness, is entirely the result of transgression *plus*—
and very much *plus*—intoxicating beverages.

A witty foreigner has said : "When, in conversation,
you wish to turn it from a *subject*, turn it to a beautiful
woman." So as I have not yet said anything about the
fair *queens* of Barcelona, I will seize the occasion and
follow such admirable advice.

There is a great deal of female loveliness in this capital
of Cataluña, but it is principally immigrant from other
parts of Spain, for the Catalan type is too coarse in outline
of face, too masculine in figure, to be fascinating. Still,
Valencia is in close connection with this port, and the fair
Valencianas are reputed to be the handsomest women of
Spain. No wonder that in Valencia the Moors placed their

paradise. And as enough of these houris are here to affect the general average, Barcelona prides itself, justly, on its pretty women.

Thanks again to the gay aide-de-camp, I have made the acquaintance of one of these lately arrived from Valencia, who is physically as near perfection as modern civilisation allows. She is quite a typical beauty of her locality, and so, fairly entitled to be described. Slightly above medium female height, inclined to fulness of figure, with most diminutive yet well-developed hands and feet, and a walk and carriage inimitable in grace; face, classical in outline; hair, profuse in quantity, of great length and glossiness, and the darkest of browns in colour; complexion, a bright, soft, clear, ruddy, light olive; and glorious eyes, the true "*ojos Arabes*," large, tender, almond eyes, breathing love, sentiment, and passion—that is to say, always seeming to, it being their natural and usual expression—exactly such eyes as I suspect Cleopatra had; eyes to "*trastorno el mundo*," as they say here, and she is just the age when Spanish women reach their perfection—twenty-four, and as sweet-tempered and kind as she is handsome; the only thing I regret about our acquaintance is, that it began so lately and has to finish so soon. But "*Vamos!*" as the aide-de-camp says, "*En la tierra el carnero, en el mar el mero.*" By which saying he intends both to console me and flatter my patriotism, meaning to infer I shall soon find at home an equally beautiful substitute for *La Capitolana*. Ah! little does my lively military friend realise the discreet decorum of respectability in virtuous England. No more *Capitolanas* for me when I return to the land of Messrs. Barlow and Pecksniff, Mesdames Grundy and Goody.

I have given away my faithful *compagnon de voyage ;* Juan and I have parted. I shall miss the dog greatly ; he was an affectionate, caressing, intelligent creature, and I have got to be very fond of him. He and " *Capi* " are two more cases of "dear gazelle ;" but it is a longish way to take a dog from here to the West of England ; he would be a great inconvenience during my sojourn *en route* in Paris ; I shall have no use for him at home ; he will then be a dog too many ; and I have got him into happy permanent quarters, which is better for him.

Juan's new master is my countryman ; a gentleman long since domiciled here, and moving in Barcelona's best circle. Like all Englishmen of his class, he was a sportsman in his youth, and having an eye for a well-bred dog, at once spotted and admired mine. From this compatriot I have received much kind politeness ; without introduction, without recommendation, excepting his private judgment, he has cordially extended to me the genial hospitalities of his house and home, and admitted me to the society of the *bien distingué,* elegant, and accomplished ladies who adorn it ; and further, he has paid me every social attention in his power ; so one day, seeing that Juan tempted him to sin against the tenth commandment, hearing him praise the dog, and the ladies declare they were in love with him, I made the reply of a true Spaniard, " Then he is yours," and insisted that, for once, the phrase of the country should be taken *au pied de la lettre.*

The present was received with such evident delight

that I was quite gratified at what I had done; indeed, I felt happy for twenty-four hours. It is so nice to confer pleasure, especially when by so doing a man at the same time consults his own convenience.

The king left on Monday. There was not much fuss made about it, only a parting salute from the guns of Monjuich.

Monjuich is much bragged of by Spaniards. They are fond of comparing it and Gibraltar, much to the disparagement of our stronghold. According to Spanish military authorities, modern improvements have rendered Gibraltar quite takable, indeed untenable, should Spain determine to repossess herself of it; whereas Monjuich is absolutely impregnable when garrisoned to its proper strength. But it is all moonshine. Monjuich is not, as confidently repeated, "the strongest natural position in the world." I have seen—I speak advisedly—hundreds far stronger. But, no doubt, "'twill serve," for it holds the city at its mercy, and can knock it into a cocked hat should its citizens again rise against military dictation—the chief use Spanish forts are put to. And the guns dominate the harbour too, and perhaps could keep an enemy from entering it; but as town and harbour can be easily shelled from, and troops landed at, places it does not command, *cui bono?*

"The hill of the Jews" is, to its extremest altitude, but seven hundred and fifty feet above the sea level, and though partly precipitous on its sea face, for the rest slopes so gradually that there are but few places where, were there not artificial obstructions, a Californian stage-driver would hesitate to put his conveyance along at a gallop up or down.

The great strength of Monjuich lies in the fact that it is not dominated by superior elevations, and that an immense amount of money has been very well laid out in earthworks, casemates, cisterns, and guns. But "*Mons Judaicus*" being not a small mountain, not a rock, but a hill, whose soil landwards is deep and easily workable, its defensive lines are as easy to sap up to, and easier to undermine, than were it an entrenched camp in the middle of a plain. However, nobody wants to meddle with Spain. If she will only leave herself alone she will do well enough.

As I do not mean to stop here for ever, I begin to think the sooner I depart the better, for reasons not at all necessary to mention ; but how to go, what route to take, know not. There are two courses, each open to objection. If I take passage by steamer to Marseilles, I shall see absolutely nothing between the two ports, for the course stretches straight out to sea and across the Gulf of Lyons. If I go overland by rail and diligence, I shall see much, but, *per contra*, may be robbed, for quite an epidemic of road agency has lately broken out in these parts adjacent. For instance, while I was *en route* from Montserrat, the train between here and Monistrol was twice stopped and "gone through." Quite lately the diligence from Figueras to Perpignan—my route if I go overland—has been "interviewed." However, I think I shall risk *los ladrones*, though I do not want to hear the cry "*Abajo, boca, á tierra*," having had some experience of its Yankee equivalent, "Throw up your hands, G—— d—— you." It is not the actual loss of property so much as the feeling of degradation at being obliged to obey such miscreants that hurts.

And, as I have parted with my gun, and do not carry a
revolver, should I be "stuck up," will have to submit.
However, in such case, I shall not lose much.   Only
a few trifling presents —remembrances from Spain—the
aluminium watch brought on "spec," to be taken from me,
and my clothes.

These last would be very inconvenient to part from, for
I might catch cold before they could be replaced, but
robbers will get no money from me, as I intend to spend my
last coin, excepting enough to feed me on the way, and see
me past the customs, ere I leave this gay city, for can I not
cash the traveller's blessing—a circular note—at Perpignan?
and I would sooner be eased of my money here by *fair*
means, than on the road by foul.   I have crossed one
extremity of *Los Pirineos;* I should like to traverse the
other.   The chances of being robbed are, on the one hand,
not greater than of being sea-sick on the other.   I would
sooner lose the coats off my back than the coats of my
stomach.

The *cafés* of Barcelona excel any I have seen in Spain,
and are no more expensive to such as frequent them than
those of the meanest inland hamlet.   Not only are they
the best of Spanish ones, but absolutely the best I know of;
very large and airy, handsome, clean, and comfortable.   In
all the leading ones are pianos, played by professionals of
no mean proficiency.   I have heard as good piano-playing
in these *cafés* as at many London concerts.   They are
almost always full of company, and though in Spain,
generally speaking, *cafés* are not considered quite the
places for ladies, here it is quite correct for the fair sex to

be present, even without a male escort, and therefore there
is almost always to be seen in them a goodly sprinkling of
Doñas Catalañas sipping coffee, sugar and water, orgeat, or
some other such light drink ; fooling with their fans and
by their fans, listening to the music, laughing, chatting,
ogling, and flirting. Many is the flirtation begun, continued,
but not ended in a Barcelona *café*. And what is the
expense to enjoy all this—brilliant chandeliers, marble
tables, velvet-covered seats and lounges, plate-glass mirrors,
paint, gilding and glitter, attentive and respectful waiters,
good professional music, a sight of youth, beauty, and
innocence engaging the experienced, brave, and knowing,
and coming off first best ? Why, only twopence-halfpenny.
You are expected to order "*uno café*"—unless you want
something else—and there will be placed before you a small
cup of coffee, milk, sugar, *eau-de-vie* in a decanter, ladies'-
fingers in a plate. For these the waiter will demand
one *real*, and leave you. He expects no fee, and unless
you want something more, and call, will not come
near you again if you sit there and smoke all night.
Nor will you be considered mean if you should, and yet
spend no more. Plenty of well-off and respected citizens
do so every night. I did not, but only because I used to
get thirsty, and besides, not playing dominoes nor being
given to flirting, I liked to have a something to sip and play
with. Why should I not amuse myself by flirting a spoon,
as well as my neighbour by spooning a flirt ? It is quite as
innocent an amusement, and somewhat less dangerous,
except to a kleptomaniac.

And its *cafés* are not the only commendable things of

Barcelona. The shops are, for goodness, elegance, variety, and choiceness of wares, quite equal to Paris or London, and by no manner of means as dear, nor are their attendants so much given to taking strangers in, though of course it is always safest for a foreigner to deal at a "*precio fijo*" shop until he learns the local values.

But, on one account, Barcelona has been to me the least interesting place I have visited since crossing the Bidassoa, for of any of them it is the one least typically Spanish; and having come to this country to see Spanish customs and ways, familiarise myself with Spanish ideas and peculiarities, that which is cosmopolitan, being neither new nor attractive, I care not for.

A study of the almost inextricable maze, jumble, and confusion together of the old beliefs and usages of Pagan, Roman, and Eastern occupation, mixed and blended with those of civilisation and to-day, which this country presents to even the least observing stranger is, and must be, a source of wonder and delight. Surely the Spain of to-day is in Europe the chief arena of the psychological contest, the *Gran Plaza de Toros*, where the *matador* of Modern Thought is pitted against the "Bull of Superstition," where in his calm hand the keen *espalda* of Science firmly encounters on its gleaming point the fierce expiring onslaught of that beast whose characteristics are tail, horns, and cloven foot. Most certainly if, going south, "*L'Afric commence aux Pyrénées,*" on the return, modernism begins at Gibraltar.

CHAPTER XXXI.

MARCH 15, 1877.—I have recrossed the Pyrenees. Spain is now to me a dream that is past—a very pleasant dream. Fatigue, thirst, dust, annoyances, and vexations will gradually fade from recollection ; but many a bright picture of fair scenery, many a joyous revel, the incidents of some few charming interviews, are laid away in memory's "dark room," intangible, invisible—treasured negatives in photographic clearness, to be reproduced at will, to gladden and beguile the lonely hours of the future.

Nor has my trip been altogether devoid of instruction. It has dissipated many erroneous, previously-conceived opinions, informed me of many an unsuspected fact. I had considered Spain to be a worked-out country : the undeveloped wealth of her natural resources is great beyond all calculation. I had presupposed a people proud, intolerant, bigoted, indolent, shiftless, lawless. I have found an upper

class courteous and considerate to their equals, kind and
familiar to their inferiors, fairly liberal and enlightened in
opinion, and very wide awake to the faults and shortcomings of their country; a peasantry full of self-respect,
of manly independence, honest, hard-working, frugal, law-
abiding, sober.

With such a grand substratum for national tranquillity,
prosperity, progress, how comes it Spain is the home of
chronic disorder, revolution, strife? Because since the
Goths she has been either the battlefield of contending
foreign forces and intrigue, or of contest between national
virtues and the powers of darkness. A gallant people,
purposely and cunningly kept in poverty and ignorance,
imbruted and cajoled, have made a long struggle against
combined priest and kingcraft. For four centuries a cruel,
subtle, inscrutable, and omnipotent conspiracy, remorseless,
omnipresent, bloody, sought to crush manhood in the dust;
mutual confidence between classes, between individuals,
was sapped, destroyed, and disappeared. Crime was the
only safe road to prosperity; to think was dangerous, to
utter thought aloud, if that thought was truth—death.
Between 1481 and 1808, thirty-four thousand six hundred
and twelve victims are officially reported as being burnt to
death, and two hundred and eighty-eight thousand one
hundred and nine as otherwise made away with by the
" Holy " Inquisition.

A nightmare of fear, distrust, lethargy, paralysed the
country. To prosper in business, to be enterprising, to
amass a little money, was to become a prey. The goods
and chattels of him who fell into the clutches of the black

alguacils were the perquisites of a body of men craving for gold and utterly irresponsible. The youth of the nobility were thoroughly demoralised by the inculcation of the most dishonourable code of ethics ever conceived—one destructive to confidence, truth, and mental improvement. The people learned that to be idle, uninquiring, servile, was absolutely necessary to life. Literature was made an engine of ignorance; government, one of plunder. The intelligence, talent, enterprise of the country was banished, destroyed, or silenced.

A people who have suffered this, and still retain such traits of character as the Spaniard of to-day, must have an innate nobility of soul, that in the end will insure to their country a foremost place among the nations of the earth.

In one thing Spain is quite behind the three countries leading civilisation's van—England, the United States, France. Spanish women do not know even the meaning of "sphere," as that word is used by the strong-minded. What are her rights, wherein lie her wrongs, trouble not her. She is content to be—and is—a careful, notable housewife, a good mother, a kind mistress. She dresses well and elegantly for her station, but not extravagantly ; loves amusement, but never neglects her home ; is coquettish and attractive in her manner, but proper in her conduct. There may be "more advanced" women— women with "higher purposes," with more "lofty aspiration ;" but more comfortable women to live with—more charming women to make love to—more gentle, unselfish, amiable, domestic, loving women, I do not think the world can show. And they seem utterly unaware of the "degradation" of being so, and quite happy and contented with their "sphere."

No wonder the Spaniard loves his home; no wonder there are so few bachelors in Spain. False start—whoa! This sort of thing will never do. It is not giving an account of my peregrinations, and I have taken no contract to furnish "reflections"—only to report progress.

Having "done" Barcelona pretty thoroughly, wished my friends *a dios*, paid my bills, got my through ticket to Perpignan, *via* rail and diligence, and put by a few *pesetas* for use *en route*, I succeeded by two o'clock A.M. yesterday in getting rid satisfactorily of my last coin, and retired to my virtuous couch to snatch a short repose, ere I should be called to catch the 'bus to the *Estacion del Norte*, advertised to start at four A.M. "to the moment."

Of course I was called half an hour after the 'bus should have departed. Of course I had half an hour to wait. Of course I was in time at the station. And at 6.45 A.M. the whistle blew and the train started for Gerona.

It was a pleasant run, and thoroughly enjoyed, though I was in solitary grandeur all alone; for, as usual on the Continent, being *au premier*, I had a whole compartment to myself.

The weather was superb, clear, bright, calm. Occasional glimpses of the blue Mediterranean, enlivened with queer-looking craft, recalling by their strange rakish rig the pictured Algerine pirates of story, and lake-like in its glassy surface, charmed the vision.

The inland scenery was varied, striking, and romantic, and several spots of interest were passed.

Soon the ancient town of Badalona came in view, surrounded with its famous orange groves and watered by the brawling Nesos ; in antiquity, a very grandmother of a city to Barcelona. Then appears a hill, crowned by *El Castillo de Mongat*, famous for a most gallant defence against an entire French army, in which its garrison lost its last man. There was no Metz about that. Then another castle —*Vilasar*—and some watch-towers of the Moors.

A little town and a fine church are passed, and we stop a few minutes at Mataro, a handsome, thriving, if small town, very Genoese in the *al fresco* ornamentation of its houses. Soon after leaving there we cross the Llevaneras by a well-built, picturesque stone bridge, run past the ruins of *El Castillo Rocaberto*, and behold, still another old-time castle—*Nofre Arnan*—appears in sight. Then we make another stop—we are at *Arenys de Mar.*

I call up the "highly-intelligent guard," and at his dictation write the names of the places I have noticed against the circles and cross indicating their situation in the little sketch-itinerary I amuse myself by making in my pocket-book as I am whirled along, adding thereto such other information as he volunteers, and obtaining his promise to "post" me about the remainder of the trip when we arrive at Gerona.

He tells me *Arenys de Mar* boasts of very fair dock-yards, and makes quantities of soap, lace, and linen. I can see that it is a prosperous and a pretty port—three P's that do not always go together. A league farther and we pass another *embarcadero*, then, by an iron bridge, cross the Rio San Pol, catch a passing glimpse of a pretty little town, cross another stream by another and much finer iron bridge —the Tordera. Ere long the town of that name is left behind, and the celebrated *Barranca*, then the junction station of Empalme, and at 10.40 A.M. we are arrived at Gerona.

Gerona is a town of some size and importance, with a rapid river flowing by it, clean and decent in its old age ; but evidently having in its youth been given to an exhausting dissipation of energy in overmuch church-building. Had the time as well as the occasion served, I would have taken a peep at its cathedral, because I had heard much of its extraordinary merits, and it has the widest Gothic vault in existence. But the *diligence* was billed to start at eleven o'clock, " *en punto*," and the inner man demanded immediate attention.

There was no time to lose. Already the coach stood before the hotel door, its driver and the helps putting in and strapping down luggage. Already the harnessed horses were in sight, being led up by the groom and straps. It was quite evident the stage was intended to start " on time."

It lacked an hour to the breakfast-time of the country. To expect to get that meal cooked at any other than the regular one, much more cooked and eaten in twenty minutes, would be a wild delusion, one I know Spain too well to harbour, so forthwith I skirmish for forage. I dive into a *bodega* and buy a bottle of wine ; into a *tienda* and procure a *longaniza*—a high-spiced sausage, requiring no cooking—and some excellent cream cheese. Then I prospect the stage and interrogate the coachman.

It is ready to start, will be off instantly. "Just a little moment."

That "little moment" set my mind at ease. Seeing my traps safely stowed away on my seat, and learning which street the coach route followed, I strolled along in the direction indicated, found a *panadera*, went in, bought some delicious milk rolls, explained the situation to the bakeress in waiting, knocked off the neck of my bottle, and, confident the *diligence* could not get by unseen and unheard, sat down, spread my frugal repast before me, and had a very comfortable "little moment" of about a quarter of an hour's duration ; after which I lit my pipe, and sauntering back to the hotel, arrived and took my place as Jehu started his team.

There were six good horses to the *diligence*, the road was excellent, and we bowled along at a good lively rate, arriving at the town of Figueras—where we changed our stage for one more fitted to mountain travel—at three in the afternoon ; twenty miles, with a considerable grade against us, in about three hours and a half.

We had passed three little villages, another ruined castle, the small town of Buscara, and some pretty *Casas de Campos*, called "*Torres*"—a Catalan word, signifying country houses. (What a chance for a derivation of the old *sobriquet* of England's Conservative party.) The view had all along been getting more and still more enchanting as we progressed, for the Pyrenean chain was in full view, getting clearer and fuller in its lovely details every mile, while the day was warm and bright as though a summer one.

While approaching Figueras, my attention was drawn to very extensive military works, covering a bench of the plain. As well as could be judged by a passing spectator, I was looking at an example, on a large scale, of a most complete system of earthwork defence, and was struck by the admirable choice of its position, its size, and apparent strength. It seemed large enough to contain a covering army of very respectable size, and the ground commanded from its embrasures to be a natural formation that was highly favourable for a strong garrison to assume the offensive over. I do not recollect that I have ever seen a good natural position better utilised. My fellow-passengers in the *berlina* of the *diligence* could tell me little about it. They were men of commerce, and it was simply a *castillo* to them. However, one knew its name—San Fernando—so I determined to seek information when we should stop in the town.

Our detention at Figueras was to be but short ; only a quarter of an hour was the *mayoral's* announcement, so I had to stir myself, for it was my last chance, for many a long day, to buy really good smoking tobacco. I had to provide also against getting hungry, appease my thirst, and learn what I could about the *Castillo de San Fernando*. An *estanco*—Government tobacco agency—was easily found, and I there laid in a small store of *Picardo Pico Fina de Habana;* then I purchased a pocketful of biscuits ; finally entered a *taberna*, and regaled myself with *aguardiente* and water.

I singled out that particular tavern because in it I caught sight of uniforms, and saw my chance to pick up

information about the fortifications in sight. An invitation
to drink immediately made the two *cabos de esquadra* my
buen amigos, and the extent of their knowledge on the
subject was at my disposal.

According to them, the fortification was the strongest
in the world ; the bomb-proof barracks amply sufficient to
lodge twenty thousand men, the bomb-proof stables to
contain five hundred horses. There were nine proof
magazines, a fine park of artillery, sixty heavy guns in
position, and "only just let the *c——jo* French try to take
it." I failed, however, in ascertaining who was the military
engineer who planned it. My informant stated his name
appeared in a mural tablet over one of the gateways, but
they did not recollect it.

A few miles from Figueras we traversed an immense
olive plantation, and in its centre passed the little village
of Molina, so called on account of its many olive mills.
Once clear of the olive wood the road became very
steep, with numerous short, sharp descents ; in fact, we
were climbing the Pyrenees. As the *diligence* progressed
very slowly, I took to walking most of the way, only
jumping up whenever we came to a level run, for, on foot,
I could better enjoy the magnificent scenery, and loiter at
such spots as afforded advantageous look-outs. Besides, I
so escaped the dust and closeness of the *diligence*, both
which were excessive. Indeed, the day was so hot that I
left coat and waistcoat in the *diligence*, and walked without
them.

We were passing the places where the late robberies
took place. Judging by the frequency we have seen pickets

of *guardias civiles* since we got amongst the spurs of the mountains, there is an evident determination on the part of the authorities to block that little game. As I am sometimes a mile ahead of the *diligence*, and without coat, waistcoat, collar, or hat—my necktie being twisted turbanwise round my head—I wonder none of them have stopped me as a suspicious character; but they have only made the salutation of the country as I passed. Perhaps they think I am a harmless lunatic or an Englishman. They have some queer notions about Englishmen in Spain.

It was beginning to get dark as we drove into the last Catalan town of La Junquera, the Spanish frontier customs station. A strong body of *carabineros* were stationed there.

The *diligence* stopped at La Junquera to change horses, and I walked on. Two passengers descended from the *banquette* and did so likewise. At a turn of the road, out of sight of the town, they struck off up a ravine to the right. I thought it strange conduct, and sat down to smoke, wait for the *diligence*, and see if they would reappear when it did. They did not, and nothing was said about it.

Shortly after we arrived at a barrier, looking not unlike an English turnpike, only the "lodge" was of stone, and loopholed for musketry, and the "keeper" a *carabinero*. We had reached the frontier.

We are halted, a light is thrown on us, we are scanned and counted by the *carabinero* and a companion. A few words are said in an inaudible tone to our driver, his reply is as *sotto voce*, then from the first *carabinero*, in a loud voice:

" It is well, go with God, your worships." A reply from us, in chorus : " Remain you with Him." A flick of the whip to the horses and we are across the line. We have left the old kingdom of the Spains, we have entered the novel Macmahondom of France.

For some time the conversation of the two men of commerce sharing with me the *berlina* had turned upon passports, permits, and *visas*, and one of them expressed a hope I had my papers all right, adding, the French authorities have been excessively strict and annoying of late. I told him I had a Foreign Office passport.

" *Visa* by the French consul of Barcelona ? "

" No."

" Then they will never let you pass."

" Just as good a thing as I want. I will return to the best hotel in Barcelona, file a heavy claim for detention and expenses, and have a jolly time at the cost of the authorities. They shall be made to respect my papers."

" Ah ! I see by your sentiments you are English or American : they will not try to stop you. It is only us poor devils they harass and plunder."

These remarks were hardly made before we arrived at the little hamlet in which is situated the French customs post, and drew up before a long shed and a knot of gendarmes. It was by this time quite dark, but the interior of the shed was dimly lit by oil-lamps, and the gendarmes carried lanterns. We were all marched into the shed. " Give me your waybill," said the gendarme in command to our driver. It was produced. The man in authority looked it and us over.

" You are two passengers short ; where are they ? "

" I don't know."

" Then you ought. Does anyone know what has become of the two *banquette* passengers ? "

This last question in a loud domineering voice, and addressed to all and sundry. A woman, who had been riding in the *interior*, volunteered a statement.

" They walked from La Junquera. Perhaps they are in the *guinguette* refreshing themselves."

" Perhaps *les sacrés scélérats* are no such thing ; they are *polissons*, without papers, giving us the slip." It looked very like it.

" Bring in all luggage to be examined, and show your papers, masters and mistresses," shouted the irate, jack-booted Jack-in-office.

The other passengers' " papers " were all shabby scraps, on which were written permits signed by the French consul of Barcelona, at a cost to them each of ten francs. They were *en règle* of course.

My " Derby " was a different affair. There was not a word of French about it, nor any, to those present, known signature attached thereto ; but it was a most imposing-looking document as compared with the shabby, crumpled scraps from the French consul's office ; large, on vellum, headed by a regal-looking coat-of-arms, sealed with most official amplitude, it certainly looked a most authentic document ; what it said was an Egyptian mystery ; whether it belonged to me or not, unapparent.

" English ? " said the chief gendarme, interrogatively.

" Yes."

It was returned with a bow and "All is regular."

I picked out my little luggage; a *douanier* asked for my keys; I slipped the hand holding them, &c., quietly in his.

"There they are."

"Monsieur has nothing to declare; Monsieur's luggage is passed;" and the official chalk marked my traps as being free to be replaced in the *diligence*. Not so simple was the process with the remainder of the passengers, and soon the counter was strewn with a varied and indescribable assortment of personal effects, and great became the vehemence of gesticulation and figurativeness of oratory of the respective owners thereof, and most especially distinguished as a performer was the vigorous female who had volunteered the information about the missing passengers, when she found herself detected in an attempt to evade a payment of a few francs duty.

After a tiresome detention, we proceeded more rapidly on our way, for the grade of the road soon began to fall rapidly. We were descending the French slope of the Pyrenees. The darkness sadly militated against seeing the face of the country, but it was perceivable that on the north side of the pass the descents were more precipitous, and the scenery far wilder and more weird than on the southern; and a castle perched on the top of an isolated peak, amongst a nest of ravines and summits, irresistibly recalled reminiscences of Doré. However it might look in daytime, by the light I saw it the scene was almost grotesquely extravagant in savage grandeur. The castle was Fort Bellegarde, built nearly two hundred years ago by

Louis XIV., and doubtless a very strong place for self-
defence. I do not think, considering the exigencies of
modern war, it is advantageously placed, either as a
menace to an invading, or a *point d'appui* for a covering
force.

It was half-past nine last night when, arrived at Perpignan, I found my way to the *Hôtel de l'Europe*, sufficiently
tired with my sixteen hours' journey, but well repaid by
what I had seen of the country passed through.

To-day I shall devote to looking around this extremely
prettily-situated place ; to-morrow take the through express
for Paris, stop there awhile, and see my artist friends and
their works for the coming *salon*, and then "GOD SAVE
THE QUEEN," and—Ho for home ! which I trust to find
blooming with spring. Certainly I have this year dodged
English winter in a highly satisfactory manner. I have
passed nearly five months very agreeably and instructively,
experienced much pleasure, and enlarged my stock of information in the most reliable of all ways ; and that, too,
at a less than no expense, for had I remained quietly in
England, I should certainly have disbursed more money
for no satisfaction in the world that I can perceive, unless
a series of trials of constitution and temper against depress-
ing weather and colds in the head can be considered as
such. And if anyone, encouraged by my example, takes
heart of grace, a light kit, a few circular notes, and his
ticket for Spain, I can promise him that, unless he there
makes himself decidedly disagreeable—which of course he
will not—every Spaniard, on learning he is English, will
treat him as a personal friend ; that his money will go

farther, and procure him better fare and quarters than at any English watering-place ; that he will find the climate exhilarating and healthy, and the annoyances and dangers of the country greatly exaggerated ; and to him I say in the phraseology of Spain : " *Vaya usted con Dios, y buen provecho le haga á usted*"—"Go you with God, and much may it profit your grace."

THE END.

BRADBURY, AGNEW, & CO., PRINTERS, WHITEFRIARS

www.ingramcontent.com/pod-product-compliance
Lightning Source LLC
Chambersburg PA
CBHW021342110726
47900CB00005B/1580